WHAT
WAS
RESCUED

WHAT
WAS
RESCUED

JANE BAILEY

LAKE UNION
PUBLISHING

Text copyright © 2017 by Jane Bailey
All rights reserved.

Published by Lake Union Publishing, Seattle

www.apub.com

Amazon, the Amazon logo, and Lake Union Publishing are trademarks of Amazon.com, Inc., or its affiliates.

ISBN-13: 9781477823156
ISBN-10: 1477823158

Cover design by Emma Rogers

Printed in the United States of America

For John
and what was rescued

This book would not have been written without the generosity of The Royal Literary Fund

I remember the night the whales came. That was the first time I didn't feel her eyes upon me, and I began to feel the consolation of forgetting. They came from nowhere, the whales, gliding alongside us like a friendly convoy. They gave long, satisfied sighs from their blowholes, like old men relaxing, and swam with us in the moonlight as if they had been sent to guide us to safety. I remember the coloured flecks of light in the water. And the stars, I remember the stars: there were more of them than I've ever seen since, plastering the sky like sea spray. But I didn't know that it was eight days we were adrift. Eight days! Our Mam said she'd thought I was dead. They had a memorial service for me in the chapel and everything.

Apart from that, I couldn't remember anything much about the boat for years . . . except for his arms, and the sense of safety I had in them. An older boy's arms and the smell of him, that's what I remember vividly. Damp wool, salty skin and the musky scent of his hair roots. Mostly I cushioned my cheek on his wet shoulder and he let me cling on, a sodden speechless creature, fished out of the sea like a sprat. Sometimes he rubbed my feet. I don't know if anyone rubbed his. We were all drenched in our pyjamas and coats; it was hard to think about anything but parched mouths and cold feet.

That was what stayed with me. And then I did remember that deeply buried thing, when I saw her again, when I caught the look in her eyes. But that was over a decade later . . .

Yes, I remember the whales — and the cold feet. To this day I can think of no better feeling in all the world than the comfort of warm socks. Except for those arms around me.

EMBARKING

1

ARTHUR

When Dora found me after all those years, I should have guessed something was being held back. What could have been an extraordinary meeting was, in fact, markedly strained. There was something going on between Pippa and Dora that I didn't know about, and when I came across them in the living room, they were clearly arguing about something in angry, urgent voices. I flattered myself that they were arguing over me. I thought that maybe Dora's arrival out of the blue had sparked some jealousy in Pippa. If I'm honest, I was touched. Thrilled, actually. The idea that Dora might want me enough to track me down and that Pippa (who had taken me for granted for some time, I'm afraid) should whip up such a passion to defend her claim on me – well, I can't deny it made me feel quite proud.

How wrong I was. If only I'd come upon them just a little earlier, if I'd heard the true content of their heated discussion, I can't say for certain what I would have done. But lives would have been very different.

Anyhow, that is not to start at the beginning. We first met in a train compartment. My brother, Philip, and I had boarded the train at

Euston, and it was all very exciting because we had no idea where we were going. We knew we were bound for Canada, but the train journey itself was a complete mystery. I think it was this secrecy that added to the sense of adventure. I remember when the big brown envelope arrived to say we had been given places; we were officially forbidden from telling anyone. We weren't even allowed to tell our school friends or neighbours.

My mother had been reluctant to let us go. She hadn't sent us off as evacuees like most of our friends and had been criticized harshly for it, I think. So she felt pleased and vindicated when they all started coming home again, full of horror stories about their host families and disgruntled at having been sent away for a phoney war. But then, of course, in that late summer of 1940 the most terrible bombing raids began over London. We hadn't seen anything like it before. Dad got us all out building an Anderson shelter. It seemed like fun at first, but it was back-breaking work, and halfway through, a boy I knew in the next street got a direct hit on his house. He was really clever and had just won a place at the grammar school. With ghoulish curiosity, Philip and I went with some other kids to look at the charred remains of the house. There was his lovely leather satchel, its pale contents spilt out on to the back garden like a burst conker. I had wanted one like that badly, but I didn't dare take it.

Pretty soon after, Dad started talking about evacuation again. Mum had heard so many stories about children being used as cheap labour and whatnot that she was still very reluctant. Then Dad spotted this advert in the newspaper about ships to Canada – escorted by the Royal Navy itself. I was dead keen. What an adventure for a twelve-year-old boy! Mum kept putting up arguments about Philip being too young, because he was only six, but I insisted I'd look after him. She still took some persuading, but the fact that the Royal Navy would be protecting us swayed her, I think.

We were in this train carriage bound for we knew not where (Liverpool, as it happened). Miss Prendergast, the woman looking after us, was in the next compartment with five other 'seavacuees' in our group, and we were on our own. Then, at Birmingham, two other children joined us. A tall woman in a fur coat, wafting strong perfume, swung open the door to our compartment and inspected us with a frown. Parents weren't supposed to get on the train. 'Here you are, darling! Keep your chin up!' She ushered in the object of her endearment. 'You needn't sit next to anyone.' She looked at us again, as if we might be harbouring a disease. 'You can sit here in the corner by the corridor. This boy will help you with your luggage.'

I jumped to my feet and lifted the suitcase she had placed on the seat next to her daughter. It was so weighty, I nearly lost it over my head as I heaved it up on to the luggage rack.

'Cheerio, darling!' The word 'darling' seemed very sophisticated to our ears, not being a word our parents used with us, but coming from this lady's lips it sounded more like an accusation. In fact, for a moment I thought it was addressed to me, and I looked up to respond, but she was gone.

I tried hard not to stare, but I could hardly take my eyes off the girl. She was about my age; she had dark hair with a glossy fringe, and the most dazzling green eyes. It was her eyes that struck me first, and then her manner, which was self-possessed and confident. She was the complete opposite of the other little girl joining the compartment who, having been hugged and waved off by a loud and weeping Welsh woman, sat sheepishly in the other corner, picking at the buckle of her bag.

It's an odd thing to reflect on now, but we didn't know then that the four of us, in that train compartment, would be the main protagonists in the rest of our lives.

'Well, I suppose we ought to introduce ourselves,' said the girl with the heavenly eyes. From her corner, diagonally opposite, she looked directly at me, and I could hardly breathe. 'My name's Pippa.'

'I'm Arthur,' I said, 'and this is my brother, Philip.'

'Philip! That's the same name as mine, sort of. I'm Philippa, really.'

Philip looked affronted. 'It's a boy's name. You can't have my name. It's not a girl's name!'

'Yes, but there's a girl's version of it. It means "horseman or -woman". Do you ride?'

Philip did not ride. Not even with stabilizers. He frowned and looked at me crossly, as if I could undo the fact that there was a girlie version of his name.

'Oh well,' she said. 'You're young yet.' Before I could think of anything to defend Philip – or indeed my own lack of horsemanship – she turned to the other girl, who sat opposite her. I hoped she wouldn't ask her the same question. 'And what about you? What's your name?'

'Dora.'

'Dora. I'm afraid I don't know what that name means.'

'It means "a gift",' said Dora unexpectedly, revealing a strong Welsh accent.

'How pretty!'

'I'm seven,' she added, encouraged perhaps by the compliment.

'I'm six,' Philip said, at last on a topic he felt knowledgeable about. 'But I'll be seven soon.'

'In eleven months' time,' I said drily, which was a bit cruel of me, because I could see it was important to him, but I just wanted to keep the conversation going. 'Anyone know where we're heading?'

Little Dora said, 'Our Mam says it's to a ship.'

Pippa looked at her sympathetically. 'Are you *Welsh*?'

Dora looked startled. 'How did you know?'

'Aha! I have special powers.'

In that moment, and for many years after, I truly believed that she did. Her glance around the compartment was regal, and her smile, to my eyes, subtle and delicious. She always claimed she had no idea of the effect she had on me that day, but I swear she did. My palms were sweating, I stumbled over words. And if she took me for just a normally awkward boy, Philip made sure she was aware of the changes she caused in me.

'Why are you smiling, Arthur?'

'I'm not. Shut up.'

'Yes, you are. You've gone all funny.'

Philip was six years my junior. Enough of a gap to make me truly resentful of his arrival in my life. Fortunately, Dora drew his attention to the comic he'd brought with him. She went over to sit next to him and began to read out clues to a simple crossword. 'Three across: "creepy-crawlies". Must be spiders – or insects. It's insects, it is.'

Somewhere between Birmingham and Liverpool, an Irish seaman joined our compartment and sat next to me in the middle seat.

'How do you spell "sex"?' Philip asked the compartment suddenly. Pippa looked out of the window, as if she hadn't heard. I was so embarrassed I could have hit him.

'Why do you want to know?'

He looked down at his comic, pencil poised. 'I've got the "in" but I can't get the "sex".'

The seaman gave a chuckle. 'You and me both, lad.'

I spotted a smirk on Pippa's face, and I released my own laugh. I'd like to think it wasn't a cruel laugh, but I remember Philip's slightly hurt and baffled look, and Dora putting an arm round him. 'Don't worry. I'll help you with it,' she said. And that made me laugh even more. I hate myself for that now. I can't help wondering, if things had been different, whether Dora might well have been the one to show my brother all the tender things a man learns from a woman. But that bewildered face haunts me.

The newcomer came to our rescue. He introduced himself as Seamus and kept up a banter that acted as a welcome sedative for us kids. (He seemed old to us, but on lists I've seen since he was only forty-eight.)

When things quietened down, he stood up and produced a hexagonal box from his overhead luggage. Opening it, he took out a concertina, which he began to play casually. Philip immediately stood up from his window seat opposite me and went to take a closer look. He planted himself in front of Seamus, and Dora went back to her corner seat next to the musician. They were both transfixed.

'How charming!' Pippa turned her lovely head towards me and caught my gaze. 'Isn't it?'

We listened to four or five tunes, relieved to be free of the need to talk. Dora and Philip plied the man with questions between the tunes, and I felt relaxed and grateful.

'What's that tune called?'

'That's "The Galway Shawl".'

Philip and Dora repeated the name, and giggled at their efforts.

'Are those real diamonds?'

Along the rim of the concertina were embedded these cut-glass stones. One or two were missing, and I noticed the cheap metal sockets like the ones in my mother's 'diamond' bracelet. Seamus ran his fingers across the sparkling stones and smiled.

'These?'

'Is it worth thousands of pounds?'

'Ah! This instrument, *macushla*, is priceless.'

Dora and Philip were awestruck, and so, I imagined, was Pippa. I tilted my head back on the seat and smiled, pleased with my silent authority.

'Are you very rich, then?' asked Philip, not entirely sure about 'priceless'.

'I am a rich man, son.' He spoke the words slowly and with a twinkle in his eye. 'Wealthy beyond compare.'

'Have you got a palace?'

'I will have, one day.'

'Where?'

'Oh . . . Clare, Connemara, Galway. Somewhere near Clare, for sure.'

'Is she your girlfriend?'

Seamus laughed. He began to play again, softly, like a murmur to himself. 'She was my first love, you could say. And she will be my last.'

I think I must have blushed at this, because I had to look away from Pippa and fix my gaze on the man's hands. The mention of what was on my mind made my jacket feel suddenly too hot. Pippa stared at the concertina too. I wondered if she was thinking the same as I was, but she burst my bubble immediately.

'Well,' she said, still staring at the instrument, 'I hope you have it insured.'

My pompous assumption that I was the only one to notice that the diamonds were paste had been roundly trumped by Pippa with that phrase. I had no idea what insurance was, except that it was a word belonging to a dull file of vocabulary in my head marked 'grown-up and boring'. We learnt that her family had recently had an expensive painting stolen. It had not been adequately insured, it seemed. Since then, the toing and froing of insurance brokers at her house had become as familiar as the visits of the Friday Fish Man to ours.

We seemed to chug slowly past the backs of some extremely tall terraced houses with line after line of washing smiling in sagging rows from each storey.

'Look how tall they are!' said Dora.

Philip leant forward to look out. 'They're amazing!'

'Utterly ghastly!' said Pippa.

Dora looked at her in awe, and I suspect she misunderstood. I saw her mouth the new word to herself, and then whisper it – 'Garsley! Utterly *garsley*!' – with Pippa's accent. I tried not to smile.

And so the journey continued, with me feeling alternately excited and deflated, and all against an impending homesickness beginning to lurch in my stomach, the swiftly receding fields pushing me further and further away from my mother's arms. Philip and Dora grew closer with each passing town, riveted by the Irishman and his magical concertina. Their shoulders touched as they squashed up together to look at it, and then they sat next to each other, having a go on it and chuckling. I envied their easy physicality.

Before we arrived, Miss Prendergast popped her head into our compartment. 'Nearly there now. How are you all in here?'

'It's dreadfully hot,' said Pippa.

'Otherwise,' Dora said politely, 'we're utterly garsley, thank you.'

Seamus chuckled, and Miss Prendergast smiled kindly at Dora. 'Well, I'm sure we'll all get on splendidly.'

I warmed to Dora straight away, but the truth is, I didn't pay her much attention. I'm sure I would have done, had Pippa not been sitting diagonally opposite me. Pippa was the sort of person who commanded all your attention, and if you let it slip, she grabbed it back without your even noticing.

It is odd, now, to think that it took a catastrophe to bring our little group together, and the chilling actions of just one person to tear it apart. One of us.

2

DORA

The first time I saw Pippa again was in a pub function room ten years later. Miss Prendergast had organized a survivors' get-together at the Wayfarer's Inn in Shepherd's Bush and had offered to put people up in her London flat if they couldn't make the journey in a day trip. I was just seventeen and had to plead with Our Mam to let me go and to pay my train fare. If I hadn't been promised a summer job at the Post Office and agreed to apply for college, I don't think she would have let me. But I had my way in the end.

I was longing to see him, of course. All the way to Paddington I was a bag of nerves, not helped by having to use the tube train for the first time when I got there. Even as I walked through the revolving doors of the pub, I spotted her. It seemed unbelievable that she should be there, smiling, sharing a pleasantry with someone near the entrance to the drab, brown function room.

I knew she'd seen me; I turned my eyes away just a fraction too late and was aware of hers tracking me as I searched for the ladies' cloakroom before I went in. Sure enough, as I came out of my cubicle, she was there at the washbasins, applying deep red lipstick. I stood at the basin next to hers and began to wash my hands. I chanced a look in the mirror and saw her eyes on mine. In that moment I knew that the magnitude of the effect she'd had on me was entirely justified. She must have registered my awareness of this, because she smiled quickly. Might she have risked ignoring me? Pretended I wasn't there? Or that she didn't recognize me, and that somehow she could keep this ignorance up for several hours before slipping quietly away?

'It can't be! Is it? Is it little Dora?'

'Yes – not so little now.'

'Oh, you're a slip of a thing. You make me feel like an old lady.'

She waited for my compliment, so I complied.

'You haven't changed a bit.'

'Lord, I hope I have! I just feel old next to you.'

I couldn't tell if this last remark required more flattery or was meant as some kind of palliative.

'And yet it seems like only yesterday,' she said, turning back to the mirror. There. She was trying to see if I remembered, but I would keep my cards close to my chest.

'It's all a bit of a blur to me, I'm afraid. I was only seven.'

'Of course.' That look again: fearful, dangerous.

I saw her now through the eyes of a young woman. She had a military straight back, well-cut dark hair, arched eyebrows and fashionably conical breasts above a slender waist. Protruding from a cream-coloured bolero, her forearms were less fashionably covered in a dark down, which moved me a little.

She snapped her lipstick shut and opened a compact. I looked away but could feel her eyes on me. I tugged at a rickety towel dispenser, which conceded no more than an inch of clean towel before it jammed. I had wanted to run my hand through my hair and powder my nose, like her, but instead I stood flapping my hands in an attempt to dry them.

'Here, have a tissue,' she said, clicking open a patent leather handbag that matched her red shoes. (I think I found her colour coordination a bit undermining.) I took it, but felt she was trying to disarm me with generosity. I stood there panic-stricken, puzzled, unresolved.

It was the look in her eyes that brought it all back, and I knew she could tell. Perhaps I swallowed too hard, perhaps I looked away too fast, but she saw straight away that I hadn't forgotten the event at sea that she had most wished me to forget.

When I'd set off on that Atlantic adventure ten years before, it had felt as though life had been jump-started after a long delay. Life at home had felt provisional for some time. Not because of the blackouts or the rationing or the fear of raids, but because just as the war started the previous year, my sister, Siân, died of diphtheria. The house was filled with the absence of her, the space she left far greater than the little space she had occupied, and the silence was somehow louder than her laughter. My mother had been there for me, and not there, in equal measure. She would hold me closer than ever, her eyes miles away. I suppose she thought that the seavacuee scheme would keep me safe, at least, although she wanted to keep me close after Siân had gone.

My father's sister in Port Talbot had had a direct hit, and that had made up his mind. He thought they'd try to bomb the mines next, after the steelworks, and ours was a mining village.

I really can't remember anything much about the journey to Liverpool, except Philip. Phil and I were about the same age, and we liked each other straight away. I remember the concertina, of course, and Seamus playing it. That was what brought us together. Arthur was there, and Pippa, but it's all a bit vague. I know Pippa's mother got on the train with her to find her a place, which you weren't supposed to do, so I knew she was a bit special. Dead posh. Also, later on, when an escort came round with a bag to collect rubbish, Pippa dropped a whole chicken sandwich into it – and half a beef one. Beautiful *and* wasteful. Utterly exotic in my eyes.

Fortunately, the next day was glorious: clear blue skies and sunshine. We were taken to the docks, past dun-coloured boats and dun-coloured buildings, and there, suddenly, floating majestically in the harbour, was *The City of India*. Each one of us was awestruck. The ship was so huge and stately and gleaming. She had two funnels with bands of white and waited regally in the sunshine for us to board her. She was, quite literally, breathtaking.

And on board! We were simply overwhelmed. I don't think even Pippa had seen anything quite like it before. We were welcomed by Indian lascars who wore bright white robes and turbans, blue waistbands, and shoes that curled up at the end. They loved children and treated every one of us like gentry. First, we were shown to our cabins. Mine had a bunk I shared with a girl called Janet, and it had its own massive wardrobe, a sink and a giant carafe of water, which was changed daily. The dining rooms were fabulous. There seemed to be no such thing as second class on this ship. There were waiters in blue uniforms and white turbans, there were six-course meals (really, *six* courses for children!) and there were forty different kinds of ice cream! This wasn't just for private passengers: this was for all of us. I could imagine Our Mam's face if she knew.

For our first meal – lunch – we had chicken. I remember it because at home we only ever had chicken at Christmas, and this was only September. I got to sit with Philip again at mealtimes, and we had so much fun together, asking the lascars about India and getting special treats just by asking for them. They would call us 'Little Madam' and 'Little Sir' and would smile and bring us delicious dishes we couldn't possibly have made up. Pippa and Arthur sat with us, which made it even more majestic. Arthur was like a grown-up to me, and very dark and handsome – I felt quite coy around him, I did! I thought Pippa was pretty too, and quite an authority. She explained a lot of the menu to us, with such confidence it was as though she could personally take credit for the entire operation.

In the end, we weren't able to sail that first day. We were so excited that I don't think we really cared. We had luxury and smiles around every corner, and we knew exactly what to do in the event of an emergency. At least, we knew exactly what to do in the event of an emergency on a gloriously sunny day with a beautifully calm sea.

People come from such different backgrounds, don't they? I hadn't come across anything quite like it before, especially with Pippa. And I don't just mean their class. I mean their experience of being loved.

I had known love from birth. It had been the temperate climate of our family life, had fluffed up our feathers and kept us warm through the Depression, and even its trembling clumsiness after the death of my sister only served to show the power of its presence in our home. It would have been unthinkable to me that some children had to lie in wait for crumbs of love, had to catch it unawares, trick it into their arms or be tricked by counterfeit copies of it. At the age of seven, I couldn't comprehend that people had different value systems to my own. I understood that Hitler was evil, and that the Welsh were good. Most British people, in fact, were generally good eggs. And so it followed naturally that everyone on this ship was generally a good person. We were all fleeing evil, weren't we? I hadn't reckoned on each passenger carrying with them their own little record of love, some with the pages crammed full, and some with the entries false or scrappy or with their ledgers almost empty.

I knew poshness when I saw it though, and I saw extremes of it for the first time on this expedition. There were levels of poshness. I was somewhere near the lower end, and at the bottom were people like the Joneses down our street, who had ten children with clothes that didn't fit and a few pairs of shoes between them. Pippa was pretty much at the top. She wore new shoes and cardigans that weren't hand-knitted. She spoke with a BBC accent, she had a mother who wore fur and broke rules, and she threw away chicken sandwiches.

Pippa dispensed advice with an authority that immediately commanded you. In the absence of parents, she and Arthur were the people we sought most readily for instruction and reassurance. The escorts, Miss Prendergast and Mr Dent, were a little more remote, and the naval officers, though kind, even more daunting for us to approach. Seamus was easy to talk to, and although he had no interest in parenting us, he was often there on deck to chat to and to play us a few tunes.

Within twenty-four hours, Seamus became our main focus of interest – second to food. He would give us his little concertina to play around on and then produce another from the canvas bag by his side. Philip and I took turns to play, although he made a lot of people put their hands over their ears and he lost interest quickly, frustrated by the inconsistency of the notes. But I liked the way they changed according to whether you pushed in or pulled out. Seamus played a slow air, and I tried to copy him. He showed me, note by note. It was tricky, but I loved it.

'Pushing in takes the air out,' he said, 'and pulling takes the air *in*, and that will give you different sounds, you see now, with the same buttons. Try these now . . .'

Philip was quite happy to let me monopolize the instrument, once he'd found three tin whistles in Seamus' top pocket with which to blast everyone on deck.

At one of these little sessions – perhaps on the second day, I can't remember – Pippa came and joined us for a bit. Of course she wanted a go, and tried 'Three Blind Mice', ignoring Seamus' efforts at tuition. She quickly ran out of air and found that the notes disobeyed her when pulling out.

'There's a little button there,' said Seamus, showing her, 'that lets you put the air in without making a sound. You have to let the air in.' Pippa ignored him and went on pushing and pulling the concertina apart loudly and roughly. 'You can't take out what you haven't put in,' said Seamus, agitated for the first time. 'Dora will show you, now.'

She released the concertina abruptly and plonked it in my hands. I felt awkwardly favoured and thought she might be angry. I started to play 'The Galway Shawl' very badly.

'I'll tell you what now, Dora,' said Seamus, 'if you can play that little tune there by the end of the trip, the box is yours.'

I was breathless. 'The concertina?'

'It is.'

Pippa, who'd got up to walk away, stopped. 'You're going to give her the concertina?'

Philip took a tin whistle from his lips. 'You're going to give it her to *keep*?'

I remember Seamus just closed his eyes and started to play gently on his other concertina. 'An instrument needs a player. I don't need that one any more, but I want it to go to a good player. Dora here is going to be a grand player.' He winked at me. 'You take it away and practise. You have to be able to play that tune, mind.'

I was speechless. My joy was only marred by the envy felt, I imagined, by Philip and Pippa, who were not receiving any such gifts.

'But what about the diamonds?' asked Philip.

I saw Seamus wink at me. 'Ah, I've no need of those, son. I've everything I need.'

Phil looked at me with eyes and mouth wide open. 'Crikey!' Then he did a little jig on the spot. 'If I can learn to play a whistle, can I keep it then?'

Seamus put his head on one side, as though giving this some serious thought. 'You take the big one away with you and practise in your cabin,' he said. 'You play me something on it by the time we get to Canada, and I'll give it to you.'

Philip was more than content with his penny whistle, and I was, of course, overwhelmed by the concertina. I spent every moment I could practising, and I drove Janet mad with the racket in our cabin. I pretty much had the tune off after a day, but I never got to perfect it. That's not because the ship sank, but because the next evening, something very odd happened.

3

ARTHUR

You can imagine how we felt when we set eyes on *The City of India*. The only time we'd seen anything remotely like it was on a jigsaw puzzle of the *Queen Mary* we kept in a cake tin at home. But this was miles better. To start with, we were dog-tired because we'd had a terrifying night of air raids in Liverpool, and now it was a glorious late-summer day with clear blue skies. Sunlight lit up this beautiful liner, waiting for us like a palace on water.

We all cheered up even more when we went on board. These lascars welcomed us with such pleasure and dignity that we felt like royalty. Philip was so excited, because after we'd been shown to a large room on board by our 'escort' (Mr Dent), we met Dora and Pippa. And, if I'm honest, I was pretty keen to see Pippa again.

For once, I was quite pleased to have Philip with me, because Pippa took quite a shine to him, and he and Dora were a good source of shared amusement for Pippa and me. Normally, I hated having to look after Philip. I was six when he was born and used to my mother's full attention. Had I been merely a toddler when Philip invaded my life, I would probably have kicked up an almighty fuss, unburdened by any need to pretend finer feelings. I would have thrown things about in a jealous rage, beheaded his toys, screamed at him and jumped on him and tried to sabotage his feeding at my mother's breast. She would have been left in no doubt as to my childish trauma at being replaced. As it was, she told the neighbours and relatives, 'Arthur adores his little brother,' and, 'He's so good with Philip. I don't know what I'd do without him.' This, the result of my attempts to please her, fed the grudge I could not speak of. I resented the way he took all her time. I didn't want mushy food and silly rhymes, but I was angry at the pleasure these things seemed to give them both. I would have been mortified, of course, if she had hugged me in front of my friends, but I ached for her to hug me as much as she hugged Philip, and I hated myself for wanting to knock down the towers they built together, for longing to go to his cot and shake him awake so that he would scream.

I suppose I wanted her to notice me, but since the little attention I got seemed to hinge on being good with my brother, I was loath to tamper with secure approval. Sometimes, when I was in the garden shed with my father, making ships in bottles (a passion of his), I would look out through the shed door and catch my brother watching me from the kitchen window. He would be helping my mother bake, and I fancied he was taunting me with the bowl I knew she would let him lick. He stared at me with slit eyes, and I felt all his cruel satisfaction at being so close to my mother. *Little git*, I thought.

Once, my father caught me scowling back at Philip, and he put his hand on my shoulder. 'You have to pay attention with these ships. Every moment counts. It takes patience and commitment.' He was holding the threads to pull up the hinged masts of an intricate finished ship inside its bottle. 'You know, Arthur, Phil is so jealous of you being out here doing men's work with me. He must feel a right Charlie making buns, don't you think?' Then he handed me the threads. That was the first time he'd ever let me do it myself. I still have that ship.

The incessant emergency drills on board were a bit tiresome, but it was still exciting. The hint of danger, constantly renewed by these drills, became mixed up in the potent thrill of adventure. I suppose we had rarely felt so much adrenaline over so short a period of time, so it's not something we could forget easily. That heady exhilaration was galvanized by news that we couldn't set sail the next day as planned, because the harbour exit had been mined. We had to wait another day for them to be cleared. Danger, excitement and endless ice cream. What a cocktail!

I shared a cabin with Philip, and he had the top bunk because he enjoyed the novelty of climbing up a ladder to bed. I tried to keep an eye on him, as I'd promised Mum I would, but he kept going off with Dora to listen to Seamus play his concertina. I have found out since that the Irishman was working the night shift in the boiler room. No wonder he liked to be on deck when he could. Dora and Philip couldn't get enough of him, and it was easy to track them down just by following the strains of an Irish jig or a polka.

It was important not to let Philip wander off too far, because every so often this bell would ring, and we'd all have to go to our muster station (a passenger lounge, in our case) and have another wretched drill. We had several drills a day, and unless he was with me, Philip often got lost. The passageways do all look a little the same on a ship, and he had only just turned six. Once, I found him being ushered out of the ladies' cloakrooms in the private quarters by a very firm woman in a mink, when he thought he'd found the gents'. And Dora, who was only seven herself, found it pretty confusing too, although she wasn't quite as clueless as Phil. She used to bring him to me and say, 'He's lost, love him,' and she'd give him a little cuddle (what she called a 'cwtch' – *Give us a little cwtch, then*) before she handed him over. She always looked so caring, though, holding his hand and turning her sweet little face towards his. Obviously I wasn't interested in her then, but I was envious of him – irritated, I suppose – because of his effortless intimacy with a girl. He just seemed to be a magnet for affection.

Anyhow, we were all assigned to a lifeboat (I was in the same boat as Phil) and actually had to sit in it to be absolutely certain we knew what to do. We were told about the dangers from U-boats and torpedoes, but we felt very safe with these naval officers drilling us all the time. We were shown where the provisions were – corned beef, sardines and ship's biscuits – and no sooner had one drill finished than another one seemed to begin. We had two life jackets, one navy blue kapok one, which we had to wear all the time, and one inflatable canvas one. These were puffy, unwieldy things, but we had to carry them about everywhere, even to mealtimes.

That first night on board there was bombing again. Bombs were landing in the Mersey, in the harbour all around our ship. We were a floating target. I don't know how we slept, but we did. Everyone was relieved when we set sail the next day on the early evening tide, even though, by then, the weather had turned to rain. We just wanted to get moving and out of that estuary. All the children were waving and cheering at the other boats as we left.

It did feel odd leaving England, watching the land recede and become a scrawl of ships and tall buildings along the horizon. I wondered when I'd next see Mum and Dad. For a moment, it felt as though I were on a giant elastic band pulling me back. It's just as well I had Philip to take care of. I don't think I could've got through that bit on my own.

I was very aware of Pippa, even then. We were segregated – boys on one side of the ship and girls on the other – but we all used to get together every moment we could. There were 'lessons' arranged for each age group and rooms allocated for them, but even these classes were segregated, and frankly a lot of us bunked off. There was a pretty impressive children's room with a rocking horse in it, so some of the younger ones went there, but the rest of us spent our time avoiding the escorts. We boys used to play Postman's Knock with the girls in Pippa's corridor. Pippa never kept the same number twice, so I never got to kiss her. Not that she was remotely interested in me then. She seemed to be a bit sweet on one of the private passengers, an older boy called Graham who used to come down from the top deck and hang about with us. I used to watch her flirt with him and I'd feel embarrassed for her. She would throw sponges at him or scream and run away from an imaginary lunge of his. It was mortifying. Graham took it all in his stride, and I'm not sure he even cared – that was the most aggravating part of it. He seemed more interested in filling us boys in with the latest news about the convoy. I was both relieved and angered by Graham's nonchalance. I loathed his common sense and his sangfroid. I envied his Fair Isle tank top and his long trousers.

Graham had found out from the crew, who had found it out from the captain, that being now so far from a German base and less likely to be torpedoed, the Royal Navy escort was turning round at this point in the Atlantic to accompany some incoming cargo ships back through the treacherous waters to Britain. At this point too, the convoy of smaller vessels was meant to disperse because they slowed us down and made us a sitting duck that could be seen for miles. 'You wait and see,' one of the lascars told us. 'We'll be streaking ahead now the navy escort has gone. There'll be no stopping us. And you won't notice any of this bad weather because we'll be going so fast!' We were all in a good mood that day, because we were out of danger and because a noticeboard informed us that our air force had downed one hundred and eighty-five German planes in the Battle of Britain.

Well, the convoy did *not* disperse as they were supposed to. According to Graham, the ship's admiral did not want to relinquish his position as commodore (which he had only as long as there was a convoy) and insisted the convoy stay together. Since he happened to be on our ship, there was a real clash of power between the captain and the commodore, and the commodore, being an admiral, pulled rank. Captain Taylor was officially in charge of our ship, and he wanted to break away (as originally instructed by the navy) and go full steam ahead to Canada on our own. This rapid pick-up in speed would also protect the passengers from the terrible buffeting of the ship in the building storm.

My interest in Graham's theories was really sparked on that fourth and last day on board, Tuesday the 17th of September. The ship was pitching and wallowing quite a bit, and the grown-ups had retreated to their cabins, seasick. We were over in the girls' passageway, racing around and playing ever more reckless games. Graham came down from the top deck to join us. Pippa noticed his arrival with delight, and my heart sank; but then he began telling me the news with a very sombre look on his face. The new zig-zag course the admiral insisted on taking to help fox any U-boats was simply slowing us down even more. He reckoned the captain was furious, and some of the crew were talking mutiny. For the first time, I began to feel very uneasy about our safety.

Mr Dent eventually appeared to disperse us, as usual, but he looked even leaner and paler than normal.

'Come on, lads, back to your side of the ship.' He waved his thin, elbow-patched arm at us, and seemed about to faint. 'People are ill; they don't need this noise. Early bath and bed. You can sleep in pyjamas tonight.'

Pippa said, 'Oooh! A bath!' and gave such a flirty, wide-eyed look of pleasure that I was condemned to spending the next few hours imagining her naked, soaking in a tub of hot sea-water and sponging herself down somewhere within walking distance of my cabin.

Mr Dent, a volunteer escort with the CORB, the Children's Overseas Reception Board, was a teacher in real life. How he controlled the children at school we couldn't imagine, and we assumed he must've been driven to this escort job as a desperate escape from the classroom. He seemed a quiet, underfed man, of no interest to anyone. We rarely paid any attention to what he said, and it was cruel, really. That evening, however, the ship was getting a bit too rocky for comfort. We felt as though we were in a recalcitrant lift that couldn't decide which floor to stop on. So we went back to our cabins and took advantage of the first bath on offer that trip and the first opportunity to wear pyjamas instead of outdoor clothes to bed. We were supposedly outside the torpedo zone and therefore out of danger. Graham and I knew different. We would wear our coats over our pyjamas anyway.

I saw Phil hanging about with Dora, and I told him to get a move on. I remember her beautiful clear blue eyes turned on me, and they seemed sort of reproachful, as if I'd interrupted something. They both looked like that. It's an awful thing to say, but it irritated the hell out of me. That was probably the last time I had a good long look at my brother, and all I could think was that he *irritated* me. God.

By the time he went to bed, he wasn't feeling too good and refused to wear his coat because it made him feel hot and worse. I should have insisted. If he'd been wearing his coat . . . Well, I didn't. And he wasn't.

SINKING

4

DORA

It was the fourth day out, and the morning was stormy. Loads of the adults were seasick, but most of the kids were fine, although we were told to stay off the decks because they were getting wet and slippery. By teatime things had calmed down, so everyone cheered up a bit. A group of us younger children were playing hide-and-seek in the cabins after tea. We were making a terrible noise, squealing and laughing, I suppose. The grown-ups used to get cross when we made a racket, and you weren't meant to run in the passageways. Mr Dent came down and told us, ineffectually, his hands clasped together, that we should stop, because we were upsetting the other passengers. We ignored him, like we ignored everything Mr Dent said, and carried on playing as soon as he had retreated apologetically up the stairs. But when we started playing again, we did so at least a bit more quietly. As I stood on deck, counting to a hundred and looking out at the sunset spreading beneath some black clouds, I didn't move my lips, and anyone going down to our cabins below might have thought them deserted.

I didn't say 'Coming, ready or not'. I didn't even get as far as the top of the stairs. I was making my way across the deck when Philip came rushing towards me, out of breath. I could see from his face that something was very wrong.

'What is it?'

'It's been nicked!'

'What has?'

'The concertina!'

I made for the steps, but he pulled me back.

He said, 'It's not there. I know where it is. I saw who took it!'

It seems he had been hiding in my cabin, under the bottom bunk. It wasn't a very sophisticated place to hide, because it was the first place you looked: under the bunks, then in the wardrobe. There wasn't anywhere else. In fact, the whole game was a bit daft; we only did it to pass the time of day and to have a giggle. I suppose we were all getting to know one another, and that was the fun of it. Well, according to Philip, this is what happened. He was under the bunk; the door opened. He thought it was going to be me, but a pair of smart shoes walked in, and he could tell it was Pippa. He lifted the bedspread, which he'd optimistically pulled down a bit to hang over the side of the bed and conceal his position, and he was about to say 'hello' to Pippa, when he saw her open the cupboard. He ducked back and waited, hearing her rifle about in the wardrobe. Then she put the concertina box beside the bunk and closed the wardrobe door. After that, she picked it up and left.

He couldn't imagine what she wanted with the concertina (unless it was for the diamonds, but she was too rich to need those), and so he crawled out and went after her.

'What are you doing with Dora's concertina?'

She turned in the passageway, startled, and he could see straight away that she looked guilty.

'It's not *Dora's*. It doesn't belong to her.'

'It doesn't belong to *you*. You've stolen it! I'm going to tell her!'

And it seems she really frightened him then, because when he ran into me on the deck, he was afraid for his life. When he told me what had happened, I thought there must've been some misunderstanding. I said, 'I'm going to go and find her and tell her to give it back.' But he put his arm out to stop me and looked at me pleadingly.

'Please, *please* don't say anything.' He was in a state of genuine panic, so I sat him down on deck. The boat was swaying quite a lot, which added to the surreal quality of the news.

'What did she *say*?'

'She said if I told you, she'd . . .' Then he did a cut-throat gesture with his hand across his neck. 'That means she'll kill me, doesn't it? And she looked at me like this . . .' He squeezed his eyes into slits. 'Don't tell her you know, Dora. We'll get it back.' Then he looked very brave and very indignant. '*I'll* get it back for you. I'll get it back tonight.'

'And I won't tell anyone – not even Arthur.'

The storm was beginning to whip up again. Our feet on the deck would be suddenly weightless, and the next moment the floor would press up beneath us. Nothing felt very real any more, and I wouldn't have been surprised to find it was all a dream.

Then we were told to go below because the decks were getting wet again and it was dangerous. I said to Philip, 'We'll sort it out in the morning.'

We went down the stairs, holding on to the rails, and then Philip put his arm around me as we walked down the passageway. I remember Arthur came and found us and urged Phil to get back to the cabin. He asked if I knew how to get back to mine, and I said I did. We must've looked quite comical, a seven-year-old and a six-year-old, standing like tragic lovers, because Arthur smiled and said something like, 'Say good-bye to your girlfriend, then, and look sharp.' I remember I felt embarrassed when he said that.

'Don't worry,' said Philip, giving me a proprietorial squeeze as we parted. 'I'll get it back for you.' That's what he said, love him. 'I'll get it back for you.'

It's hard, now, to distinguish between that feeling of nausea and the dismay at stumbling upon Pippa's betrayal. She knew so much about everything and was like a grown-up to me. She wasn't supposed to break the rules. Then I remembered her mother. The world seemed suddenly unstable, and the pushing and pulling of the deck beneath me only reinforced this sense of unease.

I kept trying to work out why Pippa had done it. It would bother me for many years, until I eventually understood. But lying there in my bottom bunk, listening to Janet talking quietly to herself as she read, I simply couldn't figure it out. However, we'd just had our first bath of the trip, so when the torpedo struck, I was, at last, luxuriously asleep.

I thought someone was shaking me awake, but then I heard a thud as Janet's life jacket fell to the floor, and then the alarm bell went off. I was confused. Janet had been almost hurled from the top bunk, but we couldn't see anything in the dark. She said we must've hit something.

The alarm was punishingly loud as we got out of our bunks wearily. We'd had enough of drills, but this seemed suddenly, scarily, like it might be the real thing.

'Janet, turn the light on.'

'I have.'

Nothing happened. It was pitch black and we had to try to find our shoes in the dark.

'Take your coat,' said Janet. 'It'll be cold up on deck.'

It chokes me to remember her saying that.

I scrabbled for my coat at the end of the bed and put it on. I remember my feet were wet. We thought the sea had come in, but in fact it was just burst water pipes. That feeling that the sea was already at our feet spurred us on though. My socks were tucked into my shoes, and I remember trying to pull them on over sodden feet. I reluctantly shoved my feet into my brand-new lace-ups, but didn't try to do them up. I remember this strange smell – a sort of sulphurous smell – which I later learnt to be cordite from the explosion. It was already seeping into the cabin before we opened the door. Janet took my hand and told me to put my life jacket on. 'It's no good carrying it,' she said, 'you have to put it on.'

She didn't make it, Janet. But she made sure I did.

Now, in the passageway, we began to hear screams above the alarm bell. Water was everywhere under our feet, and all sorts of debris seemed to be across the floor, making it hard to walk along in the dark. I just held on to Janet and we shuffled in the direction of the stairs. Eventually some blue emergency lights came on, and we could see the true extent of the chaos. Bits of wall panel had fallen through, the air was blue and smoky and debris formed drenched obstacles underfoot. Girls in pyjamas were appearing at all the doors, some with cuts and grazes, some calling the names of friends or sisters, but all filing obediently out into the passageway and joining a strangely orderly queue to get up on deck. We might have been queuing for our dinner at school.

At one point we had to crawl on our hands and knees over fragments of wall and ceiling, and Miss Prendergast was on the other side, covered in cuts, ready to help us out.

When we reached our muster station – which was the playroom – there was nothing but a giant precipice. You could look down and see the bottom of the ship. The playroom floor had become a huge hole. That was when I began to feel really frightened. I still have nightmares about that missing playroom.

Miss Prendergast made us walk along the promenade deck directly to our lifeboat. We passed a pool of blood on deck, and some of the girls started to cry. The emergency lights were dim, but the low blue gleam made that pool of blood even more eerie. I resented those crying girls. I envied them too. No one ever cried in our house – at least, not in front of anyone else. You just didn't. It was a private thing, like going to the lav, it was. You would've felt ashamed to do it in front of anyone. I held on tight to Janet's hand instead.

By now the ship was clearly listing. We grabbed on to each other when it swayed to stop us falling back towards the stern. The escorts were busy counting their protégés, and we stood and waited like children on a school outing. Some of the boys on the port side were even singing 'Roll out the Barrel'. We watched one of the other lifeboats being lowered. The ropes, or 'falls', at one end didn't unwind as fast as the ropes at the other, so the boat hung at an angle, and the children were clinging on and shouting. Then it tipped the other way. Back and forth it went, rocking like a fairground contraption, and we watched as it reached the sea, which was a huge way down – it must have been at least forty feet below. The final movement tipped the boat at a dramatic angle and tossed out half of its passengers like little dolls. We could hear their screaming but could do nothing except gawp as the boat careered away on a wave when the falls were detached.

Our boat was on the starboard side. This wasn't good, as the ship was tilting the other way, towards port, making the distance to travel down to the sea much further than it had been on our drills. Also, the boats hit the side of the ship as they were lowered. I didn't want to get into our boat when it was time, but a large seaman picked me up and practically threw me in. I landed on a lascar who was shivering – or trembling – in his thin cotton gear. There must have been nearly forty of us when we were launched, but Miss Prendergast didn't get in. She went to find a missing girl. Instead we had another woman, who said she'd take care of us and reassured us that Miss Prendergast would be all right.

Having seen what happened to the previous boat, the chaotic lowering of our boat made everyone panic. We were hurled towards the stern end, grabbing on to the falls or to each other, and then hurled back towards the bow. Several children fell out less than halfway down to the sea. Janet and I clung on to the gunwales and I closed my eyes tightly when the boat jerked and pitched, but as soon as it righted itself, it seemed to swing back in the other direction.

Just before we reached the water, the stern ropes became stuck and the bow ones lengthened suddenly, pitching us all forward into the sea.

All I remember is the boat practically standing upright and then being swallowed by this dark wave. I didn't drown, like I thought I had, because the life jacket sent me bobbing up to the surface. What I know now is that when the engines cut out, the deceleration of a big ship is very slow, and we were caught in the bow waves as it still ploughed forward. I could see the upturned lifeboat and lots of other children in the water, but the waves were taking us further and further away from the boat and the ship. It had a life of its own, that sea. I felt it suck me one way, then hurl me another, pull me up on to mountains and push me down into dark valleys. It mauled me and wouldn't let me go. There seemed no point in struggling against it, but struggle I did. Strange how that will to survive defies all the odds. I didn't think I was going to die, at least not in the sea. I just thought, *Our Mam'll kill me when she sees the state of these new shoes.*

It may seem ridiculous, but I wasn't afraid. I couldn't swim, of course. I'd never even seen a swimming pool and had been only once to the beach at Barry Island with my Aunty Ruby (a paddle in the sea and a wafer ice cream on the beach under a dome of gunmetal sky). It wasn't fear, though. What I felt as those waves picked me up and swept me about was something that stayed with me for many years. It was a deep sense of shock born of insecurity and betrayal. The Pippa incident had shaken my faith, and now the real grown-ups had sold us a lie. We had trusted them with their endless practice drills, and now their safety boats had not only failed to keep us safe, but they had tossed us into the sea like so much rubbish. I wanted badly to believe in their protection, but seeing all those children in the boat before mine flipped into the waves, screaming, and then the same thing happening to me, it was the almost callous inadequacy of the grown-up world that hurt, more than the result itself.

There was no protection after all. We were on our own in life for certain, as I had once feared when my sister died. All the grief at my mother's hopeless distance from me then resurfaced like the bits of chair and table that now bobbed up around me. So it was a wonderful release when a man's strong arms hauled me over the gunwales of a vessel and into the relative safety of a waterlogged lifeboat, seemingly jammed with people.

The safety was short-lived, but the gesture was important.

'We can't take any more! We'll sink!' a woman's voice shrieked, but the man whose arms had come to my rescue was unrepentant.

'They're children, for God's sake!'

I found myself in a boat so full of water that my knees were completely submerged. A few of the ship's crew were doing their best to bail out the water and free up the Fleming gear. It was dark, but *The City of India* gave off her mysterious blue emergency lighting, and a full moon dodged in and out of the clouds. I heard a familiar voice a few feet away. 'I've lost my brother. I promised him I'd wait.'

'Philip!' He was wedged between two shivering lascars. I waded along to him and one of the lascars shuffled into my space to make room for me. 'It's me, Dora.'

'Dora?' He clung on to me, cold and trembling. I put a stiff, sodden arm around him and gave him a little cwtch. He said, 'Don't worry, Dora, I'll look after you!'

The water was creeping up to our waists. There was no hiding the panic on board now; even the naval crew members seemed to be losing control. They knew we had to get as far away from the ship as possible, but the water in the boat was weighing us down and holding us back.

Suddenly the blackness became illuminated with pretty shining lights. It was like a firework display. All the ship's lights had come back on together. Then her bows went right up in the air and she slid swiftly down into the sea. It was a terrifying sight. The lights stayed on for a bit after she had sunk, so you could see this glow coming out of the sea, and it was so sad to think of all that loss.

No one spoke on our boat. There was an aching silence amongst the grown-ups, as if we were in church or something. I suppose they knew we were about to suffer the same fate but in a less stately manner. Then Philip murmured an utterly awestruck 'Crikey!' He heaved a loud sigh: 'What a waste of ice cream!'

5

ARTHUR

I was reading my *Beano* with a torch when it happened. There was a sound like a massive gong – you know, the one you see at the pictures when the film is about to begin. Only it was very, very deep in sound. You wouldn't have taken it for an explosion, because sound travels so differently underwater, but this was right under our cabins, so I guessed straight away. I shone the torch around the room: the wardrobe had fallen away from the wall, leaving a hole, and you could see the passageway through it. I could hear screams, and then the alarm went off.

I found the light switch, but it wouldn't work. Phil had been thrown awake and was practically hanging off the edge of his bunk. I shone the torch up at him, and he looked dazed. 'Come on!' I said. 'We've got to get our shoes on!'

There was water all over the floor. I sat Phil on the edge of the bed and put his shoes and socks on. There was no time to waste getting dressed when we should have been dressed already. Our pyjamas felt like a stupid luxury. The grown-ups had got it wrong.

When we both had shoes on we tried the cabin door, but it was stuck. We managed to climb out through the hole in the wall, but as soon as we got into the passageway we could hear Mr Dent shouting for help. His cabin door was jammed too, and another boy was trying to open it. Phil and I joined in, ramming and shoving until eventually Mr Dent came out, dishevelled and ghostly pale in the blue emergency lights which had come on.

'Thank you, boys,' he said tremulously. 'Let's form an orderly exit to the promenade deck.'

We edged our way slowly in the dim light, stepping over all sorts of wet debris. The floors were drenched. At one point we had to step around a gigantic hole in the floor at the side of the passage. I couldn't help looking down, and I wish I hadn't. You could see all the way down to the curved hull near the bottom of the ship, which was where the torpedo had struck. It was terrifying. I mean, really terrifying. I turned to help Philip pass this point without his looking down, but what I saw when I looked at him horrified me more.

'Where's your life jacket?'

He looked confused. He had left it beside the hole in our cabin as we'd climbed out.

I hate remembering this. I knew I shouldn't leave him, I *knew* I shouldn't, but he couldn't be without a life jacket. We were still edging relentlessly forward in this queue of boys, so I didn't have much time to think. I gave him my life jacket and fastened it on him securely.

'Stay with the other boys. Go to the muster station with them. I'll be back in a tick. Okay, Phil?'

'Yep.'

I went back the way we'd come, edging around dazed boys coming towards me. That's how I got to be on deck after the lifeboats had started being launched. That's how I got to be in the last lifeboat, without my brother.

The captain spoke over the tannoy: 'Take care of yourselves. Get into the boats.' We were told this was the very last boat and everyone else had left the ship except for the captain, but I wanted to look for Phil.

'Get in the boat!' A huge seaman shoved me in, and I noticed that Mr Dent was there too. He had waited until all the boys on deck were safely in lifeboats and he had gone back to check all the cabins with Miss Prendergast. She, too, sat in Boat Nine, and I felt some relief to see two familiar faces amongst the forty or so passengers and crew that were now being lowered with me into the dark ocean.

We were on the port side, towards which the ship was listing, so our descent was relatively easy. The falls were released as we hit the water and we all did whatever we could to get the boat as far away from the ship as possible. One of the crew members, Jack Heggarty, explained that we could get sucked down when the ship went under, so we had to get away quickly. Because we'd had such an easy launch compared to the other boats, we weren't waterlogged. This made it easier to work the system of paddles down the centre of the boat – the Fleming gear – and get us clear of any suction. But this great advantage – which no doubt helped to save our lives – would also be a disadvantage, as we would soon discover.

It was freezing cold and wet. The waves lashed against us and the wind was relentless. I was glad to be wearing my damp overcoat and shoes. Most of the lascars were in thin cotton clothes and they looked shocked and cold. Once we were free of the ship, we all sat for a moment, tossing on the waves and looking back at the dim lights. In the moonlight you could clearly see the shape of the majestic *City of India* like a giant sea creature nosing out of the water. There were screams and people shouting. The odd piece of ship's furniture floated by from the veranda cafe. I thought of Philip, and loathed myself for going back for the life jacket. I hadn't needed it after all. I could have kept him safe with me.

You could see a torchlight going around by the bridge, and I'm sure it was the captain, making one last check that everyone had abandoned ship safely. Was Philip still on there, on the dark ship? It was a chilling thought. I prayed that he wasn't lost somewhere in the maze of passageways, searching for me. Then suddenly the ship lit up. All her lights blazed and her bows came up. Then she went down by the stern and slid right down into the ocean very, very fast. For a few seconds you could see all her lights still on under the waves, and then it all went dark. There was a sudden silence, although you could hear faint cries in the distance. No one said anything. I wondered if one of the cries was my brother calling to me.

God.

So there we were, stranded in a storm in the North Atlantic, waiting for someone to come and rescue us. The trouble was, we had drifted further away than any of the other boats because we were water-free. Our success had isolated us. All we could make out were the distant lights of one or two lifeboats. We didn't know what had happened to the convoy, although one of the bigger merchant ships had been hit too and was on fire.

Someone fixed the light on the bow of our boat, and suddenly we could see our companions. I was quite startled to see Pippa sitting half-way down the starboard side. It would emerge later that, like me, she had gone back to fetch something from her cabin, only to be scooped up by Miss Prendergast who had missed her own boat in the process of looking for her. I caught Pippa's eye and said, 'Hello, Pippa,' as cheerfully as I could. She raised a hand in salutation and gave a defeated half-smile. I went to sit next to her, but she pulled her coat around her and turned her head to look the other way.

'You okay, Pippa?'

'Just tickety-boo.'

I felt foolish, and I looked across to the other side of the boat where Miss Prendergast was seated with a very small child on her knee. Mr Dent, in turn, was comforting Miss Prendergast and had wrapped a blanket and his arm around her.

'Look at the lovebirds,' I ventured in a low voice.

This raised a smile. 'And what a romantic!' she said – almost too loudly. 'He'll bring out his dominoes next,' or something like that.

I feel guilty, now, that my attention moved so quickly from my brother to attempting to flirt with Pippa, and guilty that Mr Dent might have heard. Because the next thing I remember, someone was shouting about people in the sea. On the port side, where Mr Dent and Miss Prendergast sat, people were turning to look. I stood up and could just make out a few life jackets at some distance from the boat. Jack Heggarty and another man grabbed an oar each and started trying to take the boat over to them, but it seemed useless.

'Have they seen us?' asked someone. 'Why don't they swim over?'

But the waves were sweeping them along, and it seemed very likely that these people either couldn't swim or were dead already. For a short while some of them came close enough to our boat for us to see that they were moving.

'They're children!' cried Mr Dent. 'They're some of ours!'

And before anyone could object, he took off the dressing gown he had been wearing since we freed him from his cabin and made a clumsy leap over the side of the boat, leaving a stunned Miss Prendergast to peer after him into the dark waves. It seemed like ages before he came back to the boat, but there were all sorts of goings-on with the men with oars, and eventually a child and Mr Dent were dragged, soaking and exhausted, over the gunwales. I can't remember much about what happened next in the rescue mission, except that Jack Heggarty seemed to take over, but I was commandeered by Miss Prendergast to look after the rescued child – a girl – while she administered to the heroic Mr Dent. I was dispatched to the bow end of the boat to find blankets. It was only when I wrapped a blanket around the child that I saw it was little Dora. Her hair was flattened against her and darkened by the water. She was speechless and shaking and gasping for breath. I found a gap on the starboard side big enough for us both to sit in, but it was a few seats away from Pippa on the same side of the boat. In any case, Dora soon took up all my attention, curling herself on my lap and wrapping her arms around me. I pulled the blanket tightly around her and tried to reassure her. She seemed unable to say anything in reply. When I did look towards Pippa, she was watching me and I felt mildly heroic. Then Dora brought my head down as she clung on to my neck, and I was lost in the new warmth of her as she began to settle down. I couldn't say that she ever completely settled on that boat. We didn't know it then, but we were to drift in that punishing ocean for another eight days and nights, and Dora barely let go of me once.

Well, it must've been just a few minutes later when Dora, whose head was resting on my shoulder and facing out to sea, spotted a child on our side of the boat. She became agitated and tried to point, and Jack Heggarty got up to look.

'There's another one on this side!' he shouted.

'Dead,' a voice said.

'No, it moved. It came right up close.'

When I managed to wrench my head round to look, there was just a distant life jacket bobbing about fifty yards away. The next thing, Mr Dent had shed his blanket, pattered to our side of the boat, and once more jumped inelegantly into the deep.

'It's too far out!' shouted Heggarty. Then he lowered his voice and said to the men around him, 'That skinny runt doesn't stand a chance. Madness. Complete madness. He'll die of cold before he makes it back.'

Later, I saw Pippa was looking anxiously out to sea. I imagined what she must have been feeling, having been so scathing about him. Mr Dent never came back.

6

DORA

Crumbs. Did we really not spot love blooming in our midst? When you think how keenly we were watching the people around us, how on earth did we fail to spot the signs? Was I moved at the time by that act of heroism, by Miss Prendergast's reaction, her slow realization that he was gone forever along with her dreams? Or did I sit there – more likely – in frozen paralysis, unaware of anything? But I can't have been unaware, because I *do* remember things. I'm just not sure how I translated the events stacking up so fast around me.

At that first reunion Miss Prendergast remembered all those lost that night. 'You all made your own attempts to rescue people, but because you survived – because *we* survived – we feel, maybe, that we have less right to be here. There may seem sometimes an unfairness about it, a throw of the dice that went our way at the expense of some-one else. But what these reunions must be above all else is a celebration of life – a celebration of the lives of those we lost, for we all lost some-one. I remember in particular, of course, those on Boat Nine, because we spent over a week together, and I wish to celebrate the bravery of a very shy and self-effacing man, George Dent – known to many of you here as one of the escorts.' Her voice began to waver at this point, but only very slightly, and with the fortitude we knew so well, she passed over it. 'But this is a celebration of our lives too. A celebration of life itself. Because if we don't celebrate this life and live it to the full, then they gave their lives for nothing. So, I give you a toast . . . to life!'

I clinked glasses with Arthur on my right and a veteran seaman to my left. Arthur turned from me to Pippa and touched glasses with her, but when I turned back to the table he was looking at the cloth intently, turning slightly away from Pippa as if he wished to avoid her eyes.

'Dora,' he said enthusiastically, but without looking at me, 'some more water?'

I touched his arm. I couldn't help it. I wanted his arms around me. I wanted to burrow into his neck. I wanted to smell his skin and his hair. Duw! God almighty. He looked up at me briefly and I could see his eyes were glistening with tears. 'It's all right,' I said, and he poured me a shaky glass of water with a frown.

'It's not all right,' he said to the table. I felt chastened. I had shown uncharacteristic confidence and it had been rebuked. 'I can never forgive myself for leaving Phil. I promised my mother that whatever happened, *whatever happened*, I would not let him out of my sight.'

'You mustn't feel guilty.'

'But I do. I have, ever since. It follows me everywhere, that thought of what I might've done, how I could've changed everything if only—'

'No. Listen, Arthur . . .' I was choked with all the things I wanted to tell him, unsure where to start or if I should. What would come out of me once I began? What inappropriate things might I say that simply couldn't be said in this company? He had already closed his eyes on my beginning, dismissing anything I could tell him before I said it. He wanted none of my balm. But if he'd had any idea what I could've told him, he would've listened, he would've been saved. But those lids came down, and my courage failed to find a foothold. 'It wasn't your fault.'

Pippa leant across from his right and blundered in with her cherry lips and dazzling eyes. 'Come on, Arthur! My glass is empty – mine's a G and T!'

He got up gratefully and went to the bar, asking if he could get me anything.

'An orange juice, please.' I didn't even know what a G and T was.

Pippa leant back in her chair and regarded me with interest, as if I were a newly arrived animal at a zoo. She took in my white blouse and my leaf-patterned dirndl (a last-minute creation I'd run up the week before) and she cocked her head on one side sympathetically. '*What's* not his fault?'

You see, you couldn't relax your guard for a minute. 'Oh, nothing,' I said, and I got up to help Arthur back with the drinks. I was waylaid by Daphne Prendergast, who called me 'My darling Dora', and I hoped Pippa was cringing.

I tried not to imagine the load that must have weighed on Arthur's shoulders all these years. I would not picture his homecoming (trumpeted by the local paper perhaps), or his mother's face as he walked through the door, or however it was that he returned to the maternal arms, alone, without Philip. I closed my eyes to the possibility that those arms felt dead, like my own mother's after Siân's death, or worse, that the arms were not proffered at all. He would have sat, like me, at a table normally laid for four, and they would have both turned to him to avoid looking at the empty space. And every now and then he would have seen his mother lay the table and hover, fourth plate in hand, before returning it to the plate rack, or else watched the backs of her arms fidget at the cutlery drawer as she replaced the unwanted – yet so much wanted – fourth knife or spoon. Yes, it was the table that announced the absence as loudly as a pulled front tooth, and I would not look at him there. I could have spared him that. I could have told him.

7

ARTHUR

The bond the two of us forged on that boat had been a very strong one.
I swear Dora didn't stop clinging on to me for eight days and nights,
and I had no wish to let go of her. I held her close to me, and I can still
smell the oily dampness of her hair, feel the milky skin, warm even in
the North Atlantic, warm where we touched, chin to cheek, neck to
neck, neck to face, face to hair, cheek to chest, arm to back, arm to arm.
I swear she kept me going, little Dora, having to reassure her, having
someone to look after, to put before myself. She kept me going as surely
as Miss Prendergast kept us all going by cheerfully telling us stories and
singing songs for us to join in with, fending off her own grief until such
time as she could be alone with it.

I wanted to spend some time with Dora at that reunion. If I'm honest . . . well . . . I hadn't really expected her to have grown up so much.
Of course, I'd been intrigued to see her again, but I'd pictured a school-
girl. Now here she was, all white and green, eyes sparkling, smiling and
youthful. No Atlantic wind in her hair. Not a trace of helplessness. But
of course the Atlantic *was* there. When she touched my arm, I felt it.
All those eight long days and nights of fear and longing and thirst and
dread and hope. All those thoughts of Philip and my stupidity, she and

Miss Prendergast brought them all back. In contrast, Pippa, who had largely ignored me on the long Atlantic drift, seemed like a safe haven. When I'd bought the drinks at the bar, she appeared at my elbow.

'Shall I relieve you of that gin?'

I smiled, and handed it over. I looked to see if I could discharge myself of the orange juice too, but I could see Dora talking to Miss Prendergast. Pippa watched my eyes.

'Did she upset you?'

'Miss Prendergast?'

'I meant Dora.'

'Dora?'

Pippa gave me a long look with those extraordinary green eyes and stirred some remote longing in me. 'I thought she might have said something to upset you.'

She put her head a little on one side. I felt all her attention upon me, and it was electric. 'Of course not. I was just thinking about my brother.' She looked down at her drink, turning the glass slowly with manicured fingers. I realized that, as children, we had been oblivious to the lists of those lost at sea and those who survived. 'He was never found.'

'Oh.' She turned her head away, and when she turned it back there were tears welling up in her eyes. 'I'm so sorry, Arthur. Poor Philip.'

'You remember him?'

'Of course. How could I forget?'

I was moved by her reaction. She was genuinely upset.

'So . . .' She looked at me with such angst I felt embarrassed for having brought the subject up. 'You've no idea what happened to him, then?'

'We're certain he drowned. Probably in one of the early lifeboats that tipped the passengers out. The life jacket wasn't enough in those freezing waters.'

A tear rolled down her cheek, and I put down the orange juice to comfort her. I touched her arm, half on the soft wool of her bolero and half on her bare skin. I let my thumb stroke her skin. She didn't flinch.

'I'm sorry! I'm just a bit emotional. He was such a sweet boy and . . . everyone seems to have lost so much.'

'And you?'

'Me? Oh, I'm all right.' She flashed me an affectionate smile. 'I have everything I could possibly want.'

I felt a little disappointed at this statement and then wondered if it was meant as some kind of provocation. I looked at her left hand, previously hidden under the base of her glass, and for the first time I noticed a large diamond sparkling from her ring finger. 'You're engaged?'

She looked down at her hand with mock surprise. 'Oh, that! I should take it off really. It's all over.' She flashed me an intense look. 'I found out he only wanted me for my money, so I had to call it off.' She fixed her eyes steadily on mine again. 'I think one should marry for love, don't you?'

'Aha! You're all here! I've got you all together!' Miss Prendergast joined us suddenly with Dora at her side. 'Pippa, how good to see you – and looking so elegant. Now, Arthur, here is your little protégée, all the way from Wales. And what do you think of her now? Somewhat changed, perhaps?'

I can't help wondering what was actually going through my mind at that time. Had I any idea that the choices I made then would change us all? Of course I didn't. But what was I actually thinking when I looked at Dora? Did I see the little companion of my darkest days? She made me melt, I know that! She made me helpless. I know I wanted to touch her, to put my arms around her. I wanted to *smell* her. But what could I do? I hadn't seen her since she was seven. It was like a madness. She had the same candid blue eyes, the same delicate features, and she hung her head slightly in the same self-effacing way she had as a child. I know I wanted to talk to her. Despite the other temptation at my elbow, she, Dora, was unfinished business, but I doubt I could've told you why.

Dora, Pippa and Miss Prendergast were the only women on Boat Nine. It was hard to believe we'd been in such an intimate space once. There had been no privacy on that boat. I remember that when any of the three needed to use the toilet, there would be a bucket passed down the boat and we'd hold a blanket up and look the other way. Whenever Miss Prendergast needed to go, the lascars would shout, 'Bucket for Memsahib! Bucket for Memsahib!' and the bucket would be handed down with a sort of reverence. The rest of us just did it over the side. And as for anything else, well, there wasn't anything going through us. We were so hungry. All there was were ship's biscuits and a few cans of sardines and peaches, and we had to make it last. We had one of the ship's stewards with us, and he sorted out the food. We got one ship's biscuit per day each and one slice of peach or a sardine. Those biscuits were like rock, and you needed something to wash it down with. All we had to drink was one beaker of water each per day – and those beakers were one inch in diameter and about eight inches deep. So we were always hungry, but after the first two days it was the thirst that got to us. That's all we could think of: water to drink. We did have a bit of a squall on the second day, I think it was, and we all got empty cans ready. By then we'd found the sail wrapped up under the boards and we'd rigged it up so that all the rain would wash off the sail and into the beakers and cans. But of course the sail was covered in brine, so we couldn't drink our lovely rainwater. That was a real blow.

The first night we thought we'd be picked up, but because we'd drifted so far away from the others, the ship that was sent out to rescue everyone, HMS *Alexander*, didn't spot us. When it got back to the Firth of Clyde a couple of days later, we were all added to the list of those missing. It must have been unbearable for my mother.

Well, anyway, after we'd got through that first night, we could begin to see each other more clearly and see the state of the waves.

They were mountainous. They had been lashing at the boat all night and soaking everyone to the skin. I was lucky in my coat, even if I was drenched. Most people were in their pyjamas, and the lascars were huddled together for warmth in their flimsy cotton gear. When the sea did calm down a bit, on the second night, it was actually rather beautiful. It sounds funny saying that, but there was a sort of phosphorescence to it, and if you put your hand in, it would become all glowing. And the stars . . . I've never seen stars like them. You felt you were just stuck on this little planet suspended in space, space that went on forever. And it was a sort of comfort, somehow, to feel the vastness of it all. It made our problems seem small – for a moment or two at least.

It's hard to explain how cold we were. The pads of our fingers were permanently wrinkled, as if we'd been in the bath too long. There were little icebergs around us too – 'growlers', they were called – so that gives you an idea of the cold. And the thirst was like nothing else. Daphne Prendergast told us all to suck on a button, and that sort of helped. Also, she came around the boat rubbing our feet to keep the circulation going. I don't remember anyone doing it for her. She got us all singing too. We sang 'Run, Rabbit, Run' and 'When You Wish upon a Star' and 'Let's Call the Whole Thing Off'; she really kept our spirits up. She told us stories, made us tell her what we were going to do when we got back, what we were going to eat, what we were going to drink. And we all talked about what we'd do when we were grown-up. I was going to join the Navy, like most of the other boys. Actually, most of them did, and I became an aeronautical engineer, so I design bits of planes. Funny, that. It didn't put many of us off. I can't remember what Pippa's ambition was. Dora never talked. She didn't say a word all through that voyage. I rubbed her feet and her arms and held her close. She clung on to me and rubbed my back. Never said a word.

One night we had a pod of whales next to us. Minke whales, according to the seamen on board. It was magical. We forgot how cold and thirsty we were for a while and were just mesmerized by these enormous, gentle creatures. Then someone reckoned they liked to rub up against the bottom of boats, so we were all splashing like mad to shoo them away. Still, I remember the enchantment of that night when the whales came.

Then on the sixth day one of the kids spotted a ship. No one believed him at first, because we were always imagining ships, but when you focused on the spot in the mist, you began to see it *was* a ship. We'd set up a canvas awning over the bows to provide a tiny bit of shelter from rain and wind, but at this point we threw it overboard to speed us up and worked the paddles like mad. We set off our last remaining smoke flare, and we were all cheering and shouting like mad. I swear we were within fifty yards of that ship – you could see the crew walking around on deck. Then, to our utter amazement, her propeller started up, there was a belch of smoke from her funnel, and off she went.

She *must* have seen us, but she was heading away from us. That was the worst day. That really was torture. Up until then we'd all had hope, but after that we were down to half a beaker of water a day, and it wasn't enough. We knew we were slowly dying of thirst. No one could make any sense of what had happened. The only thing anyone could think of was that German U-boats sometimes followed lifeboats, waiting for a rescue ship to come along, and then they'd torpedo it. That was the only reasoning we could come up with.

So there we were, marooned in the Atlantic, weakening day by day with hunger and thirst, all hope now gone, and what did Daphne Prendergast do? She said if there was one ship then there could easily be another, and she started singing. She must have been feeling as despondent as the rest of us, and privately grieving for a lost love, but she sang her heart out. That's Daphne Prendergast for you, and we owe her everything.

8

DORA

There was a newspaper photograph of us on board the rescue ship, and Our Dad cut it out. There I am with a sailor's hat on, and Arthur's wearing one too. And there's Miss Prendergast. 'Aunty Daphne' we called her. If it weren't for the photo, I'm not sure I would've recognized her at all at the reunion. I had a sense of her as a person, but not a visual one. So the photo filled things in for me. I've looked at it a lot over the years, and all the faces are like family, almost.

I was surprised when I saw Arthur again. He was still very recognizably himself, but the face was longer and the jaw more pronounced, altogether more manly than I'd imagined. I'm not sure what I'd expected – he was nearly twenty-three after all – but I certainly wasn't disappointed. As I said, Pippa hadn't changed significantly (you'd recognize that triumphant, pigeon-shooting stance anywhere), but Miss Prendergast seemed determined to tell everyone how transformed I was. It was wonderful to see her there, looking pretty much as she does in that photo, but so strange to be singled out by her and to be the object of so much attention and affection. I thought I looked totally different to my seven-year-old self. I'd been surprised that Pippa knew me in the ladies' cloakroom, but at least she had taken a few moments to work it out. Miss Prendergast found me so instantly familiar, she might have seen me only the day before. And yet her insistence, like a visiting relative, on how much I'd grown (as if this were a surprise after ten long years) did at least make me feel that my efforts with the sewing machine had been worthwhile. I was blushing with embarrassment and pleasure in equal measure.

In retrospect, she was probably surprised to see me in fresh summer clothes instead of a grey ship's blanket, my hair flattened to my head with sea spray. She would've remembered every detail of those eight long days with a greater poignancy than the rest of us. I was also, of course, living proof that her dear Mr Dent was indeed the bravest of men. I was his successful rescue attempt. My life lent something crucial to the meaning of his passing. But aged seventeen, I wasn't thinking any of this. I was thinking about Arthur touching Pippa's arm at the bar.

Daphne Prendergast was asking me all sorts of questions: where I lived now, what my plans were, whether I needed any references and so on. I don't think I asked her a single question about herself. It makes me shudder to think how socially inept I was. But she was always on the ball: I think she could see where my attention lay.

'Aha, here they are! So Arthur, what do you think of little Dora now?' That's what she said, or something like that. I was mortified, and a little bit thrilled.

And there was Pippa, of course, shocked to find herself standing face to face with me and to have Arthur's attention wrenched away from her by the very direct question. I looked down at the floor, where Pippa's red patent shoes trounced my little white ones and the brown suede pumps of Miss Prendergast.

'I think, Aunty Daphne, that she's radiant.' He held Miss Prendergast's hand in both of his own and turned his smile on me. 'Of course, I would've expected nothing less.'

'Do you know,' she continued, grabbing my elbow, 'that watching you and this young Dora was one of the things that kept me going? You were so affectionate towards her. It was wonderful – really moving – to see a young lad take so much care of a little one.' She patted my arm with her other hand. 'It warmed my heart.'

Pippa closed her eyes in a slow blink, clearly bored. Arthur looked intently at my arm, as if expecting to find an appropriate reply written upon it. 'I . . .' He looked up at my face and our eyes met. 'It was important.'

That's what he said: *It was important.* That's all he said, but it was enough to keep me hoping. Pippa broke the moment, saying the do was marvellous and what a super idea of Miss Prendergast's to bring us all together, and had she seen Jack Heggarty yet, and so on. I suppose she hoped to move the conversation away from Arthur and me, but it gave us the opportunity to look at each other urgently and awkwardly, interrupted suddenly by the exhortation of one of the bar staff to eat up the sandwiches at the buffet or they'd all be going to the pigs.

'Addresses!' Miss Prendergast said suddenly. 'I must remind everyone to write down any new addresses.'

Pippa put her glass down on the nearest table, confidently slinging someone's handbag over a chair to make way for it. 'Arthur!' she said, leaning in close to his ear (but I could still hear her). 'Can I speak with you privately a moment?'

He followed her out of the function room to the entrance hall. He never came back.

9

ARTHUR

'Arthur, I really need to get away from here. Will you take me somewhere?'

'What is it? Are you feeling unwell?'

She looked disorientated, and a frown appeared. 'I just need to get away. It's all been too much – too many memories. I can't see how people can be enjoying this. It's dreadful.' Her voice began to wobble. What could a man do?

I took her out on to the street, vaguely thinking I might take her to a nearby cafe for a sit-down and a chat, but looking up and down the street, there seemed to be nowhere inviting. She grabbed my arm and breathed deeply. 'Let's get a cab – let's get out of here altogether.'

Obediently, I hailed a taxi.

'Where to, sir?'

'The Ritz,' she replied for me, sinking into her seat as though she had just escaped a nasty incident.

I thought of the wallet in my jacket pocket. I had no idea how much tea at the Ritz would cost, but I had taken out three pounds from the bank to pay for an overnight stay if necessary. I think I would have panicked more had Pippa not leant into me slightly, and that gentle pressure seemed to tell me any cost was worth it. The taxi drove right up to the front entrance, and Pippa waited for the door to be opened for her, turning her back as I paid the taxi driver. She had plainly done all this before, whereas I was a total novice.

We were shown into a high-ceilinged, elegant hall called Palm Court, where the white-clothed tables were set out for tea, and where the buzz of conversation was softened by the rippling notes of a grand piano. There didn't seem to be any prices displayed anywhere, so when the waiter came round and Pippa said, 'Shall we have tea?' I nodded and asked the waiter for tea for two. There followed a series of questions about which type of tea, choice of sandwiches, choice of scones and so forth. I felt such an idiot, and couldn't help wondering if she had taken me there to test me out. I think I fumbled by okay, but I remember that awkward feeling of not quite knowing what she was up to.

'So, what are you doing with yourself?' she asked after the tea had arrived (a silver tea service and a three-tiered plate with sandwiches and cakes). 'Are you a doctor or a lawyer, or a sad little man in an office?'

'I'm none of those,' I said quietly, pouring the milk into the teacups.

'Oh!' She smiled benignly. 'Milk afterwards, not before. So do tell.'

So I said, 'I'm an aeronautical engineer.'

'An engineer? How ghastly. Don't they wear overalls and get covered in oil?'

'I don't wear overalls or get covered in oil. I design engines for aircraft.'

She looked confused. There were only two types of men in her experience: landed or professional, and the only professions allowed were medicine or law. She sipped her tea and then placed the cup back in its saucer purposefully. 'So do you earn an awful lot of money, then?'

I shifted in my seat. I wasn't used to this level of directness. 'I'm doing very well, thank you. I've been able to save, and next year I'm hoping to have enough to put a deposit on a small house.'

'A house? How wonderful. Is there a Mrs Arthur in the background?'

'No.' There she was again, direct as anything. 'Not yet,' I said.

'Not *yet*? So they're queuing up, are they?'

I didn't like the way she had hold of the conversation. Back at the reunion she had seemed distressed, in need of me. Now she seemed to be laughing at me. I could be back at the pub talking to Dora. I *wanted* to be talking to Dora, to touch her, to hold her. 'Well, *you* seem to have men queuing up. How many more of those diamonds have you got stashed away?' I nodded at her ring finger.

'I don't like your implication.' She looked genuinely indignant, then smiled coquettishly. 'The trouble with women in my position is that men want you for all the wrong reasons. A woman has to protect herself. I'll give the ring back, I suppose, but then again, I might just keep it.' She munched defiantly into a smoked-salmon sandwich, and I thought it quite possible that she would.

'Why did you want to leave the reunion?'

She thought for a moment, staring gravely at the tablecloth. 'I find it so painful, remembering that time. Don't you?'

'Actually,' I said, 'I think it's good to remember it with people who were there, people who understand. I wasn't quite sure what I'd make of it when I got there, but I found it . . . well, sort of consoling.'

'Well' – she reached across the table and stroked my wrist – 'we can remember it together if you like.' This was typical of Pippa. One minute she made you feel like a fool, and the next she would seem to need you more than anyone.

'I can't remember much about you on the lifeboat,' I said. 'You kept yourself very much to yourself.'

'Well.' She folded her lips together as though trying to prevent them from trembling. 'It was a very frightening time.'

'Yes, but we were all in it together. Don't you feel that? Even Miss Prendergast admitted at the reunion that she had almost lost hope on that sixth day after the ship had turned tail. She did a great job of pretending, for our sakes.'

Pippa left her hand on the tablecloth, and I took it. We had been through this terrible thing together, and I wanted to talk about it. After that ship ignored us, we were all tested to the limit. And apart from one poor lascar, all of us survived, and that was an extraordinary thing. We were parched, we were starving, we were suffering from hypothermia. And yet we sang. We made plans to collect rainwater, but the weather turned beautiful, and we sat, on the most glorious late September day, adrift and miserable under a cloudless blue sky. I felt for the first time that I was going to die. And then, on the eighth day, when we were barely moving at all, one of the boys said there was a plane. No one took much notice, because we all kept imagining spots on the horizon or in the sky. But this other boy, he got all excited, and none of us had the energy to be that excited over nothing, so we looked, and at about the same time you could begin to hear the distant drone of the engine. It was a seaplane. The crewmen started trying to signal to it, and Miss Prendergast lent her petticoat so that it could be flown on the mast. One of the lascars even unwound his turban to wave madly, and everyone began to get excited. Then the pilot signalled with his Aldis lamp. It was a good job we had Jack Heggarty and his men with us, because we wouldn't have been able to understand that signal: he was low on petrol, but would send a relief plane and a ship, which would be along in about an hour. Anyway, the plane dropped us a little raft with supplies on it, but we couldn't row to it. That gives you some idea how exhausted we were: we couldn't even row to the raft, which had food on it! But we were so happy. The mood change on the boat was remarkable. Suddenly we were going home. And by the time the relief plane came – a Sunderland – we were all waving our arms. It signalled to us that a rescue ship was on its way and it dropped supplies, and this time there was a long cord attached which fell next to the boat, so we were able to haul them in. I still remember those gulps of fresh water! Corned beef? Never been happier to taste anything! And there was a big red flare for us to use as well, but in any case that Sunderland kept circling us to make sure the ship didn't miss us.

HMS *Anthony*. That's a ship I'll never forget. She came right up beside us, and it was an odd mix of feelings then, because it was so reminiscent of the last time we had been right next to a huge ship, being lowered into a raging sea – so frightening, you know – but at the same time we were thrilled to be rescued. We were just so glad to see it. The sailors put these nets over the side of the ship for us to scramble up, but of course, none of us was up to it. Not one of us – not even the men – could climb. We had trench foot, you see. We all had to be carried up one by one by the sailors. I remember being slung over a sailor's shoulder, and it was a long climb up like that!

Pippa didn't seem to remember any of this – or, at least, she didn't want to. She made that very clear. I was still reminiscing when her eyes filled with tears. 'Stop, please! I can't bear it!'

'I'm sorry. I should have thought . . .' I handed her a newly pressed handkerchief. 'Look, I won't mention any of it again. Is there something I can do?'

She held the handkerchief to her nose and shook her head. Now that the tears had come there seemed to be no stopping them; they spilt over from her pretty green eyes and rolled down into the white cotton. She was really distressed, so I shuffled my seat around to hers and put my arm around her. She melted into me, leaning her head on my shoulders, as if that was what she had wanted all along. I rested my cheek on her perfumed hair and felt blessed. This was Pippa: the girl at the heart of so many of my teenage fantasies. Here she was, pressed up against me, vulnerable and fragrant. 'Are you sure there's nothing I can do? Would you like some fresh air?' In truth, I didn't want to move her from this position in case she never held herself against me again, but I was at a loss, having not seen this coming at all.

'Don't leave me!' she whispered urgently, turning her face towards mine. 'Stay with me.'

My strong feeling of unease at having left the party in such an underhand manner resurfaced suddenly. I really ought to get back there before people started to go home. I calculated that I could probably just about make it back there with Pippa, without it looking too rude if we left now. The bill arrived. I willed myself not to look at it, but squeezed Pippa closer to me. 'I won't leave you. But we should be getting back to the party.'

'No! Don't make me go back there, Arthur.' The use of my name sent a shiver down me. 'Stay with me tonight.'

I couldn't think of anything to say. I couldn't believe she was inviting me to bed with her. Women didn't do that sort of thing in 1950, at least not any women I'd ever met. Was she suggesting we got a room? Would I be able to pay for one? Did she live nearby? Did she have twin beds, by any chance?

'You're upset.' I held her shoulders gently and turned her towards me. 'I'm not sure you realize what you're saying.'

'I want you to stay with me tonight. We'll get a room. Stay with me. I want you with me.'

I was so out of my depth, I can't really believe I said anything sensible, but I do know I was determined to do the right thing. It wasn't easy, though, because I didn't want her feeling rejected. 'Dear, sweet Pippa, I don't think you realize what you're asking of me. I couldn't spend the night with you without . . . I couldn't possibly . . . you would regret it in the morning. I won't take advantage of you like that.' She looked down at the tablecloth and began to breathe deeply. 'I don't think you're in a very good state to make the right decision now, so I'm making it for you.'

'I see.' Her face was inscrutable.

'I'll pay the bill, then I'll see you to your train.'

I had the feeling that I had annoyed her – humiliated her even – although in later years she would tell me she had loved me for that decision (and in later years again, that she had hated me for it). I glanced at the bill and mustered all my effort not to look shocked. Could this be right? Two guineas for *tea*? We're talking about I-don't-know-what in today's money – enough to buy a good pair of shoes at any rate. And then there was the tip – I was expected to leave a tip as well. I had less than three pounds left in my wallet – which I had hoped would last me all week – and I placed two pound notes and a half crown on the little silver dish with the bill.

'Don't worry,' she said, recovered from her tears, 'I'm staying in town, anyway. Just get me a cab to Knightsbridge.'

The change was placed on the table with two complimentary mints. I left a shilling as a tip, and she instantly told me it should be ten per cent. *Two shillings!* More still if you took into account they'd asked for guineas rather than pounds. I fumbled clumsily in my pocket for another half crown and added it casually to the dish. She stood up and didn't wait for me as she started walking towards the entrance lobby. I caught up with her and went to open the front doors, but I was beaten to it by a footman. No doubt he expected a tip too, but I followed her through the doors. I could see a free taxi hovering in front of the hotel and saw her hesitate briefly before making her way towards it.

'Pippa,' I said, holding on to her arm, and I could feel a thrill as I came into contact with her warm skin once more. 'I'd like to see you again.'

She turned by the taxi door. 'Well, you'd better play your cards right, then.' It was more coquettish than sulky, and when I had given the taxi driver a ten-shilling note in advance, she looked at me from the back seat with those heart-stopping green eyes and smiled knowingly. She knew full well she would see me again.

I stood on the pavement and watched her go, slowly aware that I didn't have enough change to get back to Shepherd's Bush. I would have to walk – no, *run* – all the way. What were my chances of seeing Dora before she left?

RESURFACING

10

DORA

From the moment I saw Pippa again, I knew life was going to take a strange turn. Even so, I had no idea quite how far she would go.

It wasn't easy to start with. Daphne Prendergast gave me Arthur's address, but there seemed no point in contacting him, not after he'd disappeared with Pippa. I mean, if he'd wanted to speak to me as much as I wanted to speak to him, he would've stayed at the party. In fact, leaving like he did was nothing short of rude. He didn't even say goodbye to Daphne, and she had been looking forward to catching up with him. There was also a crewman from the rescue ship – the one which picked up the other boats – who had wanted to speak to him about something.

Then, out of the blue, I had a letter from him a week or so later:

> *Dear Dora,*
> *I'm so sorry we didn't have time to chat much at the reunion. I had been really looking forward to a good old chinwag with you! It was my fault, of course, and I apologize. Pippa was feeling unwell and needed escorting home, and then I found myself on the wrong side of town with no money for a bus! I did go back, but only found*

*Daphne and Jack Heggarty. I hope you don't mind, I
asked her for your address.*

*Well, let me know your news. Are you going to col-
lege? Are you planning to stay in South Wales? I'm in
London at the moment, but expecting to be sent to Bristol
very soon, so you can write to me at the above address (my
parents') if you like. I'd like that very much.*

Warmest wishes,

Arthur

I had had some time to wonder about the implications of his leaving
with Pippa. My fears varied from what she might tell him about me, how
she might tell her version of events, to full-blown seduction on her part.
And there was also the fear, which I had tried not to dwell on, that he might
actually have planned to leave with her, that he had had his eye on Pippa
all along. I was consoled by his letter – more than consoled. I examined his
handwriting, touched the paper that he had touched, held it to my cheek,
to my nose, to my lips. I kissed the stamp that he had licked. I memorized
his parents' address near London. I looked at the brochure of teacher training colleges at school, and I decided to apply to Cheltenham and Bristol so
that I could be closer to him. I know it's just a letter, well-worn and a bit
raggedy now. But there's something almost primitive about a letter: it can
have a powerful physical impact on you. The words are not just words but
marks made by someone's hand, in a way that only they can make them.
They choose the pressure of the pen, the width of line spacing, the slant of
the words. It is something precious and unique. Here's my reply:

Dear Arthur,

*Thank you for your letter. We did wonder what had hap-
pened to you at the reunion. There was a crewman from
HMS Alexander – the ship that rescued all the other
boats – who was looking for you. Anyway, it's good to*

hear from you, and I'm glad that you managed to get back from your adventure in time to catch Aunty Daphne. Did she fill you in about the crewman?

I don't have much news, but yes, I am hoping to go to college in September. I'm applying to Cheltenham and Bristol, so you never know, we might bump into each other! How is your work going? I saw a huge plane fly over our house yesterday and wondered if you had designed it.

Love,

Dora

I rubbed a little *L'Aimant* scent on to the envelope and hoped I hadn't gone too far.

We wrote to each other like this for a few months, exchanging information in a friendly and inquisitive manner. I think there was little doubt that we were interested in each other, but although I picked up on the clues from him – hungry as I was for them – I was far too lacking in confidence to acknowledge the evidence. I just kept writing back innocent, newsy letters in the hope of a breakthrough of some kind, although I wasn't quite sure what nature it could take. I spent a good deal of time daydreaming about romantic meetings on cliff tops and in exotic places I'd seen at the pictures, like Capri, Casablanca and Devon. And then, in July, after my eighteenth birthday, there was this:

Dear Dora,

I've been looking at the train and bus services and realize that you are really not that far away from me. I thought it might be nice to pay you a visit. What do you think? I've never been to Wales and think it's about time I did! Are you free next weekend?

I could arrive on the 10:30 Joneses' bus from Newport, which, according to the timetable, will take me all the way to Gwern Road. Please don't worry if this is inconvenient. Don't trouble your mother about food or anything. If the weather's nice, we can take a picnic somewhere, and if it's not, I could take you to a cafe.

  Love and good wishes,

  Arthur

You can see how many times I've read this letter – it's falling apart. It was the first use of the word 'love' in his letters. Of course, I was on top of the world, but I was terrified too. There were no cafes where I lived, only the workingmen's club by the Co-op. There wasn't anywhere I could imagine taking a picnic to either, unless he wanted to sit in sheep droppings with a view of the coal tip. It was a far cry from Casablanca. I would have to improvise.

He came.

  Our Mam put on lipstick and wore a fake pearl necklace. She put us in the front room, which smelt musty because it hadn't been used since Siân's funeral. The house was one in a long terrace, which ribboned along a mountain. It was on two floors at the front and three at the back. Downstairs at the back was the kitchen and parlour, which looked out over the valley to the tip on the mountain opposite. It was a bright room, but the chairs were covered in newspaper to stop Our Dad's coal dust getting everywhere, and the other furniture was covered in coal dust and laundry. It was unthinkable that Arthur should see our parlour, so Our Mam had put a little vase of flowers up on the table in the front room along with the best china.

  If Arthur was disappointed with our humble house, he didn't show it. In fact, he was really polite about everything, and of course that went down well, as you can imagine. I'm afraid to say, though, that I was probably a little bit ashamed of my parents. They were trying too hard and it made me feel awkward. Mam kept bobbing in and out with trays and a huge red-lipsticked smile, and Our Dad, who had been sleeping after a late shift, came downstairs with a tie on to say hello. He shook Arthur's hand, which I'd never seen him do to anyone before, except the pastor. I suppose I'd never seen them through anyone else's eyes before, but suddenly my father's hands were nicotine-stained and his clothes reeked of smoke, and my mother's hands were red-raw and her cheeks were ablaze with tiny blood vessels and she said embarrassing things about me.

'Our Dora made these. She's a good cook, Our Dora.' She might as well have added, 'And would make someone a lovely wife.' In fact, I was convinced she would if she were allowed to stick around long enough. I knew she meant well, but her constant trays of tea had two very bad consequences. The first was that – at least, as I saw it – Arthur would think I was incapable of making tea myself, and that I was still a baby whose mother did everything for her, which was not true. The second consequence was a little more dire: all that tea meant that Arthur had to pay a visit 'to the bathroom'. Not only did we not have one, but also the lav was outside the back door, and to get to it you had to go downstairs and through the parlour.

I ventured a look at his face when he came back, but there were no visible signs of trauma. If he was shocked, he was dealing with it pretty well. I had to get him out of there.

We went for a walk up the mountain and looked out across the valley to the next mountain and the tall tip. Grey sheep nibbled the sparse grass around us, and we sat down in the sunshine. 'I'm afraid it's not Capri,' I said.

He laughed, and I laughed too.

'You get sheep thrown in here, though,' I said.

'And mountain air . . . and a pretty girl.'

My pulse thumped loud in my head and I could feel my cheeks heat up even in the cool air. His arm brushed against mine. I wanted to be wrapped in those arms again, but this time with a strange urgency. It was all I could do not to jump on him. I loved the skin of him, familiar but surprising. The pull of his closeness sparked a startling turbulence in every part of me. He leant over gently and kissed me on the lips.

Let me say that again: he leant over gently and kissed me on the lips. It was the most wonderful thing that had ever happened to me. Of course, I'd never been to Capri, but I doubt it could have beaten that kiss on the mountain.

11

ARTHUR

Dora and I wrote to each other for some time, and occasionally we met up. The first time was when I went over to Wales to see her. When she met me off the bus, it was like seeing her for the first time all over again. I had to reacquaint myself with small details I had forgotten: the tilted head, the shy smile with slightly crooked teeth, the blue eyes that disappeared with that smile, the way she had of holding one arm at the elbow, the apologetic shoulders, the milky skin, the slender waist, the utter loveliness of her. I felt oddly tearful when I saw her standing there in the crisp sunshine. I breathed in the fresh air all around her. She was oxygen to me. I wanted to take her in my arms and inhale her. Instead I held out my hand, and she gave me hers to shake awkwardly, cool and soft.

I liked her parents. They were gentle, modest people. I knew they would be. As soon as they spoke, I was transported back to the exciting moment when I first heard Dora speak with her Welsh accent on the train. It was thick and easy, with a rhythm so foreign and exotic that I had to stop myself from listening to the music of it rather than what was being said.

Her mother was slim but sturdy, with calves shaped on the steep roads and mountainside. Dora's father was a short, skinny man, but even so his jacket, fastened tightly with one button, indicated that it had been bought a decade or so earlier for a younger version of himself.

The house smelt homely, of coal and baking and gas. I liked the frugality of her surroundings, and I was pleased to see where she came from. Dora was made here: unspoilt and practical; she appreciated everything.

After a few sandwiches in their front room, we decided to go for a walk. Whilst waiting for her to fetch her coat, I stood studying the photographs on the wall in the hallway. There was a picture of a male voice choir in which I spotted her father; a picture of what must have been her maternal family, with a teenage version of her mother; then there was a photograph of two little girls. The smallest one, pretty and grinning, was undoubtedly Dora, but the older one, who had her arm around Dora, was a real beauty. She looked out of the picture with more steadfast confidence than the little one, who appeared so excited that she needed the steadying arm.

'That's Dora and her sister, Siân,' said Dora's mother, coming into the hallway.

'Oh, I didn't realize she had a sister. Does she live here too?'

'Oh, no. Siân passed away twelve years ago. Diphtheria, it was.'

'I'm so sorry.'

'It was a long time ago.'

'But these things don't go away, do they?'

'Oh, Arthur, bach, have you lost someone too?'

'My brother.' It felt so easy to say. Just a word to represent a whole person, a whole life. 'He was never found after the ship . . . after the disaster.'

'Oh, your poor mother!' She pronounced the word 'your' like 'ewer', and I was so fascinated that I was distracted for a moment from the truly interesting thing about this remark. She had not consoled me.

72

She had gone straight to my mother. I suppose it was to be expected that she would put herself in another mother's shoes. Siblings were not expected to feel the great loss with such intensity – and perhaps that's true – but I could see now that Dora and I had more in common than I thought. I wanted to understand her mother's thinking.

'Yes. My mother took it badly.'

'Oh, yes! Poor thing!' Then she grabbed my arm and said brightly, 'But she has *you*!'

I smiled. 'It's funny, though. I never really felt I was enough for her after that.'

I waited for her reply. It was going to be important. She was going to tell me what my mother truly felt.

'Didn't you, love?'

Her face, upturned sideways to mine, was full of feeling, but what it expressed I couldn't tell for sure. I needed more words.

Dora came up the stairs from the parlour wearing a dark green coat and a headscarf, and so the next words her mother gave me were, 'Enjoy yourselves my lovelies! And come back for some tea!'

Dora's house was on the side of a mountain. The back looked down into the valley and the front faced up the mountain. We walked up the mountain opposite their front door and looked down at the houses streaming along the valley, their windows edged in white stone against the grey. And we looked across the valley at the opposite mountain, tall and golden with bracken behind the dark coal tip. 'See those springs and streams along the mountainside?' she said, pointing. 'There's one under that great tip as well. Our Dad's mad as hell with the Coal Board. Says the tip'll come down and cover us all one day.' Along the valley to the left was the giant wheel of the pit-head, and to the right was the only exit, a slim pale horizon down the valley between the walls of the mountains. It was a beautiful early August day, and the stiff breeze seemed to push the sun in and out of the little clouds, so that we were alternately warm and cool in quick succession. Dora took on a new glow for me. As I saw her climb ahead of me, as sure-footed as any of the ragged sheep across our path, I realized that she would have already lost her sister Siân when I first met her in the train compartment, and lost her quite recently too. She would have been sent away to keep her safe, to keep *her* from dying as well, and that would have been an agonizing decision to make. I recalled the frantic Welsh woman hugging her on the station. Had I been a little envious at the time? Had I wanted more displays of affection from my own mother, whose hugs were largely for Philip (because I would've turned away in any case, awkward and ashamed)? And little Dora, sitting there in the compartment alone with strangers, had been feeling just as I did when I got home: not quite enough for her. Loved, but not quite . . . *enough*.

The grassy mountainside was covered in sheep pellets, and bleating from all directions reached us from time to time on the wind. We were sitting on our coats and the sun was on us. I felt a sudden rush of tenderness for Dora. I needed to hold her, to give her all the warmth she had been missing, to feel – as if some essence might be transferred from her bones pressed against mine – how she had coped with her need so well.

The scent of her skin took me straight back to Boat Nine when my arms were wrapped around her and her little limbs were clinging on to mine. As a boy, there had been an instinctive need to hold her and protect her, and I know she was the reason I survived. On that Welsh mountain the smell of her was like coming home. But it was far more powerful than that because we were no longer children. There was something else. I could have drowned in her. I ached for her.

I leant over and kissed her. It was a wonderful feeling. I had found my woman.

12

DORA

Life at college was pretty dull. I shared a room with a buttoned-up girl called Edith who saw images of Jesus in the pattern of the floor tiles. On the weekends, if I wasn't seeing Arthur, I went to the pictures with another girl called Jenny, a bubbly second-year student who lived out in a flat in a smart part of Cheltenham. She was trying to convince me to join her the following year, as she thought I'd have more fun out of college. One particularly bleak weekend she invited me to a party that her landlord was throwing. Apparently he was young but had his own house and he came from landed gentry or something. I had nothing better to do, so I went along.

I first came across Ralph in photographs. I was standing in the hallway of his Georgian terraced house, and there he was: straining on the oars of a boat, biceps flexed, neck splayed with tendons like the base of tree. There were other young men behind him, and the picture oozed masculinity. It is odd, in retrospect, that this was my first image of him. Rowing requires such commitment and team spirit, and Ralph possessed neither of these qualities. I would later discover that he was only standing in temporarily on the day the photograph was taken, and that he was booted out of the team even before the injured rower he was replacing returned. Next to the rowing photograph was a picture of him standing on a mountaintop, his arms folded, his legs apart. He looked as though he had conquered the world. Again the moulded muscles stood out and flaunted themselves at the camera. In another photograph he stood on a beach, in bathing trunks, with a pipe in his mouth, a trilby on his head and his arms around two girls, and in yet another he playfully appeared to be leaning on the Eiffel Tower, although it was tiny and in the distance whilst he was huge and in the foreground. On the opposite wall to these pictures in the hallway was his framed degree certificate from Cambridge. Although I would return to inspect them later, I first observed all these things quite fleetingly with Jenny, as we made our way upstairs to her 'flat'.

There were two bedrooms and a living room with a kitchenette in one corner. The bathroom on the landing was shared with the rest of the house, where, according to Jenny, the landlord lived with assorted glamorous people who came and went. I could not have been more excited at the prospect of securing a room somewhere like this for my next year of college. The shared living room to the flat had a view over a park, in the middle of which was a beautifully painted bandstand. The room was full of light, and I spotted a sewing machine in the corner.

'You sew – like me!' I heard myself say.

'*Do* you?' Jenny's face lit up. 'I'm absolutely hopeless!' She picked up a partly finished dress and showed it to me. 'Can you do zips?'

'Yes.'

'Okay, Dora, you're moving in! We're going to have some fun together, you and I! Come on, that sounded like Ralph coming in. You'd better meet him.'

'Hasn't he got to approve of me first?'

'He'll do as I say! I'm afraid we can't let a good seamstress slip through our fingers. Anyway, you're pretty. He won't say no.'

I was flustered, but I followed Jenny down the stairs and into a huge, high-ceilinged front room, which she entered without knocking.

Two young men sat in opposite corners and didn't stand up when we went in.

'This is Dora. She'd like to move in.'

The chestnut-haired man she was addressing put down a pile of papers he had been studying and looked directly into my eyes, so intently that I had to look down at the floor. 'A Dora? I adore her!' He laughed at his own little joke. 'And where do you come from, Dora?' He pronounced my name as if it were something unusual, or a piece of pretentiousness on my part to be its owner.

'Wales,' I muttered.

'Where in Wales?'

'The Valleys.' I had learnt never to mention the mining village I grew up in, partly because the pronunciation of it provoked mirth and partly because no one in England had ever heard of it.

'The mining valleys?'

I nodded.

'A true proletarian,' he said. 'You're in, Dora. Welcome to your new home!'

This was my first glimpse of real freedom, and I genuinely wanted to move in the following September, but I explained that I was committed to my accommodation at the college for now.

'We'll have to see if we can persuade you, then.'

The man in the opposite corner, silent until then, started playing a guitar, and Jenny beckoned me to come and sit down on a sofa to listen. He had bright orange hair and closed his eyes as he played. At first it was jazz, and then he moved on to some Nat King Cole hits, which we sang along to. Despite his skilful playing, he was clearly more modest than his friend, who busied himself with drinks and banter.

As the daylight faded, more people began to arrive, and soon the high-ceilinged living room was filled with voices growing ever louder above the music. The red-haired guitarist paused for a drink, and someone put on a record player. People began to dance. Now it may seem strange, but it was the first time I'd ever drunk alcohol, and although I'd had only one glass, I was beginning to feel light-headed. Ralph came to sit on the arm of the sofa and said something to me.

'Pardon?'

He leant in close.

'Have you travelled much?'

'No.'

'Where have you been?'

What could I say? Newport, Bristol, here, my aunty's village in the next valley, Barry Island.

'I set sail for Canada once.'

'Canada! Now there's somewhere I've never been. Not yet, anyway. What was it like?'

'I don't know. I never got there.'

He looked confused, and then intrigued. 'What happened?'

'Ship sank.'

'Oh!' He leant more emphatically on his arm, which was resting behind me on the sofa. 'That wasn't *The City of India*, was it?'

I nodded, a little impressed that he remembered it from so long ago.

'I knew someone on that ship.'

'Did you? Who?'

'You probably wouldn't know her. Philippa Barrington-Hobb. Different deck, I should think.'

'Not Pippa?' I felt suddenly alert, as if I had just heard some shocking news. 'There was a Pippa in our group. She did have a double-barrelled name.'

'Dark hair. Amazing green eyes.'

It was her. I resented the allusion to her eyes. If she could dazzle Ralph, she could dazzle anyone. Why did she keep turning up in my life? I had tried my hardest to bury that particular memory. I didn't want any trouble. I must have nodded.

'Well, I'll be damned!' he said. 'What are the chances? Did you know her well?'

'Well enough.'

'Poor Pippa. She's had a rough time.'

Now he really had my attention. I swivelled round to face him. 'What's happened to her?'

'Didn't you hear?' Then he suggested we go somewhere quieter.

I could hardly say no. We were beginning to bellow at each other. I followed him into the kitchen, which was also high-ceilinged and grand, if a little tatty, but that was also filling up with noisy people pushing for drinks from the large oak table. He opened a French door into a small sunroom. It was dark and cool but suddenly quiet.

'How's your drink?'

I looked at my empty glass. 'I'm fine.'

He insisted on topping me up. He produced an open bottle of wine from his side, which he must have taken from the table as we passed. 'There. This is a bit quieter, isn't it?'

'Tell me about Pippa.'

'Pippa? Ah, well. You knew, presumably, that her family had fallen upon hard times, because that was why she was on that ship, basically.'

'Hard times?'

'Her father ran off with someone-or-other and left her mother with nothing, just the big house to live in. Huge great place, but impossible to run without an income.'

I pictured this huge great place and found it hard to work up any sympathy. 'Couldn't her mother sell it?'

'Lord, no! Ashleycroft Hall is the family estate. You can't sell that. Anyway, it wasn't her mother's to sell.'

So I asked what they did, then, and he said that her mother started selling off the paintings. 'Fetched a fair whack for some of those. Then the poor thing got burgled, and there was no insurance. Bastard had let it run out. So then she sends Pippa off to Canada as a seavacuee, while

79

she shacks up with a millionaire – if she can find one. That was the plan, anyway.' He was taking swigs straight from the bottle. 'All goes well for a bit, but he leaves her too. Bit of a hard one, her mother. Have you met her? Bit cold. Beautiful for a woman in her forties, but not going to keep a man around for long. No warmth. A man can soon tell when he's being used. So it was all down to poor old Philippa. Had to land herself a big fish.'

'You mean marry someone rich?'

'That was the plan. And you've seen Pippa. *Not* difficult, I would say.'

'So what happened?'

'She got her man. Jeremy Finlay-Funny-Fanny or something. Rolling in it. Perfect match. He had the money; she had the blood. New money marries breeding, that sort of thing. Even Pa thought it a good match, and he's a stickler for good blood. "Best of a bad job!" he said. Anything to keep the stately homes of England from going to the dogs, you see.'

'That makes sense. She was wearing an engagement ring when I saw her the September before last.'

'Oh, you saw her? Oh, well you'll know then. All went up the spout. Poor Pippa. There she was pretending to be the loaded inheritor of a vast estate, and there was he pretending to be just plain loaded. Which he had been. Owned all these shares in a gold mine in South Africa. Except he didn't. It had all been gambled away the year before. Just able to borrow enough for the bluster – decent ring and all that. When she found out he'd deceived her, she had to ditch him.'

'But she'd deceived *him*.'

Ralph smiled and put his arm around me. 'Oh, you are delightful.'

I pushed his arm away. 'Why don't *you* marry her, then? If she's so beautiful and you don't need the money?'

He pressed his hand against the wall above my shoulder and leant in towards me. 'Because, dear Dora, I am a socialist. I like my women to be from honest toiling stock.' He kissed me on the cheek, and I backed even harder against the wall. His breath smelt of alcohol.

'I've got a boyfriend,' I heard myself say. It sounded odd. I'd never called Arthur that before, but now I knew that's what he was. Ralph straightened a little and considered me intently.

'Beautiful, honest *and* unavailable.' He smiled. 'I like a challenge.'

13

ARTHUR

Let's see, how on earth did it happen? Dora came down to see me in Bristol during her Christmas holidays – right at the beginning, it must've been. She had her suitcase with her and she was catching the Newport train later, to head back home for Christmas.

I had a surprise lined up for her. I'd been looking at houses to buy for some time, and I'd finally whittled it down to two that I liked and could just about afford. I wanted to show them to her, and had arranged two consecutive viewings with the estate agent. I can still remember her face when we were looking around. It was so full of awe and delight.

'An *indoor* bathroom!' she squeaked in the first house, a very modest terraced home in Redland. 'A fitted kitchen!' she marvelled in the second one, a small semi-detached place in Horfield. We must've been in every room three times at least, and her eyes seemed to grow wider with each inspection.

'Oh, look! There's even a fridge!'

'That belongs to the owners,' I laughed, 'but we could get a fridge.'

She looked at me awkwardly for a moment, and I realized I had given myself away with that 'we'. It was meant to be a surprise for the day I got the key and showed her the house I actually owned, and I still intended to leave the marriage proposal until that moment, but somehow the word hung in the air.

'I'm hoping we'll be a *we*, if that's all right with you?'

She nodded, smiled and buried her face in my armpit. So it was sort of understood, but I was going to surprise her with a ring when I moved in and she came to help me choose the furniture.

'So which house is it to be? You choose, Dora.'

'Really?'

'Really. I've looked at them both three times now, and they both look okay to me.'

'This one then.' She turned around in the kitchen, looking up at the ceiling in wonderment as if there were a chandelier hanging from it.

'And will you help me choose the furniture?' She looked at me with happy, tear-filled eyes and said nothing. 'I'm relying on you to help me, Dora. I don't know a fawn from a beige.'

So that was it. Unofficially, we were engaged. I went to a jeweller's to look at some rings. I hadn't really thought about this; I thought they were all pretty much the same until they started to shunt tray upon tray of different rings past me on the counter. Also, I didn't know her size. They suggested that the lady might like to make her own choice and that I could pop the question with a family heirloom or a dress ring. If I liked, they could even trade it in for the eventual purchase when I brought her in. This seemed to make sense, so I arranged to borrow a dress ring from my mother (a mock emerald) and bought a new box for it.

Then something odd happened. It must have been prompted by that Christmas letter from Daphne Prendergast and the updated list of addresses that was enclosed, because in the New Year I had a 'late Christmas card' from Pippa.

Dear Arthur,
Just saw your new address and wondered how life was
for you these days? Do you still see anything of the old
crowd? (Dora, Graham etc.?) Are you going to Daphne's
do in September?
　　Lots of love,
　　Pippa

I suppose there was nothing especially unusual about that, and I replied fairly briefly and politely that yes, I wrote to Graham from time to time, and yes, I still saw Dora and, in fact, she was coming to see me in a few weekends' time, and yes, I was hoping to go to the do in September. But the events that followed were mystifying. Until now, of course.

I arrived home from work a few days later – January 1952, this was – and my landlady, Mrs Peet, said there was a visitor for me. She was a kindly old soul, and she gave me a bit of a nod and a wink. She knew about Dora, but this visitor was decidedly unexpected and a whole new kettle of fish. She opened the door to the never-used front room to reveal Pippa, semi-reclining on the modest wooden-armed sofa and wafting expensive perfume into the musty unused air. She was such an unusual sight, surrounded by Mrs Peet's cheap ornaments, copper knick-knacks and photos of dead relatives, that I couldn't quite believe my eyes at first.

'Pippa?'

She smiled but didn't get up. 'Have I changed that much?'

I don't know why, but I felt ambushed by her. I was uncomfortable in my work clothes and felt like relaxing after a long day. I wished she'd given me some notice.

'Of course not. If I'd known you were coming . . .'

'You'd've baked a cake?' She grinned with her shapely lips, swinging her legs around in front of her, as if beckoning me to sit beside her. 'Don't worry, we can go out somewhere.'

That was how it was with Pippa. You could always go out somewhere and spend a fortune on cucumber sandwiches or cocktails.

'What brings you here?' I said, trying not to sound irritated, and sat down opposite her.

'I was just passing through Bristol, visiting a friend, and I thought, why not look up Arthur? So here I am. I won't stop. Just thought I'd call by and have a quick catch-up.'

I said it was good to see her, of course, and she was looking well and so on. She smiled and looked directly into my eyes. That's what she used to do, Pippa. It was her way of capturing you. Or of checking whether she needed to capture you. There was no escaping those eyes. I asked how she was doing.

'I'm extremely well, thank you. So, tell me all about you. You're seeing the lovely little Dora, then?'

I looked down at the floor. 'Yes.' I don't know how she made that 'yes' feel guilty, but she did. 'Would you like a cup of tea?'

'Your landlady has already plied me with tea, thank you.'

I was parched. 'Good.'

'Do I hear wedding bells?'

I should've just said yes. Why didn't I? To this day I can't fully explain. It's not as though I was trying to avoid admitting that I was seeing Dora. It was almost as if I was afraid she would interfere. I told Pippa plainly that Dora and I had been seeing a lot of each other and that she was even coming down in a few weeks, after completion on my new house, to help me move in.

'Are you intending to move in together?'

'Dora's still at teacher training college in Cheltenham.'

I knew exactly what she meant, of course. I tried to look away, but it was hard. She was wearing a close-fitting dark green dress, which accentuated her breasts and her hips. Around the neck was some green fur or something fluffy and soft. It made you want to touch it. She had crossed her legs again and let the heel of her shoe dangle off a little, flopping it to and fro.

'So, you're dating little Dora! What does she say about me?'

'I don't think she says anything about you.'

'Oh, come on. You know she's never liked me.'

The truth was, I *had* detected a little animosity between Dora and Pippa, but I had put it down to girls being girls. The feminine world was a world I didn't understand. I had no sisters, and the only women at work brought tea and gossiped about fashion and film stars. I was vain enough to imagine it was normal for two pretty women I knew not to like each other.

'Why would she not like you?'

'Oh . . . it's silly, childish stuff. She probably says I'm a liar, doesn't she?'

I shrugged.

'Well, if she does, I'd better tell you it goes back to our time on the ship. I never mentioned it before because it involved Philip, and I didn't want to . . . I didn't think . . .'

'It's okay.' I was really curious.

'Well, it was the day of the sinking. I borrowed that concertina to have a little go on it. I was jealous, I think, because she played it so well. So I went into her room and borrowed it from her cupboard, and Philip saw me take it. They were playing hide-and-seek, you see, and I didn't realize. Philip accused me of stealing it, and I'm sure he told her, and she would've thought me a thief or something. But then, of course, the ship went down, and . . . you know the rest. But it's always stayed with me. I'm sure she thinks I'm a thief.'

'I'm sure she doesn't.'

'Well, no need to bring it up if she doesn't mention it. But you know what she's like – loves to make up stories about people.'

'Does she?' I said. 'I've never noticed.'

'Haven't you? Dora? She was always making up stories. Lord knows what she's said about me. I'm not saying she's like it now – and I love her to bits, I really do, such a lovely girl – but when she was little . . . I'm just saying, that's all. If she says anything, be warned.'

This struck me as very odd. In all the time I'd known Dora, she'd come across as the most honest and decent person. I didn't like what Pippa was saying, even if she was making excuses for it. And, if I'm honest, I was a bit startled at the mention of my brother. The idea that he had witnessed something that I didn't know about – however trivial – felt like an important revelation. I didn't like the idea that his last impression of the world was of someone he trusted appearing to be dishonest. It was odd that Dora had never mentioned it.

'Are you sure Philip got round to telling her?'

'Oh yes. I could tell from the way she looked at me.'

'If you're worried about it, why don't you explain it to her yourself?'

'Well, if she's really forgotten about it, best let sleeping dogs lie. It was all such a long time ago. So what date are you moving in to the new house?'

I told her I'd move in on the 6th of March. And then, because I felt the need to arm myself against the breasts and the fluffy neckline, I added, 'Dora will be coming later that day to help me buy furniture.'

'How exciting!'

We continued to chat for a while, and she told me again how much she liked Dora and what a sweet person she seemed to have grown into. After an hour or so she left. She said she was meeting a friend, and that, I thought, would be the last of her.

14

DORA

We went for this walk in the hills before term started again.

'You'll never guess who I heard from over Christmas.'

'Oh yes, Aunty Daphne! Isn't it wonderful?'

'Daphne? Oh, that. Yes, it is. No, it was someone else as well.'

I was disappointed. I wanted him to talk about Daphne. She had written to all those of us from Boat Nine with a list of addresses, asking if we could update them if necessary, because she was sending out invitations to a rather special reunion the following September:

> *I know it's a bit earlier than you might have expected for*
> *our next reunion, but I'm getting married, and I'd love*
> *all of you from Boat Nine to be there. We went through a*
> *lot together, didn't we? And I hope it's a nice surprise that*
> *the groom is Jack Heggarty! There will be a short service*
> *at St Peter's, and the reception will be at the Wayfarer's*
> *Inn, where we all met last time. So hope you can make it!*
> *(Details to follow later.)*

We were standing on the summit of Leckhampton Hill, looking out over Cheltenham and the Severn Valley. On that evening it was spectacular. In the distance, the Black Mountains of the Welsh border sketched a faint blue line, and to the right, the buxom-breasted Malvern Hills stood out perkily. Further to the right again was Clee Hill in Shropshire, and beneath us the wide valley of the Severn basked in the golden light and long shadows of an early sunset.

'Who then?'

'Our old friend Pippa.'

I felt suddenly dizzy. I held on to his arm and tried not to look down. I looked instead at Wales, but it seemed a long way away, too far to reach.

'Pippa?'

'Yes. She sent me a late Christmas card. Must've been Daphne's address list. Did you get a card from her?'

'No,' I said thinly, the word little more than a breath. I continued to look at Wales, searching for home.

'Well, that's odd. Even odder that she called by a few days ago . . . on her way to somewhere-or-other.'

Now I could hardly breathe. *What? What!* I wanted to shout. I took a deep breath but nothing came out. I let go of his hand.

'What is it?'

'She came to your *house?*'

'Not the new one. Just the digs. She just happened to be in Bristol, so she thought she'd look me up.'

'Did she?' I said woodenly.

He shifted his weight awkwardly from the balls of his feet to his heels.

'You two don't get on very well, do you?'

I asked what she'd said. What *had* she said? I could see it all now: a flutter of those eyelashes, a hand on his arm. *Don't trust Dora. She doesn't like me. I don't know why, but she never has.*

'We just talked about this and that. She asked after you.'

'And what did you say?'

He looked nonplussed. 'I . . . said . . . you were well, of course. Was that okay?'

I sighed. He took my hand again and gave it a squeeze.

'I'm sorry,' I said. 'I just don't trust her.'

'Why's that?'

I couldn't think what to say. 'It's just . . . I don't think she's entirely honest.'

'Oh, you're thinking of the concertina, is that it? She told me all about that. She took it from your room to have a go on it and Philip thought she was stealing it. Don't worry, she told me all about it.'

Then I looked at him, trying to convey something that I knew was impossible to explain without words, but which could never be spoken. I just started to stutter. I don't think I was going to tell him, but I was so close. 'I think . . . Don't think that . . . It's just that I'm . . .'

'Lost for words,' he said. He gave my hand another squeeze, and I felt sick. Wales went all wiggly and melted, and I realized that tears had welled up in my eyes. I smelt him, close to me then, that wonderful Arthur odour that had fuelled my unconscious love for him since we sat curled in the boat together. It was raw and woody and powerful. It was my lifeline. He was my life. She could destroy it all. But if I told him . . .

I had tried not to relive what I had witnessed, half hoping it had been an illusion. I knew, of course, the moment I saw her again in the Wayfarer's cloakroom, that it had been no dream.

The sea . . . the sea numbs every bit of you. Your voice, your hands, your feet, your lips, your legs, your chest, your arms, maybe even your heart. And when you are fished out of it, after many hours, the feeling comes back slowly, but in reverse order. Your heart, your glad and grateful heart, your arms, wrapped up in another's, your heaving chest, your forgotten legs, your lips, brushing on warm skin, your feet, rubbed tenderly back to life, your hands, held, squeezed, warmed between the two kind hands of another. But you can't relax, because you know that, minutes before, there was someone else with you, floating in the bitter sea. You both try to hold on to each other, but the hands give way. They stop feeling the grip and let go. And he is swept away, but never quite out of sight. When the moon comes out from behind the clouds you see his bobbing head, up and down on the giant heaving waves, in and out of sight, up and down, to and fro. And you hope he's alive. And on the boat you know he's been spotted. You know she's seen him. You can see him over Arthur's shoulder. He's by the boat. He's reaching up. He's alive! He's alive! You want to shout to Arthur, but no words come out. Your lips haven't thawed. Your voice is still lost. But it's all right, because *she* has seen him. She offers down her oar, and he grabs it. She is pulling, but she isn't asking for help. She's looking around, and everyone is looking at you and at Mr Dent. The lascars beyond her are huddled together, not looking at her. She is pushing. *Pushing.* She is *beating* him off. She's beating his head with the oar. Philip lets go and is swept away. Someone spots him: there's someone in the water! Maybe another child! Mr Dent jumps in. She sees you looking at her. How long have you been doing that? Everyone else is fixated on the heaving black waves that push Mr Dent out of sight and swallow him whole. Mr Dent doesn't come back, and you are still looking at her. Two lives lost now. She sees you looking at her, and she knows.

At the most important moment of your life – and of Philip's – your voice has failed you, and it continues to fail you all the way home.

Now that I had my voice, it felt so wrong to hold this truth back from the one I loved above all others, but I couldn't bear the hurt it would cause. What could he do with this new information? His mother would be broken by it all over again, and she might not be able to piece together anything resembling herself this time. His indelible guilt at having survived his brother would be relived, and he would have to trawl through new varieties of pain for no good outcome. Too much time had passed, and I had hoped that with those years I might somehow come to realize that the memory was a mere hallucination. But an unwanted memory is like a smell. It bypasses all language and logic. You can cover your eyes and block your ears, but it will still flood your feelings and wrench you back to a single moment, and it can ambush you when you least expect it.

'Don't worry,' said Arthur gently. '*You* are my girl.'

'Promise you won't see her again.'

He smiled, flattered. 'Stop worrying.'

'Promise me.'

He rubbed my hand between his two. 'I promise.'

Secure that he would keep his word, I let the chance to tell him slip away, and I was almost relieved.

15

ARTHUR

Before the completion date on my house I invited Dora up to London to meet my parents. I was embarrassed by their enthusiasm. Ever since Philip died, I had become the focus of all their aspirations, and my mum made it very plain to me on numerous occasions that I was her only hope of grandchildren. If I'm honest, though, I could not have been more pleased with the fuss they made over Dora. She was everything they could have wished for in a daughter-in-law: polite, pretty, kind and anxious to please. Before I left, my mum cornered me in the kitchen and whispered, 'She's the one! Don't waste any time, now, or someone else will snatch her up!' and she slipped her dress ring into my pocket. 'Let her choose a new one this weekend!'

This had been my ulterior motive in going to see them, but I realized I should have brought her sooner. I was so proud of Dora. I felt mighty and kinglike with her on my arm. My dad was clearly taken with her too, and when we left, Mum clung on to Dora's hand with tears in her eyes. 'It was *lovely* to meet you, my dear. We'll be seeing much more of you, though, I'm sure.'

I often remember that look my mother gave me, her eyes glistening with excitement, and I want to put my arms around her and say 'I'm sorry'.

I picked up the keys to my new home on the 5th of March and moved in on the 6th. It was pouring with rain, and the boxes I took out of the boot of the taxi were soggy by the time they reached the hallway. In one box I had a lamp, a few old knives and forks from Mrs Peet, my landlady, and a kettle I had bought, along with one saucepan, a frying pan and some tea. In another box were some bed linen, a blanket and a pillow, and in the third box were my books.

After a cup of tea, I emptied the boxes, made a makeshift bed and sat down to write a list of the things that Dora and I could buy together. I still felt huge and mighty. Walking through my own house for the first time, waiting on the arrival of my own woman, a woman whose love filled me with confidence and longing and made me swell up with emotion. The certainty of Dora's love for me was like a drug. That she could love me as she did authenticated me in some way and added to the fieriness of my love for her. All my self-doubt had ebbed away since I'd known her, and I couldn't wait for her knock on the door and for all our tomorrows to be spent together.

I made two trips to the shops. I returned with tins of food, milk, cereal, fruit, bread and a new pillowcase, a sponge, some cleaning products, toilet roll and a dishcloth. I paced around the house making notes on where we should start first. The priority was a bed and some chairs – and a table, of course. The curtains were a good quality and wouldn't need replacing, but the floors were bare and in a sorry state. We would have to buy some rugs. At around midday I allowed myself a can of corned beef and sat on the floor of my dining room eating it. I could have sat there cross-legged all day making plans, but the sound of my own front doorbell interrupted me.

Through the misted glass I could see the figure of a woman. I opened the door, elated. I hadn't expected her until seven o'clock.

'Hello, Arthur!'

'Pippa?'

'Just passing. Didn't really expect to find you here, if I'm honest.'

'How did you—'

'Your landlady gave me your address. Hope I'm not disturbing anything.' She raised her eyebrows mischievously. 'Aren't you going to invite me in?'

She glided past me and started to look around, commenting on the curtains that had been left by the previous owners. 'Did they leave that ship in a bottle too? Lord, isn't it ghastly?'

'It's mine, actually.'

'Oh, well. I'm sure Dora will like it. She'll probably make you some new curtains as well. Isn't she here yet?'

'It's Friday. She has college. She'll be along later. Where are you "passing" to?'

She inspected my face as if she were a teacher looking for traces of insolence. 'I'm on my way to Devon, if you must know. A house party.'

'Well, since you're here,' I said, 'let me show you round properly.'

I showed her the kitchen, the narrow garden, shaking off the drab winter with a few daffodils and some yellow kerria; I showed her the bathroom with its white tiles and brand-new white towel, and I showed her the three bedrooms.

'Well, the third bedroom is rather petite, but this one is fit for a king.' She smiled her winning smile. 'And you are something of a king, these days, aren't you?'

'How do you mean?'

'I mean, Arthur, that you are a salaried man with your own home. It's impressive at your age.'

'You mean for a man from my class.'

'I mean for a man of any class. You've done well.' Then she looked me in the eyes with what seemed like tenderness. 'I admire you.'

'Would you like a quick cup of tea?'

We sat on the dining-room floor and had tea and biscuits. Afterwards, she produced from her bag a bottle of champagne and insisted we toast the new house. We talked about this and that, and before I knew it, my watch said three o'clock.

'You'd better be off or your friends will be wondering where you are. I'll see you to the station if you like.'

I went to use the bathroom, but when I came downstairs she had gone. All that was left was the empty champagne bottle and the teacups. Then I noticed her coat still slung over the bannister in the hallway. I found her in the bedroom, looking out of the window at the splashes of yellow flowers.

'Pippa?' She didn't answer, and when I reached her I saw that her face was covered in tears. I said, 'What is it?'

She sobbed. 'I'm so envious of Dora. She's so lucky . . . having . . . you.' Her voice broke up and she fell on my shoulder. I didn't want to console her too much, for fear of how it could be construed, but she wept so copiously it was hard not to put a hand on her hair.

'Please don't cry. You must have lots of admirers.'

'That's just it. I was engaged again and once again it's all fallen apart.'

'What happened?'

'Usual thing. I found out he only wanted me for my money.'

I held her away from me by the shoulders. 'Listen to me, Pippa. Whatever else a man may want you for, it will *never* be just for your money.'

She attempted a smile. 'You're so good to me!' She hugged me very hard. I should have extricated myself, but I felt it right to console her for a few moments. She really was in a terrible state. She began weeping again. 'Do you *really* think that?' she sniffed.

'Yes, I do. You're a beautiful woman, Pippa.'

And her lips were on mine.

I know how it sounds, but really, *she* kissed *me*. I know that's absolutely no excuse for what happened next, but you need to know what she was like. Her hands, they were everywhere. I was a virgin; I wasn't prepared for that sort of thing. I mean, well, she took me by surprise. She took me by storm. That woman knew exactly what she was doing.

The thing is, my coals had been stoked for Dora, so to speak. I was already on fire waiting for her all day. But even so . . . It was my fault. I should have found a way to stop her – and to stop myself. At the time it felt as though a 'no' from me would have seemed like a further rejection, like the last straw for a woman who was already down and distraught. Oh God, even as I say it, it sounds so pathetic.

I was woken by a bell. It took me a while to find my bearings. The ceiling was alien. I was in my new house, of course. I could hear bare feet on the carpetless stairs. I pulled on my trousers and rushed out of the bedroom, only to see Pippa at the bottom of the stairs. Pippa, face flushed and sleepy, wearing a new white towel, opening the front door.

As long as I live I shall be haunted by that look on Dora's face. She was so bewildered and hurt. Pippa might as well have slapped a child for no reason, the incomprehension was as painful to witness. Those eyes, they took in Pippa, the towel and then me. I had always thought them pretty eyes, but I had never noticed how beautifully limpid they were. If Pippa's dazzled, Dora's at that moment could have nailed me to the wall.

I stood there speechless on the stairs, still giddy with what I had just done with Pippa, woolly-headed with the doze that must have followed. Fleetingly, it seemed possible that this moment could be easily explained. For a split second, it was no more than Pippa turning up unheralded again, and I would tell Dora and roll my eyes and she would tell me not to trust her in future. But the thought scuttled away, chased by the devastation on Dora's face, visible over Pippa's naked shoulder, and by the brisk movement she made to pick up the little brown suitcase that she had set down on the front step. She turned swiftly and fled.

I would have done the same.

Pippa had said something overzealous like, 'Oh, Dora! It's you! Come on in!' I just stood on those stairs, hating myself, hating Pippa, hating her smugness, but then, as soon as she turned around, aching to take the towel off her and hating myself for wanting her again.

'You knew she was coming,' I said, incredulous. 'You planned it!'

She came right up to me where I had slumped down on the stairs. She inserted a leg between my knees and dropped the towel. 'And you loved it.'

16

DORA

Over the weeks that followed, all this lovely cherry blossom puffed out over the sun-warmed pavements of Cheltenham, daffodils trumpeted along every grass verge, and the whole world seemed to be having a heartless celebration of my crushed spirit.

He wrote me a postcard, begging to see me and explain. He said that what he had to say couldn't be explained in a letter. No, it certainly couldn't. He wrote me another postcard, imploring me to please give him a chance. I couldn't think what explanation could possibly make it all right. He had known I was coming. He knew I was arriving at seven o'clock, and I was on time. I wasn't even early. *I was on time!* He knew I didn't want him to see Pippa again. He had promised that he wouldn't. And yet there she was, all pink and tousled. And *naked.* And then there *he* was, coming down the stairs in nothing but his trousers, his pale chest covered in dark hair, and all I could think was that I had never seen him like that before. I had been seeing him for months and he had told me I was his girl and I had never seen him how *she* had seen him. I felt a pang of lust and grief come crashing together. I had touched his chest and put my cheek against it when we had kissed. I had felt his skin under his shirt when we petted in the sunshine. But I had never seen him naked to the waist, his braces dangling down, coming down the stairs of the house I thought we were to share together, coming up behind a woman who smiled sheepishly and whose attempt at surprise was as obnoxious as the perfume she wafted too close to me. I would have known her with my eyes closed. Since that time in the cloakroom at the Wayfarer's Inn, I knew the smell of her.

I couldn't cry. I stood on the station that evening looking for trains to Newport, but I couldn't cry. I knew he would follow me, so I hid in the ladies' cloakroom until the train arrived, then scuttled on at the First Class end, where I knew he wouldn't be looking. I didn't look out to see if he was standing there on the platform. I couldn't bear to see him. Perhaps he didn't come after all.

On the train I started to shake, just a little at first, and then so violently that I had to sit on my hands. It was terror that I felt then, not grief. Not yet. It began to sink in that I had lost everything, that this terrible wound could not be mended. My whole future would be different now, and I would have to rethink it. There would be no life with Arthur, no shared house, no waking up together or shopping together or children together. All that was gone. He had vanished into thin air and taken my future with him. But the woman he had betrayed me for was the worst part of it. If he had known the truth about her it would never have happened, and I was the one person who could have told him.

'Are you all right, love?' A woman sitting in the opposite corner of the train compartment was studying me anxiously.

'Just a bit cold. I'll be fine, thank you.' I realized my teeth were chattering, and she encouraged me to put on my coat.

My parents' house was like a warm blanket. Outside the newborn lambs were crying to their fat mothers, who replied with deep, curdled bellows. The house smelt of home: coal dust and gas and onions and carbolic soap. Our Mam wasn't expecting me that weekend. She made a fuss of me and fetched me bread and dripping. Then I cried.

What sort of fool was I to imagine he would want to marry a girl like me? It wasn't as if he'd asked me or anything. But why had he hinted so strongly? I remembered us touching each other once so ravenously that it had been hard to hold back. He had made me moan with the pain of it all, but I had said that I was saving myself for the man I married, and he had whispered very slowly and deeply in my ear, 'Well, let's hope he bears an uncanny resemblance to *me*.' It seemed cruel, and the more I thought about it, the crueller it became. There could be no explanation that would do. Supposing Pippa had just turned up. Supposing she had just turned up and asked to have a bath . . . and he had just chosen that moment to change his clothes . . . *What was I thinking?* She opened the door. She opened the door to our house. She had scent-marked the place. It was hers now, and she was welcome to it.

Then I remembered what Ralph had said about her. I didn't think she would set her sights so low – in monetary terms, at least – but if she had been desperate enough once to steal what she thought were diamonds, she might certainly feel inclined to settle for a steady, good-looking man who was doing all right for himself. A pity she hadn't thought of someone else to steal off this time. But I knew, even then, that there's no such thing as theft in love. No one can be taken if they don't want to go, and Arthur had gone.

A rumour swiftly spread around the college that I must have 'fallen out' with my boyfriend. I did nothing to dispel it, and nothing to enlighten anybody either. When Jenny asked me why I was so shaken, I told her a version of events that left an open door for things to work out. I didn't mention Pippa. I said I wasn't sure about Arthur any more and needed some time to reflect. She said she understood and would keep it under her hat.

It's interesting, looking back, that I didn't tell Our Mam either. I must have thought that, against all the odds, there was some sort of hope. She cottoned on straight away, of course, as mothers do. There was only one reason for that level of grief beyond someone dying, and that was betrayal. She knew there was something going on and guessed straight away it was another girl. But even though I acknowledged it – because I needed to tell someone, and because I knew I could trust Our Mam if no one else – I gave her a safer version of it, one where another woman merely answered the door. There was no nakedness, no hint of sexual betrayal. There could have been a hundred reasons for her being there, and Our Mam must've tried out dozens of them on me for consolation, but I omitted the one detail that would have damned him forever in her eyes. And I knew that in so doing I was throwing a lifebuoy to hope. One day, just possibly, she might still need to approve of him.

It must have been a couple of weeks later – maybe less – when Jenny asked me round one Friday for a musical evening at her flat. I guessed Ralph would be there, and he was.

An exciting array of bohemian types turned up: bearded men, women with berets at a carefully jaunty angle, men and women with duffle coats and battered instrument cases. The red-headed guitar player was there again, and it was a relief to sing along to familiar happy songs, although the lump in my throat at some of the love songs took some concealing. I would need some practice, I knew, before I was back on my feet.

Ralph did a careful job of ignoring me, after the initial 'hello', that is. He busied himself chatting to everyone else, and I sat in a corner on a cushion, studying the ceiling rose or the chords of the guitarist with ridiculous interest. It was a huge relief when Jenny came over to chat.

'Don't you just wish you could play something? Or perhaps you do?'

'No. I gave up piano after "Three Blind Mice". I did have a little go on a concertina once, but that was ages ago.'

'A concertina? How exotic! We'll have to find you one.'

'Don't bother. I only knew one tune on that as well.' We laughed at our hopelessness. 'Thank you for inviting me.'

'Are you enjoying yourself?'

I nodded. The tightness around my chest was beginning to fade, and my hands were shaking less. People talk about a broken heart, and that is where it hurts. I felt someone was squeezing my chest so hard it had been difficult to breathe freely for weeks. I thought I might explode with pain. There was nowhere to go with it. And now the music made me tap my feet, and the slow numbers gave my aching heart some curious form of balm, giving me permission to feel moved. Most of all I felt alive. I felt the fast numbers in my bones and in my blood. Smiling and laughing with Jenny, however forced, was the release my face had longed for. So I sat and smiled and tapped my feet and let myself be lulled by the music and the wine into a state so like happiness that I could nearly believe it was.

Perhaps because I was speaking mostly to Jenny, who lived there, I didn't really notice when people started to leave. I became slowly aware that it was later than I'd thought and that only a handful of friends and cohabitants remained. I still felt invigorated and a little disappointed that the evening was drawing to a close. The red-haired musician, whose name I learnt was Tighe, filled my glass up with wine.

'If you look behind that pile of papers in the corner, you'll find a box,' he told me with a wink. I was fascinated and went to investigate.

The box was instantly recognizable. That is, it was clear from its shape what it contained. Gently I slid open the fastener and lifted out a well-worn concertina. Tighe had put down his instrument and was talking to Ralph and some people who were leaving. Tentatively, I tried a note or two. No one was listening, so a tried a few more, seeing if I could capture something I thought I had forgotten. Through trial and error, I got the first few bars. Very softly I played them again. Tighe turned and looked at me. He walked over and picked up his guitar and went straight into 'The Galway Shawl' for me. Then he smiled. It was such a simple tune, but it made me shiver. We played it together, painfully slowly at first, then slowly with feeling.

'I didn't know you played,' said Ralph, coming back into the room after farewells in the hallway.

'I don't – isn't it obvious? I'm a one-tune girl.'

He studied me intently. 'It's a pity you think like that.'

There was nothing flirtatious in his tone. He sat down on the floor beside us with one elbow on his upright knee and watched patiently as Tighe taught me a new tune. I kept getting the notes wrong and soon realized that I had had too much to drink to concentrate properly. I held out my glass when he produced the bottle again, but Ralph quickly put his hand over the top.

'Be careful, Dora. You're not used to drinking, and I think you may have had enough.'

I was indignant. I should have been grateful, but such was the effect of the alcohol on my inhibitions that I was quite happy to be rude. Tighe stood up tactfully and disappeared to the bathroom.

'I'll drink what I like. I don't need you to tell me what I can and can't do.'

'You have to get home somehow.'

'Says who?'

It was wildly provocative, and I couldn't believe the words had come from my mouth. I lay back on the cushion and leant on my elbows, body stretched out in front. He gently took hold of my stockinged feet. 'Dora, you're squiffy, and I'm going to walk you home.'

He stood up and went to fetch my coat. I should have heard this as a compliment, but all I heard was that I wasn't enough to tempt him, and he wanted me gone. I felt humiliated, stupid. I tried to stand but felt dizzy, so I put a hand on the mantelpiece for support. What a fool I was making of myself. Suddenly I wanted him to want me, this man I had tried to shake off before. Now even he didn't want me. I was worth more than this.

He walked me back to my accommodation through the bitterly cold Cotswold night. I felt sick a few times, but I don't think I threw up. He supported me with a strong arm around my shoulder and under my armpit. I leant heavily against him and must have muttered some foolish things. When we eventually arrived back, it was only just before midnight and he was afraid the place would be locked. They did that in those days. You couldn't stay out after twelve. I was almost pleased.

'You'll have to take me home with you,' I remember saying.

'I don't fancy sleeping on the floor.'

'You wouldn't *have* to, would you?'

This much I do remember: the large house I lived in with the other women was still open. He pushed me against the wall to steady me, and he took my head in his big hands. 'Dora, you've had too much to drink, and I'm not going to take advantage of you. But don't think for a moment that I don't want you. I want you when you know exactly what you're doing, when you remember every detail. I want you when you want me so badly it hurts. And you *will* want me.'

Then he kissed me lightly on the lips and left.

17

ARTHUR

I'm not proud of this period of my life. It makes me cringe to think of it. However, I think, if I'm honest, that although I was devastated by what I had done to Dora, and although I would have given anything to have her love me again, I was also a bit elated. It's a big thing to happen to a man. I mean, it wasn't how I'd expected it to happen, but Pippa . . . she overwhelmed me. I don't think any man could've resisted her. No, that's just making excuses for myself, I know. But I felt like a king. I was riding on the crest of a wave. I was ecstatic. And at the same time . . .

I couldn't imagine anything I could possibly say to Dora that would make her forgive me. I knew she was a sweet-natured and forgiving person, but I also knew that Pippa was someone she had warned me off, and so I had let her down pretty emphatically. I sent her a postcard asking her to see me, to give me a chance to explain things, but I had no reply. I sent her another one a few days later, begging her to see me, but in the intervening days, I'm ashamed to say, Pippa called by again, and again I weakened. That probably sounds pathetic. I loved Dora more than I can say, but . . . Pippa made me feel so alive, so powerful, so electric, I almost didn't *want* to resist her.

Pippa became quite sulky when I told her I had to see Dora.

'I see, so I'm just your plaything, am I?'

'Look, I didn't ask you to turn up and stop me getting engaged.'

'Oh, so you still want to marry her. I'm all right for a bit of fun, but she's the one you'll marry!'

'Dora wouldn't touch me with a bargepole now!'

'But you'd still marry her if you *could*, is that it? So you really are just *using* me!'

She stamped off down the stairs, taking her clothes with her. I followed, bewildered at this new turn of events. If I asked Pippa to marry me she would scoff at me. I stood naked, watching her step into her flouncy petticoat and carefully roll up her stockings and attach them to her suspenders, and I felt helpless.

'What do you want from me?'

She wriggled into her dress and pouted. 'Why don't you come and visit my family home?'

'All right. I will.'

She softened, then, and wrote down the address in Gloucestershire on a notepad in the kitchen. Next weekend, she said. She didn't stay, though. She left me with that thought: that she wanted me to meet her parents.

I had pictured myself going up to Cheltenham that weekend to see Dora. I would tell her everything: the way I had been surprised by Pippa's arrival, how she had got hold of the address from my landlady, the way I had been overwhelmed by Pippa's crying . . . Was I going to tell her about my repeat performances? I would have to leave those out. It already felt like a shabby way to excuse myself.

Now it occurred to me that I could combine my visit to Pippa's home with a visit to Dora. At the very least I owed her a face-to-face apology. After all, I wasn't sure if anything else was possible, but I knew I had to talk to her, to see her face again. It was too wretched a way to leave things as they stood. There had been no reply to my postcards.

I had even phoned the college on three occasions but was told on the last two attempts that my first message had certainly been forwarded.

My work at the aeronautical company was frenetic. I had recently been promoted and needed to stay too late after work to be catching trains on a Friday. Instead I arrived at her accommodation block at about eleven-thirty on the Saturday morning. I was told she was out, so asked when she might be back. The lady in charge had seen me with Dora in the past and said she would go and ask her room-mate for me. While I waited, I looked at the half-open front door which flooded the lobby with April-green light, and I wondered what on earth I would say if Dora walked through it right then. But Dora was out until lunchtime, it seemed, and so I went to sit in the garden. It was an unusually clement day and the little wall I chose to sit on was warm. The blackthorn blossom was out already, and squirrels scampered about the base of the beech trees that stood between me and the front door.

I don't suppose I was there more than half an hour, but it seemed like an age. It didn't occur to me to chicken out, but I was feeling sweaty, and the more I thought about what I would say, the more pointless it seemed being there at all. I was looking at the squirrels and wishing that I, too, could dart up a tree, when I heard her voice. Heard her laugh, to be more precise. I looked up and saw Dora in a full swirling skirt and a white, tight-waisted blouse. Her hair was swept up in a chignon that I had never seen before, and she was smiling. I allowed myself a wave of relief at her high spirits, but then my stomach did a little somersault. The cause of her smile was a man: a young, good-looking man with brown curly hair and a slightly bohemian air to him. I had started to get up. Now I sat down again, and from my position on the wall I saw him stop, cup the side of her face in his hand, and kiss her gently on the lips. 'See you at seven,' he said. Then she said 'okay' or something I couldn't quite hear, and he called back to her, 'Say thank you to your father for me!' And then he added, louder still, because he was already some way off and she was climbing the steps to the front door, 'I'll thank him myself when I meet him!'

I was furious. Ridiculous, isn't it? What right had I to be angry? I stood up and marched over to her.

'Dora!'

She was about to disappear behind the front door when she saw me. I can't describe her expression. Still bearing the traces of her delight with the other man, it was sad and lovely and intelligent and utterly beautiful.

She closed the door gently behind her.

I knocked heavily. There was a delay before the woman I'd first seen came to answer it, telling me that Dora did not wish to see me.

I waited another half-hour, hoping she might come out and go to eat somewhere, but she did not. If I'd been half a man I would have waited there all day and all night. I would have watched the dawn come up and still have been there, bedraggled yet determined, when she came out in the morning. That's what I wish I'd done. Instead, I took a piece of paper out of my pocket and studied some times I had written down. If I went straight to the bus station, I could still be at Pippa's family home, as agreed, for the afternoon.

18

DORA

The week after the party Ralph telephoned to ask if I would like to meet up with him on Saturday morning. Apparently he was writing a book about the plight of coal miners, and he wanted me to help him with his research. He was thrilled at the possibility of gleaning some first-hand experiences from me. I was flattered of course, and considering his gallantry on the last occasion I'd seen him, it felt safe to accept.

We met in a little coffee shop in Montpellier, not far from his house. I didn't drink coffee, so I asked if I might have a cup of tea instead. He looked nonplussed for a moment, and then delighted, as if he had learnt something new to add to his collection of knowledge about the working class.

'Of course! A pot of tea for two it is, then!'

When I had gone home to my parents straight after the discovery of Arthur's betrayal, I had sought out my father's scrapbook and brought it back to Cheltenham with me. I had done so because in it, amongst all the cuttings on local mining accidents, was a photograph of the children rescued from Boat Nine. There was Arthur sitting on deck with a naval officer's hat on his head, sandwiched between a grinning Graham and myself. In fact, we are all smiling, because the man who took the photo made us say 'cheese', and it is only Pippa, sitting a little apart, who has barely a trace of a smile. I had pored over this grainy photograph over the last couple of weeks, studying the faces for signs of what was to come. Of course, I knew why Pippa was unable to look fully happy, and I knew as well the secret torment in Arthur's head. If he'd had news that his brother was alive, that safe smile would have been a joyous one. I looked at that dear face, and I couldn't see any hint of a deceiver. What had happened to him? I had reached the point where I couldn't look at that photo any more and was planning to take the book back home, when Ralph suggested I help him with his research. Now I relinquished the fat scrapbook I had been hugging to my chest and placed it on the table.

'I thought you might find this helpful. It belongs to my father. It's mostly stuff about mining accidents where the authorities have been negligent.'

He gently opened the first page, then turned to the second and the third, a look of charmed amazement lighting up his face. 'Oh, Dora. Dora, Dora! This is wonderful. This is . . . *exactly* the sort of thing I need. And he's written in it too. He's added his *own comments*! This is priceless. May I borrow it?'

'Yes, but he doesn't know I have it, so please be careful, won't you?'

'Of course. Perhaps I can come and meet him sometime?'

I tried to picture a meeting between Ralph and my father. My father would undoubtedly think him a toff and feel patronized by his interest. And what would Ralph make of the newspaper on the chairs and the tin bath by the fire and the outside lav with its squares of newspaper on a string? I smiled at the thought. 'Perhaps.'

I gathered from Ralph that he was the eldest son of a wealthy family, set to inherit a title and a country manor he did not wish to have. His father was exasperated with him, convinced that his socialism was a fad or a childish attempt to annoy him. He had given Ralph the house in Cheltenham on loan and allowed him to keep the tenants' rent by way of having something to live off, but he expected him to find respectable employment. He had threatened to disinherit Ralph if he didn't 'make good' before the end of the year.

'So you've found work as a journalist?'

'I've set up my own newspaper. It's called *Plight*.'

It took me some time to realize that this was a pattern with Ralph's 'set'. You had a house on loan but allowed people to think you owned it. You started up a newspaper of your own which you tried to give away on street corners and you called yourself a journalist. You fancied writing a book, so you called yourself a writer. You fancied a girl, so you called her your researcher. But, as I say, it took me some time to work all this out. Back then I was young and keen and easily impressed. What did *I* know?

'Where can I buy a copy? I'd love to read it.'

'Would you? Well, I think I can let you have a copy for free, as it's you.'

'Thank you! And what about the book? What's it called?'

'It's going to be called *The Working Man's Struggle*.'

I didn't think this was a very catchy title, but I suppressed anything negative I felt. Ralph was so positive about everything he did that I began to feel caught up in his enthusiasm. And when he later gave me a copy of *Plight*, a thin pamphlet with very dense print and clichéd views of class in which every working man was some sort of hero with his own detailed plans to bring down capitalism and put the world to rights, I said I thought it was wonderful, and to my shame, I probably convinced myself that it was.

When the waitress brought our tea things we sat quietly while she set them out carefully before us. I could sense him watching me, and when I looked up he was studying me intently. He waited for the waitress to leave us.

'You're beautiful, Dora.'

I didn't know where to look, so I poured the milk into the cups. Then he added something very cunning, because (as I later found out) he already knew about my disastrous engagement from Jenny, who had not been able to keep a secret: 'I'm sorry,' he said. 'I realize you are already spoken for. It just slipped out.'

'That's all right.'

'What I meant to say was that I find you intelligent and perceptive and exactly the sort of person I'm looking for to help me with this project. Please say yes.'

I smiled. 'Yes.'

'And please let me take you out to discuss it further tonight.'

'Well . . .'

'On a friendly basis. A work basis. I won't call you beautiful, I promise.'

I smiled again. 'All right. If you like.'

When I returned to my accommodation, I had a real shock. I had just said goodbye to Ralph when Arthur came running up behind me towards the steps, shouting my name. You can't imagine how much I had longed for him to do this. Every night I had been here since that fateful day in Bristol, I had imagined him beating a path to my door. I lay in bed wondering if he was waiting outside for me. I crept down each morning in search of post before anyone else saw me, and I checked outside the front door to see if he was waiting on the steps. I made excuses for him, picturing him trying to make it but being held up by work, or delaying his visit because he was waiting for some special gift he had ordered to arrive in a jewellery shop, or else one of his parents had fallen ill and he had to be by their side, when all the time he longed to be with me, and telling me what had really happened and that it was not how it seemed at all. There was a perfectly logical explanation. But now three weeks had passed, and I had given up hoping.

Or rather, I hadn't given up, but any gesture he made now would have a ring of insincerity about it. How could any man be sincere with such a lack of urgency?

'Dora!' he shouted.

I looked at him briefly, the face of all my dreams and cherished hopes, and I saw his dear, pleading eyes. For a moment I wanted to bury my head in his shoulder and cry in his arms. I wanted to hold him and feel him press himself against me like he used to with such frenzy, but his timing was too irresolute to be excused. His half-heartedness seemed to blot out all the honest pleading of his eyes, and I found myself closing the door on him. And when I had done it, I felt stronger.

I went to my room and heard him hammering on the door downstairs. Miss Locke came up and asked me if I wanted to see a visitor who had called by earlier, and I said no. I lay on my bed for twenty minutes or so and then tiptoed on to the landing to see through the window if he was still there. He was sitting on the wall, gazing wistfully at the front door. I went back to my room, elated. I would have to go over to the canteen, and I would pass him. It would give him a chance to show me what he was made of. I must have still entertained a hope that he could convince me to go back to him.

Of course, when I opened the front door to walk over to the dining hall, he was gone.

Ralph took me to a restaurant that evening. He had chosen a slightly downmarket one and ordered shepherd's pie to be more working class. I didn't like to tell him there were no restaurants where I came from, and nobody 'ate out', unless you counted the chip shop.

'So,' he said, after ordering me an Irish coffee and telling me I would like it, 'I saw the cuttings of the ship that sank.'

'And did you recognize anyone?'

'Well, I recognized you, of course. You haven't changed a bit!'

I laughed. 'That's what *you* think!'

He smiled and stroked my knuckles across the table. 'Who's the boy you're snuggled up to?'

'I'm not snuggled up to anyone.'

'Oh yes you are. You couldn't be closer. Don't tell me you don't remember him? Arthur Fielding?'

I felt a wave of horror but quickly realized he had read the names printed underneath in the caption. 'Ah yes, Arthur. So you spotted your old friend, Pippa, too?'

'Funnily enough, I didn't recognize her at first. She's looking a bit glum, isn't she? But yes, I can see it's her all right. Fancy you two meeting up like that. It was such a huge story at the time, that ship going down. Gosh, you've been through the wars, haven't you? I know you told me about it and everything, but it really brought it home to me, seeing that picture.'

'So, have you seen anything of Pippa, lately?'

'No, I told you – our paths hardly cross any more. I only used to see her if I went up to town, really. Though I did go to a couple of house parties at her place, ages ago.'

'Where's that?'

'Hickleton. Here in Gloucestershire. Ashleycroft Hall. Place is falling apart a bit now, not surprisingly.'

'Poor Pippa. So she's not much of a prospect for anyone, then?'

'Not on the material side, anyway.'

I tried to sound as casual as I could, desperate not to let this topic peter out before I had learnt something new. 'She's a very attractive woman, though. I should think most men would be happy to marry someone like her.'

He laughed with a slight sneer. 'Most men of my class, Dora, are looking for one of three things: money, if the family pile is falling apart, or a family pile, if they didn't inherit one.'

'And the third thing?'

'Oh, well, if they've plenty of money and no need of property, then they'll go for the looks alone. But of course they'll want a woman who's unsullied.'

'Unsullied? You mean . . . ?'

'A beautiful virgin. If a man wants heirs he wants them to be half decent to look at and *his* without a shadow of doubt.'

Now he had my interest. I lowered my voice. 'You mean you think Pippa's not . . . unsullied?'

He threw back his head and chuckled. 'Pippa? Philippa Barrington-Hobb? And my Aunt Nelly!' I was confused, and I must have shown it. 'Dear Dora, I don't want to besmirch the name of a gal I've known for years, and Lord knows she could do with a spot of luck, but I wouldn't put money on it.'

I was suddenly struck by a vile thought. 'My God, Ralph, *you* haven't slept with her, have you?'

'*Me?*' He smiled benignly. 'No, I'm looking for a virginal, salt-of-the-earth sort of girl. The sort who values honesty and loyalty. The sort I can trust.'

I could see he was flattered by my concern, so I tried to appear a little less bothered about him and more bothered about Pippa. 'So *no one's* interested in her, then, poor thing?'

'Oh, don't you worry about Pippa, young Dora. She can take care of herself. She knows a trick or two.'

And then Irish coffee arrived and he changed the subject, and I was left with the horrible thought that Pippa knew a trick or two. I was desperate to know what her tricks consisted of. But Ralph knew a trick or two himself.

'Tell me about your boyfriend.'

'I'd rather not.'

He looked me in the eyes. 'I respect that. I respect your loyalty to him.' Then he took a sip of coffee and was silent for a while. 'He's a lucky man,' he said at last. 'He knows what matters in life. Not wealth and flighty girls but good, strong values. That's what I'm looking for too. These are the values I treasure most: loyalty and honesty.'

When he walked me home, I still half expected to see Arthur jump out of the flower beds, but he did not. Ralph gave me another of his respectful but tender goodbyes, and I was left to lie alone, tormented by his slight kisses and by his thinly veiled promises of loyalty. What if Arthur never came back? What if he had misunderstood my closing the door on him as a gesture of finality and not, as it was, of injury? What if he fell in love with the woman who had murdered his own brother? It was unthinkable. But I couldn't tell him now. I couldn't say what she'd done *now*, not now that I knew about their betrayal. He would just think I was being spiteful. There was only one thing I could do. I could warn her. I could tell her that I knew what she'd done, and that I remembered everything. Tomorrow I could check up on the place name Ralph had mentioned. Hickleton or Hickleford or something. In Gloucestershire. Ashleycroft Hall, Hickleton. I thrashed about under the covers, unable to get comfortable and unable to find sleep. When it eventually found me, I was rudely awoken by Edith's alarm clock, set for her God-awful early church communion, and I was dreaming about Pippa. She was standing in the bedroom wearing a top hat and a purple cloak. When I asked her what she was doing, she smiled slyly, produced a rabbit from under my pillow, and said she was just teaching me a few tricks.

19

ARTHUR

Yes. I took directions from the pub to Ashleycroft Hall. It was a ten-minute walk down a country lane with hedgerows so high that the house took me by surprise. It stood back from the road some fifty yards, a greying Cotswold-stone building with the pale yellow it had once been visible here and there beneath the budding creeper. It was a symmetrical building with grouped tall chimneys, crenellated parapets, and stone mullions and transoms at the panelled windows. I would later discover that it dated back to the fifteenth century and was built by a prosperous wool merchant. But then, on that long-ago spring afternoon, it merely looked daunting.

The door was answered by Pippa, looking relaxed and kittenish in short slacks and a soft pullover. Her hair was tied up with some chiffon in a petite ponytail. I had never seen her look so casual, and it thrilled me.

'Let me show you to your room, sir,' she said mischievously, and I followed her up a grand staircase that split off in two directions. She took me to the left, and we entered a modestly decorated guest room with a view to a fine lawn at the back of the house.

'Crumbs, this place is huge,' I said foolishly. I'd managed to buy a bunch of roses for her mother near the bus station, and I was still holding them. I put them on the bed awkwardly while she took my coat.

'Come on, let me show you the rest of the house.'

'Hadn't we better say hello to your parents first?'

'Oh, Arthur! You are a sweetie!'

She took me by the hand and pulled me off to visit the many rooms. There was the library, filled with musty books that looked ancient. 'Daddy likes dark red books best, so the brown ones are over in that corner. It's all colour coordinated. He's never read any of them.'

'Oh. I imagined him to be an educated man.'

'Lord, no. More of a Neanderthal.'

'A Neanderthal?'

'Well, a bit of a monkey, anyway.'

I didn't pursue this, as I was being invited to take in the drawing room, with its heavy dark furniture and sunlit shards of dust motes so thick they looked solid. The chairs were elaborate and hard, and I tried to picture her monkey father sitting here and smoking a pipe. Where was he? Presumably in another room. We visited the grand hall, the kitchen, the pantry, the dining room and the orangery. I could hardly take my eyes off the dark wisps of velvety hair on her neck and the floating of the chiffon as she moved her head. All the rooms smelt faintly of damp and polish, apart from the kitchen, which had the sweet aroma of slightly rotting food. I felt like a small boy who had been invited to play at a friend's house and who didn't understand the rules of another family.

'This is Mummy's favourite room,' she told me as she slumped into a wicker chair in the orangery. From giant green pots on the tiled floor, great palms and rubber plants emerged, and strange hothouse plants I had never seen sent huge luxuriant stems in a tangle across the glass ceiling. It was warm and humid in there, and I was surprised by the room's lush, jungly tang.

'It's lovely. Where *is* your mother?'

'Oh, Mummy's away for the weekend. She's gone to town.'

I was a little put out by this. Was she playing games with me? I had understood that she wanted me to meet her parents, but perhaps I had been wrong.

'What about your father? Where's he?'

'Oh he's . . . he's away.'

So she had merely invited me here to tantalize me. I felt suddenly exasperated with her.

'So you're here alone?'

'Yes! Isn't it *wonderful?*'

Well, of course it *was* wonderful. A beautiful woman and a house in the country all to ourselves – what man could resist? But if I had managed to repress my sense of guilt for the time being, I was now hampered by a feeling of hurt. It took me by surprise, like so many of the emotions that Pippa aroused in me. I excused myself and went to the bathroom, where I tried to take stock. I had to get back to Dora. I wanted her arms around me, her softness, her gentleness, her certainty. I wanted to retrieve all her love and respect. Pippa's tricky behaviour made me feel stupid and furious and weak. And excited. When I returned to the orangery she had brought a tray of tea and fruit and placed it on a low table between the opposite chairs. She sat in one of them, facing me, naked to the waist.

She held out a peach in her hand. 'I thought you'd like some refreshment.'

I went over to her and kissed her breasts. Then, in the exotic foliage of the jungle around us, I urgently removed her slacks. She lay back and let me explore her under the leathery leaves of the indoor plants until she was so soft and wet it was too much for me. There was no resistance left to draw on.

That was Pippa, you see. She seemed to be a man's dream: wild, beautiful and unpredictable. It was that unpredictability that knocked you off guard, that facility for ambush that swung it for her every time. And the irony is that, with hindsight, she is probably one of the most predictable women I have ever met.

That evening we ate in the kitchen by the warm range. She lit candles, and we shared a cold game pie and a bottle of red wine from the cellar.

'What do you think, then? Do you like my house?' She waved her wine glass at the room.

'It's a very fine house.'

She looked steadily at me and said, 'It'll be mine when Daddy dies.'

'Well, let's hope that's not for a long time.'

She laughed a little. 'I should think it could be any time. He drinks like a fish. Or at least he did the last time I saw him.'

'Haven't you seen him for a while, then?'

'Not since a few months before you first met me, actually.' She looked down at her plate and frowned. 'That's why I was packed off on *The City of India*, you see. Daddy did a runner, and Mummy needed a bit of time to . . . get herself organized.'

'I'm sorry . . . I didn't know. You must've been feeling—'

'Really, it's okay.'

I admired her pluckiness, remembering that train journey and her mother coming on board to see her off. How lonely she must have felt. We were all being sent away for our own safety, and Philip and I had *wanted* to go. She had been dispatched not so much because of German bombing but because her presence was an added problem. I watched her face as she said it was okay. It was clear that she still carried the hurt behind the clipped response.

She looked over at me breezily. 'Tell me, Arthur, where do you see yourself in five years' time?'

I found I was keen to tell her about my promotion. 'Well, there are a lot of big developments in aerospace at the moment. I'm the youngest and most qualified engineer they have, and I've been given shares in the company. That little house in Bristol is just a beginning. In a few years' time I'll be able to move on to something far bigger.'

She studied my face thoughtfully. 'I'm sure you will.'

I wondered then if she was thinking of Ashleycroft Hall. Despite the disappointment of her parents' absence, I wondered if she might be considering me as a prospect after all. Did I spare a thought for Dora at that moment? I can't remember. I can still hear my eagerness to impress Pippa, even as I was breaking Dora's heart.

What happened next, of course, changed everything.

FLOTSAM

20

DORA

It must have been when I was looking for a map to show me where Pippa lived that I had the oddest experience. I was in an unusual little bookshop that smelt of mildew and fresh coffee. There were shelves of second-hand books with faded spines and displays of brand-new books with glossy jackets; there were rows with quirky handwritten labels pasted on to the ends: 'Birds and the Like', 'Good Reads (if you share my tastes)', 'Scary Novels' and so forth. I found the map I was looking for in 'Local Interest', and I had just pinpointed Hickleton when I heard a voice behind me.

'Dora? *Dora!*'

I turned, and at first I couldn't see the person who had addressed me, as they had circled around to my other shoulder.

'I thought it was you! You'll have to forgive me for not coming to see you, but I only arrived yesterday and I'm heading off today. How *lovely* to see you!' Daphne Prendergast gave my arm a squeeze.

'Daphne! I didn't expect to see you here!'

'I popped down to see my uncle who's not well, and we're just trying to find him a present to cheer him up. That's my cousin, Hazel, over by "Green Fingers". He likes gardening, Uncle Albert.'

'Well,' I said, folding the map quickly and replacing it on the shelf, 'I'm glad to have bumped into you. I wanted to congratulate you on your engagement, but I'm afraid I haven't got round to writing to you yet. Congratulations! I'm looking forward to it!'

'Oh, you *can* come! Good, good! We thought we'd go with the Wayfarer's for the venue, but I'll write to you nearer the time.' She looked genuinely thrilled to see me, and her unexpected presence made me both happy and slightly nervous. I felt I had been somehow caught off my guard, doing something I shouldn't have been doing. She may have noticed my furtiveness, for she gave me a conspiratorial look. 'And I hear congratulations might be in order for you too . . . ?'

I could feel the blood pounding in my head. I had to stay calm. What had Daphne heard? Stay calm. Look pleased. I did my best.

'Who told you?'

'Aha! Well, if you must know, I phoned Arthur's mother. He told me in his last card he was hoping to move, and I only remembered it after I'd sent the note about our wedding. So I had his old home address and number and spoke to his mother, and she just happened to let slip that you'd been up there the weekend before and he'd asked her if he could borrow a ring so that he could propose to you. I expect he's bought you the real thing by now!'

While she was speaking, I thrust my left hand into the pocket of my coat. 'No . . . not yet.' I tried to look as delighted as she did.

'Well, I'm *so* pleased. And presumably you're both coming, then? In September? There'll be a proper invitation later.'

'Oh yes,' I said truthfully. 'He said he was looking forward to it.'

'Splendid! Only his poor mother was having kittens about him. Said she hadn't heard a word from him since, and she was all of a doo-dah wondering what had happened. But she did say he'd been terribly busy with his work. An engineer now, isn't he?'

'Yes, yes he is. Oh, but Daphne, it's such wonderful news about you and Mr Heggarty. Everyone will be so pleased. You deserve to be happy. Really you do. And when—'

Cousin Hazel came over with a paper bag and displayed her new purchase. I was introduced, and shortly afterwards they left the shop. I stayed on a while, as long as was necessary to look like a serious shopper, then I replaced a book on direction-finding by the stars and left, elated and tormented, with my new piece of knowledge.

I did contact Pippa. I wrote her a note: short and to the point. I wouldn't be aware of the impact it had for quite some time. In fact, I'm not convinced I was ever truly sure about it until now. One thing is certain, though, and that is that it did not have the effect I'd been expecting. But I'm rushing ahead of myself.

I didn't hear anything from Pippa, and I was glad of it. I had had my say, and I knew it would have shaken her. I heard nothing from Arthur, and as the weeks passed I learnt the pain of losing someone who is still alive to love you if they wish. Had he chosen not to love me because he had fallen in love with someone else? Or had he never loved me enough to withstand other women? Had he simply fallen out of love with me? I longed for big gestures from him, like the waiting outside my door. But that had turned out to be a limp imitation of a grand gesture. I had to face it: his love was simply not robust enough to want to win me back. And then, of course, I wondered if it ever had been. I replayed endlessly the scenes of our courtship. I saw again his face light up as he stepped off the Joneses' bus and looked at me standing there on the pavement; I saw him meet Our Mam and Our Dad, and I watched his face carefully this time for signs of disappointment, but there were none; I studied the tenderness in his eyes as he leant in to kiss me for the first time; I felt his passion as he laid me down on the mountain and as his heart galloped against my chest; and when I said I was saving myself for the man I married I detected no change in his interest but felt again the heady vibrating whisper in my ear: 'Well, let's hope he bears an uncanny resemblance to *me*.'

I lived again the long embrace of our time on Boat Nine; I smelt him over and over, the same notes I had inhaled years later, and I pined for the odour of him. I touched his face in a photograph his landlady had taken of us, and I kissed it foolishly, as if the silver nitrate surface could yield up the scent of him. I wondered if I could have done things differently. If I had slept with him, would we be planting spring flowers in our new garden now? Had he expected me to sleep with him when he invited me down that weekend? But no matter how often I revisited these scenes, there was nothing, not one thing, to suggest that he wasn't happy about us – about me. Even his mother dropped heavy hints about forthcoming events and he hadn't flinched. All of which left me with the conclusion that Pippa was a temptress beyond compare. That her box of tricks was so captivating that the most loving and loyal of men were prepared to risk everything to have more of her magic.

I can't begin to say how devastated I was. I've never known grief like it. I shouldn't say that, I suppose, not with my sister having died and everything. But I tell you, this was something else. I felt as if my body was detached from me, as though everything I did was not quite real. I needed someone to bring me down to earth. And it is very easy, when you have all these unused feelings, like unopened packets of pleasure bursting at the seams, to let someone else open them and release the contents.

Ralph was playing a waiting game. He knew from the first that I had been jilted, and had I been more alert I would have questioned why he never once asked me about the state of my relationship with the boyfriend I was supposed to have. Instead, he nursed the wilting plant, watering it with compliments and affection, waiting patiently for the day it would stand tall and lush and flower in his hands. April passed into May, and he had the whole of the summer to work on me – and the whole of leafy Gloucestershire, puffed out suddenly in the brightest green, as the back-drop for his wooing.

Don't forget, it had already been agreed that in September I would become his lodger, so he had to play a very careful game. He held back. He took his time. He spent the hours that he might have passed luring me to his bed seducing me instead with words and, without actually spelling it out, images of the life I could live with him if I came to my senses.

'I have an aunt in Paris who owns a delightful farmhouse in Provence. Why don't we go there this summer?'

'Has she invited us?'

'I'm always invited. She keeps asking me to go. And she'd *love* you. I know she would. Anyway, she doesn't live in the farmhouse. It would be ours.' Seeing the dubious look on my face, he added, 'There'll be a crowd of other friends, of course, if you want.'

I protested that I didn't remember much French from school, but he was adamant that I wouldn't need any. And the more he painted a picture for me of the vineyards and the almond trees, the markets full of lavender and peaches and honey, the smiling locals in the little cafes, the smell of coffee and freshly baked bread, the more I weakened, until eventually he said that I should be more adventurous, and he knew that little challenge would be all it took, and it was.

One day in July we set off from Victoria station to Dover. We took a morning ferry and, aware that I was afraid of the ocean, Ralph took the trouble to make everything as special for me as possible. He tied a headscarf around me and stood with me on deck to watch the white cliffs of Dover disappear, waving goodbye to England as if it was all new to him. He took me to a lounge bar and gave me champagne, toasting my first trip to the continent. He seemed acutely aware of the memories that being on the sea might provoke in me, and he took my hand at the first sign of a sway and said, 'Don't worry, old fruit, the sea's as calm as glass today. That lurch was a one-off. We'll be on dry land before you can blink.' Then he made me hold a blink for five seconds, and when I did he kissed me, and we laughed.

In Calais we took a train to Paris, and he made sure that we caught the Metro straight to the Eiffel Tower so that the city could fulfil all of its cinematic promise for me. He wanted my brief stay to incorporate everything I had seen on the big screen, so that I would associate our time together with film stars and glamour and the good life. I took photographs with his Brownie box camera. I snapped him in several different poses because I have always thought that photographs of views are a waste of time. I took a picture of him with the Eiffel Tower in the background, and as I did so I recalled the Paris photograph of him hanging on the wall in his hallway. It would have made more sense for him to take a photograph of me, but he did not offer. Eventually a middle-aged American couple asked if I would take a picture of them together, and when I did so, they offered to return the favour. I still have that picture. We both look so happy. It's funny, I still find it strange how we shape things for ourselves. I mean, how, when things seem to be going our way, we so happily and unconsciously sweep the inconvenient facts under the carpet.

We had drinks in a cafe by the Seine and took a taxi down the Champs-Elysées, Ralph and I singing 'La Vie en Rose' all the way. Eventually we were dropped in the Avenue Foch, where his aunt had an apartment. I began to feel a little nervous, craning my neck to look up at the buildings. It seemed impossible that anyone could have built such grand and elegant buildings to be so high. 'Don't worry, *ma chérie*, there's a lift!'

Aunt Beatrice had a very thoroughbred air to her, speaking in an English I had only ever heard on the radio, but she was very friendly and wore a profusion of brightly coloured chiffon scarves around her neck in an arty fashion, suggesting that she, like her nephew, was making a little protest at her aristocratic roots. She joshed with Ralph like a schoolboy and teased him about me relentlessly. I could see he was a favourite nephew. 'She's perfectly adorable – you're perfectly adorable, Dora – and we could do with some Welsh in the family! We could! Enrich that weak and watery blood a bit. The Welsh are so passionate, aren't they? I do love a bit of passion. Are you passionate, Dora? I expect you're hungry for life. Are you *actually* hungry? Because I've organized afternoon tea. They call it *le goûter* here, but it really is a pale imitation of afternoon tea. *However*, I am rather fond of the patisserie, so we have the best of both worlds.' Then she said something in what sounded like impeccable French, and an elderly Frenchwoman looked around the door: '*C'est tout prêt, madame. Je vous sers?*' And to my astonishment, the low table between the chairs we were sitting on rapidly became covered in tea things without Aunt Beatrice having to move an inch. A silver teapot, china cups and saucers and little pastries on tiered plates appeared as if by magic, the old servant scuttling in and out so quickly she was barely noticeable.

'Bee,' Ralph said, 'shall I be mother?' And he poured us all tea, much to the surprise of the servant, who disappeared behind the door again.

'Now, Ralphie, *mon cher*, I hope you're not going to let me down. I'm banking on you staying at Les Amandiers.'

'Of course!'

'And are you staying with him, Dora darling, or just holidaying?'

I felt myself colour, and looked at Ralph for enlightenment. To my surprise, he appeared rattled and fiddled with the cake stand as if he might be able to adjust it. His aunt looked at him too, and he took in a breath, as if a little exasperated. 'Dora is coming down for a few weeks. *D'abord.*'

'*Ah, tant mieux!* You'll love it, Dora, and you'll be able to give it a feminine touch. But you, Ralphie, you're going to stay, aren't you? You can't go back on your word now – I've given the tenants their notice.'

I detected an awkwardness in Ralph that I had not witnessed before. It was quite clear that one of us – his aunt or me – was not being told the truth, and I suspected it was me.

'Bee, stop worrying!' he rallied quickly. 'Of course I'll be staying. I have everything under control!'

21

ARTHUR

After that weekend at Pippa's, I sent her a postcard thanking her for the very 'special' hospitality. She didn't reply, and within a few days I was feeling foolish again. I began to think more and more about Dora, and by the end of the week I decided I would write her a letter. That was the very least she deserved, after all. Composing it in my head was like grieving. I kept seeing her dear face smiling up at me. I saw her clear blue eyes gazing at mine as she propped herself up on her elbows in the long grass of Leckhampton Hill. We had a place there we called our sunny spot, because it was warm and sheltered. We used to lie there together under our coats, and she would let me touch her. I felt the velvet of her again as I composed that letter; I drifted into the scent of her skin, I heard her soft moans, felt her breath on my neck, and I wanted her back. I couldn't believe what I'd done. Out of pure lust – for there wasn't any other motive behind my dalliance with Pippa – I had thrown away my best chance of happiness. And Dora was more than that. We had a history. No, that's not it either. Lots of people have histories. A history isn't irreplaceable. We had something else, something visceral, born of that voyage in the boat, of the closest possible contact during the most frightening week of our two young lives. Pippa had been in the same boat, of course, but she had been distant. She hadn't wanted to know me. And as I've said, I think Dora – and caring for her – was the reason I survived.

I dreamt of the sea. A towering monster tossing me about like a toy in its paws. I saw Pippa's pale, inscrutable face in the boat, which became the figurehead at the prow, chin uplifted to the sea, cold and wooden. And I dreamt of Dora's arms around me, of her nuzzling into me, warm and salty in the icy wind.

I wrote that letter in my head dozens of times, but in the end work was too pressing and I found no time to write it down. And even if I had, there was always the nagging feeling that nothing I said, however well expressed, could possibly excuse what I had done. How could Dora ever forgive me? I remembered the look in her eyes as she closed the door on me. I didn't blame her, but I knew it was a lost cause. Even so, I felt that I had to try. I resolved instead to go and see her at the first possible opportunity, which was the following weekend. I bought a train ticket to Cheltenham for Saturday morning. She could close the door on me if she liked, but I *would* see her. Nothing was going to stand in my way.

Or so I thought.

On the Friday evening, while I was packing an overnight bag, the doorbell rang. I considered not answering it, for I had a list of things to do before I was done for the evening, but some pathetic optimism told me it might be Dora, so I went to the door.

'You're invited to supper. Mummy wants to meet you!'

Pippa was glowing. I must have looked alarmed, because she reached out and touched my arm and said, 'Don't worry, old thing. She's got the car. She's waiting for us at the end of the road.'

Her presence startled me. This sudden wish to introduce me to her mother when, it seemed to me, I had not been quite up to the mark before, flattered me. Of course I couldn't go, and I said as much. I had an important meeting in Cheltenham the next day.

'Cheltenham? That's no problem. Stay over tonight and you'll be on the doorstep.' Her perfume wafted in with her confidence, and it curled around my resolve, gently detaching it.

'I'm sorry, Pippa. Why couldn't you have given me a bit more notice?'

'Well, I couldn't. Come on. All you need is a toothbrush. Mummy won't take no for an answer.'

It seemed to me that it didn't really matter what time I saw Dora, so long as I stuck to my guns and saw her. The idea that Pippa's mother was waiting for me in her car struck me as both ludicrous and enticing. I already had my overnight bag. All I had to do was say yes.

Lady Barrington-Hobb was not quite what I'd expected. She was glamorous, certainly, and younger than I'd expected, but she chain-smoked as she was driving and spoke with a gravelly voice, every other word – it seemed to me, anyway – being 'bloody' or 'darling'. I sat next to her, and Pippa sat in the back seat, so most of the time all I could see was the mother's profile, which was dainty and totally at odds with her voice. Her hands on the wheel were veiny and long-nailed and glittered with rings, including a diamond I couldn't possibly imagine any man being able to afford. I tried hard not to cough during the journey and was relieved when we reached Ashleycroft Hall, so that I could have some respite from smoke and stilted conversation.

'Oh Lord,' she said as we went through the front door, 'Could you pick up the post for me, darling?' I think she was addressing Pippa, but I bent down and collected three envelopes from the mat. She took them without a glance at them or at me. 'Well, I suppose you'd better go and have a chat with your young man, and we can have a little snifter in the kitchen. At least it's warm in there.' She leafed through the mail. 'Here's one for you, darling.'

As she handed the letter to her daughter, I couldn't help noticing the writing on the envelope. It would have had no impact on me had it not been for the very familiar loops and the quirky capitals of 'Barrington-Hobb', which I had seen so often in my own 'Fielding'. A chill went through me.

I wanted to seize the letter and read it myself. I was jealous of Pippa at that moment, and frightened. I had the feeling that events were out of my control, the waves coming over again, throwing me up and sucking me down.

She tore it open and her expression stiffened. She replaced the single sheet of familiar blue writing paper in its envelope and pushed it into the pocket of her coat. 'Come on, Arthur. Let me show you to your room.' So, I had to pretend that I hadn't been there before, and this sudden demand for deception only served to double my discomfort.

We took off our coats and I followed her upstairs. Once inside my room she sat on the bed and tapped the space beside her. 'Arthur, I don't know quite how to put this, but there's something you need to know.' She looked suddenly very fragile, and her shoulders drooped as she looked at the carpet.

'Tell me,' I said, slipping an arm around her.

'You must promise not to be cross.'

Now I was nervous. Had she said something to Dora that prompted the letter? I swallowed hard. 'Go on . . .'

'Promise?'

'I don't know what it is yet. Just say it.'

'Well . . .' She continued to look down at the floor and folded her lips together as if willing them to stay shut. 'Well, something that should have happened . . . hasn't happened.'

It sounds ridiculous now, but I didn't cotton on straight away. Did she mean meeting her family? Did she mean I should have proposed to her first before sleeping with her? And then she touched her belly and looked at me with those big green eyes, and I felt dizzy.

It seemed to me that she was twelve years old again, but this time without the confidence. There was something touchingly vulnerable about her hopeful expression that made me want to weep. I had hurt her. I had thought she was in control, but I had hurt her.

It would take me years, of course, to realize that she was utterly in control, of this moment as well as all others.

'I was using this special method, with dates and everything, and I thought . . . I thought it would be all right. I honestly didn't think it could happen. Honestly, Arthur, I would never have . . . I just don't understand it.'

I gave her a squeeze because I didn't know what else to do. A wave tossed me right upside down, and I didn't know which way was up. She leant into my shoulder and started to sob gently.

'Does your mother know?'

'Yes.'

My heart sank. I felt trapped. All my plans . . . I slowly began to see that there were no options now. The rest of my life was being drawn up by my stupid, selfish actions. Was I going to have to marry her? Was her mother going to approve? Would I spend the rest of my life being not quite good enough? Would I be expected to live here with them? Would I inherit this house? Did I want to be a father yet? Yes, yes, as a matter of fact I did, in a year or two at least, but I had pictured Dora as the mother.

'What . . . what would you like to do about it?'

She pushed me off. 'What do you mean, what would I like to do about it? For God's sake, Arthur! Are you suggesting I get rid of it?'

'No! No, not at all. I mean . . . I don't know, you seem so . . . so modern, I just wasn't sure, that's all.'

'Well I'm not "modern", for your information! Not *that* modern, anyway.'

'But you seemed so . . . you seemed to have done it before.'

She slapped me hard across the cheek. 'How *dare* you!'

'I'm sorry.'

'So you should be. If you'd thought to use some sort of protection, like most men, this wouldn't have happened.'

I felt too ashamed to pick up on the 'most men' reference. It was all my fault. I had to do the manly thing. 'Surely you don't want to marry me. I mean, of course I'll marry you, Pippa, but surely I'm not good enough?'

She softened slightly. 'Well, clearly someone with your income would not be my mother's *first* choice . . . but then I don't *have* a choice, do I?'

This wasn't the way I had hoped to make someone my wife. I didn't want any woman to 'make do' with me. I wanted her – as I knew Dora would – to be bowled over with delight at the prospect of a future together. I wanted someone loyal and loving and excited by me and all I had to offer. I realized now for certain, and with a somersault in my stomach, that all of this, everything, was with the wrong woman.

'We'd better go and talk to your mother, then.' I smiled weakly and kissed her neck so that she couldn't see the terror in my face.

In the kitchen her mother was waiting for us at the big oak table, cigarette in hand and bottle of cognac open in front of her. I saw for the first time that her face was deeply lined, and her mouth had the drawstring creases of a serious smoker. She looked up at me under heavy lids and said, 'Well, you're still alive, then? I expect you'd like a stiff drink.'

It soon became clear that it was Lady Barrington-Hobb who liked a stiff drink or two. She proceeded to quiz me on my income and my property whilst knocking back several glasses. 'So you're an engineer?'

'Yes.'

'Any chance of promotion?'

'I've just been promoted.'

'But you have a small house.'

'Yes,' I said proudly. 'I have a property of my own.'

'But a small one. Any chance of owning a larger one?'

I felt foolish. 'I have a very high chance of further promotion. My area of expertise is in great demand at the moment. I expect to be earning considerably more within the next few years.'

'Well, I suppose you'll do, Archie.'

'*Arthur*, Mummy,' Pippa chipped in.

'Arthur. How very traditional. I suppose you'll have to do, Arthur. Make sure you do it soon.' She looked at her wristwatch. 'I'm off to bed. Goodnight, darling.' She looked across at me. 'You can call me Cynthia, but only in private.'

Pippa heaved a sigh when she was gone. Her mother had not thought to ask me if I was prepared to marry Pippa, and I realized I had absolutely no say in the matter. My heart was pounding. I had been cross-examined on my manhood and survived. Why was it, then, that I felt it had just been taken away from me?

Pippa said goodnight to me on the landing. 'I do love you, you know,' she said, and kissed me on the cheek.

I lay in the cold guest bed and stared into the gloom. I lay on my right, I lay on my left, I threw out a pillow, I clawed at the sheets, and then I flung back the eiderdown. I listened to the silence; I sweated; I breathed heavily. I had the gnawing feeling that there was something I had meant to do – something important. And then, at about four in the morning, I remembered.

I tiptoed down to the hallway cloakroom. Pippa's coat was hanging next to mine, and I slipped a hand into the pocket and retrieved the letter. I don't know why, but I had the feeling that a lot rested on that letter; and so it did. I opened the little sheet of Basildon Bond paper with trembling hands and had to close the cloakroom door so that I could turn on the light. My eyes blinked at the sudden glare. I looked down at the writing:

Pippa,
I know what you did.
Dora

I reread it, confused. This didn't sound like the Dora I knew. This was an accusing Dora, a Dora accusing Pippa of sleeping with me, when in fact it was all my fault. If Dora blamed anyone, it should have been me. I didn't like this underhand way of dealing with it. I couldn't blame her, of course, but this wasn't the girl I thought she was. This showed a little streak of spite. This wasn't my Dora at all.

22

DORA

The train journey seemed to go on forever. At first, there was a trace of familiarity in the grey stone buildings and endless telegraph posts. The cows in the fields looked the same as the cows in Gloucestershire, although Ralph insisted they mooed with a French accent. We passed through station after station, coming to a slow, screeching halt, and hearing urgent French voices and doors slamming. Each time I felt a growing distance from a world where things were certain and familiar. I was glad of Ralph's company and felt a little shock of panic if he left me even for a minute or two.

After Lyon, the landscape changed. There were fewer grey roofs and the meadows began to run out. The rooftops turned to a salmon pink and the houses were more often ochre-coloured or pale and rendered. The fields became increasingly parched, and the only green came in the form of vineyards and tall, dark trees. At Montélimar, Ralph reached overhead for our suitcases and ushered me on to the platform. I followed him into the windswept town, dazed at all the signs for *nougat*. There was a Bar Nougat, a Café Nougat and even an Hôtel Nougat.

'We'll stop here for a bite to eat,' said Ralph. 'It's near the bus stop. There are buses every hour, and we've just missed one, so we can take our time.'

We laughed as we entered a little restaurant called Le Restaurant Nougat, and he explained that the lavender in this region produced wonderful honey, and the almond trees were abundant, so Montélimar combined the two in its world-famous nougat. Ever since Paris I realized that being on foreign soil put Ralph very much in control. I could only look on in awe as he ordered tickets, put our luggage on the right train, chatted to Frenchmen or summoned waiters. Without him I was lost. I'm not sure if I was uncomfortable with this state of affairs straight away or if it was a discomfort that grew, but it would set the tone for the summer.

By the time we boarded the bus for our final destination, I was already jittery with homesickness. The landscape now was utterly alien. The fields were pale and arid, stitched occasionally with neat rows of short, green vines. There was none of the softness of England. Everywhere there was row after row of dry, knobbly trees, bent over by the wind.

We alighted at a village called Valréas, on an ancient, circular road with heavily pruned plane trees blocking out the intense afternoon sun. We went into a bar for some mineral water, and clusters of old men wearing berets looked up from their drinking or their cards to stare at us. I rested my eyes firmly on the bar, where two cool glasses of water arrived for us, but I could feel the eyes on my back. I had been aware of a strange way of speaking French on our bus journey, and now the heavily accented barman demanded 'veng-senk'. To my astonishment, Ralph understood and handed him twenty-five francs. The men had begun to resume their banter and their card games, but as soon as I spoke to Ralph they looked up again with renewed interest. Some younger men in a far corner began to joke with the barman, and I knew they were talking about me. What was this strange place Ralph had brought me to? How did he understand them when they didn't even speak proper French?

As soon as we'd finished our drinks, one of the men in the bar walked over to us and said something to Ralph. We followed him out into the brightly dappled light and down a side street, where a sleepy-looking mule was waiting with its cart. I couldn't imagine how the poor animal could pull a cart, three people and our heavy luggage, but it seemed quite content to saunter through the streets until we reached the open countryside, where the scorching sun was relentless. I wished I had brought a sunhat, and I watched with increasing agitation as the little mule dragged its head up and down with each step.

Les Amandiers was nothing like the villa I had expected. I stood on the tinder-dry grass and looked at its flaking golden walls, its faded green shutters and curving pink roof tiles, several of which were piled up, broken, by the side of the house. The mule relieved itself on the road, and I asked Ralph if we couldn't get it some water. This suggestion was met with a wave of the hand, and he and the cart-driver laughed as money was exchanged. I thought of all my excitement at the station in Cheltenham, and then at Victoria, and of the night in Paris, and the relentless fields and rooftops and small towns and slamming train doors and the miles and miles of telegraph wires slumped between post after post and all the vastness of the unfamiliar earth that stretched between this arid place and home. As the mule walked off, I felt as abandoned as the house, and the thought that I had carefully packed, in the suitcases at our feet, my best dress, high-heeled shoes and a new toilet bag that Our Mam had bought specially, brought a constriction to my throat.

Despite the mule's recent delivery, there was a sweet smell in the air. As we walked down the path towards the house, we kicked at wild thyme and rosemary. The brightness was so overwhelming that the cool darkness inside the front door came as a release. I had to blink several times before I made out a flagstone floor and a dark stone staircase. In front of us was a rectangle of light through which was the promise of a kitchen. I followed Ralph upstairs with the luggage and slumped down on a bed.

'We will take a siesta if you like, dear Dora. But first we need some light refreshment and some exploring.'

In the kitchen were a long oak table and a sink as old as the one my grandmother had back home. I noticed the curling flypapers hanging from the ceiling, each one plastered in fat insects.

I must have looked bewildered when a young man appeared, because he said, in slightly accented English, 'Don't worry. We were supposed to move out by the summer, but Ralph says we can stay. Is that okay with you?'

'Of course.' I looked at Ralph for some clues.

'Sylveng,' said the man, holding out his hand.

I took it and smiled. 'Dora.'

'This is Sylvain,' said Ralph, pronouncing his name in correct French, as though the man's own rendering of his name was inadequate. 'He's a carpenter, and I'm very envious. If only I'd done something useful with my life; I'd like to learn how to make things out of wood.'

'There's still time,' said Sylvain. 'You are young.' He pronounced this last word 'yong', and I warmed to him.

'Well, yes, I suppose I am.'

'*Et moi, je suis Claudine*,' chirped a voice from underneath the table. I looked down, and a girl of about eight emerged carrying a colander of strawberries. '*Et je* speak English.'

'It's true, she does,' said Ralph. 'She's the daughter of Patsy, who runs the house for us.'

'You have a housekeeper?' I asked.

'Aunt Bee does. We won't really need a housekeeper for the long term, of course, but Bee is very attached to her, and she sort of comes with the house.'

'*Tu ne vas pas renvoyer maman?*' The little girl shot him a defiant look.

'No, your *maman* is fine with us. And so are you, Claudine. What would we do without your strawberries?'

Claudine smiled proudly and proceeded to chop off the heads of the strawberries with a massive knife she had selected from the knife rack. 'I can bring you rabbits too,' she said to me with great authority. 'You stick with me and you'll eat like a queen.'

'I think I will stick with you, then,' I said.

For some reason, the sight of the little girl topping fruit, and of her smiling English mother coming in from the pantry with an armful of bread, and the smell of something aromatic roasting in the range, made me feel less homesick. I didn't know what Ralph meant by not needing a housekeeper in the long term, or who he was referring to with 'we', but I allowed the scent of the roasting meat, the taste of the aperitif and the sound of Claudine humming 'I'm Gonna Wash That Man Right Outa My Hair' to herself to ease my mind. If there was something about Ralph's plans I needed to worry about, it would become clear soon enough.

23

ARTHUR

Work was busier than ever. I was responsible for six new recruits, and if it hadn't been for a colleague a couple of years older than me, I would have found it hard to keep my head above water. Len had a parallel role to mine, working on jet engines. He had a wife and a child, of whom he talked proudly, and there was another baby on the way. It had been Len who had suggested the area in which I bought my house, for he had bought one a year earlier just a few streets away.

One lunchtime I broached the subject of Pippa with Len.

'I thought you were seeing a little Welsh girl.'

'I was. The thing is . . . well, I'm seeing Pippa now, and we're going to be married next week.'

'Next week? Fast work there, mate.'

'Yes.'

He gave me a knowing glance, which turned rapidly into a sympathetic one as he saw the truth in my face.

'Do you . . . um, do you love her?'

I hesitated. 'Yes.'

He put his hand out and patted my shoulder. 'Anything I can do? Do you need a witness at the wedding?'

I hadn't thought of this. 'Yes, please. That would be helpful.' It was a relief to tell someone and to find Len – who was a good, upright human being – so non-judgemental and kind.

'Maureen's aunt has a house by the sea in Blackpool, if you want a short honeymoon.'

We were married in a small gothic church with only the vicar, Pippa's mother and Len present. Afterwards we went back to Ashleycroft Hall, where Cynthia had the perfect excuse for a 'snifter' and uncorked a bottle of champagne. Then we had salmon sandwiches and an hour of awkward conversation, Cynthia clearly finding Len impossible to grasp or impress or intimidate. I was mildly amused, and I was disappointed when he said he had to go. As Cynthia didn't offer to drive him, Pippa and I walked with him back to the village to catch the bus, and the three of us waited in the pub, toasting the marriage and, following Pippa's lead, allowing ourselves to laugh at Cynthia's pomposity. When the bus came and we waved Len off, I saw for an instant the rescue ship that turned tail and left us in the ocean, adrift.

Telling my parents about Pippa was not easy. Quite apart from the disappointment I was sure they would feel about Dora, I knew I would have to face their hurt at not being invited to the wedding. In the end I decided to visit them the week after we were married and to see them alone at first, to field their reaction. I left Pippa in Oxford Street with some of her London friends, while I took the tube as far south as it would go and then caught a bus to my parents' house in Middlesex.

My mother was not the sort of woman to cry, but I could see her eyes redden when she realized what had happened. She understood straight away that I would never have given Dora up lightly, and that something serious and shameful had occurred to make me sneak off and get married 'on the sly', as she called it.

'Where did we go wrong?' she asked the fireplace. 'What did we do to you, Arthur?'

'Mum, please . . . You've done nothing wrong. I slipped up, that's all.'

'*Slipped up?* Is that what you call it these days?'

My father gave me an indecipherable glance, and the three of us sat for a moment, in the same three chairs we had sat in since Philip died, with the fourth chair empty, as it had been since then.

'Your mother is disappointed, that's all. She likes Dora a lot – we both do. She seemed such a perfect match for you. I'm sure we'll get to like this – what is it? Pippa? – just as well, given time.'

'Do you love her?' asked my mother. This was the second time I had been asked the question in a week, and it was like a reprimand, reminding me that love, not lust, should have driven my decision to marry.

'Yes,' I said, with practised assertiveness, 'I do.'

Mum looked me in the eye then. 'I thought you loved Dora? How can you be sure you love this woman?'

I said nothing in reply but brushed some imaginary dust from my trousers.

'I *wondered* why you hadn't been in touch. I've been out of my mind with worry.'

'I'm sorry.'

'You're all we've got left, Arthur. Since Philip . . . you're all we've got.'

Something in the way she said it made me feel like a remnant, something with which she would have to make do. It was a childish feeling, but Philip always brought back that gut sense of being displaced, of being second best. And worse, since his death, Philip was my perpetual burden of guilt. Philip would not have let them down. Philip would have married someone like Dora and made them proud. Hell, he prob-ably would have married *Dora*.

'And what does poor Dora make of all this?'

I looked up at her.

She must have seen my distress, because she softened then and poured me some tea. 'Well, we'll just have to make the best of it. I hope she's worth it.'

My father came rushing up alongside us in his lifeboat. 'What's she like, Pippa?'

'She's beautiful. I mean . . . she really is . . . beautiful.'

'Are you going to introduce her to us?'

'Of course. I'm going to pick her up from some friends in town right now.' But even as I said it, I knew they would never take to Pippa as they had taken to Dora. This made me feel protective of my new wife, and I said, 'Please be nice to her, won't you?'

I think my mother tried very hard. She must have sensed, with the confidence of that first 'hello' and the manicured hand she was given to shake, that this was someone outside her familiar orbit. She must have clocked Pippa's slow sweep of the living room and the inscrutable half-smile on her face. I was relieved when Pippa refused tea, because she might have asked for 'Darjeeling'.

My father took her to his shed and showed her his ships in bottles, and she smiled, unlike Dora who had been thrilled by them. 'How very clever of you,' she said, 'but what do you do with them?' Then, as we were coming out of the shed she stung herself on a nettle, and my father apolo-gized profusely. 'Don't worry,' she said. 'But I should sack your gardener.' Poor Pippa, I don't think she knew what she was doing, but she managed to save the day by simply being beautiful. I had told her beforehand that all she had to do was smile. This she did, and winningly. I think they were so dazzled by her green eyes and her refined accent and the prospect of their grandchild inheriting her magnificence that they managed to forget that she was the sort of woman who slept with men outside wedlock.

24

DORA

That first evening Ralph showed me the terrain. In the golden light things looked kinder. The bleached earth was now peachy, and the air was alive with the sound of cicadas, or *les cigales*, as I was to come to know them. It was a sound like none I'd heard before, and the relentless croaky purr they made was immediately exotic to me.

As we climbed the fragrant wooded slope behind the house, I became aware of another aroma. To the smell of thyme and rosemary was now added a new scent, one that I warmed to with each passing step. At the top of the slope was, I now saw, a field of dramatically violet-blue lavender, great bushy rows extending as far as the eye could see. I breathed it in hungrily: a familiar, intoxicating smell but with a sweetness to it far removed from old clothes hanging in a wardrobe. We walked along a path until the trees no longer blocked the view down towards the house. I realized that Les Amandiers was larger and more sprawling than I had first thought. Newly built, it would have been a highly desirable residence. The main building was symmetrical, with a tall double door flanked on two floors by green shuttered windows. Although faded and peeling now, the green emphasized the pinkness of the roof and the yellowness of the stucco walls, so flaky that it looked as if they had been covered in wallpaper that someone had idly started to scratch off. There were several outhouses and sheds, outside which was a neglected car that belonged to Aunty Bee. Around the house were fig trees and almond trees. To the front of the house and to one side, I could see now that the land stretched out in rows of what appeared to be waist-high trees.

'Those are vines,' said Ralph. 'They've been a bit neglected over the years, but I'm going to get them back in shape. There should still be some good grapes this autumn, though. Enough to make a bit of wine, anyway.'

'You're going to make wine? Do you know how?'

'No, but Denis does.' He pronounced the name 'Dunny'.

'Dunny?'

'Patsy's husband – Claudine's father. He's French. He helps look after the place, but he has his own vineyard.'

'So that's why Claudine speaks such good French.'

'She speaks French because she goes to school here.'

We entered the pinewood again and made our way back down to the house on a winding path through its glorious resiny smell.

I had carefully let pass his reference to getting the vines back into shape and all the references so far that seemed to indicate something more than a summer holiday here, but I determined to broach it with him soon. Did he expect me to return home alone? What sort of holiday invitation was that? And if, on the other hand, he had notions of my staying with him, he would have to think again. I had my teacher training to finish first. And Daphne's wedding to go to in September.

In the evening there was a meal in the kitchen at which everyone I had met so far seemed to be invited, as well as Denis, the housekeeper's French husband. They all sprawled around the long table, clinking glasses and chattering loudly. Some conversation I could follow, but none of the French made any sense to me. Ralph spoke in French a little more than he needed to, I felt, given that the women present spoke

English. I supposed, however, that he was just showing off to me and had not considered how it excluded me. At length he caught my eye.

'We always have communal meals,' he said. 'It's one of the best things about living here.'

'Oh.' I was embarrassed not to have taken part in any of the preparation for this small feast. Food was still being rationed in England, and what was on offer here had been cooked with great care. 'Surely, then, we should have done something to contribute to it ourselves . . . if they're communal?'

Patsy, the young housekeeper, laughed. 'Well said, Dora! You tell him!'

Ralph looked at me coldly then, as if I had in some way made him look a fool, but all I had intended was to offer my services, to muck in with everyone else. 'Everyone does what they can,' he said with authority. 'If you have cooking skills, then your help will be welcome, I'm sure. But don't forget that your main role is to help me with the book. You are my researcher.'

A few words were muttered in French by Denis at which Sylvain laughed. Ralph flared his nostrils and said something emphatically to them both, and Denis raised his hands in a gesture of mock defence. Patsy turned to me and started asking about my home and my teacher training course. Claudine stood up behind me and started plaiting my hair as if I were a school friend, and I quite forgot about Ralph and the chilling look that had so unexpectedly crossed his face.

A couple of days passed. Ralph and I did little except walk and eat and take siestas. At no point did he attempt to sleep with me, and I began to feel that his interest in me had diminished. But then I didn't know Ralph very well at all at that point. I didn't know what a calculated game he played.

After maybe three days he took me on a walk and said, 'Well, Dora, what do you think?'

'Of what?'

'Of the house. Of Les Amandiers.'

'It's striking. It's like nothing I've ever experienced.'

'And yet you're not happy.' He stopped in his tracks and held my shoulders.

'What do you mean?'

'I mean, I can tell that this isn't quite what you had in mind, is it?'

'Well, no, perhaps not.'

'In what way?'

I hesitated. I didn't want to see his look of disapproval again. 'Well, I suppose I just didn't expect so many people. I thought we'd be alone until Tighe came out with his friends.'

'Ah, Tighe! He's coming out next week. We'll have some fun then!' He drew me close to him and kissed my neck. 'My poor Dora. You wanted some time alone, just the two of us.'

I didn't know what to say. It wasn't really true. I wasn't sure I had wanted time alone with him, except that his avoidance of it had, it was true, left me feeling a little neglected. I had almost gone from fearing he would make a pass at me to longing for him to make one. And of course he knew that far better than I did myself.

'Dora,' he whispered, 'I've been neglectful. Tomorrow we'll go for an evening picnic – just the two us.'

It was about six-thirty in the evening when we set off. The sun was still warm, but we walked at a leisurely pace for a couple of miles until we came to the edge of a wood overlooking another lavender field.

'This is the place,' said Ralph, dropping the basket he was carrying and turning to smile at me. 'Let's spread the rug here, in the shade.'

I helped him lay out an old, grey service rug, and he proceeded to unpack wine and bread, pâté, cheese and strawberries. It was a feast. It was the sort of picnic you read about, not the sort I had ever been on. He even handed me a linen napkin, took two carefully wrapped glasses out of the basket and uncorked the wine. When he poured it, glugging into the glasses that I held out, it was the only sound except for the cicadas.

'Here's to . . . *us*!' he said, winking.

We clinked glasses. Did I want an 'us'? Did I want an 'us' with Ralph? We ate and drank and talked. The sun moved soundlessly towards the violet skyline. We ate and drank and giggled in the lavender-scented air. We drank and touched. We touched, we kissed, we lay down. Everything was golden now, except for the lavender, which was magenta. There was no one else around: just us and the cicadas.

He ran his hands over my breasts, my hips, my thighs. I let him touch me in places that only Arthur had ever touched me before. I let him do this with a weary, drink-smudged abandon. I was aware of a sense of betrayal: I was betraying Arthur. But, I reminded myself, he had betrayed me. He could hardly expect me to remain intact for him, if he *did* ever want me back . . . but then I would be lost to anyone else . . . How much I wanted . . . I wanted . . .

'I know you want me,' he said.

'I'm . . .' I heard myself murmur, 'I'm saving myself . . . for the man I marry.'

I felt my cheek being stroked. How I wished it were Arthur. Arthur smiling, crazed with desire. *Well, let's hope he bears an uncanny resemblance to me.*

Ralph leant in close to my ear: 'Good girl.' Then he held one of my arms down hard to the blanket and kissed me. 'But you *know* you want me,' he said softly. 'It's all right, Dora. It's all right. I can wait, because it won't be long.'

Then he pulled away from me and started to pack the things, leaving me flushed and aching, outstretched to the violet and reddened dome of the sky.

The next couple of days seemed hotter than before. All I wanted to do was stay in the cool of my room and lie on the bed. And I could think of nothing but my desire, uncorked and breathing heavily in the Mediterranean heat. But when I recalled – as I did almost every moment – Ralph's hands on my body, memories of Arthur kept winging back to me. He was like a scrunched-up letter in a waste bin, moving and opening long after it had been thrown away.

Tighe had arrived, along with a girlfriend who played the flute and a male friend who played the fiddle. Each night we ate outside on an old wooden table. I covered it in clean linen cloths and Claudine put flowers in little pots to decorate it. Flypapers were strung from the trees to catch the mosquitoes, and we ate and talked and laughed until the sun went down and the moon rose over the vineyards. Then the music started: fiddle, flute and concertina, old Provençal songs from Denis and Sylvain, and the latest hits from Claudine. There were foot-stamping jigs and reels, and when there were waltzes and polkas everyone who wasn't playing got up to dance.

How we danced! They were heady times. I began to fall in love with the place. Bleached and burnt out in the day, it became rich and exotic by night. I only wished Arthur were here. If only he could see me now. I wondered what he would think if he knew I was having so much fun. Would he want me back? I imagined telling him about it all at Daphne's wedding in September. He would ask me what I was up to these days and I would casually say that I had just spent the summer in the south of France – with friends. I would walk away from him and mingle, and later he would follow me, intrigued, just as he had been intrigued by Pippa. He would buy me a drink and comment on my tanned arms, and perhaps he would comment too, with a little jolt of despair, at the sight of a giant diamond ring on my finger. 'Are you *married?*' he would ask in panic. 'No,' I would say, 'but I'm engaged.' I would sense his relief mingled with agitation. Just time, he would think, if I'm quick, to win her back. But, of course, he would need to woo me like no one on earth to win me back after all that had happened. I could stand it, though, perhaps, being wooed like no one else on earth . . .

One afternoon – I can't remember when, exactly, but some time after Tighe arrived – I was lying on my bed taking a siesta. It was too hot to wear a petticoat, which was what I usually stripped down to, and I had on just my underwear. I heard footsteps on the flagstones out on the landing. I listened, wondering if there was something to cover myself with but having no energy to get under the coverlet. The footsteps stopped. Whoever it was, they were in no hurry: listening, perhaps. Ralph came in and closed the door behind him. He said nothing, but took off the rest of my clothes as if I had been waiting for him. His arrogance shocked me. But perhaps it wasn't shock it stirred in me. I was so . . .

There was no excuse for it. I could blame the sunshine or the music or Ralph – or Arthur – but I knew what I was doing, and I kept on wanting it. In the days that followed, I wanted Ralph more, not less. I wanted him to make love to me all the time. He was like a drug, and I began to wonder if I wasn't, perhaps, in love with him after all.

25

ARTHUR

Married life with Pippa was a whirlwind. I had to keep rebuking myself for making comparisons with what it might have been like with Dora. But the truth was I enjoyed coming home at the end of the day to find Pippa busy in the kitchen. I would go and slip my arms around her waist from behind, running my hands up and down her curves, and she would shoo me away or turn around and kiss me, and I would never know which it was to be. Sometimes there was the smell of cooking in the air, and this pleased me more than anything after a long day's work. At other times, and this happened quite often, there would be a smell of burning, and she would be in a foul mood as she threw a tray of charred meat on the hob. On the whole, though, she seemed to enjoy playing housewife in those first few months. It was like a new game for her. There would be pots of flowers on every surface and music playing on the radio, and she filled the house with new tea towels, salad bowls, vases, cushions and colourful bedspreads. I was impressed with her style. It is true I was less impressed with our joint bank statements, which ran into several sheets of paper instead of one, but then I was earning good money, and I told myself it was gratifying to see it put to good use.

Sometimes I would watch her dressing or putting on make-up and I would hardly be able to contain my pride at having such a gorgeous wife. The way she held her hair up as she sat at the new dressing table, the little wisps of hair at her neck, the pout as she applied her red lipstick, the way she folded her lips over a tissue to blot them: all these things thrilled me. I would pick up the tissues with the imprint of her lips and marvel at them, then remind myself that I didn't need mementos, because she was here with me under my roof. She was mine, and mine alone.

Sharing a bed with Pippa was another joy. Again, I had to stop myself wondering what it might have been like if Dora . . . Well, anyway, it was a new experience for me, wrapping myself around a woman, skin on skin, all night long. And I no longer had to feel awkward about things, wondering if I could or couldn't make love to her. She was my wife, my woman. Coming home to her each day, eating with her, sleeping with her, touching her, making her moan with pleasure and taking my own: these were the delights of this marriage I had once feared.

I could hardly believe my luck.

As the months went on and the evenings became long and warm, she began to reject me sometimes. At first, I barely noticed. I was tired myself and occasionally fell asleep straight away. By August she would roll away from me in bed, refusing even the gentlest of cuddles. Len told me it was usual for a woman to be a little less active as pregnancy progressed and explained that it was because she was tired. He gave me some tips on relaxing her, which had worked well with Maureen, and they had even made love on the night their son was born. I tried these on Pippa. I brought home fish and chips one evening to save her cooking, I put her legs up on a cushion and played soft music, I massaged her feet and stroked her skin and took her to bed at seven o'clock. She allowed me to carry on stroking her for nearly an hour, then pushed me away and called me a brute.

Len told me to be patient. I had no choice. I would come home from work and find her slumped on the sofa. There would be nothing cooking and the fridge was always empty. She no longer shopped, except for luxury items, and I began to think that pregnancy must be some kind of illness, and felt guilty for putting her through it.

'There's a tin of salmon in the cupboard,' she murmured one day when I came home. 'You can make us a sandwich if you like.'

I put down my briefcase and went to kneel beside the sofa. I noticed the ship in the bottle had disappeared from the mantelpiece and had been replaced by a bronze statuette.

'What is it? Are you all right?'

'Of course I'm not all right! I'm five months pregnant! Look at me. I can't get into a decent dress. I'm disgusting.'

'Oh no, you're not. You're beautiful, Pippa. You're beautiful in your clothes and even more beautiful naked.'

'Naked? Uh! Have you seen what you've done to my skin? *You* did this to me, Arthur! *You* did this! I look like a hippo!'

I put my hand out to stroke her and she flung it away. I went into the kitchen and put on the kettle to make her some tea and opened the tin of salmon, which sat alone in the empty cupboard. There was no bread; there was no butter. Unwashed knives and forks and pots were stacked up in the sink. I began to wash them and noticed that the washing-up liquid was low and I had to turn the bottle upside down and shake it. As I held a dirty saucepan under the tap, some spots of tomato sauce spattered my jacket. I put on the apron hanging on the back of the door and continued washing and scrubbing until they were all clean. Then I took her a cup of tea.

'Oh, for God's sake!' She propped herself up from her reclining position on the sofa and closed her eyes slowly with disdain.

I placed the cup beside her. 'What? Would you prefer cocoa?'

'Oh for crying out loud!'

I looked at her for clues. She seemed utterly repulsed by me, but for what reason at that precise moment I couldn't be sure. I studied the cup of tea I had put down for some guidance.

'Oh, for pity's sake, look at you! Standing there in a pinny!'

'I'm sorry, but someone had to clean the dishes.'

She rolled her eyes emphatically. 'Oh, so *that's* it, is it? I'm not as domestic as you were expecting, am I? Well why can't we do like everyone else and get a cleaning lady?'

'A cleaning lady?' The thought had never entered my head. No one I knew had a cleaning lady. It was ridiculous, and I must have laughed or smiled or something, because she hit the roof.

'What's so offensive to your plebeian ways about that? I'm five months pregnant, let me remind you. Five months pregnant. How am I supposed to go shopping and do the washing and the cleaning *and* cook for you? Mmm?'

'My mother had two children and never had a cleaning lady. None of the women in this street have cleaning ladies, and a lot of them are pregnant.' I thought of Len's wife, Maureen, who was eight months gone with a toddler in tow, and he still had fresh socks each day and a meal on the table when he got home. 'Most other women seem to manage it.'

She swung her legs round and stood up, her face rosy with rage. 'Well I am *not* most other women. I wasn't finished in Switzerland to be a skivvy in a backstreet house in Bristol!'

I didn't know where to start. 'You weren't "finished" in Switzerland, were you?'

She looked awkward, but only briefly. 'Well, I *would've* been, if Daddy hadn't buggered off with some tart or other. But that's beside the point. I wasn't meant for the slums!'

'And no one has put you in a slum!'

'Oh no, I suppose this pathetic little house would seem like a palace to your sort, wouldn't it? That little Dora of yours, she'd have lapped it up! And I suppose she'd be out heaving bags of shopping at nine months pregnant or herding bally sheep on a Welsh mountain!'

How I wished she hadn't said that. It immediately conjured up the memory of Dora skipping up the steep mountain path ahead of me, sure-footed as a goat. Despite the vitriol with which it had been delivered, I think we both knew there was truth in Pippa's diatribe. Dora would have been happy with this home. She would not have complained about its shortcomings, she wouldn't have been ashamed of a model ship, and I knew she would have taken the ups and downs of pregnancy in her stride like all the women in her family before her, blooming more with each passing day, and excited to be bringing a new life into the world.

The shops were all closed, so I said I would go out and fetch us fish and chips from the chip shop a few streets away. She pulled a face at the thought of it, but she was crying now, great dramatic sobs that must have worried the neighbours. I went to the bathroom to get her some tissue, but there was no toilet roll, just an empty cardboard tube hanging in its holder.

At the end of August my parents came to stay for a long weekend. They still hadn't seen the new house and were anxious to establish good relations with Pippa. They rarely travelled, so I invited them for the week, but my mother was adamant that Pippa should not be put out, what with her being pregnant and me being at work. They would come instead for the bank holiday weekend, and when I told Pippa the plan she nearly hit the roof.

'That's *three whole days!*'

'But they're coming from London. And they haven't seen the house yet.'

'Well, that's your problem. Why didn't you invite them when you moved in? Then that little Welsh girl could've cooked them pie and mash every day.'

'We'll find a way of . . . I'll sort out the meals, somehow. You won't have to cook. Perhaps just the first day? It would be nice to welcome them with a meal.'

She clenched her jaw and glared at me. I swallowed hard.

'They're my parents. They only want to see where we live, how well I've done for myself.'

'How well you've done for yourself!' she sneered, repeating each word as if she were holding it up for ridicule. 'Well that won't take them three days!'

'Why don't we invite your mother to stay soon as well?'

'Well, *there's* a treat!'

'Pippa, I promise I'll make this as easy as possible, and I'll make it up to you.' I had a sudden inspiration. We hadn't had a proper honeymoon – just a weekend in Bath – as I'd been unable to take the time off work at such short notice. 'Why don't we plan a holiday for ourselves? Where would you like to go?'

She exhaled slowly, as if containing her patience.

'Please don't tell me you want me to get my bucket and spade and go to Weston-super-Mare with you?'

As a matter of fact, I had pictured us walking along the sands at Weston together, but I tried to think on my feet. I could see I'd aroused her interest, though, because she put her head to one side.

'Well, if I'd married Jeremy, he was going to take me on the Grand Tour.'

I didn't know what the 'Grand Tour' referred to, but I imagined it was abroad. I knew I couldn't afford anything like that, but I tried to be as glamorous as possible. I knew an island would tempt her.

'I was thinking maybe . . . the Isle of Wight?'

'*The Isle of Wight?* Can't we go to Austria? I have friends in Austria. Or France? I'd love to go to Monte Carlo again.'

When I said it would cripple us to embark on a foreign holiday and that very long trips now would tire her out, she began to cry. She sobbed that her life was pointless and joyless and that all she had to look forward to was getting fatter and cooking spam and eggs for my parents. I began to think it was unreasonable of me to invite my parents. I started to make rash claims that I would do everything myself, that she would barely have to lift a finger, that I would make some excuse to shorten their visit to two days, because after all she was pregnant and tired.

They arrived on the twelve o'clock train from Paddington and I brought them to the house in a taxi. They swept into the hallway behind me, Bill and Elsie, bringing gifts and smiles for Pippa and cries of astonishment and pleasure for me. My mother was so pleased for us both that her eyes were buried in her smiling and only emerged to pop open wide at some new delight: the toaster, the new radio, the carpet on the stairs, the fitted bathroom.

'You look radiant!' said my mother, squeezing Pippa's hands. 'Radiant – doesn't she, Bill?'

'She looks smashing.'

Pippa did not offer to take their coats, but I did, and I hung them by the door as she showed them into the front room.

'He's a lucky man, our son. Ah, here he is . . . I was just saying . . .'

I put my arm around my wife and she smiled for them, before saying that she had to go and see to the lunch. My mother followed her to the kitchen carrying her basket with an enormous apple pie in it, 'To save you making dessert – or to keep till later – I don't want to replace anything you've prepared.'

I sat down with my father and we chatted about the upcoming football season, doing our best to make contact through the safety of the Arsenal and Tottenham Hotspur. I had put the ship in the bottle back on the mantelpiece. I knew Dad would be pleased to see it in pride of place. I wanted to say, 'Dad, have I made a mistake? And if I have, please tell me what to do – what would *you* do?' But even as I strained

161

to convey this to him from behind my screen of normality, I knew exactly what my father would have done in my shoes. For a start, he wouldn't have weakened before wedlock, and even if he had, he would have done the honourable thing, exactly as I had done, and lived with the consequences, for better, for worse. Even if I could have bared my soul to him, he would have counselled me to do no differently. And before they left, I think they both saw my soul stripped naked, without my having to share a single thought.

'All right, Elsie?' he said, as my mother came back into the front room.

'Yes!' Her stricken face lit up with another smile, and I could only sit and wonder what had happened in the kitchen.

Lunch was a strained affair, with both of my parents and myself trying to keep the conversation going. My mother, a past master at filling gaps, would not allow a second to go by without a syllable in it. This gave the exchange a dislocated, sometimes quirky thread, but I was grateful to her for coming up with words when the rest of us were stumped, and for changing route when some hurdle was put in her way.

'So you were in the same boat as Arthur? Boat Nine?'

'Yes.'

'What a coincidence! I bet your parents were relieved when they heard the news of the rescue.'

'I doubt my father even noticed. And I think my mother was disappointed that someone else wasn't going to take me off her hands after all.'

Mum found this one hard to take in in one gulp, so Dad came to her rescue.

'Do you have any brothers and sisters?'

'Not to my knowledge. Only daughter meets only son, I'm afraid.'

There was a short silence, which my father curtailed.

'It's a pity you never met Philip. Arthur had a little brother called Philip. Well, perhaps you did meet him, of course?'

'Yes. Yes, I did meet him.'

Mum put down her knife. 'You knew him? You knew Philip?'

'Only a little.'

'He was . . . lost at sea.' Mum looked lost at sea too.

'I heard. How absolutely dreadful for you.' I was pleased that Pippa was managing some empathy. 'How *awful*! I can't imagine what that must have been like. That poor, poor boy. I was so fond of him.'

'Were you?'

'Oh, he was adorable. Just adorable. Friends with that odd little Welsh girl, though. Don't think she was a very good influence. What was her name? . . . Dora.'

Dad's radar kicked in fast.

'This is a wonderful shoulder of lamb, Pippa. How good of you to go to all this trouble. We really weren't expecting anything like this.'

'It is a tasty bit of lamb, all right,' said Mum, reluctantly leaving her favourite subject, but making a mental note to revisit it at her leisure. 'You not having any more than that yourself? You'll waste away, Pippa.'

'I'm fat. I don't want to get any fatter.'

'Nonsense. You look a picture.'

'Yes, but a picture of what? A Botticelli cherub, perhaps – or a beached whale.'

'A botty . . . ? Elsie's right. You look a picture.'

'And you've got the gravy just right, Pippa.'

'Yes, I like a thick bit of gravy. Elsie'll tell you, I don't like it too runny, do I, Else?'

'No, he doesn't like it runny.'

'Oh, for God's sake!'

I thought she was going to get up and leave the room, but she didn't. She just sat there, with Elsie and Bill not knowing where to look and gazing earnestly down at their lamb and beans for a clue. Maybe there was some mileage in the firmness of carrot?

Pippa carried on as if nothing had happened. She chewed silently on some food and then enquired about their journey, which Bill jumped on eagerly and which had been, it seemed, wonderful. Mum continued to fill the gaps to ensure that none of us felt uncomfortable, but from then on I noticed her hands shaking a fraction, and her smile faltered a little from time to time.

In the afternoon we all went for a walk on the Downs and looked at the view from the Clifton Suspension Bridge. More gasps of delight and wonderment. More scathing silence from Pippa. When we reached home, I made us all a cup of tea – with my mother desperately trying to help. Once alone in the kitchen with me, she tapped my hand, whispering excuses for Pippa's behaviour and telling me not to worry. My parents' sympathy for my wife's tiredness was overwhelming, and Pippa's response to their kindness was to sit without saying a word, occasionally closing her eyes on some comment they made, then wearily opening them again.

'Oh God!' she said suddenly, 'What's that piece of trash doing back on the mantelpiece?'

On Sunday morning they remembered that they had promised to feed a neighbour's cat on the bank holiday Monday, so would not be able to stay another night. Pippa's sarcasm as she said 'Oh, what a shame!' lacked any of the subtlety she may have supposed it to have amidst people like my parents.

God. When I remember them smiling that day, it breaks my heart.

26

DORA

It was the third week in July, I think, and I was beginning to find the heat overwhelming. My hair had grown long and unruly and Patsy said she had a sister-in-law in Nyons who was a hairdresser and who would cut it for free. So on the next market day, she got out Bee's old Renault and took Claudine and me to the little town of Nyons.

There are so many, many smells that bring that place flooding back to me. It's a dangerous thing to have a smell association. There's no controlling it. Smell bypasses all the normal routes in your memory and makes its own magical way direct to your core. The lavender harvest was over and the oil was being extracted in the lavender factory. Nyons was full of the smell of it: so sweet and invasive it was hard to ignore. The intensity of it filled me with a kind of joy. And when, passing the different market stalls, more fragrances filled my head – of freshly baked bread, of garlic, salami, rosemary, honey, cheese, olives, pizza or coffee – I felt I was discovering my sense of smell for the first time. The awnings of the market stalls cast cooling shadows, and the morning sun had not yet heated the pavements. If I close my eyes, I can still bring it all back. And if I smell any one of those things . . .

Anyway, Patsy led us through the market to a little hairdresser's shop, where her sister-in-law was just holding a mirror up to the back of her client's head. Loud exclamations of joy followed, with multiple kissings on each cheek. The client paid and departed, and more delight followed. Maryse, the sister-in-law, looked at me with glee. She held my hair as if it were an injured bird and stroked it behind my ears, putting her head on one side. Then she showed me to the newly vacated chair. I tuned out the loud chatter between the women and allowed myself to enjoy the feel of her hands running through my hair and combing it and parting it, lifting and stroking, all the time smiling at me and talking to Patsy and Claudine, asking me questions which they answered for me. I was taken to a small sink where my hair was gently washed, then I was seated again at the chair, a cover was swung over me, and a glass of iced tea was placed in my hands. I felt like a child, devoid of responsibility, and I was happy to let the women take control. Never in my life had I been to a hairdresser's: Our Mam had always trimmed it for me with the kitchen scissors. Now I sat and let something more creative happen to my head. I gazed in the mirror and saw a bronzed young woman, slimmer than I remembered myself to be, and more confident. As the little snips let hair drop to the ground, I felt more alert, more alive.

When Maryse brushed the back of my neck I felt my spine tingle, and as she held up the mirror for me to look, I could hardly believe it was my head she was showing me. The women cooed and hooted with approval. I was made to stand up, brushed down and instructed to turn around.

'*Tourne-toi! Tourne-toi! Qu'elle est belle!*'

I could barely look at myself; I felt more fashionable than I had a right to. Maryse had given me a beautifully styled bob, the long top layers showing off my newly sun-bleached hair and the short bottom layers like velvet at my neck. I swung my head from side to side and did a mock fashion twirl at which they all laughed. I went back into the market with them, feeling like a model.

There was an aroma of warm bread and salami as we entered the kitchen. The men had heated up the morning's baguettes, unable to wait any longer for lunch. Sylvain, who had his feet up on the table, swung them down and whistled. '*Tourne-toi! T'es magnifique!*'

Ralph looked up from the salami he was cutting as I spun around. His face froze.

'What have you done?'

'I've had my hair cut. Do you like it?'

He put the knife down. He looked furious. 'It's horrible! What have you done to yourself?'

Patsy and Claudine protested, and Claudine said she was going to have hers done like that next week, and it looked lovely. I felt stupid. I didn't know where to put my hands and fumbled for the hair that I normally twirled when embarrassed, but I found nothing to hold on to and held on to my shoulders instead. Ralph stood up and went to the oven, his jaw clenched.

'Well,' said Sylvain, 'me, I find it very . . . *chic*.'

'It goes you well,' said Denis.

'He means it suits you.' Claudine, unable to contain her excitement, added, 'Don't worry about Ralph. He has no idea about fashion. Look at his trousers!'

People laughed, grateful for the opportunity to diffuse things, but Ralph did not raise a smile. The women unloaded the market produce on to the table, and we used the enthusiasm for the cheeses and the fruit and the olives to cover up the sourness of Ralph's unexpected mood.

Ralph didn't speak to me for the rest of the day, but instead of keeping up his mood in public, he carefully hid it from the others by becoming jocular with them. He found reasons to make jokes with Denis and Sylvain, teased Claudine about a boy he knew she liked and praised Patsy's mayonnaise, grabbing her round the waist and doing a little waltz with her round the room. No one noticed that he did not so much as look at me, or address a single word to me. At bedtime he did not come to my room, and I did not go to his. I can't remember how long he kept up this sulk. Perhaps it was only a day or two; in my memory it may have grown. It seemed to last forever. I remember going to his room during a siesta and sitting on his bed.

'What have I done? Is it really because you just don't like my hair?'

He remained motionless for some time, staring at the dusty light fitting hanging from the ceiling as if it held the answer to my question. Then he propped himself up on one elbow. He took a deep breath in and exhaled slowly, giving him a slightly exasperated air. 'I'm just concerned about you, that's all. I don't think you realize how you come across.'

'What do you mean?'

'I mean that you have absolutely no idea how men here look at young women like you – young English women especially.'

'I'm Welsh.'

He smiled then, and reached out to stroke my hand. 'Dear Dora, you're so innocent and lovely. It just hurts to see you corrupted in any way. And that haircut . . . it looks so . . . it makes you look . . . well, I don't like to say.'

'Tell me.'

He stroked my hand some more and extended his caress to my arm. I suppose I was so grateful that he was speaking to me again that I was relieved. 'You look like a woman who's asking for it.' I pulled my arm away and looked at him in horror. 'Of course I don't mean you are. I mean *here*, where we are in this part of the world, you can't just swan about on your own looking like that.'

'It's a *haircut!*'

'Oh, Dora, my sweet little Dora! You saw the way Denis and Sylvain reacted. And they're friends. I can only guess at what would happen if you walked alone through a street looking like that. And that dress you wore to market . . . it leaves nothing to the imagination.'

I looked at his face. It was deadly serious. My dress had been an ordinary summer one, sleeveless, with a modest neckline and a dirndl skirt.

True, I had worn a bra that enhanced my bosom, but that was the fashion, and frankly, the bodice of the dress didn't fit without it. He was smiling at me in a slightly avuncular way. I had never understood him less.

I sat for some time, stroking the coverlet, which had a lozenge pattern repeated in different colours. 'Do *you* like the way I look? My hair . . . and my dress?'

He sat right up on the bed then and pushed me back on to it. 'I like the way you look with no adornments.' He began to unbutton my blouse. 'I like your simplicity.' He pulled off my bra and tossed it aside with mild disgust. I thought about hitting him. He ran his hands over my breasts and up the inside of my thighs, and my building anger and panic dissolved almost instantly. 'I like my sweet little Welsh girl, who was innocent until I touched her, and is innocent for everyone except me.'

I remember that August as a haze of music, sunshine and dancing on the warm terrace. We must have done other things with our time, but those are the most vivid memories. I did ask Ralph about his book and remind him that I was supposed to be his research assistant, but he simply said irritably that he was still at the planning stage. After that, though, he disappeared to his 'study' each morning for an hour or so after breakfast. This was an upstairs library overlooking the terrace, and sometimes, if I stayed on chatting over coffee in the shade with Patsy or Claudine or Sylvain, I would look up and catch him watching me before he quickly looked down at his 'work'.

Patsy and her daughter Claudine became my firm friends. Patsy introduced me to coffee and enjoyed gossiping over it – especially about the men. Claudine, for all her eight years, had us all worked out. I liked her company especially because she could diffuse any situation. Once, when we could hear Sylvain and Ralph arguing loudly in French, she came out on to the terrace rolling her eyes.

'What's happening in there?' I asked.

'Nothing. Just the usual. Sylvain is telling him to stop being a pompous . . . arse, and Ralph is telling him that when the revolution comes he won't talk to him like that, and Sylvain says when the revolution comes Ralph will be put on a bonfire, and Ralph says Sylvain is only good for chopping wood, and Sylvain says he only says that because he can't hold an axe and because he has a tiny, tiny' – she held her forefinger and thumb up to signify the smallest measure – 'dick.'

Patsy, who was always busy cooking and cleaning, was delighted to have me around. I enjoyed helping her, not just because I learnt so many new things to cook but also because her company was a tonic. She was calm and playful whenever she spoke to me or Claudine, but when she spoke French to the men she would become a harridan. Her voice would be raised and a flood of words would come speeding out of her mouth, peppered with insults.

One day, as I sat shelling peas with the women, Claudine mentioned the grape harvest. 'It's lovely here in October. Everywhere smells sweet. There are great big vats of crushed grapes, and cartloads of grapes in every village, and they drop all over the road and get crushed and look like *blood*! And everywhere is warm and not too hot. Of course it gets really cold in November, but we have great big log fires to keep us warm and it always snows on the mountains and we buy wool from the market and make *huge* jumpers. You'll love it!'

I looked at Patsy, but she was smiling at the thought of it all, looking down at her peas. 'It does sound lovely,' I said, 'but I won't be here in the autumn.'

They both looked up at me, astonished. Claudine was appalled. 'Why not?'

'Well, I have to get back to my studies.'

Patsy put her hands on her aproned knees. 'Ralph told us you'd finished with your studies. He said you were staying with us permanently.' She sounded indignant, and I wasn't sure if it was with me or with him.

'I'm training to be a teacher. I have another year to do.' In those days the course lasted only two years.

'But we need you here!' Claudine protested. '*Maman*, tell her! She can't go! I don't want her to go!' Her faced collapsed, and her bottom lip began to tremble.

'Are you sure you have to go?' Patsy asked almost tenderly. 'We'd love you to stay.'

I couldn't find any words. Claudine had rushed over to me and was buried in my armpit, and Patsy was looking at me anxiously, as if her daughter's happiness – and her own – depended upon my reply. My chest was tight. My fingers were clenched around the pea pods. It was hard to take in what Ralph had done. I stroked Claudine's head, but I could barely contain my fury.

'Where have you put my ticket?'

'What ticket?'

'My return ticket.'

'We didn't get returns.'

'Why not? You knew I had to go back!'

Ralph closed his eyes as if he were dealing with a difficult child. He stood at the window of what had become 'our' bedroom, and I stood squarely in front of the closed door.

'Look,' he said, 'I felt certain you would want to stay once you'd been here a bit. And you seem so happy.'

'That's not *your* decision to make! I have a course to finish!'

'But what's the point? You can live here. You've seen what it's like now. This is communal life. This is the future. Don't tell me you haven't enjoyed it, Dora, because I know you have.'

He approached me and put his hands on my hips. I shrugged him off.

'I'm not your puppet. I *do* love it here, but I want to finish my course before I make any permanent decisions. You have no right to make that decision for me. You *knew* I intended to return in September!'

'Okay, okay! Return you shall, if you must.' He shrugged, as though defeated. Then, seeing my determined face, he smiled. 'You little goose. I'm only thinking of you. You don't know the sort of people who can give you good advice about your future.'

'My parents, you mean. There's nothing wrong with my parents!'

He put his hands up defensively. 'Of course not. They're salt of the earth, I don't doubt, but you come from the sort of background where teaching is seen as the only escape. It's teaching or teaching. Don't you see?'

'Well that's *my* choice, not yours.'

'Come on, Dora. I'm giving you a real alternative. You're not cut out to be a crusty old schoolmarm.' He pushed his hands up the side of my torso and pulled me towards him. 'You're too sensuous.' He ran his palms over my breasts. 'You belong here with me, making love and *salade niçoise*.'

I stood there, wanting a man who made me feel that he had me in the palm of his hand. I stood there in that bedroom, knowing I should storm out of the door but unable to do so. I thought about Arthur, but that didn't help. He only increased my desire. I thought about seeing Arthur one more time. If I could just see him one more time, maybe . . .

I had no money for the return ticket. Ralph had promised it was an 'all-expenses-paid' trip. I reminded him of this, and he went out of the room coldly. I sat down on the bed and felt too trapped to cry. I trembled.

He returned fifteen minutes later with a bunch of notes. 'Patsy can take you to Montélimar station next week.'

I began to gather my things in my suitcase as surreptitiously as possible. He must have noticed the clothes disappearing from the wardrobe, and all he would have had to do was to lift the lid of the case to see them folded neatly. Ralph's idea had only been that I should buy the ticket next week, not that I should leave, but it was already the last week in August, and I had to be in England for September. My plan was to catch the train from Montélimar the day I bought the ticket. It would be a shock, and Ralph might be angry, but if I had my case and my passport already in the boot, he could hardly stop me.

The only hitch was that I did not have my passport. I thought I had left it in my suitcase inside a little pocket, but now it was clear that it wasn't there, and I remembered that Ralph had taken mine for safekeeping after going through customs in Calais. I started to look through his things while he wasn't there. I went into his old room, now inhabited by a friend of Tighe's, and rooted about inside the wardrobe. I pulled out drawers furtively and stood on a chair to check the top of the wardrobe. As the search remained fruitless, I began to open books and instrument boxes. I went to the kitchen and looked inside tins and cupboards. I peeled back rugs; I emptied linen cupboards; I lifted flowerpots; I trawled his study; I rifled through his pockets. I was not proud of myself, but my rising panic made me desperate.

Eventually, with forty-eight hours to go, I asked Ralph if he had my passport. I asked him at the dinner table, in front of everyone. He hesitated.

'You took it for safekeeping, remember?'

'Ah . . . yes. Yes, it's with mine.'

After dinner we went to the sitting room. He opened a drawer in a little bureau and took out his passport. 'That's strange. I had it with mine. I saw it yesterday.' I knew this wasn't true, for I'd opened this drawer two days before and found only his passport. A chill went through me. I would never get home.

27

ARTHUR

At the beginning of September, something arrived in the post that disturbed me. It posed so many difficult questions and brought back such troubling memories that I put it in the letter rack and tried to forget about it. But a day or so later, a similar envelope arrived for Pippa, forwarded by her mother in a batch of letters inside a brown envelope. Feigning interest in my newspaper, I watched as Pippa read her letters and cast them aside. When she came to the little cream envelope, she opened it dismissively, as she had all the others, then I watched as her lashes swept back and forth over the handwriting. She swallowed hard, then placed the little card back in its envelope and looked across at me.

'Daphne seems to want us all to celebrate her wedding in a pub – at the Wayfarer's.'

'What do you think?' I asked casually, taking a sip of tea.

'I think, we didn't invite the world and his dog to *our* wedding.'

'Well, it was a little rushed.'

'Perhaps we should take this opportunity to tell everyone.'

I put down my tea, feeling suddenly nauseous. I couldn't bear the thought of announcing my marriage in front of Dora, but I was pretty certain Dora wouldn't be there. But then again, if she *was* there, I could see her. I could explain. The questions I thought I'd put aside in the letter rack began to leap out and demand to be answered.

'Well, that's a good idea,' I said, because I knew she thought I would object. I knew she would think I would be ashamed in front of Dora and that the possibility of Dora being there – seeing her face – was what attracted Pippa to the idea. 'Let's do it. Let's go.'

She was immediately contrary. 'Oh Lord! Do you really think I'd want to be seen like *this*?'

'But you look blooming.'

'I look like a boulder.' There was a strange panic in her eyes. She began to gather the breakfast things in an unusual frenzy of domesticity. 'It *would* have been a nice idea, had you not got me in this condition.'

'But people will understand—'

'I'm not going like this, and there's an end to it.'

I wondered if there was any way I could go on my own – engineer a trip to London on that day, perhaps. Even as I thought it, I knew I didn't want to lie to Pippa.

'*You* go, if you want,' she said suddenly. 'I know you want to see Dora.'

'I doubt very much she'd be there if she thought we were going.' I let this idea sink in for a moment. 'I suppose I could go – and announce our news. At least that way, everyone would know. I suppose it *would* rather steal Daphne's thunder if we both went.'

'God, you just can't wait to see her, can you?'

'What do you mean?'

'Dora. You just can't wait to get her alone. Well, let me tell you something, Arthur. If that woman's going, *you aren't*.'

I got up and went out into the hallway. I put my coat on for work without looking at her. She came after me, seeking the goodbye kiss she normally begrudged. There was something pathetic about her terror, because that's what it was: she was terrified about my meeting Dora, and I hadn't realized until then just how afraid she was. I cupped her jaw in my hand with a sudden tenderness. 'Find out if she's going if you like. I'll only go if she isn't.'

She kissed me. 'Thank you.'

The wedding party was to be held on Saturday the 21st of September, the first Saturday after the date we all remembered, the sinking of *The City of India*. It would have felt wrong to go to London without visiting my parents, but somehow I wanted to keep the whole day free, just in case. In case of what, you might ask. I still hadn't steeled myself to ask Daphne if Dora would be there, and I wasn't sure if I was going to. It's true that all sorts of scenarios were running through my mind, and it was hard to disentangle real possibilities from fantasy. In my fantasies I was suddenly and unaccountably available to Dora again, so there was no guilt involved when we slipped off to a hotel together and renewed our loving properly. In my dreams I would introduce her to lovemaking, and she would be a coy but fast learner. She would be like tinder waiting to be lit, and I would light her touchpaper with the gentlest of strokes. Soon we would be making love fiercely and tenderly all night through, unable to get enough of each other. And there would be no end to this daydream . . . except the realization that I was married and expecting a child, and that Dora would probably never speak to me again. Nonetheless, out of a curious respect for this self-delusion, I wanted to keep the day free. Perhaps I imagined that a stolen moment with Dora in a bar after the wedding was a remote possibility.

So I arranged to visit my parents the weekend before Daphne's wedding and asked Pippa if she would like a stay in London. Of course I knew she wouldn't want to see them, and it was because of her rudeness towards them that I wanted to smooth things over with them, but to my surprise she was enthusiastic. Not until we were due to set off did she announce that she would be staying with 'friends' in Kensington.

Despite my annoyance that she so consistently made changes at the last minute, I have to confess I felt relieved. However, I was determined to nail down these 'friends' she so often referred to and to whom she had never introduced her husband, so I waited until she did her predictable 'Bye, darling!' at Paddington, before letting her know that I would be accompanying her to her friends' house, since I was not comfortable with her taking the tube on her own at the moment.

'Oh, no, darling! I shan't be taking the tube in this condition. Lord, no!'

I felt foolish. 'Well, in that case, let me at least walk with you and carry your bag.'

'Oh, for God's sake, Arthur. I'm taking a taxi. I don't need you to carry my bag.'

We hailed a taxi and I got in too. She looked at me in horror. 'What do you think you're doing? Are you checking up on me?'

'Can't a man make sure that his pregnant wife arrives safely at her destination?' She rolled her eyes. I added lamely, 'What if they're not in?'

They were in. 'They' appeared to be two other young women and a young man, not that I would have known any of this if Pippa had had her way and shooed me off in the taxi. Instead, I went up the grand steps to the front door, carrying her small suitcase like a butler. A red-haired woman in her twenties opened the door and squealed in delight. A further young woman came up behind her and squealed also. Pippa apologized for my presence and said I wasn't staying.

'Oh, come in! Let's have a look at you! We've heard so much about you.'

'Oh, Pippa, he's gorgeous! Where have you been hiding him?'

In the vast, high-ceilinged living room – or drawing room, or whatever they called it – there sat a young man smoking a pipe. He stood up when he saw me and shook my hand. 'Ah! We encounter the husband at last. Pleased to meet you. I'm Miles. We were beginning to think she'd made you up!'

'Yes, well he can't stay. He has to go and see his parents, and they live in Chiswick.'

'Chiswick?'

'Off you go!' Pippa ushered me away with a wave of her hand, as if I were an over-enthusiastic dog.

I went. I have no idea to this day who these people were – not one of them – but they were responsible for delivering some terrible news, news that in one way or another changed the course of a life. Dora's, actually.

28

DORA

Claudine stayed very close to me after the news that I had to return to England, and I found her company comforting. We sat in a little sewing room near the kitchen and made clothes for her doll. There were lots of scraps of material, ribbons, old zips and buttons that Patsy had accumulated, and I spotted one of the bedspreads that had been discarded after moths had nibbled great holes in it, too numerous to patch up. It had the same beautiful lozenge pattern in rainbow colours as my coverlet, and I asked Claudine which were her favourite colours. She liked the blue, where it turned into violet and indigo, so I snipped out a rectangle, selected an old trouser zip and set to work on the sewing machine in the corner.

'What is it going to be?'

'Wait and see!'

I had looked everywhere I could think of for my passport, and I felt certain that Ralph knew exactly where it was. I'd been very attracted to Ralph, there's no doubt about it: attracted by his confidence and his certainty at a time when I was devoid of both. But the appeal of someone who was in control of things changed dramatically when I suspected that he wanted to be in control of *me*. I turned the handle of the machine aggressively, enjoying the loud growl that it made as I sped along the cloth. Claudine observed me carefully, watching for clues.

'Are you angry with me?' she asked at last.

I laughed and handed her the pencil case I had made for her. She came and hugged me and marvelled at it. She ran off and came back with a fistful of crayons and pencils and zipped them inside. Her thrill gave me a moment of peace. Then she stood beside me and stroked my hair tenderly. 'Is it him? Has he upset you?'

I looked her in the eye and wondered what she knew. Her pale gaze fixed intelligently on mine, and I could see she was deadly serious. 'I can sort him out for you if you like!'

I smiled. 'There's no need.' She looked relieved that she had restored the status quo, and I suggested we make some lavender bags. 'Does Ralph usually spend a lot of time here?'

'Off and on. It's his Aunty Bee's place, but he always pretends to be in charge. The men don't take him very seriously.'

Claudine was already laying out a piece of muslin on the floor and brandishing some scissors. 'Would you like me to bandage your arm?' I let her practise bandaging with old strips of cloth while she carried on about Ralph and how much she would miss me when I went. My right arm was so tightly bound in a sling that Claudine had to cut out the squares of muslin on her own.

Later on, with all the squares cut out and ribbon cut into equal lengths, we went out to one of the outhouses where great bunches of lavender hung from all the walls.

I looked at the task ahead and then at my arm. 'You do a very firm bandage, nurse. I think you may have stopped my circulation.' Claudine laughed and released me from my sling. I began to push the dry florets off the stems into a bucket, but my fingers were soon sore and burning with the threat of blisters. Claudine climbed on to a wooden crate. 'There should be some gloves here somewhere.' She was rifling through boxes on a shelf. 'There – catch!' She threw me a battered old leather glove. 'You have that one, I'll have the other.' She rifled a bit more and found its partner.

'Good. Now we'll make quick work of this lot.' Suddenly it was simple. The lavender fell away into the bucket with swift, easy strokes. I collected quite a pile of brushy stalks, but Claudine was still on the crate, glove shoved under her armpit.

'There's a picture of you here!'

I looked up, startled.

'In a book!'

'Let me see.' She handed me my passport. It had been buried under the gloves and trowels and other gardening knick-knacks in a box on a shelf in an outhouse. Now I knew for certain. My fury transformed itself into something like fear. I had known from the moment Ralph showed me the empty drawer, but I had kept a little hope for other explanations, had tried so hard to let him off the hook. But soon all fear was taken over by elation, as I slipped the slim booklet into my blouse. 'Thank you. I wondered where that had got to.'

She eyed me curiously. 'Is it important?'

'Sort of. Identity papers. Are you going to put that glove on and help me?'

She sighed. 'There are so many boxes here. You never know what you're going to find in a box.'

We made twenty fat lavender bags and fourteen little ones, each tied up with coloured ribbon. I made a decision not to tell Claudine and Patsy about my plans. I was afraid one of them might unwittingly give the game away, but it meant I couldn't say goodbye. At least, I reasoned, I would be able to tell them when we got to the station, and I could explain exactly how things were with Ralph and they would understand. It was going to be an emotional farewell, but I could think of no other way.

I went to bed that night with the fragrant smell of lavender and the even more enticing scent of freedom. My pulse galloped like that of a prisoner poised for escape. I pictured where all the items were that I hadn't yet packed and how I would gather them swiftly after breakfast tomorrow. Then I would slip my suitcase into the boot of the car, and Patsy would drive me to the way home.

The following morning, I rose while Ralph was still asleep. I left the suitcase under my bed and went down to make breakfast. I put the milk on to boil, cut bread and made coffee. Ralph emerged sleepily and went out on to the terrace where Claudine was already laying the table in the shade of the house. I was so excited. I remember trying to stop my hand from trembling as I poured hot milk on to the coffee in Ralph's bowl and on to the chocolate in Claudine's. Patsy arrived and took over, gabbling curses to Denis as he put his feet up on the table and moved the cloth. It seemed to go on forever, but eventually Ralph made his move to the study and I sloped up to our room for the suitcase and put it into the boot of the car.

My relief – I can feel it now – was so mixed with adrenaline that it was a heady feeling. I pottered about in the kitchen, waiting for Patsy to tell me she was ready. Before she arrived, Ralph came into the kitchen: 'Change of plan. Patsy's not taking you to Montélimar.'

'What? But I—'

'I am.'

Something seemed to wrap itself around my stomach and squeeze hard. I could taste the apricot jam I'd had for breakfast in my throat.

'I need to go to the bank, and Patsy's happy to take you to Montélimar next week instead.'

I tried not to look disappointed. I could hear my own pulse in my head. He must have seen me put the suitcase in the car. I could still go. He couldn't stop me. How could he stop me? I pictured a struggle on the platform. What if he'd already removed the suitcase? I still had my winter coat and shoes back in Wales. I would manage.

I eyed my handbag on the kitchen chair and folded my lips together, afraid of the words that might come out if I opened them. In the bag were my passport and the money he'd given me. They were in there for certain – I had checked the moment before he came into the kitchen. I picked up my handbag. It might be all I took home with me on the voyage, but he wasn't going to stop me. I was getting out of there and I was going home.

He said very little on the way to the station. When I looked across at him his jaw was clamped shut, and I knew – from the twitches in the hollows of his cheek – that he was angry. I made small talk, for my own benefit rather than his, because I couldn't bear the silence. I was so convinced that he knew of my plans that when we parked at the station I went straight to the boot and opened it, calculating that, if I had the suitcase in my hand and he tried to wrench it from me, people might come to my aid.

I still don't know for certain if he had guessed my intentions, but he gave a very convincing appearance of astonishment. 'Why on earth have you brought that? What are you playing at?'

'I'm not playing, Ralph. I'm going back to England to finish my course.'

The thick dark eyebrows came down and the nostrils flared. 'You said you were just buying the ticket today.'

'*You* said that.'

'But your course doesn't start until next week.'

I looked at his fury. My hands were weak and sweating. I had nothing to say.

'Well?' he demanded.

And suddenly I knew I didn't have to explain myself to him. He talked to me like a schoolmaster admonishing a wayward child, but I had every right to return to England. I moved away from him decisively in the direction of the ticket office. No one else was waiting and I bought my ticket to Calais.

'*C'est pour aujourd'hui?*'

I swallowed hard. '*Oui.*'

The man behind the *guichet* asked if I wanted a single or return. I could feel Ralph at my shoulder, but I asked for a single. '*Un aller simple,*' I muttered. The man told me about the changes I would need to make and that there was a train to Paris running late if I wanted to get that one.

The ticket was slipped under the glass and I snatched it like a child in danger of losing a balloon. With that voucher for freedom securely in my purse I marched out on to the platform. Ralph followed.

'What the *hell* do you think you're doing? Running away like a thief in the night . . . When was I going to find out? Didn't you even plan to say goodbye? Is that your thanks for my taking you to the south of France?'

He could hardly draw breath. There was such rage in him that I instinctively backed away. He came right up to me, grabbed me by the shoulders and shook me. '*When* were you going to tell me?'

I pushed his hands away. 'You told me we were going to France for a holiday. You lied to me. You *lied* to me, Ralph.' It felt good, telling him that. It felt good, but I was still afraid. I was aware of a bunch of other people on the platform (uncomfortably looking away from us, but there, nonetheless) and I was grateful for that delayed Paris train. 'I'm not your prisoner. I didn't tell you because I knew you'd try to stop me.'

I turned and faced the platform, gripping the suitcase in my trembling hand and clutching my handbag tightly against my torso. Then something rather bizarre happened.

As I waited, wondering what he was going to do next, I heard him catch his breath in an unfamiliar way. I could feel my heart pounding inside my ribs. My head was aching. I longed to shove him away, but I feared he might throttle me, there and then, in front of the other waiting passengers. You heard of things like that happening in France: men would be acquitted for murder if it was considered a crime of passion . . .

Eventually he grabbed my shoulder and turned me round. I was about to push him away when he sobbed my name. His face was contorted in grief.

'Please, Dora, *please*, I beg you, don't leave me like this. I didn't mean for you to feel imprisoned . . . I just love you . . . so much!'

The train heralded its arrival with a distant hoot. I couldn't believe the look in Ralph's sad eyes. There was suddenly so much tenderness, such a transformation. I put my suitcase down and wrapped my arms around him. The noise of the approaching train was growing louder. It seemed like a warning. *No! Don't weaken.* Louder, louder, and a long screech of brakes. The steam enveloped us, and in its cover I grabbed my case and ran for a door. A man with a briefcase held it open for me, and I scrambled in, holding my own case in front of me, and made my way in a rushed, ungainly fashion down the carriage to the nearest compartment with an empty seat in it. I was helped to lift my luggage on to the overhead rack. When I sat down, Ralph was banging on the window. Embarrassed, and afraid he would get on to the train and make a scene, I made my way out of the compartment and back to the train door. In a hurry to get this late train on its journey, the signalman had already slammed the door and was busy slamming others, working his way down the length of the platform. To my horror, Ralph opened the door and got on.

'I know you love me, Dora. Don't let this silly misunderstanding stop you coming back. Say you'll come back.' He squeezed me very tight and I was afraid and confused. He was kissing my neck and holding my buttock and, when he suddenly grabbed my face between his hands, I saw that tears were making his eyes glisten. 'I'm sorry I upset you; I just didn't want to lose you! I love you so much, Dora!'

The signalman came up and babbled angrily at Ralph and at the open door. Ralph backed off the train and the door was slammed shut between us. A whistle was blown, long and loud. Through the open window he grabbed my hand. 'I want to have children with you, Dora . . . Dora . . . do you understand what I'm saying? I can look after you . . . you won't need to teach . . . I want to spend the rest of my life with you!'

The train emitted a laconic thud, then chugged with increasing enthusiasm. Ralph's sad, contrite face tilted to one side like a puppy dog, his wet brown eyes imploring me to forgive him, to love him, to be his woman. And as he grew smaller, so my confusion grew. I watched him shrink before my eyes to a mere dot on a distant platform, and I couldn't help feeling that I had done that: I had shrunk him.

29

ARTHUR

'Heavens to Betsy! There it goes again! Look at it!'

'What is it?'

'Look!'

Pippa grabbed my hand at the breakfast table and placed it firmly on her belly. 'Can you feel it?'

I felt my child wriggle and kick for the first time. Until that moment, none of it had seemed real. Now I had a child; I was a father. A rush of pride went through me, and I noticed something extraordinary: Pippa was smiling. In fact, she had seemed a great deal happier since we had come back from London. She sang around the house. She had a meal ready for me when I came home, and there was less often a pile of dishes in the sink. Sometimes, now, she even smiled at *me*, and I mean the sort of smile that wasn't prompted by sarcasm. I couldn't imagine what had come over her, of course, but I was pleased.

Our little trip to London seemed to have proved a success all round. She had returned in better spirits and I had had a chance to make up to my parents. I say 'make up to' because I had done them a terrible wrong, I think, getting married to Pippa when they were expecting me to marry Dora, and cutting them out of the picture.

I had sat beside my mother on the sofa when I visited, while my father was shaving one morning. I recalled Philip entwined in her arms here many years ago. Philip the baby, the beloved. How I hated myself for my sibling jealousy, even now. The room seemed filled with pictures of him, prominently displayed, although actually, I think there were only three, and I was in two of them. My mother listened to my sad story and placed a hand on mine.

'We thought Dora was lovely. We *were* sad when we heard you weren't marrying her, but only because we thought she'd make you such a loving wife. You seemed so right together. But if you're happy with Pippa, then we're happy too. We only want you to be happy, Arthur. That's all that matters to us.' She squeezed my hand and I tried not to blink because my eyes were welling unexpectedly. 'You are happy, aren't you?' I didn't answer. I swallowed and nodded. The pressure on my hand again. No words, but an understanding. I wanted to entwine myself like Philip. Instead I gave her a hug. 'She has beautiful eyes,' she said reassuringly. 'You're going to have a beautiful child.'

Now Pippa waltzed around the house, a new woman. If my mother could have seen her, all sadness would have lifted. I began to feel hopeful myself. She even let me hold her in bed and stroke her back – although that was all. But I was hopeful.

'Did you ask Daphne about whether Dora was coming to the wedding?' she asked breezily one morning at breakfast.

'I'm afraid I haven't got around to it yet.'

'Well, don't bother; there's no need.'

I looked at her, quizzically. 'Why not?'

'Because . . .' She was savouring the moment. 'She won't be there.'

I began to panic. What could have happened? Was she alive? I thought of that little note again. Were Pippa and Dora in contact? Had

Pippa said something to her? My stomach tightened. I looked at my newspaper and tried to sound nonchalant: 'Why's that?'

'*Because* . . . she's living in France.' She sounded triumphant. Even in my peripheral vision I could tell she looked triumphant.

'France?' I had to catch my breath.

'Yes! The London gossip is that she ran off to live with someone I vaguely know. Someone who's set to inherit a fortune.'

I had to put the paper down because it was shaking, and the little trembles in my hand translated into giant shudders at the edges of the paper. 'I wonder *you* didn't marry him, then.' I surprised myself when this slipped out, but she only laughed.

'I doubt Ralph Rowanwood will inherit unless he stops his silly revolutionary ideas. Apparently he's set up a commune in the south of France and little Dora has gone with him.'

'Well, good for her,' I managed.

'So you can go to the wedding without me if you want. Get a bit drunk. Loosen up a bit. Do you good.' She was Madame Bountiful, she was beaming, she was relaxed, and I couldn't help wondering – given the apparent lack of passion I inspired in my wife – what had passed between her and Dora to make Pippa so relieved to have her out of the way for good.

I heard nothing else that my wife said to me after breakfast that morning. I caught the bus in a daze. Nothing I had eaten was being digested, and nothing I had heard either. It made for an uncomfortable journey. I changed buses without noticing, and I arrived at work half unconscious that I had done so. It was the busiest of times. I had an office of trainee engineers to oversee and two trained engineers who reported to me. One of these approached me with a roll of paper and a design question the moment I hung my coat on the door. I said I would be right with him, and asked my secretary if she could bring a cup of tea to my study. She looked confused: I never asked for tea this early in the morning.

Alone for a few moments, I forced myself to assess things. Despite my shock and my unaccountable feelings of desperation and grief, the truth was that Dora had been lost to me from the moment I betrayed her. The only problem was that I had been unable to accept that. In some fantastical corner of my mind she had remained vibrant and loyal and longing and mine. That she hadn't *been* there with me all this time had seemed almost irrelevant. I had conjured her up, a yearning, playful, tender lover, and therefore she was real. But *now* . . . now there could be no more self-delusion. Dora was gone. She had made a conscious decision to be out of my life, to be as far away as possible.

It hit me suddenly, as I took the first sip of tea I didn't want, how afraid I had been of seeing Dora again and being unable to stop myself from wanting her, from touching her, from betraying Pippa. Now I need worry no more. Yes, that was the way to look at it. I left the cup of tea on my desk and went out of my study and into the drafting office to face the day.

'It's not *probably* for the best; it definitely is.' Len sipped his beer, perched at the bar of a large, noisy pub he had brought me to. 'Everything will change when the baby's born – you'll see. Being a father – there's nothing quite like it.'

'I'm not sure Pippa is ready to be a mother.'

'You wait and see.'

There was some music playing in a room upstairs – folk night, it seemed. Len and I drank beer after beer. He told me intimate things about his wife, and I told him that all I saw of mine these days was her back. A beer or two later he was telling me what I could do with a back, and soon after that I rushed to the gents' and was sick in a toilet and on the floor.

When I got home that night I felt purged. I tried a few of Len's hints on the curved back in bed beside me, and was batted off like a fly.

30

DORA

At Calais I bought a ferry ticket, relieved that I still had the money that Ralph had given me for the journey home, and I reflected on how my handbag with its money and passport was all that stood between me and destitution on the streets of Paris or Calais. In fact, it wasn't the fear of destitution that made me cling so tightly to my bag and case, but the fear of not getting back and seeing Arthur again.

I won't go into details, but you can imagine how I felt on that crossing. It brought it all back: travelling alone, a sea crossing, a calm day. It was the waiting to embark that was the worst of it. The morning sun shone at exactly the same slant, with exactly the same crisp glow on the calm sea as it had twelve years before. I half expected to see *The City of India* waiting in the docks. The cross-Channel ferry was a very different affair, but its modest size did nothing to cancel out the huge-ness of the sea, threateningly calm and visible from each deck. I found a seat inside, clutched my bag tightly and closed my eyes, startled to be listening to English words from the loudspeakers: Perry Como singing 'Hello, Young Lovers'.

I caught the train from Dover to London and then from London to Cheltenham. I decided to call by Ralph's house before I went back to Wales, just to see if I still had my room as arranged. I had phoned in advance so Jenny was expecting me, and we spent a couple of days together, settling me in for the new term. It was odd being back there, living in Ralph's house without Ralph. Jenny told me that his father had visited to see about letting out the ground-floor flat, but that nothing had been done about it. I asked what he had been like, Ralph's father, and she rolled her eyes: 'You know, posh.'

So we had the run of the house, the pair of us, and I could see that Jenny had been enjoying it for some time. Her laundry was pegged up in his kitchen, and her magazines were strewn across Ralph's living room. I couldn't resist a snoop around his bedroom, although I hardly dared to touch anything in case he somehow appeared at my shoulder. I did leaf through a few things on the floor beside his bed, though. Books and papers were piled scruffily next to and under the bed. They were mostly copies of his self-published 'magazine', *Plight*. I was about to walk away, guilty at my intrusion, when I spotted something familiar. A dark red cover, battered and creased at one edge where it had been thrown under the bed. I fished it out. I smoothed the cover back into some sort of shape. He had gone to France without it, without any of his 'research' materials, and yet he was planning not to come back. Had he ever intended to write that book, or was it yet another project he started but couldn't see through? I will probably never know.

I took the scrapbook back to Our Dad, who didn't know it had gone missing. Mam baked me an apple batter, got all the neighbours round to see me, and they all gawped at my new hairstyle and said, 'She da talk proper posh now.'

I'm ashamed when I think of that visit. I think I may have been critical about the lack of fruit and salad in the house and the use of ketchup on everything and garlic in nothing. I probably – oh, I cringe to think of it – insisted on drinking from a bowl in the mornings, rejected my cornflakes and turned my nose up at sliced bread. What a little prat I must have been. It must have really hurt Our Mam and Dad, but they didn't show it.

On the Sunday I refused to go to chapel with them, saying I didn't believe in God any more. Our Mam was worried for my soul. Our Dad was upset too, but I think with him it was the 'any more' which hurt, suggesting to his mind that I had outgrown something which he, by inference, was childishly clinging on to. I'm not sure I saw all this then, any more than I understood what my indifference cost my mother when, a day or two into my visit, she placed on the table in front of me some lettuce from Mr Price's allotment and a bottle of salad cream, a modest and expectant smile on her face.

Anyway, the long and the short of it is that I made it to the wedding. I moved back to the flat in Cheltenham, and on Saturday the 21st of September 1952, I was there at the wedding of Daphne Prendergast and Jack Heggarty.

I timed my arrival carefully. I didn't want to have to turn around in the church to see if Arthur had arrived, so I made certain I was there only just in time, with three minutes to spare before the service. I sat in a pew behind the rest of the congregation, alongside an elderly lady who must have been some relative or friend of Daphne or Jack.

I couldn't see Arthur from where I was, but there were quite a few heads in the way. If he was there – and Daphne had said he would be – he would see me walking out of church ahead of him. Then it would be up to Arthur. I was certainly not going to approach *him*.

31

ARTHUR

I reached the venue for the wedding early, so before the church service I slipped into the Wayfarer's Inn for a drink. The groom was there with some of the other guests, and he offered me a pint.

Till my dying breath, I will wish Jack Heggarty had never spoken to me on his wedding day. That conversation will haunt me.

It was light-hearted enough. It was well intentioned. Jack asked me how I was and I told him. I asked where they were going to live, and he told me Battersea. He asked about work and where I was living now, and I told him. I congratulated him on his fine choice of wife, and he asked if I was married yet.

'I am, actually.'

'Wonderful! Have you brought her with you?'

'Er, no. She's five months pregnant.'

'Congratulations!' He looked thoughtful for a moment. 'Not Dora then. There was some talk a while back . . .'

'Ah . . . well . . . yes, actually . . . actually it's Pippa.'

'Philippa? From Boat Nine?' His eyes widened. 'Phwoar! You did all right, matey. Bit of a stunner as I recall from the last reunion. Well!

You don't waste much time! Bit of a dark horse, eh?' He winked at me. He was in a jovial mood. It was his wedding day.

'The thing is—'

I really don't know what I was going to say. I wasn't going to apologize for marrying Pippa. What sort of man was I? I smiled weakly as he was overwhelmed by a group of men offering him a drink, and I was left awkwardly marooned.

I arrived at the church deliberately late, with just two minutes to go before the ceremony. I didn't want to make small talk beforehand with people from the boat; someone was sure to have heard news of Dora, and I needed to prepare myself. There would be time for all that later back at the pub.

I sat down in the last pew with anyone in it: an elderly gentleman I didn't recognize. He must have been somebody's relative. The church was echoey with chatter, and I felt happily anonymous at the back. The organ music changed suddenly to a rousing piece, and voices hushed. I turned my head to the left to see Daphne, dressed in a modest ivory outfit, walking gracefully up the aisle, unaccompanied. I couldn't see Jack – there were too many heads in the way – but when the organ music finished and we were asked to be seated, I could see him standing and beaming at the front of the church, unfamiliar in a tailored suit.

The words of the service passed me in a sort of blur. I fixed my attention on the neck of the girl sitting a couple of pews in front of me. Her skin was golden brown and swept down to a wide semi-circle of pale print fabric at her neckline. It swept up to the softest nape, topped with velvety short fair hair. On the crown of her head, the hair was honey pale. As it reached her neck it formed the gentlest of peaks, pointing to her very slightly protruding vertebrae . . . *and therefore not to be enterprised, nor taken in hand, inadvisedly, lightly or wantonly . . .* When she stood for a hymn she displayed her whole back. The wide

195

folds of the skirt narrowed into a belt at her slender waist. The backs of her arms showed under her little capped sleeves, and they were soft and smooth. Her face and hands were invisible, but I tried to imagine them, and I had to check myself. By the time we stood for the next hymn ('Glorious Things of Thee Are Spoken'), I realized I was having very inappropriate thoughts. Whatever was I thinking? This wedding service, which I tried not to hear, was a stark reminder of my own, with all its confusion and guilt and uncertainty, and all I had ever wanted was to marry my lovely Dora and be faithful only unto her. *For the mutual society, help and comfort* . . . There was no mutual comfort in my marriage. Would there ever be? I longed to touch the bare skin of the woman whose neck I could see, and I loathed myself for my weakness. I yearned to make love to a woman. I had tried so hard to make love to my wife. God knows, I could have made myself content with just the odd occasion, but . . . *till death us do part* . . . I found I was clenching the order of service sheet and had half crumpled it. The old gentleman next to me sent me a curious glance. At least, he turned his head briefly to look at me and I felt awkward. I hoped there was nothing else that showed. I mouthed the words of the hymn but couldn't sing. No words would come out.

32

DORA

There were tears in my eyes during the service. I'd heard of that sort of thing – you know, women crying at weddings – but it had never occurred to me that I might ever be moved enough to shed tears. And yet there they were, unbidden, making my vision swim. I wasn't quite sure what to do about it, because I didn't want Arthur seeing me like that. He might think I was upset that I hadn't married him or something. I needed to look cool.

Fortunately, by the end of the service I had rallied. I had resisted blinking until my eyes hurt, and the tears had evaporated with the help of a bit of dabbing with a hanky. I turned to follow the old lady out of my pew, my attention straight ahead of me. I couldn't see him, but I felt somehow his eyes were on me. I walked as demurely as I could out into the bright September sunshine, where I waited on the grass of the tiny graveyard for the rest of the congregation to emerge and for the photos to be taken. In my awkwardness, I pretended to read the gravestones. I stood with my back to the church entrance, intent on a very bland 'Rest in Peace' to some woman called Elizabeth or Charlotte who had died in the eighteenth century. How long could it take to read these few words? I passed my hand over the stone, as if fascinated, and moved on to 'John Miller', whose relatives had had a little more to say in valediction, but not much.

'Dora!'

I felt it before I heard it. Fingers placed inside my elbow – a charge sent right through me. I turned. I must have looked as shocked as I felt. 'Arthur!'

He looked unchanged. Of course he would – it had been only a few months. Look cool. Look *cool*. I smiled – but not too much. I waited for him to speak. He was staring at me.

'I didn't expect you to be here . . . I heard you were abroad.'

This threw me a little. I couldn't imagine how he could have heard about France, and it took the wind out of my sails. Now I couldn't impress him; he had already been impressed. 'I *was* in the south of France.'

'Hence the tan. And the hair . . . I would hardly have recognized you – I *didn't* recognize you, actually. I was sitting behind you during the service.'

Oh God! Hearing his voice again, seeing his face, his awkwardness. And his touch! My body was still fizzing from the fingers on the inside of my arm. He might as well have caressed my thighs. *Cool, cool,* I told myself. 'Were you? I didn't see you.'

'No.' He hovered. A serviceman stopped to say hello. Photos were being taken, rice was being thrown. 'Dora, I have to talk to you.'

One of the boys on our boat came over and grabbed my hands in his. 'Little Dora! How you've changed! And Arthur! Never see one of you without the other – you were *glued* together on the boat! How are you both doing now?'

Arthur babbled some stuff about his work and I said I was training to be a teacher, and then someone interrupted the young man.

'Come on,' Arthur said. He took my elbow again. 'Let's make our way to the pub. I want to talk to you.'

He didn't ask me if I wanted to talk to him. I was a bit disappointed that he somehow had the upper hand. There should have been some grovelling. I should have shaken him off. But I wanted his skin on mine, and I let myself be led.

In the Wayfarer's Inn we were greeted by people who had not attended the service. Arthur went to buy me a drink, and by the time he came back with it I was in conversation with some ex-servicemen from the rescue ship. He hovered by me for a while, then was scooped up himself by someone else. It was okay, though. There was no sign of Pippa, and we had plenty of time. Knowing his eyes were on me, I chatted and giggled and smiled for England. I was a woman of the world, chic and nonchalant. I would speak to him at some point. He would have to wait for me to be free.

33

ARTHUR

When the service ended, the golden-skinned woman turned to go out of the pew, and I saw her profile. I stood and gawped. She followed the elderly woman out and crossed right in front of me, obscured only briefly by the elderly chap in front of me who let her pass before he went into the aisle himself. Would you believe it? It was Dora! It was Dora, and I hadn't recognized her! And she hadn't seen me.

Then I couldn't get out of there quick enough. People kept pouring into the aisle, women and older folk; I couldn't just barge past them. I saw her disappear out of the church door, silhouetted against the light, but moving away from me. What if she didn't come back to the reception? What if she'd seen me and ignored me? What if I didn't catch up with her now? I could hear my own breathing above the sound of the organ music, which, despite the gay occasion, seemed to be pulling me back and holding everyone up in its sluggish tempo.

Then I spotted her. Of course it was her! She seemed slimmer, more graceful and willowy, yet now that I saw her moving between the gravestones, there was something unmistakable about her slight gaucheness. I must have practically shoved people out of the way. I didn't stop to think about what I was going to say to her; I had nothing planned – I hadn't expected to see her. All I could think of was *reaching* her. If I could just get hold of her . . . I could hear people say my name, people who wanted to talk to me, people who would stop me getting to her . . . She was touching a headstone . . . 'Dora!' I had grabbed her by the arm. I hadn't meant to take hold of her like that. I didn't know what to do next.

'Arthur!' She looked surprised to see me, and I couldn't say she looked pleased. I couldn't tell what she felt. She was so aloof and inscrutable. Now I had nothing to say. I looked at her, at the tanned face and the clear blue eyes and the stylish hairdo. She had changed, but jealously I wanted her to be the same as she had been with me. And yet . . . and yet she was still . . . I had absolutely nothing to say to her, but I realized my mouth was open, ready to speak. I let a few words out. 'I didn't expect you to be here . . . I heard you were abroad.'

I can't remember what she said next. I really can't picture anything except her beautiful remembered lips moving, and her lovely remembered eyes that told me she was not so very changed, for all her sophisticated appearance. Some dreadful chap came up and said hello, and I had to dart my eyes away rudely to keep him from lingering, and then some other chap came up and took hold of both her hands in his and I wanted to scream, 'NO-OOO!' I wanted to shove him away, I wanted to lift her up in my arms and carry her off, I wanted her all to myself and I was in such a panic that I might end up with none of her, that she would be wrenched away from me by one of these jolly chaps, that I took her by the arm and propelled her away. I said I had to talk to her. It was dreadful. What right did I have? I mean, what right did *I* have, of all people? But she didn't put up a fight. She let me take her out of the churchyard and on to the road.

It was a good two hundred yards to the Wayfarer's, and I can't for the life of me imagine what my conversation was like on the way. She chatted fairly blandly about the service and how nice it had been, and I probably agreed. When we arrived, I was exasperated to find there were already some people there. People! How I hated people on that day. If only they'd all been somewhere else! By the time I'd bought her a drink, she was already surrounded by servicemen. God, how I loathed them all with their clean haircuts, their clean smiles, their clean uniforms and their dirty thoughts. I suspected every one of them of flirting with her. I was whisked away by Graham, my old friend from the ship, and he really wanted to talk. I kept trying to see Dora, but she disappeared, and then later she reappeared, and I found it hard to keep track of her. He must have noticed, for eventually he said, '*She* scrubbed up nicely, didn't she? I always thought she was a bit plain, but it just goes to show . . .'

I felt irritated by him then. We both looked over towards Dora, who was beaming and radiant amidst a group of entirely different people. People! I tried to catch her eye, but she didn't look my way. For a full half-hour I couldn't catch her attention, and every time I tried to move in her direction, someone stopped me with an urgent 'Hello!' or 'How-the-hell-*are*-you?' Then there was a gong, and someone shouted that the buffet was waiting, and I chose that moment to barge through everyone.

'Excuse me . . . excuse me . . . sorry . . . excuse me . . . *Dora!*'

I tailed her as she collected a few modest sandwiches on her plate, and I found a little table for two for us to sit at. She didn't seem unhappy to be sitting with me, but neither did she seem overjoyed. I kept swallowing hard, preparing to say something but then finding no words. I cleared my throat to see if that would help, but repeated clearings produced nothing of any interest, only comments on the sandwich fillings and the pleasantness of the 'do'.

She told me about France and how she had had an offer to stay but had decided to finish her studies first. Then, it seemed, she might very well return to the south of France to write a book about poverty with a young journalist.

'Dora!' I said, barely able to breathe. 'Dora, I have to talk to you. We can't keep pretending nothing has happened. The truth is . . . the truth is . . . I made a terrible mistake. A *terrible* mistake.'

She chewed slowly on her sandwich. 'Yes, you did,' she replied coolly.

'And . . . and . . . and I shall regret it for the rest of my life.'

She turned to look at me then, a long, searching look that lifted my spirits. I put my hand on hers and squeezed it. 'Oh, Dora! I'm so—'

Someone was tapping on a glass with a spoon.

34

DORA

He couldn't keep his eyes off me. Every time I risked a look in his direction, he was staring at me. I smiled and giggled at nearly everything anyone said, knowing he was watching. I was enjoying myself. Let him wish he could make me laugh too. Let him dream!

I underestimated his keenness. When I'd filled my plate at the buffet he practically dragged me to a table and sat me down with him. I kept very cool. I could tell he was nervous, but I was as cool as my cucumber sandwich. I told him all about Ralph and how he had asked me to be his research assistant and how he had a house in the south of France. He seemed genuinely rattled by that. Good. I said Ralph had asked me to move in permanently but that I wanted to be an independent woman and finish my training first. Then I would consider it. It must have had an effect because he suddenly took hold of my hand and squeezed it.

'Dora!' he said, right in my ear, right up close. I could feel his breath, and it sent a shiver through me, just as it used to. 'Dora, we have to talk. I made the most terrible mistake.'

'Yes,' I said, as nonchalantly as I could, 'you did.'

He got very worked up then and said, 'And I'll regret it for the rest of my life.'

You can imagine how I felt. I knew he was going to tell me something important, and I was so excited. But right at that moment, *right at that very moment*, someone chimed on a glass with a spoon. It was dreadful timing. No, I mean *really* dreadful timing.

Everyone stopped talking and looked towards the table where Jack Heggarty, next to his new wife, had stood up ready to make a speech. 'Ladies and gentlemen, I won't talk for long, because, as many of you know, I'm a pretty boring chap . . .' People laughed. 'But one thing I do want to do is to thank you all for coming. I know many of you have travelled long distances for this – and one person even from France! Thank you for that. And of course I want to say how lucky I am to be married today to the most wonderful woman any man could hope to meet.' Cheers went up all round. 'And we met, of course, in the worst of circumstances. Difficult times sometimes throw people together, they sometimes bring out the best in people, and I can only say I'm glad – despite all the terrible loss of life and tragedy that touched us all back then – that something good and joyful has come out of it.' I felt a pressure against my knee from Arthur. His hand, which was palm down on the table next to mine, edged a finger alongside my own. 'I *was* going to say that we are the only couple to get together from that boat, *but*, it seems, someone has got there first . . .' He looked over at Arthur. 'Ladies and gentlemen, congratulations are in order for *another* couple from Boat Nine . . .' My blood galloped through me. What had he heard? What had Arthur told him? Daphne looked over at me and beamed with unreserved delight. She placed her hands together like a child. I could feel myself blushing with the thrill of it. 'And they've beaten us to the altar and are already expecting a child!'

I stopped breathing. Daphne's face dropped. She nudged Jack. He leant down to hear her say something. Everyone was looking at me, raising their glasses, some delighted, some looking confused. I couldn't look at Arthur. I fixed my stare at the edge of the tablecloth in front of Daphne and Jack. I could tell Jack was shaking his head. There was a murmur or two. I wanted to run. Heart racing, hands sweating, the adrenaline had been provided in bucketfuls. Run. Run! Get out of there! I sat, quiet as a mouse except for my foolish thumping heart, gazing intently at the surface of that table: a white damask cloth with a bunch of fake flowers in a blue china vase.

'Unfortunately Arthur's wife can't be here today, but ladies and gentlemen, raise your glasses to Arthur and Pippa!'

'Arthur and Pippa!' People were *clapping*.

And here's the worst of it: I think I may even have clapped too.

For dignity's sake, I sat out the rest of that short speech and then, without a backward glance, I ran out choking into the street, where the shop fronts were all distorted and the lamp posts were bent double and everything swam in my tears. I just kept running.

35

ARTHUR

Oh God. Well . . . Oh Christ . . . this is the worst thing . . . I can hardly
bear to remember this . . . Of course, he announced to everyone that
Pippa and I were married and expecting a baby, and he *toasted* us. He
meant well – he's a lovely man, Jack Heggarty. I've so much respect for
the pair of them. But I could feel Dora sitting next to me like a stone.
And people cheered and the speech went painfully on, and as it did I
thought . . . well, what I thought was, he's *said* it now, he's said it for me.
What more could I say to her? My throat was thick. There was nothing,
nothing that I could possibly say to her to make it better. Nothing.

I know it sounds weak, but when she got up and left without looking at me, I didn't even call after her. And people were chatting again
by then, so I could have done – easily. I did start to get up, instinctively,
to follow her, but then I caught Graham's eye. He was standing by the
door, where he had been all through the speech, and he gave me an
emphatic thumbs up. People were coming up to me to congratulate me,
and then, of course, as soon as they did that I felt trapped – everything
was wrong, just wrong, and I had to find Dora urgently.

I edged my way out into the entrance hall and waited about by
the ladies' toilets. That, I thought, was where women went to hide and

to cry and to collect themselves. But Graham came up and tapped me on the shoulder. 'She's gone. She took her jacket from the peg and ran outside. I don't reckon she'll be coming back. Was there something between—?'

I dashed out into the street and looked up and down it. Of course, she wasn't anywhere in sight: I'd left it too late. I began to gasp for air. Paddington station. She'd be going back home. I started to run in the direction of the nearest tube station.

'By the way,' I vaguely heard Graham call out behind me, 'congratulations, old chap!'

It was the longest, most sluggish journey I have ever taken! I'm not joking: the train stopped between stations near Holland Park for no apparent reason, and even people who looked to be in no hurry at all began to get fed up. It was just a nightmare. God knows how long we were stuck there, but I was sweating and my pulse was racing. I was so agitated; I swear I could've murdered someone. It's a good job I didn't get my hands on the train driver. And then at Notting Hill Gate I seemed to wait forever for the Circle Line train. Oh, just remembering it makes me feel . . . nauseous.

Anyway, I got into Paddington, and there was a train due to leave for Swansea, calling at Newport, which was where Dora would get off. I bought a platform ticket and ran alongside the waiting train, looking in every compartment, but couldn't see her. What if she was in the toilet? I got on to the train and pushed my way past people in the corridors, checking all the toilets. They were all empty, of course, because you're not supposed to use them at a station. The whistle blew, and I got off just in time to watch the wheels sigh into action and take the train slowly away from me. She wasn't on it.

I asked the man at the ticket gate when the previous train for Wales had departed, and he told me an hour beforehand. She couldn't have made that one, so I went to look at the timetable to see if she could have changed somewhere like Swindon or Bristol or . . . And then it struck me that she might have gone to Cheltenham. Of course! It was already term time, or about to be, for the training colleges. The bright, warm weather had lulled me into a sense of summer, but the new terms were beginning. I grew impatient with the timetable and raced back over to the man at the ticket gate. 'Which platform for the Cheltenham train?'

'Platform eight,' he said laconically, as if mocking my urgency, 'but you'll have to wait for that one. Not due in for an hour. There was one just left, though it wasn't direct. You had to change at Swindon.'

I remember practically crumbling in front of him. I must have been so melodramatic – not in character for me at all. I wandered back into the wide entrance area and slumped on to a bench. Though if I *had* found her, what could I have said?

JETSAM

36

DORA

Jenny was puzzled. She had been looking forward to my return so that I could tell her something exciting. She was realistic enough to know that I might not come back from London with my engagement restored, but she hoped for some passionate titbits. Finding me face down on the bed and convulsing with sobs was a let-down, but even more so because I couldn't – wouldn't – give her any explanation.

'Please talk to me, Dora. It's always better to talk.'

I wept silently into the candlewick bedcover, punctuating my wordlessness only with loud snotty snorts. Jenny patiently put her arm around me and I shrugged her off. She went down to the kitchen and made me a cup of tea with the best china, and when I wouldn't drink it she knelt down by the bed and stroked my hair, murmuring softly, 'Poor sweetheart . . . poor lamb . . . poor, poor Dora . . .'

Of course I told her eventually. I held back because I couldn't bear to hear her run Arthur down. Just as I hadn't been able to tell my mother everything because I feared so much that a bad account of Arthur would stick forever. But even as I spoke, I realized that this no longer mattered. There was never going to be a reconciliation. Never going to be a time when I introduced Jenny or my mother or anyone

I knew to Arthur and craved their good opinion of him. Arthur was married and soon to be the father to another woman's child. That was the end of it. It was a finality that terrified me and consoled me in equal measure. No more would I have either the balm or the indifferently cruel anguish of hope.

What a bastard. You're well shot of him. He doesn't know what's good for him. More fool him. And so on. I endured these well-meaning platitudes for hours on end. I drank tea. I sat in my pyjamas with Jenny and ate toast with strawberry jam. Slowly my weeping subsided. My head ached and I was exhausted. She wouldn't let me go to bed until she had asked about Ralph, and she fetched some of his whisky to help loosen my tongue.

'Did you two *do it?*'

'*It?*' I said, disingenuously.

'Come on, Dora. You've spent the whole summer in his château, for God's sake. He must've tried it on.'

'Château? His type have such a way of glorifying themselves, don't they? Did he tell you he had a château?'

'Jesus wept! Shut up, Dora. Did you or didn't you?'

'What's it to you?'

'Because I want to know. What was he like? Was he romantic? Manful? Passionate?'

I said nothing and picked at some bobbles on my winceyette pyjamas.

'Did he woo you? Or did he hold you down and' – she held on to my wrists and tried to look smouldering – 'tie you to his four-poster and make free and passionate love to you without so much as a by-your-leave?'

'Okay,' I grinned. There seemed nothing to lose any more. 'We became lovers. Happy?'

'Not happy enough! How? What happened?'

'He wooed me, like you said.'

'How? Are we talking flowers? Champagne? Offers to meet his family?'

'Champagne, lavender fields, picnics . . .' I warmed to my subject. My face had stopped aching, and the whisky warmed my cheeks. 'He asked me to marry him when I left.'

'Dora!' Her voice was a bellow as low as a foghorn. '*Dora!*'

We stayed up very late as I told her what I could. 'My God, Dora! You get me all sympathetic for you weeping over some twerp who's cheated on you, and all the while you've just happened not to tell me you've been *proposed* to and could be the next Lady Rowanwood and rich as Croesus! Blimey, Dora, you really do take the biscuit!' As the whisky set in, my tongue became looser and our shared humour raunchier, but I also remembered less.

The following morning I paid for my revelry. I was so hung-over that I became morose again. From the upstairs window, I watched people walk their dogs in the park opposite, listened to the band play something jolly in the bandstand and felt wretched. The morning after that, the first Monday of term, I could not get up. I lay in bed and felt sorry for myself. The day after was the same. When I did go in I was summoned by my tutor, a kindly faced spinster who terrified me with her generosity and the knowing understanding that she seemed to exude about matters of the heart, no doubt from a lover who never returned from the Great War, or who returned a broken man. She had guessed it was trouble with love, but I didn't want to reveal myself in case I fell apart. I knew I wouldn't be able to bear her sympathy.

I told her I was thinking of leaving the course. I didn't think it was for me. She told me I was an exceptional student, and it would be a waste to throw it all away with only three terms to go. 'You know,' she said, her eyes filled with scary compassion, 'I nearly gave up like you once. But it's so important to have that qualification. You never know when you might be on your own. It gives you independence if you need it.' I looked down at the edge of her desk, biting my lip to stop it from wobbling. 'I'm not saying you *will* need it, of course. I expect you'll get married and have children one day, but . . . well, until then, it will give you independence. You will never have to marry for money.'

When I got back, I went straight upstairs to our flat and took a long look at myself in the mirror. I put my hands to my cheeks. I looked worn out, but I was still here. I'd been through the wars, but I thought of my tutor. I saw her lover's name chiselled into the memorial stone in the centre of her village. If she could do it, so could I. I pushed my shoulders back and flared my nostrils. What I saw, fortified by my tutor, was an independent woman.

And an independent woman I might have stayed, had Jenny not rushed in breathless with some news that made me giddy. 'Dora! You'll never guess who called round today! I told him you weren't here, so he said he'd come back later – and he has!'

'Who?'

'He's waiting in the front room downstairs – quick!'

I put some lipstick on hurriedly and pinched my cheeks. I hardly dared to hope . . . No, I did not hope. I went slowly down the stairs, trying to exude an air of calm, all the while my pulse pumping violently. I stood in the hallway, the pictures of Ralph beaming at me on all sides, and pushed open the door.

There, in an armchair opposite the door, sat an imposing figure: handsome, chestnut-haired and with eyes that sparkled when he saw me. He looked contrite, and his combined timidity and pleasure at see-ing me softened me. 'Dora!' said Ralph, getting up. 'I'm sorry I behaved badly. Please, *please* forgive me. I was just so scared of losing you.'

There was a little bead of sweat on his forehead, and I was moved by it. He looked like a giant puppy who had chewed a favourite slipper and wanted forgiveness. 'Ralph!' I said. I couldn't think of anything else, so I said it again: 'Ralph.' In the context of his hangdog appearance, I thought it sounded a bit like a 'woof', and I gave a little smile.

He smiled back. He stood there smiling at me, and it was so unlike him to be this vulnerable and nervous that I wasn't quite sure what to make of him. I half hoped Jenny was listening outside the door (as I was sure she was) in case he suddenly turned on me.

'I wasn't expecting you.'

'No . . . The thing is . . . the thing is, I had to come and see my father anyway . . . at some point . . . soon . . . so I, I thought I'd do it now, while you're here, and see if you'd like to meet him.'

He swallowed hard, and my heart went out to him. 'I see.'

'Please say you will, Dora. There's no obligation on your part or anything. Just come and see my home. I know he'd love to meet you.'

'Would he? Are you sure? I would've thought he'd find me quite a joke. I should think he has someone far better lined up for you.'

He approached me tentatively. 'Dora! Please say you'll come.' He put his giant arms around me and all my hostility melted away. Yes, it was that easy. I was suddenly being rescued by the strong arms of a sailor in the mid-Atlantic. *Just let go, that's it; I've got you now!*

Did I go with him to meet his father? Of course I went.

The first I saw of Ralph's father was his shadow, a long pole of a thing stretching out across the grass diagonally from behind us as we made our way over the lawn towards the family pile. As it intercepted us and blocked out the low autumn sun, we looked up to see its owner.

'Ralph!' Again, the barking sound of his name but this time more convincingly canine.

'Father! I've brought Dora to see you. Dora, this is my father.'

'Richard Rowanwood.' He held out a massive hand. 'I've heard a lot about you.' I saw him take in my appearance with a barely perceptible sweeping glance from head to foot. I wondered if my silk neckerchief was a step too far, if my wide-skirted dark green dress was too dressy for the occasion.

'All good, I assure you,' Ralph said, squeezing my hand.

'Of course! Oh, Zorro! Pliny!' He shouted at his hefty dogs, who had run over and laddered one of my stockings by jumping up at me. 'Come on, then! Let's go and have something to eat. I feel a crepuscular chill in the air.'

I had no idea what a crepuscular chill was, but it sounded mildly infectious, so I pulled my bolero tightly around me and followed the men swiftly to the house. When I say 'house', it wasn't the sort of thing you or I would call a house. Not that you would call it a stately home, as such, but a manor house certainly, and grander than anything I had encountered before. There was a gravel drive at the front and steps up to a double oak front door spanned by a gothic arch. The deep-red autumnal creeper revealed patches of yellow stone that was dappled in lichen. An archway to the left of the house led into a quadrangle of stables, and a sister arch, to the right, into a walled garden. These things were pointed out to me as we approached the heavy front door, which was opened by a man in a bow tie who inclined his head to each of us as we went inside.

Ralph had driven me there in a very flashy dark red car, borrowed from his father, and had parked it inside the entrance gate so that we could walk up to the house and see it in all its glory. He had filled me in a little about his father – but only a little as, he said, he wanted me to 'be myself' with him. This was all very well, but I was at a distinct disadvantage. I knew nothing of Lord Rowanwood's ways and manners – let alone his personality – whereas he seemed to have heard 'all about me'. The first hurdle was the 'snifter' before dinner. Should I accept one? Was it snuff? Was it tobacco- or alcohol-based? Seeing my hesitation, Ralph said, 'She'll have a cocktail, I think, won't you, Dora?'

I nodded and prepared myself for an evening of careful copying and acquiescence. However, after a cocktail and a generous glass of deep red claret at the dinner table later, I began to feel more relaxed. Lord Rowanwood – or Richard, as he asked me to call him – looked like a grey-haired, moustachioed version of Ralph. He was a huge, imposing man with two huge, imposing, smelly dogs who slavered and farted by the fireplace while we ate. The dogs seemed more important to him than his sons – but for the fact they couldn't produce heirs. Lady Rowanwood sat quietly opposite me: a well-groomed woman with a stiff platinum-blonde perm that made her head look like a scoop of vanilla ice cream. There were a few awkward questions from the father, asking whether I rode (by which he meant a horse) and where I was 'finished', both of which Ralph helped me with, but after that I managed pretty well on my own. I was, after all, an independent woman.

'Are you interested in politics *too*, Dora?' asked Richard.

I suspected it was a key question. 'Not really.'

'Excellent! That's how a woman should be, I always say. Don't clutter your mind up with things that don't concern you. That way lies trouble.'

'Father!'

I felt sorry for Ralph, and even more sorry for him as I found myself shamefully nodding in his father's direction.

'Ralph here thinks he's a Marxist! What poppycock! I hope you're not a Marxist, Dora. What does your father do?'

I swallowed hard. 'He's a coal miner.'

'A miner! *A miner!*'

I felt myself colour. I surprised myself at how brazenly I wanted to please this man. I was the shallowest of independent women. I wanted to be able to tell him how I competed in point-to-point, had been 'finished' in Switzerland and generally enjoyed a good game of croquet on a summer's evening.

'That's a noble profession. Though I suppose he's a red, is he?'

'Oh no. I don't think he has any strong political views.' Did I tell him how my father had drummed into me Labour's five 'giant evils' of Want, Squalor, Disease, Ignorance and Unemployment? Did I explain how much my father hated the ruling classes? How he campaigned tirelessly to get our tip moved to a safer location? How, when one hundred and forty-six boys and men died in the 1860 Risca Black Vein mine explosion, it was reported as 'A severe financial loss to the owner', a fact I was never allowed to forget? Oh, shame of shames! My father, the passionate Labour voter, was being denied, Judas-like, as the cock crowed.

'Is he in good health, your father?'

'Oh yes. Very good health.' Important to have a healthy family, I thought, and I added, 'And my mother.'

'And do you have any brothers and sisters?'

This was the fertility question. I wanted to say I had a string of siblings called Lettice and Lavinia and Tertius and Claude. 'I had a sister, Siân.'

'Oh?'

Ralph stepped in for me. 'She passed away.'

'I see. What did she die of?'

This was the healthy stock question again. 'Diphtheria. It went through our village.'

There was a pause. Richard chewed on a piece of steak and took a sip of wine. 'But *you* survived.' Did I ask why he hadn't expressed his sorrow? No. I felt quietly triumphant. I could survive plagues. 'Jolly good! Aha! Here comes dessert! Apple Charlotte. I hope you'll have some, Dora. You look like you could do with feeding up.'

'I'm sorry to hear about your sister,' said Lady Rowanwood. 'Were you very young when it happened?'

'Thank you. I was six.'

'How dreadful for you – and your poor parents.'

'Eat up!' said Richard. 'Eat it while it's still warm!'

Virginia – as Lady Rowanwood asked me to address her – took me to a modest room with a coal fire that overlooked the walled garden. Ralph's father had taken him off for an after-dinner chat, and I felt like someone from a Jane Austen novel, banished to female company while the men did manly things like smoke cigars or gamble or take snuff.

'You did very well, Dora. He can be frightfully blunt at times.'

I smiled, not quite sure that any agreement would be appropriate. 'I hope . . . I hope I . . . I'm not very used to this sort of thing.'

'Don't worry. He's very keen on you for Ralph, I can tell.' She paused a little, to observe my reaction – which was another smile. I hated myself for my passive smiles, but I was out of my depth. 'He's very anxious for Ralph to be married and produce an heir.' She offered me some tea that she had poured by herself from a tray brought in by a woman. She observed me again.

'Oh. I thought he disapproved of Ralph's political beliefs and was going to disinherit him, or something.'

Now she smiled. 'Ah. Well, I'm not sure it's as easy as that. Ralph is his eldest son and he inherits. But he is worried about Ralph dying without any offspring.'

'I thought Ralph had a brother?'

'Oh yes, he does. But, you see, Richard doesn't want the estate left to Peregrine, because then there would definitely be no heirs and it would be left to some distant third cousin or something.'

'Can't Peregrine have children?'

'I expect he can, but he's determined not to.'

I had heard very little about Ralph's brother, but it seemed they both dug their heels in when it came to their father. 'That's a shame. I can't imagine not wanting children – at some point.'

She put her cup down carefully in her saucer. 'Between you and me, Peregrine is what Richard so tastefully terms "a Nancy Boy".'

'Oh, I see!' I felt a little shiver of pride that Virginia had entrusted me with this information. 'So he *can't* have children. Poor man.'

'Oh no. That's not the problem. Richard would be perfectly happy for him to get married to some poor unsuspecting woman and produce offspring. That's not a problem at all. No, the problem is that Peregrine *won't*. He refuses point blank to get married. And so you see, the weight of responsibility lies even more heavily on Ralph's shoulders. And if he refuses to marry a deb or someone considered suitable, then Richard really isn't too concerned any more. Money isn't a problem.'

My eye caught the coals in the fire, and I couldn't help thinking that my father had hewn those coals out of deep seams with nothing but a pickaxe and eighteen-inch wooden pit props, lying on his belly in the dark.

'And what about . . . well . . . class?'

'Class? Well . . . a healthy young woman with a few manners who knows her place is more important than the odd title.' She shot me a look that was unmistakably mischievous. I smiled again.

'What was Ralph like as a little boy?'

'As a *little* boy? Well, I'm not too sure what he was like as a very small boy. You know I'm his stepmother? His mother left when he was four or five.'

'Oh dear! No, I didn't know. Oh . . .' I wanted to know why she had left but didn't dare ask.

'I know, it's a terrible shame. The boys were about eight and six when I married Richard. Ralph was already off at boarding school. I think it hurt them very much.'

'Poor Ralph.' I couldn't imagine how any mother could leave her children.

'The really dreadful thing, though . . .' Virginia gazed out of the window and looked suddenly very pained. 'The dreadful thing is that he told them she had abandoned them. They were brought up believing that.'

'Didn't she leave, then?'

'Yes. Oh yes, she left, but she tried to take them with her. He took legal action against her, so that he could keep them. They know the truth now. She turned up at their school when Ralph was eighteen and told them.'

'So why did she leave? Surely . . . couldn't she have stayed for them? For her own children?' I stared out of the window with her, as if the answer might be found in the feathery wisps of dead clematis.

'I can't say,' she said, turning to meet my eyes again. 'But between you and me – strictly between you and me' – she waited until I nodded – 'I think he was . . . I think he may have . . . treated her rather badly.'

Even so, I thought. You wouldn't catch me abandoning my children for a bit of bad behaviour.

'He can be very . . . *difficult*,' she added, with feeling.

He was blundering and opinionated and arrogant. I could quite believe he could be cruel. But to leave your children . . . Poor Ralph. I warmed to him then more than I ever had done. Suddenly the controlling man on the Montélimar station became a man with a terrible fear of abandonment. Once more abandoned by a woman he loved. Who could blame him for wanting to cling on so tight?

37

ARTHUR

When I got home I was surprised to find that there were no lights on in the house at all. I looked in the living room, and there was no sign of Pippa. In the kitchen there was a saucepan on the hob with dried food hardened on to the sides and a wooden spoon propped inside it. Next to the sink was a crumb-laden plate with a buttery knife. I went upstairs and turned the landing light on. I had dreaded facing Pippa, but now this silence bothered me. I was primed for casual sarcasm, not an empty house.

On the bed was a scrawled note:

Darling, Frightful bore being here alone in my condition.
Gone to Mater's for rest of weekend. X

I scuttled back downstairs to our new telephone, which sat on a pretentious 'phone table' she had bought and which you had to ease yourself around as you went down the hallway. I hoped she – and not her mother – would answer my call.

I was disappointed.

'*Philippa!* Come and speak to that useless mechanic of yours . . .'

Pippa sounded tired when she reached the phone, as if she might have been snoozing by the fire. 'Hello?'

'Pippa, are you okay?'

'Well, as okay as any woman can be, left all alone in the house and five months pregnant with absolutely nothing to do.'

'I wish you'd said something. I don't like the idea of you catching buses or trains in your condition. Not on your own.'

'Well, I didn't.'

'How did you get over to your mother's?'

'By taxi.'

'*Taxi?* That must've cost a for— I see. Were you that bored?'

'For God's sake, Arthur. If we had a car like other people, I could have simply driven. But no, even on your salary – and you claim to be doing so well – we can't afford the basics.'

'What do you mean, "like other people"?'

She sighed heavily. 'Your colleague Andrew has a car, and he's younger than you.'

'He's also single. No expensive wife and no child on the way.'

'*Expensive!* I'm hardly an expense! You expect me to stay cooped up in that little house. We don't even have a *television*! I don't know how much longer I can bear this! Life is so *dull!*'

It occurred to me momentarily that Pippa might have left me. I was surprised to find that this made me panic.

'I'm sorry, Pippa. We do have to live within our means. But I will look into getting a television. Perhaps we could afford to rent one.'

I heard her blow air out of her mouth.

'I promise. It's too late for me to catch a train now. But I'll come over tomorrow.' There was a silence. I found that I was afraid of it. 'I'll get us a television next week. You get some sleep now.'

She said goodbye without too much fuss but still sounded petulant. There had been times over the previous few weeks when I had fanta-sized about my wife leaving me. I had actually imagined her going to live with her mother and leaving me free to be with Dora. I even took this fantasy forward to dealing with the practical details of having a baby. Pippa would feel overwhelmed by motherhood and leave the baby outside the door in a basket, and somehow Dora would be happy to bring it up as our own. Dora would live modestly, without the need for a car or a television, and we would soon be able to afford a larger house to accommodate our own children too. She wouldn't run me down in front of people or say she had me 'well-trained', and she would never say she was bored.

In this fantasy, Pippa just drifted out of my life with ease, and I gave her no more thought. Now, faced with the possibility that Pippa might indeed go to live with her mother, I was panicky. I was exhausted by her constant challenges but determined to step up to the mark. I needed her back home with me. I wanted to provide for her myself, like a man, and to provide for the child that was on its way.

Early the following morning, I caught a train to Stroud and waited an hour for a Sunday bus to Hickleton. From the village pub where the bus stopped, I made my way down the lane to the Barrington-Hobbs' home. It was a damp morning, and the leaves of overhanging branches stroked my face wetly as I walked the rough stone road. I could hear voices up ahead, and a car door slammed. A maroon-coloured car nosed out of the bushes at the entrance to the driveway, then turned towards me and drove by. I stepped back against some brambles to let it pass. It made no effort to slow down, although the driver must have seen me. I saw him turn his head after he'd driven past, but I didn't get a good look at him. Arrogant, jumped-up bastard. A jumped-up bastard who had visited – or at any rate *was leaving* – my wife before noon on a Sunday morning.

'How was the wedding?'

Pippa looked radiant. She was wearing a sapphire-blue velvet maternity dress with pearls at her neck. Her thick eyebrows had been plucked into such an arch that her glance was formidable. Her movements, though, were less graceful than they had been, giving her an air of vulnerability. I hadn't imagined a pregnant woman could look so breathtaking, and I wanted to rip her clothes off and make love to her there and then, in front of the family fireplace. However, I thought I detected a familiar reproach in her eyes, despite the smiling lips. I couldn't be sure.

'Did you have a good time with your *old friends*?'

She knew.

'What do you mean?' There was a silence as she turned her back to me. She didn't see me swallow hard. I rallied quickly. 'I might ask you the same question.'

She turned around. '*What?* You're asking me if I had a good time? Why do you think I came here? It hasn't been a night on the town for me *here*, I can tell you. Although Mother dearest seems to have a night on the tiles every night. The kitchen tiles, at any rate.'

She was doing well at deflecting me, but I wasn't going to let this slip. 'Were you alone? Was it just the two of you?'

'None of her fancy men turned up, if that's what you mean.'

'Any of yours turn up?'

'What on earth do you mean?' There was indignation and a hint of panic in her tone. She traced her finger along the edge of the mantelpiece. I could feel my pulse in my head.

'Who was the man who visited you?'

She put her head on one side, and without turning round, she said breezily, 'Oh, that was just an old friend of mine whose father lives nearby. He called by this morning.' Then she turned and challenged me with her penetrating green eyes, but I held firm.

'This morning? That's a strange time to visit.'

She laughed. 'Oh, Arthur! Oh, my darling, you didn't think he arrived last night, did you?' She smiled benignly at this. Then she opened her eyes very wide, courting the thrill of danger. 'What would you have done if he *had*?'

'What was he doing here?'

She lowered herself into an armchair and blinked slowly. 'He came to ask about . . . he came to tell me – as he is just in the country for a few days – that he's going to settle down with someone, at long last.'

'And how did he know you were here?'

'Because he didn't know I'd got married. He came here because this is where I've always lived.'

'So you told him – that you were married?'

She looked down at her bump. 'I should think so!'

'I see.' It sounded plausible. It was difficult recalibrating my emotions. She chose the moment to pounce.

'And as it happens, the person he's chosen is a friend of *yours*. Well, ours, I suppose. That was his interest. In fact, he was almost pumping me for information about her. He'd heard that I knew her from the *City of India* disaster. It's not every day you meet one of the thirteen surviving children, is it? So quite a coincidence.' I remained silent. 'Reason enough to come and see me, don't you think? Before he whisks her back to France permanently?'

I thought she pronounced the last word with some relish, but I may have been wrong. She knew. She knew I'd seen her. My pulse was booming so loudly I could barely hear my own thoughts.

'That explains it, then. That explains why she turned up to the wedding.'

Pippa smiled slyly at me. 'You weren't going to tell me, were you?'

'I was going to tell you. I barely spoke to her. She left early.' It was the best I could do, handicapped as I was by a heart rate that shook my ribcage.

So that was it. Marriage. France. It really was all over.

OCEANS APART

38

DORA

The crossing was rough. I was sick in the toilets, but worse, it didn't put an end to my feeling of nausea, and I found myself shaking the whole time. Ralph was wonderful, holding me throughout the journey, reassuring me. It takes very little – even now – to bring it all back. No need for a choppy sea or a floor that rocks you erratically like an unloving mother. Back then, after the rescue, I would often wake suddenly and find myself trying to scream, but nothing would be coming from my mouth except a little squeak. The sea towered above me. *Towered.* It was way up high, an impossibly high wall, blocking out all hope. The next minute it was buoying me up, cradling me high in the air, giving me a view of our forlorn ship and the frantic lifeboats. But then it would be sucking me down again, beating me crossly, enticing me, rejecting me: a savage, unpredictable parent, spinning everything I thought I could rely on into a whorl of terror. I had grown up loved – so very loved – by my mother and father. Whatever hardships we faced, there were always arms to hold me at the end of the day, there was always the floury smell of my mother's work-coat and the delicious oily scent of her hair as she tucked me in and kissed me goodnight. And Our Dad too, if he was off his shift, would come up and sing to me sometimes (a hymn or a music-hall song), and his ancient, earthy smell of coal dust would take me deep underground to a safe, dark, sleepy place. *Just a song at twilight, when the lights are low . . .*

When my sister died, the arms were still there, but they clung too tightly, or too limply, and their owners were far away. 'Love' was not a word we used in our house, but I had always felt it, and I knew when there was a different feeling, a feeling of absence. Suddenly, I wasn't enough to make them happy. Their sadness was so huge and over-whelming that I knew I must have always been less than half of their happiness, otherwise there would still have been half of it left when Siân died.

Then I was sent away. For my own good, of course. I wonder how many children still grapple with that one. We care about you so much that we're sending you away. To another country, even. You'll be safe, you'll be well looked after, there'll be things we can't give you. But most of all, you'll be safe.

And you can sleep in your pyjamas tonight; we're out of danger. Boom! And the screaming, and the rocking, and the water coming in; the strange blue light and the shock and the queuing, and the grown-ups getting it wrong, getting it *wrong*: packing us into boats and tipping us out into the great, swirling cheat of the sea.

> *Gentle Jesus, meek and mild,*
> *Look upon a little child;*
> *Pity my simplicity,*
> *Suffer me to come to Thee.*

Yes, Ralph was wonderful. He stroked my hair and told me it would be over soon. He tried to distract me with stories of our future together. 'I'm going to make you the happiest woman alive, Dora Powell. You wait and see.' He told me nothing could ever stop him loving me – not even the reek of vomit – and he put his great strong arms around me, like the sailor who rescued me, and I knew I was safe.

Years later, people would ask me why I hadn't seen the signs. The truth is, I just didn't. I suppose you don't see what you're not looking for, and more importantly, as Patsy often said, we women have a tendency to see one piece of a man we like and then fill in all the rest with what we'd like to see.

When I arrived back at Les Amandiers, I thought it would be difficult to explain why I'd left in such a hurry. But nobody gave me a hard time. Everyone seemed thrilled to see me, and especially Claudine, who literally danced around the kitchen in excitement. Within a few hours, it was as if I'd never been away.

The very first afternoon after we got back, Ralph took me out in the car to visit a neighbouring farm that had been bought up by some Parisians. 'They're turning it into a holiday home. And this is our big chance!'

It was a hot day, and the farmhouse we visited looked bleached out by the sun. The stone path outside the door warmed the soles of our feet through our shoes. The new owners were friendly and invited us in for a *goûter* of runny cheese and bread and some of the famous local wine. They were trying hard, Ralph reckoned later, to cast off their Parisian reserve and adopt the typical Provençal bonhomie. I attempted to follow the conversation but got lost after a few smiles and references to me, which included the word *fiancée*, to my unexpected delight. It wasn't until much later that we were taken around the back of the house to view something. It turned out that the 'big chance' took the shape of a huge metal vat, still – we were reassured – in perfect working order.

Everything Claudine had promised about October came true. It was mellow and warm, and the streets of the nearby villages were splattered with the blood of crushed grapes that had fallen off carts. Every donkey and mule for miles around seemed to converge on the streets, pulling carts overloaded with wobbly grapes. The local fruit was dark and musky, and the smell, when the pavements were littered with its flesh and juice, was so sickly sweet that you had to hold your breath at times. The area became peopled with fruit pickers. There were the old hands, short locals whose diminutive stature seemed to have adapted itself to the height of the vines and whose limbs were just as brown and gnarled. Then there were the students who came down from Paris and Lyon for the grape harvest before returning to their studies. There was money to be made for people who relied on seasonal work. It didn't pay well, but for those prepared to work long hours, it was well worth the travel. Ralph was quick to offer some of these temporary workers lodgings, at no charge if they were happy to pick some of his own grapes for a pittance. Most workers did better elsewhere, but word soon got around amongst the students that Les Amandiers was a bit bohemian and that there was good food and music every night.

That was how we came to have a house full of people, and how we came to like it. Of course, there was a lot more cooking to do, but Ralph was generous with his housekeeping allowance, which now seemed to include support from his father as well as Aunty Bee. His aim, of course, was to get the grape vat working properly and turn the vineyards into a useful income. His enthusiasm was infectious. Even Denis and Sylvain were caught up in it, helped along by having been promised equal shares in the profits after they'd taken the wine to a local co-operative. Patsy, I think, was more sceptical. I usually had her unedited views via Claudine. 'Ralph hops from one idea to the next, doesn't he?' she said once, while we were washing up alone in the kitchen. 'Last week it was writing a book, this week it's winemaking, next week it will be fly fishing in the Camargue.' She'd say these things like a gossipy old lady, and it was hard sometimes to remember that she was only eight.

The evenings were drawing in slowly, and despite the warm weather, it was cooling down quickly after the evening meal. It wouldn't be long before we would have to retreat into the house until the spring, but in the meantime a spot of dancing helped to keep us warm as the stars came out. We danced and danced. Tighe and some friends came back for the grape harvest, and the mixture of Irish and Provençal music was electric. It was almost impossible to keep still. One student grape picker whirled me round so fast that my feet left the ground for a long time. I was dizzy and laughing as he lowered me gently to the ground, and I felt glad to be back. This was home now. I had finally moved on.

Around about this time, I received a large envelope from England containing a note from Jenny (asking when the wedding was going to be, and could she be a bridesmaid) and three or four letters from my mother. Our Mam wrote to me every week in college. She never said anything much, just kept in touch with a few lines of her careful handwriting. I usually wrote back. Jenny's package reminded me that I hadn't yet had the courage to tell my parents that I'd left college.

Mam's first letter wished me luck for the beginning of term and reminded me to eat plenty of vegetables. The following letters showed an increasing level of anxiety at not having heard from me. I wrote immediately, explaining what had happened. I had to give them my address, so there was no point in trying to deceive them. I emphasized how well placed Ralph was financially, and I hoped they would be happy for me.

The letter I received ten days later was the longest she ever wrote. I still have it.

> *Dear Dora,*
> *Your father and I were very upset indeed to hear that you have given up your College course. We can't understand why you didn't tell us earlier, so that we could have talked things through.*

Of course it is wonderful news that you are engaged to be married but you are not married yet and you have made a very important decision based on thin air. Education is freedom, Dora, as you know. I hope at least he has given you a ring and a date.

There's no use beating about the bush. Your father is really upset and also he has not been well. You were his pride and joy going off to Coll as you know. Maybe the College people would consider letting you re-sit your second year next year. You did so well last year too. It's important to have a qualification under your belt. You never know. Could you come home and visit? The sooner the better. We'd like to meet your young man.

Lots of love,
Mam xxx

I wrote back and said I would try to visit soon but that it all depended on Ralph's 'business affairs'. I knew I was making excuses for him, but I brushed the thought aside. There had to be a justification for what I'd done, and any idea that I'd made a mistake was unthinkable. Most of all, I needed to console them. I thought if they could still be proud of me, it would make everything all right.

I didn't show Ralph the letter, but I explained that my parents wanted to meet him, and he said that would be lovely – maybe at Christmas. I felt vindicated. I wasn't sure they would be impressed by him. His manner might irritate Our Dad. I would have to give him some tips in advance. But one thing was certain: they'd see straight away that he was from a wealthy family and that their worries for my future were unfounded.

Ralph and I shared his room. It wasn't what I wanted, really. I would have preferred to have my own room to retreat into from time to time, although I was happy to sleep with him. That may not sound much now, but back then . . . well, nice girls waited. Anyway, I was reluctant to give up my room before we were married.

'I know Tighe needs somewhere, but can I have my own room back later?'

'Of course, but it's not just Tighe. We've got the students to think about, haven't we? Or is that precisely what you *are* thinking about?'

There was an edge of sarcasm in his voice suddenly, which startled me. 'How do you mean?'

He faced me by the side of the bed and smiled benignly, and then whispered, deliberately, 'Frédéric?'

I was almost relieved by his change in tone, but utterly confused. 'Who's Frédéric?' As soon as I said it, I guessed he was the student who had danced with me.

I didn't see it coming. I can't remember seeing anything. In fact, I don't think I would have believed it had happened at all if I hadn't found myself suddenly on the floor looking at the hem of the patterned bedcover and feeling sore about the jaw. The feeling of soreness increased rapidly until it was very painful. When I put my hand to my mouth, it was wet with blood.

39

ARTHUR

I took her into town and hired a television. It wasn't the one she wanted but the one we could afford. I took her to the cinema and to the theatre, although she complained about how uncomfortable the seats were. I promised her dinner parties after she'd had the baby, and we picked up brochures about holidays in the south of France. I also set up a bank account for her in her own name and gave her a monthly allowance. This was entirely pragmatic, as I could no longer let her have free rein over our joint account, which was now so often overdrawn that I was frittering away our savings in order to top it up. Pippa was delighted with the new bank account, having not realized that she would have to limit her spending. There was no overdraft facility, and cheques would simply bounce when she overspent.

I suggested we spend a weekend in London. We could stay with my parents, who were longing to see us again, and Pippa could look up her old friends. I knew Pippa needed a change of scene, but I just hoped she would behave herself.

We arrived on a Friday evening in mid-October. My parent's semi-detached house had the last embers of sun on its eaves and looked mellow and welcoming. My parents had pushed the boat out. I could see, when they opened the front door, that Mum had had her hair permed and Dad was wearing a new jacket and tie. In the front room sat brand-new cushions, and there was a framed picture of me and Pippa on the mantelpiece.

'Welcome to our humble abode,' said Dad, grinning.

'Ah, new cushions!' I said.

'Sit down! Sit down! Make yourselves at home!'

And then Pippa, who had a fixed, closed-lipped smile on her face, bent down to the sofa seat and gave it a gentle, almost imperceptible, brush with her hand before sitting on it. I tried to pretend to myself that my mother hadn't seen it. I sat down quickly in the hope of masking it. I talked loudly about the garden, about the photograph, about the journey. I tried not to see my mother's face collapse and then rally brightly into a wide smile.

'Now, we have a choice of tea or coffee or Ovaltine. What can I get you? Pippa?'

'What sort of tea?'

Mum chewed her bottom lip. She had thought of everything, but she hadn't bargained on different types of tea. 'Just . . . ordinary. Or . . . we have coffee.'

'Coffee, then, please.'

Mum almost genuflected as she took this order. I followed her out into the kitchen. 'I'll have Ovaltine with you and Dad. And Mum . . . make the coffee strong. And no milk. Let her add it herself.' I knew Pippa would make some comment about it if it was weak, and I couldn't bear to think of her face if she were presented with a coffee with the milk already added. But even as I said these things, I was conscious that my mother thought *I* was being pretentious. I gave her a big squeeze from behind. 'I'm sorry,' I said. 'She can be a bit . . .' All she needed was some reassurance, but I couldn't say the word. I couldn't find one that was fair to both of them.

We sat and talked over our hot drinks, and my parents held the conversation valiantly, despite Pippa's general unwillingness to make any effort to be civil. She clearly saw my parents as something to be borne, having married me. We came as a job lot, and she would just have to put up with them, but she had no intention of trying to get to know them or enjoying any aspect of their company.

'Well, Pippa, you look blooming!'

'Not for much longer, I suspect,' said Pippa, barely concealing her disgust at the coffee.

'Have a ginger biscuit – they're home-made.'

'Yes – eating for two, you know,' said Dad, winking.

Pippa sighed.

'Well, *I* will.' I grabbed a couple and dunked them provocatively in my Ovaltine. Pippa looked at me askance, and I gave her what I hoped was a challenging look. 'Yummy!'

'Show Pippa those clothes you made, Elsie,' said Dad. 'She's knitted some cracking little clothes for the baby. She was up all night finishing them.'

'Oh, shush, Bill. I was not!' Mum shuffled over to the corner of the room and produced a knitting bag. Out of it she pulled little knitted garments in white and green, and spread them on Pippa's lap. 'Those are bootees, and there's a little all-in-one—'

'Like Churchill wears!' said Dad.

'Yes, like Churchill wears – only smaller!'

Pippa picked up a bootee and examined it. 'Green. Hmm. Well, he will be well decked out.'

'Or she.'

'He or she . . .' She waved a hand, as if uninterested in the child she was carrying.

'What are you hoping for? Do you have any names lined up?'

'Oh God! If anyone else asks me that question again . . .'

'Pippa's really tired,' I said.

They insisted on putting us in their own bedroom. There was a new bedcover on their double bed, not one I'd ever seen before. And on each bedside table was a little jar with a late red rose in it from the garden. Mum had even folded a towel on each pillow. On Pippa's pillow was a present wrapped in mauve paper.

Suddenly I heard the oddest noise coming from Pippa. I turned to look at her and she was sobbing, great snorting wails. I sat beside her and put my arm around her.

'I'm sorry. I'm so sorry!'

'It's okay.' I stroked her hair in amazement.

'Your poor mother! Your poor, poor mother. She lost her son!'

When I look back now, I think it is this moment I try hardest to recall. A single time when Pippa showed her vulnerability and perhaps some real contrition.

'I'm so sorry! I'm so sorry about Philip!' She let herself go completely and wiped her nose on her arm. I kissed her head and waited for her sobs to die down.

When her breathing became normal again, she unwrapped the present on her pillow. It was a bed-shawl, handmade by my mother in pink crochet.

'Oh Lord. How utterly ghastly.'

With the first contractions, Pippa insisted on going into hospital by taxi. There we were told that she was not yet in labour and that we were to go home again. She was furious.

The baby eventually arrived – on the third visit to hospital – at the beginning of January 1953. We named her (or rather, Pippa named her) Felicity, because she made us both so happy. That was the theory, anyway. In fact, Pippa refused to speak to me when I was at last allowed in to see her. She sulked for hours because of what she had been 'put through' by me. When she eventually did speak, it was to refuse the baby at her breast. 'She's just biting me. Take her away!' The nurse assured her that babies couldn't bite, but she was adamant. 'I can't do it! Isn't there a wet-nurse or something?' The nurse gave me a wry look and offered me the baby to hold.

Felicity. What can I say? She was perfect. Dark, downy hair, tiny nose as soft as marshmallow, and dark blue eyes gazing into mine, seemingly fascinated with me. I fell in love with her. She didn't sulk or moan, just gazed appreciatively, and through the cotton swaddling I felt the warmth and the helplessness of her tiny body. My throat engorged and my eyes filled up and spilt over. I'm going to look after you, little one, I thought. I will move mountains to make you happy and keep you safe.

The nurse said briskly that it was all right: a lot of men cried like babies with their first child. I felt foolish, but still elated. Felicity changed everything.

Well . . . Pippa and motherhood. The first few weeks she went into a tailspin of self-pity and moroseness. I couldn't blame her. I know she *had* been through a lot. I can't imagine what women go through in childbirth, and I was certain she wouldn't have chosen to become a mother just yet if it hadn't been for my dissolute behaviour before we were married. Now I had to look after her. She was vulnerable, and I had a wife and a child to take care of. They were my responsibility, and responsibility was something I took very seriously.

If I had taken my responsibilities more seriously once before in my life, my brother would still be alive. I should never have left him. I know I meant well, but I should've thought! *Don't leave him alone for one minute. Stick by him. You take care of your brother.* That's what they'd said. Those were the last words of my mother when she waved us off. *Take care of Philip. Don't leave him on his own.* And I did. Ah, you say, but you gave him your own life jacket. Yes, but then I went back to get his for myself. It wasn't a real sacrifice. I just thought I'd be quicker than him, and that he'd get lost if he went, and that we might both be drowned if we went back together. I know I thought I was making a sacrifice, but in the end I was the one who was saved. How can I ever live with that? I can't look my mother in the eye and say his name. Those giant, opaque waves. To think he was tipped out into them; it must've been terrifying. Dora told me what it was like. He was only six. *Six.* Imagine – I often imagine – falling from that height in the dark, people screaming all around; imagine hitting the cold water like a hard surface; imagine the cold slap and the sense of betrayal; imagine being delivered into the safety of a lifeboat by strong arms, only to be tricked into peril; imagine wondering where your big brother is; imagine being lost in the waves, those heaving, monstrous waves, wondering why your brother has forsaken you.

We were told it was normal for some mothers to feel a bit low shortly after childbirth, but Pippa just seemed vindictive. 'Look at my belly! Look at it! No, don't! Don't look at me! It's disgusting. See what you've done? I'll never look good in a dress again. Never.'

She already looked good in a dress. In fact, within a few weeks she was out shopping for new dresses. Len had warned me to expect a wife who was not herself for a few weeks, who went about the house in a dressing gown and with unwashed hair. Not Pippa. After a few days of no make-up and endless whinging, she started to take care of herself again. She wore a red silk kimono. Before breakfast she did sit-ups while I fed Felicity from a bottle, and then, after a few weeks, she would put the baby in the pram for the rest of the morning and leave her at home while she whittled her allowance down to zero. I had no idea she had been leaving the baby on her own for hours at a time until, having stupidly left some important documents at home, I came back while she was still out one lunchtime.

I could hear Felicity crying before I opened the front door. Inside the house, the noise was heart-rending. She was lying in the pram, hot and red-faced and distraught. Her nappy had leaked, and there was some mess in her hair and on the covers. I took her to the bathroom and lay her awkwardly on the floor while I ran a shallow bath. Then I took off her things and dunked her in, talking gently to her until she stopped crying. There is something especially moving about a calm baby still with tears on its cheeks from previous distress.

'It's all right,' I said. 'That's better, isn't it?'

I emptied the muck out of the bath and rinsed her in lukewarm water. I wrapped her in a towel and held her close, savouring her warmth and her calm. There were no clean nappies anywhere for her, so I did the best I could with a folded hand towel and a nappy pin. I stood at the front door, holding her. There was no sign of Pippa, so I scribbled a note and went round the corner to Len's house, where his wife agreed to look after her. I handed Felicity over in her gigantic pink-striped nappy. Len's wife was cheerful, but I could tell she was concealing a certain shock at the circumstances. I didn't go into any detail, just said that Pippa had had to go out and would be round later.

When I eventually came home from work, Pippa was sitting reading a magazine with Felicity lying on the sofa beside her.

'Where were you?' I tried not to sound accusing.

'We'd run out of baby milk and washing powder.'

'There's a shop on the corner.'

'I had to go into town for the bank. I've no money.'

'What about the ten pounds I gave you yesterday?'

'I had to buy some new outfits. You can't possibly expect me to wear those old sacks when I've nearly got my figure back to what it was.'

'What about the clothes you used to wear?'

'They don't fit me, no thanks to you!'

'I told you, I've put more money into your account, and I gave you ten pounds. Where's it all gone?'

'I need to buy more nappies!'

'We bought a dozen. Why don't you wash any of them?'

'What am I now, a skivvy? I didn't marry you to wash excrement out of nappies!'

'Well, someone has to do it.'

'I want some help. We should hire someone.'

I phoned my parents from work. Two days later my mother arrived with a little suitcase. She cooked lunch for us both and propped Pippa's feet up on the sofa. She soaked and washed nappies, sterilized bottles, prepared the baby's milk and fed her. She showed Pippa how to do these things too, but Pippa looked bored as she explained things. 'You're just a little down, dear,' she explained. 'It's perfectly normal. It'll all get easier and you'll feel on top of the world soon.'

My mother's intention was to stay a few days or a week, just long enough to give my wife a break, but Pippa showed no signs of wanting to take over from her. If my mother handed her the baby – all washed and fed – she would look up from her magazine and say, 'Oh, not now, Elsie,' and if my mother offered to show Pippa how to sterilize a bottle, or suggested she help with a feed, Pippa would say, 'Yes, of course,' and then ten minutes later would add, 'Actually, do you mind awfully doing it yourself this time? There's something I want to watch on the television.'

Around my mother I was still childishly jealous of Philip. Every time I saw her, I felt guilt like a wound, and an inadequacy compared to my dead brother. It was so good to see her, and so gratifying to have her help us out, but I knew that Philip's wife, had he lived to have one, would never have been this much trouble. Nor would my wife have been any trouble if I'd married Dora. I was a constant source of disappointment to my mother, for certain. I would sit in the evenings sometimes, cocooned in the privacy afforded by watching a television programme, and imagine what might have been. Dora and my mother discussing children, swapping recipes, shopping together, laughing at the same jokes. I could see Dora hugging her as they said hello or goodbye; I saw my parents' faces light up when we arrived for visits or when they came to see us, welcomed by all sorts of treats and baking smells and cheerful gossipy news. The daughter they never had, helping to make up for the son they had lost.

'You think I'm a bad mother, don't you?' Pippa challenged her one day.

My mother looked as if she'd been ticked off. 'Oh, no, dear, not at all. Not at all.'

'It's okay. I know I'm not cut out for this sort of thing, and that's that.'

My mother's deeply furrowed brow softened, and she put a comforting hand on Pippa's knee. 'Actually, it's very hard to be a bad mother. All you need is to love your baby, and the rest takes care of itself.'

'How can a baby understand love? All it wants is to eat and to cry!'

Elsie folded her lips together, holding back while she found the right words to come out of them. 'A baby understands being fed as being looked after, and it understands being paid attention when it cries as being looked after. Lots of cuddling will do the trick. That's the sort of attention a baby needs most. That's how a baby learns that she's loved: food and attention.'

She said these things very gently – anxious, I suppose, not to seem to be a know-it-all. 'It's hard for first-time mothers.' Then she added something generous and surely untrue: 'I think you're doing really well.'

I was sorry to see her go. It had been ten days, and she had to get back to Dad, who phoned her every night from the telephone box on the corner of their street. My father found it hard without her. And it wasn't just the diet of corned beef and condensed milk. It was the first time they'd spent more than one night apart in thirty years. When she stood at the doorway with me, all packed with what I now saw was just a zipped-up shopping bag, Pippa was slouching on the sofa, reading a copy of *The Tatler*. I wished I had a car so that I could drive my mum to the station, but she said she would catch the bus. The taxi I'd ordered arrived bang on time, and she chided me for wasting my money.

'Now, I've made you a fruit cake, and it's cooling next to the cooker. That should last you a few days. And there's a bacon-and-egg pie I've made all ready to go in the oven. It's in the fridge. Pippa will know what to do.' She made this last comment without much conviction. Then she put a reddened hand on my arm and squeezed it, looking me in the eye with a kindly gaze. 'Don't worry, Arthur. You're doing so well. Me and your father are so proud of you.' She placed her hand on my cheek and gave me a quick peck. 'But remember, we're just a train ride away if you need us.'

I saw her into the taxi and watched her disappear around the corner at the end of the road with a pain in my throat. She had abandoned her beloved Bill for ten long days, all for me: food and attention.

40

DORA

He was so sorry. I could see him trying to get me alone all day, and as soon as he did he came up behind me and kissed my neck softly, promising it would never happen again. 'I was jealous, that's all. You can't blame me. I love you so much.' He had that way of twisting everything to make you feel it was a compliment. I should be grateful that he'd lashed out. It was proof of his love for me. And it worked. I was lulled into a sense of intense security. Strong arms. Thankfulness. Relief.

I did the predictable thing and pretended I'd had a fall. The weeks and months passed in a flurry of busyness. The wine was going to be accepted by the local co-operative since it had the right balance of Grenache and Syrah grapes, and if all went well, it would be bottled as Côtes du Rhône-Villages. The profit, after paying the grape pickers, would be minimal, but the note of promise by the co-operative was a cause for much merriment and bottle opening. 'Next year, we'll double it, and the year after that we'll double it again and bottle it ourselves: *Mis en bouteille aux Amandiers!*

All this time, Ralph was very tender towards me. The bruise completely disappeared, and it became our secret, as secret as the caresses we exchanged at night. I was surprised every time by the lust he inspired in me. Sometimes at the kitchen sink or peeling potatoes I would be overcome with a sudden ache for him, and I would close my eyes and think of a touch or a look from the night before. I would happily have sprawled in the potato peelings for him or crawled on all fours for him in the cold pantry or wrapped my feet around his neck in the shed or stood, knees trembling, against the metal of the wine vat behind the outhouses. I pictured our wedding in the spring, the guests arriving at his father's house in Gloucestershire (I knew he wouldn't want a church). I dismissed the objections of Our Mam and Dad, who would be bowled over by the gardens and the marquees. Would there be marquees? Yes, and there'd be a band, and the French crowd would come over too, with little Claudine all dressed in silk and Patsy so happy for us both, and me dressed in . . . ? White silk. Did I have the right? Ivory, then. Something ambiguous. And then at some stage, some far-off stage, we'd move into the house ourselves, and our children would play in the grounds, safe and free. And Arthur would hear about it, of course, and then he and Pippa would be almost neighbours. But we wouldn't invite them. I wouldn't have Pippa in my house. Arthur would catch glimpses of me from time to time, perhaps in Gloucestershire at a local fete, and he would wonder if he hadn't perhaps married the wrong woman; he would imagine what it would be like to lie with me, in a four-poster bed or on the side of a mountain, and take me, willing and ready and all for himself.

Always I came back to Arthur. I hadn't got over him. I hadn't allowed myself the time to grieve, and sometimes he would just pop up, unannounced like that, in the middle of another thought that had nothing to do with him. I would not go near enough to explore, because my feelings about him were an unexploded bomb. My reluctance, of course, didn't stop its timer ticking. I couldn't comprehend his motives. That was as close as I could get: a series of questions. Why didn't he . . . ? When he could so easily have . . . ? What did he intend by . . . ? Why did he . . . ? Why? Why? Had I got him so wrong? Was I such a fool? Yes, of course

I was. A fool. A gullible fool, not pretty enough, not clever enough, not sophisticated enough, not . . . enough. Enough, and I could go no further. The stealthy creeping up to it ceased, and I would scuttle back to Ralph and the safety of his erotic power over me.

And then one day just before Christmas, Ralph said something astonishing. We were alone in the kitchen one evening because everyone else was at a choir concert in the nearby village of Dieulefit. The radio was on, and he took me in his arms and swayed me gently on the tiled floor by the stove. His one hand caressed my buttock, and after a while it crept under my skirt and between my legs.

'Did he do this to you?'

I was on the alert straight away. There had been no students in the house for months. I felt myself go rigid. 'Who?'

He didn't stop his gentle movements, but I began to tremble. 'Did your dear Arthur do this to you?'

I pulled away.

'*What?*'

He held on to my shoulders. 'The man you were engaged to before me.' He looked me gravely in the eye, as though I had committed a sin.

I took in a breath. I couldn't get enough air. A wave slapped over me. I tried to surface.

'Come on, Dora, don't pretend you don't know what I'm talking about.'

'How did you . . . ? I was never engaged to him. He asked someone else instead.'

'Why was that, do you think?'

I could feel my jaw wobbling. I had to clench my teeth to stop them chattering. My eyes were swimming, and I felt the wetness and soreness of tears spilling down my cheeks.

'Ooh, I see I'm right. He did, didn't he? Mmm?' He clutched my shoulders tightly, pinching the skin hard. 'Did he touch you like me?'

I wept and gasped for air. Still he squeezed – even harder.

'Mmm? Mmm? Like this? Did he touch you like this?'

He reached for my intimate parts again, and I put my hand up to slap him, but before I managed it he defended himself by grabbing my wrists and hurling me against the stove. I hit my head as I fell down, and I found myself sitting at his feet on the cold red tiles. He turned and left.

Before everyone returned that night, he came back to the kitchen to find me sitting at the table with my head in my arms. He went to the sink and wetted a clean dishcloth, and then he gently bathed the back of my head. When he had finished he patted my hair dry and pulled up a chair to sit beside me, putting an arm around me. 'I'm sorry,' he said, sobbing. 'I just can't bear the thought . . . I can't bear the thought of another man touching you.'

I must've lifted a very blotchy, tear-stained face to him, because I had been crying for ages. 'He didn't. We didn't.' I remembered the times by the bilberry bushes when Arthur's touch had made me melt against him, but I told myself that that was not really what Ralph was interested in. He wanted to be the one to take my maidenhead, and he had. 'I bled. Can't you remember? I bled.'

He drew me into him, contrite as it was possible to be. 'I'm sorry, Dora. I'm so sorry. I just can't bear to think of any man . . . I just love you so much. I needed to know.' And then later: 'You promise he didn't even . . . ?'

I promised.

When the others came back, and when we were in bed, I ventured to ask why he thought I'd been engaged to Arthur, and how he knew his name. He turned to face me and stroked my hair, holding my gaze very carefully. 'I went to see Pippa when I was back in England. She's married to him.' That gaze, ready to pounce on a mere morsel.

'I know.' Steady as she goes.

'They have a baby on the way.' Any sign, any sign at all.

'I heard.'

'Well, anyway, she seemed to think you'd been engaged to him before her.'

'No. That's not the case.'

'I see.' He continued to stroke my hair, still paying attention. 'So, anyway, she seemed to think he was as dull as ditchwater and you're well out of it.' He was pushing so hard, no doubt certain that this would produce *something*, surely. Some flicker, if I was lying.

'Well, maybe I am.' I smiled as warmly as I could and kissed him to stop him from seeing any strain on my face.

How dare she. How dare she seduce him and ruin my life and then dismiss him as *dull*. Was a little part of me relieved? No, not at all. All right then, yes. Yes, it probably was.

I suppose it was the coffee that first alerted me. I'd made the coffee at breakfast time and was pouring it for Patsy, and I realized that I didn't want any myself. The smell of it made me nauseous, and I told her.

'*Ça y est!* You're expecting!' she whispered, even though we were the only two in the kitchen at the time. 'I wondered when that was going to happen.'

I looked at her in dismay. Of course, it shouldn't really have been a surprise, but I was ridiculously shocked. Ralph had told me there was no chance of a baby because he had a special way of doing things, and that he was keeping me safe. It had occasionally come to my notice that his special way may not have quite worked, but I knew nothing much about these things and trusted his methods.

A letter arrived from Wales telling me that my father was very ill. Our Mam was not a manipulative person. She would not have said it if it hadn't been true.

We knew it was his lungs, but now they say it's his heart. He's home from the hospital in Cardiff now but he is

not well, Dora. Try to come home. Show your young man
this letter. However busy he is he'll understand about family.
Please try to come home and see him.

I did show it to Ralph, and he said he'd think about it. He'd said
that before, of course, and nothing had happened. I wanted to go home
and see Our Dad and make him proud of me again.

There was still time. We could go to Wales, get married swiftly
somewhere, and then organize a big party at Ralph's father's later on in
the summer . . . in the spring . . . no, we would have to forget sunny
garden parties. But there was still time to make them proud and happy
to see me married.

I thought of Ralph on a little tour of the neighbourhood: Ralph
at number 17, eating Our Mam's *bara brith* in the parlour. Our Dad
sitting in the only armchair. Mrs Price popping her head round the
door for a good nosey and saying, 'There's lovely. I da like a young man
with a healthy appetite, I do. Where'd you find him then, Dora?' Mrs
Pritchard at the Co-op giving him the once over, telling him the spam is
on offer: 'Gwon, take it! Two for the price of one, it is. They don't have
it in France, do they? Better than all that foreign muck, it is. You have
it, love, as a treat on me.' Big Bryn showing us his new van and patting
it: 'They don't make engines like this very often. She's a beauty. Ralph,
is it? You can try her out if you like, since you're a friend of Dora's, like.
I'll show you how to work the gears. Driving's like riding a bicycle.
Gwon – have a go!'

Could I really see him fitting in? Even for a day? I was probably
torn between showing him off and being a little ashamed of him, wanting him to be the man I wanted him to be: the man who loved me, no
matter what, who wanted *me*, not a type.

I thought of the child inside me. I hadn't wanted one yet, but now
that it was there, I felt its presence. The tender little aches in my womb
made me feel its attachment already, although I knew from Patsy that

it was early days, because that was when the nausea came on. No, I definitely wasn't ready for a baby, but now that it was on its way, I felt protective. Strange not knowing if it was a boy or a girl, a Ralph or a Dora, a Rora or a Dalph. Strange to be so satisfied at being grown-up but afraid and excited at the same time. I held on to my news for as long as possible, and that really wasn't very long. I couldn't bear the thought of having a baby before the marquees and the public vows. I was terrified, so I turned to the only person who could help me, the person who would transform things and put them right.

'I'm pregnant,' I said to Ralph's back.

He was at his desk in his study and turned around to me. His puzzled frown melted after a second, and he beamed. I felt a rush of relief. 'An heir! Oh, my little Dora, come here.'

I went towards him and he sat me on his lap. He stroked my face tenderly. 'How are you feeling?'

'All right.'

'Not ecstatic, then?'

I braced myself, but I had rehearsed this moment, so I said what I had to say.

'I'm not . . . not yet . . . I'd like to be . . . I don't want to have a baby until we're married.'

He scrutinized my face as if I had said something difficult to comprehend. He gave a sarcastic, breathy laugh and shook his head. 'Dora, Dora!' He took a deep, exasperated breath. 'I thought you were better than this. I thought you supported me.'

Now it was my turn to look puzzled.

'I do! You know I do. What do you mean?'

'You want me to marry you, is that it?'

'Well, you said you wanted to marry me.'

His jaw dropped open melodramatically. '*Did* I? I can't remember asking you to *marry* me.'

Humiliation came over me like an allergic rash, so sudden and unstoppable I was sure he could see it. 'You said you wanted to spend the rest of your life with me.'

He smiled benignly then. 'And so I do. So I do, darling Dora.' He kissed me gently on the forehead. 'But you must know I don't believe in marriage.'

I drew back.

'Oh, come on, Dora. I'm a socialist. Marriage is a bourgeois institution. We don't need a piece of paper to tell us we can love each other the way nature intended. We're free. We're liberated from all that stuff.'

I stood up. 'My father's a socialist, but he still respected my mother enough to marry her before having children.'

'Well, I'm sure he meant well, but—'

'Your "heir" will be a bastard! No child of mine is going to be a bastard!'

He shook his head. 'So you don't want our child?'

'No, not if we're not married.'

'What exactly do you intend to do about it, then?' I hated the challenge in his voice.

'I'll get rid of it!'

'Oh no you won't!' He rose to his feet as he said it.

'If you hit me, I'll scream!'

He clenched his jaw, clearly signalling an end to the patronizing stance.

'I'll get rid of it!' I challenged again. 'If you don't want to marry me, I'll get rid of it!'

He grabbed hold of my wrists. 'Bribery now, is it? You think you can force me into marriage? You thought you could trick me into it, did you? Thought you'd enjoy the family fortune?'

'I don't want to force you into anything. *You* tricked *me* into coming here with you. *You've* got me into this mess. *You* can get me out of it!'

He threw me backwards, but I was ready for it and stepped back quickly enough to save my head from hitting the wall. He came up to me and grabbed my throat. 'You will *not* kill my child! Do you hear me? You *dare* try to kill my child! You just dare.'

By now he was speaking through clenched teeth. I was choking. I knew that when he let go there would be a shove with it, and I was right. My chest and head hit the wall behind me and I was winded. He left the study, and left me gasping for air.

In retrospect, I don't know why any of this surprised me. Nor do I know why I was surprised that he stopped my visits to the market with Patsy, or that he prevented me from using the telephone by having it disconnected. However, what happened next was enough to surprise anyone. I certainly didn't see it coming.

41

ARTHUR

Let's see. It would've been spring 1953. It must have been about two months after the baby was born and just a day or two after my mother had left. I returned home from work and had a real shock.

The baby was sleeping in the pram in the hall. I edged past to greet Pippa in the kitchen, but she was not there. There was some sign of culinary activity, though: a tin had been opened and the oven was on low. Not in the living room either. I called her name, but there was no answer. I went upstairs to use the bathroom, half expecting to find her there, luxuriating in a bubble bath. When I came out, I became aware of the sound of gentle music. With the roar of the flush still whooshing about the landing, it took a few moments to realize that the music was emanating from the bedroom. Our bedroom.

We only had one radio and that was downstairs, so I couldn't imagine what was going on. The bedroom door was ajar, so I pushed it very gently open.

All I could see to start with was our record player, sitting beside the dressing table and plugged into the socket we normally used for a lamp. The room was in semi-darkness, as the curtains were drawn and the sun was already low outside. When I walked in, the first thing I saw was a candle flickering by the bedside. We never used candles. Then I saw Pippa, lying on her front on top of the bedcovers. She had on black stockings and suspenders, and her beautiful – and now slightly fuller – backside was adorned in pale lacy silk. Her back was completely bare, and her head turned away from me. As I took this in, she propped herself on one elbow and turned her head towards me, her body following. She ran her free hand down the length of her curves, stopping at her hips. She looked at her breasts, as if surprised to see them naked, then looked at me. It was an unmistakable look, the one she had given me almost a year ago.

I kicked my shoes off clumsily and lay down beside her, and she placed my hands where she wanted them. It was too much. I was on my feet again, cursing the buttons and zips on my clothes until I was beside her again. She was magnificent. She wanted me so much. She whimpered and moaned and I could hardly contain myself. I didn't contain myself.

If I'm honest, I had spent most of the previous few months fantasizing about a girl in our office called Vivien. I would wake early in the morning and think about how it would be to creep up on her from behind and bend her gently over the drafting desk, lifting her little pleated skirt. Usually she had let me take her before Pippa woke up. Now it was all coming true with my wife: *my wife*! She was everything I had once thought she was and more. I was deliciously helpless. I was a wreck.

I must have slept afterwards for a little while. When I opened my eyes I still had my leg over hers, and she was pushing at her nails with a cuticle stick. I watched her for a few moments before she noticed me, then she stroked my hair and pulled herself towards me again, assuming a languorous, eyes-half-closed look.

'Darling,' she whispered gently into my ear, 'wasn't that wonderful?'

I probably nodded.

'Wouldn't you like to do that more often?'

Ditto.

'If we had a nanny, we could do it whenever we liked.'

I sighed.

She pouted.

As if on cue, Felicity woke up and started bawling.

'A nanny would deal with that.'

I slumped away from her and looked at the ceiling, my arm across my face as if to protect myself from her pouting and her wiles. 'We can't afford a nanny.'

She was relentless. She rubbed her body against mine with the hint of a whimper.

'You do still want me don't you?'

I had to stand firm on the nanny business. We really didn't have the money. That was the last I saw of her silk underwear. She tried to sabotage my resolve with the occasional innuendo or lustful look, but it all evaporated far too quickly when I said, 'No nanny.' After a while, the insincerity of her lust began to hurt. If it had all been fake, she was astonishingly good at it. Unfortunately, the speed with which she could turn it on and off said it all, and I was pained to remember – couldn't help but remember – our first sexual encounter. Though I couldn't, for the life of me, imagine why she might have wanted to trick me into marriage.

Before long, my Vivien fantasies started up again with a vengeance. She was a sweet girl and she smiled a lot. She didn't smile at me in particular, she smiled at everyone. She had a gentle and generous nature. Nothing was too much for her. She would fetch me cups of tea and dry my coat near the radiator if it was wet; she would ask after my baby and my wife and give me magazines she had finished with for Pippa to read. I usually put these in the bin on my way home, because I couldn't bear to watch Pippa scoff at the knitting patterns and the sherry trifles. Vivien wore soft knitwear, on the tight side. She had short-sleeved jumpers in pastel blue, pink and cream, and with each she wore a matching cardigan and a string of plastic pearls. She put her hair up on each temple with blue plastic combs, a little old-fashioned for a twenty-year-old.

Sometimes, in the room between my office and the main draftsroom, I would catch her reapplying her lipstick or powdering her nose. I used to imagine that she did these things for me, but I knew it was just that she was going out over her lunch break. Once, I saw her change her flat shoes for a pair of maroon high heels that matched her handbag. She wore those high heels in my dreams. She never took them off, not even . . . And once, once I saw her going through her handbag and take out a little . . . you know . . . woman's thing, and for weeks afterwards all I could think about was where she put it and that she put it there under the same roof as my office – yards away, probably, only yards away.

I could hardly bear it. I thought about asking if she could be transferred to another office, but I couldn't bear the thought of that either. Once, when I gave her some files, her cardigan brushed against my wrist. I must have almost flinched.

'That's very . . . soft . . . soft wool.'

'It's angora.'

'Ah.'

'British Home Stores, if your wife's interested.'

I looked at her standing there in front of me, the pastel cardigan over the tight soft jumper, the breasts bursting to get out, the pleated skirt that I had so often lifted at dawn, the big, candid eyes gazing expectantly, waiting for something more, hoping to please me if she could find more clues to my well-being.

'No, I'm afraid my wife isn't interested.'

She looked puzzled. I had knitted her brow. I was a monster.

'Doesn't she like fashion?'

I wanted to touch her. I was glad there was a desk covering my lap. I loathed myself. This wasn't who I was.

'She's just not as interesting – interested! – as . . . as you.'

Vivien beamed. She smiled in a way Dora used to smile, with every sinew of her face. I started to follow her movements. I followed her out one lunchtime to see where she went (a meeting with a stumpy-looking girlfriend in a cafe). I even bought silk underwear for her – the sort she wore under her skirt in my fantasies (plain virginal white with lace) – although I never gave it to her, of course. I kept it locked in one of my cabinets and took it out from time to time and fondled it when no one was there.

In May I hired a home-help for Pippa. She came for two hours a day. At least the baby got fed and the beds were made. It didn't help our marriage much. Pippa was holding out for a nanny or nothing, so all I had in bed was her back and a series of exasperated sighs, until sleep and Vivien blocked them out.

To be honest, I was crawling up the walls. I think I went a bit mad. I was afraid of what I might do next.

One cold spring morning Len called into my office.

'Fancy a jar at the pub tonight, mate?'

It was odd: the breezy message did not tally with the frown on his face.

'I don't think I will, thanks.'

He stood there, still frowning. 'Only, I need to have a word.'

'Oh, well . . . lunchtime, then? It's just that Pippa won't like it if I go out. You know how it is.'

'Actually . . . it was Pippa I needed to talk to you about.'

He was fumbling with a file in his hands, flicking the corner of it and looking anxiously at the edge of my desk. I asked him to shut the door and invited him to sit down and tell me what it was. I could see he would much rather have a pint in his hand, but my interest had been sparked now, and anyway, I wanted to keep my lunch hour free in case I had an encounter with Vivien.

'The thing is . . . the thing is, Arthur, my Maureen is a bit worried about Pippa, and I promised her I'd say something to you. It's none of my business, so please don't think I'm criticizing or anything, it's just that Maureen's at her wits' end.'

'What's been happening?'

'What's been happening is that nearly every day now your Pippa calls by and leaves the baby with Maureen. She always has some good reason: has to go to the doctor's, has to go and see her sick mother, has to go to the dentist's, needs something urgently in town. You know, it's probably all true and that, it's just that Maureen has her hands full herself. She's got three of her own to cope with, and like she says, she wouldn't mind popping into town herself sometimes. And the thing is, Pippa doesn't come back and pick up the baby. She's away all day sometimes. Just gets back at five or something. Maureen says I have to tell you. She doesn't like to say "no" – how can she? She's a good, kind woman is Mo, and she can't imagine refusing someone in need. And it seems your wife is always in need.' He sighed heavily. 'I'm sorry, mate. I've got to look after my wife, haven't I?'

It took a few seconds for this to sink in. I had, for many weeks, heard accounts from Pippa about how dull her time had been, spent all day at home with the baby, and I had felt guilty because of it, had planned to take her away somewhere special, and to buy her little treats to make up for it. 'I had no idea. Len, I'm really sorry. I'm sorry. You mean she's left the baby there all day?'

'Lately, yes. It started off with just an hour or two, but lately she says she'll just be an hour, and then she leaves it all day. I think Maureen made an excuse yesterday. Said she was going away for the day, but then she felt guilty and didn't dare leave the house in case your wife saw her. That's no way to live, is it?'

'No. You're absolutely right.'

I put my head in my hands. 'I don't know what to do.'

'Maureen reckons she should see someone. I mean, she thinks Pippa might be going a bit . . . you know.'

'Bonkers?'

'Well, I don't know. Maureen says it happens sometimes, after a baby.'

I stared out of the window at the blank grey-white sky and pictured Pippa in a mental asylum and poor Felicity motherless. How would I cope? For the briefest of moments, Vivien swooped into my head and took care of my child. And she took care of me too.

'I'll, um . . . I'll see what I can do. I'll have a word. She won't bother Maureen again, I'll make sure of that.'

So she had her way. A full-time nanny, which I couldn't afford, and days spent doing what the hell she liked. I made it clear that the nanny option was dependent on her seeking help. Of course there was all sorts of drama about that. Did I think she was mad? Was I going to lock her in the attic like Mr Rochester? And so on. However, after a few days she surprised me. A London friend of hers had recommended a psychiatrist, and she would agree to see him once a week in London. This meant more expense: three guineas per session! Not to mention the travel. I agreed, but only for two months. After that she would have to find someone cheaper and local. I also travelled up to London with her one Friday afternoon – time off I could ill afford – in order to take her to the first session. I didn't trust Pippa, and I had visions of her taking my money and sloping off to Harrods on a spending spree. I still had an uncomfortable feeling there was nothing wrong with my wife except her own personality, but what did I know?

Life, after that, became far easier. The nanny was a young girl called Beryl who showered affection on Felicity, cooked simple, wholesome meals and kept our bathroom clean. She wore a white apron over fitted skirts and tied her long, fair hair up in a ponytail. It was all I could do sometimes to refrain from touching the little wisps at the nape of her neck or from openly eyeing the changing shape of her skirt as she shifted neatly inside it. Still, Pippa came home from her expeditions refreshed, and she was better company slumped on the sofa watching television and not lifting a finger to help with her baby than she had been before, grumbling and moaning but still not lifting a finger to do anything. She was no better company in the bedroom, though, and I reminded her of how she'd said that a nanny would make our lovemaking possible again. But, of course, there was no logic with Pippa. She never played a fair game. She would simply yawn and turn her back on me with an implied 'Yes but not tonight', or she would tease me and get me excited and then pout, saying I should make love to Beryl if I was that desperate. Then she would turn her back on me as if I already had. She would let me coax her back at enormous length, allowing me to touch her and pleasure her, but when I reassured her that I hadn't laid a finger on Beryl, she seemed to lose her interest completely. Well, I don't need to go into all that. Let's just say that she didn't keep her side of the bargain.

Some things about her did change, though. Her psychiatrist was a tall, calm man called Eric Dumonnier. I've no idea if he was French or not, because he spoke with a well-to-do English accent. When I first shook hands with him, I remember thinking, *I don't know if you're going to have an affair with my wife, but good luck, mate*. Actually, I don't know if I really thought that or not. I'm probably just making it up because it's what I'd think now. I've no idea whether they had an affair. I do wonder if Pippa had any real passion for sex at all, or whether she simply knew how to use her sexuality for her own ends. She was good at seduction, but that was it. There seemed to be no artless desire, no passionate joy for it. However, Eric Dumonnier was to have a huge impact on our lives, one way or another.

After two sessions of analysis with Dumonnier, Pippa began to tell me in the evenings how she was suffering from post-partum anxiety. It didn't have a special name then, but I suppose the specialist had seen post-natal depression enough to recognize it and was smart enough not to see it – like everyone else did – as a form of madness. I wasn't convinced he had got this right; Pippa seemed too easily transformed by a spending spree to be depressed. However, as the weeks went by, she mentioned new insights that he had given her, and one of these was what he called 'survivor's guilt'. At first I was sceptical, but the more she talked about it the more I empathized with this myself. Was this me? Did *I* have survivor's guilt? I became intrigued, but after hours of hearing my wife enthuse about the idea I began to resent paying bloody 'Eric' three bloody guineas an hour to state the ruddy obvious and give it a special name. Of course she had survivor's guilt! We all did. Although I couldn't for the life of me see why Pippa was a special case. *She* hadn't lost a brother or a sister, and I was pretty sure she hadn't lost much sleep over anyone else's.

She seemed to become so self-absorbed. I suppose I should have been grateful to be paying someone else to take all that off my hands, but somehow she just talked about herself even more and became increasingly cheerful about her own special psychological problems. She was enjoying being a victim, although of what I'm not sure, and I don't think she was sure either. But she felt special and entitled, and in a couple of months she felt so special that she had an idea to write a book.

Yes, a book about herself.

Of course, if you knew Pippa, it was a totally logical next step. All about her. And that Dumonnier chap encouraged her. He was the person who put the idea into her head. To be honest, I don't think he saw Pippa as an individual. As soon as he learnt about her extraordinary childhood experience, he simply saw her as a victim of *that*. He saw the sinking of *The City of India* and eight days starving and thirsty, adrift in the mid-Atlantic in a small boat, as the defining feature of my wife. All right – put like that, it does seem pretty significant. It's not an everyday occurrence, but what I mean is that I don't think he looked *any* further. He was so excited by it. Well, that's how I saw it, anyway. Of course, Pippa would say I was just jealous because I hadn't thought of writing a book about it myself, but I don't think I was. I was *cynical* – and of course far too busy – but actually I was really quite pleased to see her so enlivened and happy. She stopped moping and became truly engaged in something for the first time since I'd known her. She would sit for hours writing, catch the train to London to see Eric, to see her old friends and to scout around the literary agents, and she would come back with cheeks aglow and eyes sparkling. She smiled a lot more. She had a sense of purpose. There were 'things she needed to say', and she had the chance to tell the world.

I suppose, like every partner of a writer, I hoped to God I wasn't in it.

42

DORA

It must've been the early spring of 1953, a few weeks into my captivity. Patsy had shown considerable concern about Ralph's restrictions on my movements but had been told how worried he was about my health and my state of mind. He didn't want me doing anything stupid, he said, that might lead to the loss of the baby. She knew exactly what he meant by that, and I think she would've told him to make a decent woman of me, had she not been so concerned for their jobs. Anyway, she and I were poring over Claudine's homework when Ralph came home with an unexpected guest.

The woman was in her late twenties: quiet and aloof, with short, brown curly hair. It was her quietness that fooled you. She had what was known then as a 'gamine' look, but she was very pale and seemed fragile, almost breakable. Ralph introduced her as 'Sophie'. Ralph sat her down at the kitchen table with us and nodded at me and in the direction of the pantry to fetch some bread and cheese.

It was startlingly quiet.

'Are you married, then?' asked Claudine, who was always uncomfortable with silences.

'Her husband is in Paris,' Ralph replied for her, a little gruffly I thought.

'Why has he left you here?' Claudine was unperturbed.

'He hasn't left her here. *But*, Sophie will be staying with us, so I want you to make her feel at home.' He smiled at Sophie, who managed to smile back, but only at him.

Ralph rejected all my attempts to find out more about her. I became so angry and frustrated with him that I went off to sleep in Tighe's empty room and reclaimed it for myself. He seemed to make no objection. Sophie was housed in a small bedroom which had been used to store junk but had recently been decorated by Denis, and for which Patsy and I had made curtains in early preparation for the baby. I'm not sure how much Sophie slept in it, though.

There were local rumours that Sophie had been beaten up by her husband and that she couldn't have children. *Out of the frying pan*, I thought. Anyway, I got nowhere with Ralph about it, and then one evening Denis came right out and asked him over dinner. Ralph replied in French, and Denis threw his hands in the air, making sounds of disbelief, while Sylvain blew air from his blown cheeks, a little less dramatically.

'A commune?' said Patsy. 'You're creating a commune here?'

'I've made no secret of it for some time.'

'What's a "commune"?' asked Claudine.

'It means we're all equal. We're all working together, we'll share the profits. This is my philosophy: what's mine is yours, and what's yours is mine.'

'*N'importe quoi!*' said Denis under his breath, throwing his hands about again.

'No one owns anything. We share everything.'

'Can I have the new bedroom, then?' asked Claudine, hopefully. 'Sometimes?'

'*Ta gueule!*' said her father.

'There's no need to worry, Denis. Nobody comes off badly. No one *owns* anything: people or property.'

Patsy tried desperately to introduce a note of humour, terrified that her husband might blow his top. 'You hear that, Claudine? You're not mine and Papa's any more. You belong to everyone.'

'Maman!'

'Take her – you can have her!'

'*Maman!*'

'It's okay, *chérie.*' Claudine was genuinely distressed. 'No one else will want you.' She put her arm around her daughter and pulled her in close, kissing her loudly on the head.

'Sophie is going to live with us permanently. And this is just a start. We'll add more rooms. We'll expand.'

I thought about ways I could leave Les Amandiers. Patsy would not dare to assist me openly. Despite her private sympathy and her feisty nature, she was too afraid for their future. I didn't know how to find help in France. The only way I could terminate the pregnancy was to go to England. Even there it would be illegal, and I would need money. I don't think I seriously considered getting rid of it; I just felt cheated and trapped. I wanted choices. I was angry at all the closed doors. But what if I *was* free to go home? I saw myself retching on the swaying cross-Channel ferry, disembarking with a heavy suitcase at Dover. I pictured the train journey from Dover to London, from London to Newport, and the Joneses' bus from Newport up into the Valleys. There would be no fanfare for the arrival of an unmarried daughter with a swollen belly. Hadn't I caused them enough shame? And yet home was where I wanted to be. If only I could persuade Ralph to take me.

Home. I longed to see Our Dad before anything terrible happened to him, to smell his old musty jacket and hold his fag-yellowed fingers, and I longed for the wisdom of my parents. They would know what to do. I might heap shame on them, but they would know what to do. Ralph no longer seemed a reliable source of wisdom. A part of me would happily forgive his outbursts and settle for a man who loved me enough, if not always in the way I'd hoped for. But what I found hardest of all, as I thought about the child growing inside me, for better or worse, was that I was totally on my own. This was a decision I would have to make for myself, and whether I chose to stay or to leave, I knew it was going to be a struggle.

I had written to Jenny, and she had written back, telling me she could try to help, but I must get myself over there *soon*, before the pregnancy was too advanced. After that there were no more letters – and no letters from home either. Ralph always went to meet the postman early each morning and would bring the letters to the table. There were never any for me after that.

I knew my passport would not be in my suitcase, and I was right. Life repeated itself. Whenever Ralph was out of the house, I searched. I looked in every room, under every mattress and bed, in curtain linings, in shoes, in pockets, in books. I even managed to search the outhouses, and Patsy searched the car for me, but there was no sign of it anywhere. I don't think I wanted to leave him for good. It wasn't that. I wanted to go home, to visit my parents. I wanted the freedom to choose.

'Don't you think it's a stroke of luck, coming across Sophie like that?' Ralph said one morning.

'Is it?'

'Come on, Dora, keep up! She can't have children.'

'I see.'

'And you don't want yours,' he said, 'so you can give your baby to Sophie to bring up.'

I was aghast.

'I'm not giving my baby away to anyone.'

'But you don't want a baby – you said so.'

'I don't want a baby outside marriage, that's what I said. Outside marriage. *You* keep up, Ralph!'

He made as if to come towards me, but stopped, breathing deeply. 'Sophie will have your baby. She'll bring it up. What's yours is hers, remember?'

43

ARTHUR

My wife seemed to have come home at last, but all I saw of her was the back of her head, and all I heard from her was the aggressive tapping of her typewriter. I was pleased for her, because she seemed to have found a purpose, and that released me from a certain anxiety I had about her sense of entrapment by motherhood. On the other hand, I sometimes felt I was supporting two live-in lodgers, and only one of them did anything useful.

Felicity flourished under Beryl's care. She warmed to the regular feeds and the regular bedtimes. She smiled and gurgled a lot. By May of that year, she was four months old and would turn her head and beam at me when I arrived home, and when she did her eyes nearly disappeared. They were changing, and I could see she was not going to have Pippa's dazzling ones but my grey-blue ones. A cloud of dark hair was sprouting from her soft head, and her cheeks were peachy. What a joy she was to come home to! It was a far cry from the days of her long-faced mother and tins of corned beef. Now I had a yelp of delight from Felicity and braised beef with two vegetables from Beryl. Just the tapping from Pippa, of course, but to be honest, I was glad to have her out of the way.

Work had been very stressful since the previous year, when our jet engine developed difficulties and was found responsible for a couple of air crashes. Many of us thought we would lose our jobs, but I was still there, hanging on, and it looked as though a new project for a passenger jet might save my bacon.

Pippa had been oblivious to all this, since she never asked me about my work. She saw me as a man who went out of a door in the morning and came back through it in the evening. Regular as clockwork and boring as hell. She even started sleeping in the study. Whether Beryl had really told her that the tapping was keeping the baby awake or not, I'm not sure, but it was an excuse to move the cot into Beryl's room, and soon Pippa was giving pretexts about late-night inspiration and not wanting to wake me. It wasn't long before it became permanent, and I became a lonely man in our double bed. Still, she was happier than I'd known her, and she often went up to London to see 'Eric' or her friends or someone with literary connections. I encouraged her in this. It was almost a relief to have her out of the way. What I hadn't bargained on was her deceit.

Ah! You might imagine I was going to say that Pippa was unfaithful, but that's not what I'm referring to. No. She had been lying to me since I had first known her, as I was about to find out.

44

DORA

Everyone said the spring of that year was slow coming, although to me it was early. March was brighter than any March I had known. But then April burst out, opening every bud and warming the earth long before breakfast. I had never seen anything like it. The skies were a deep blue with crisp clouds over the mountains that overlooked Les Amandiers from a distance. The beauty of it all was a torment. I longed to be back home, where I knew the rain was probably lashing the mountainsides, and the wet window panes would be distorting the outline of the coal tip out the back of Our Mam and Dad's house.

I did not attempt to go to Ralph in that time, and he didn't attempt to come to me. I lay in Tighe's old room at night and thought about Sophie in the 'nursery'. Once or twice I got up in the small hours and hovered by her door on the way to the bathroom. Once I thought I heard her breathing, mostly I did not. Sometimes I would rise early in the hope of seeing if her room was empty or not, but the door would be closed, and I would be none the wiser. I wondered if she was trying to see if he could perhaps give her a baby, if it wasn't after all some difficulty of her husband's and not hers that had led to her childlessness. I wondered if I should warn her about Ralph's temper.

In the end I did nothing. I slept, I got up, I did chores, I slept. Patsy found an earring, which wasn't mine, when she was changing Ralph's sheets. I avoided Ralph as much as possible, nursing my hurt privately. Patsy and Denis could see my wounded heart, of course, and were especially kind to me. Claudine would often come into my room at night saying that she couldn't sleep so that she could snuggle up to me. I would tell her stories about Wales, or about princes and princesses, or animals that could talk, and we would drift off to sleep together. She was a cheeky little thing, perky, cheerful and nosey, but I loved her. There was a simplicity about her tenderness for me that always moved me; and when she rested her little head on my shoulders and said she felt safe after a bad dream, the feeling of being needed filled me with something like joy.

One night I was woken by Claudine's arm across my chest.

'Dora?' she whispered. 'Where's Forth With?'

'What?' The shuttered blackness gave no hint of the time.

'Where is it?'

'No idea. Why do you ask?'

She sighed heavily. 'I went into the living room when Ralph was burning stuff on the fire, and he got really stern and told me to leave Forth With. How can I leave somewhere if I don't know where it is?'

'It's not a place,' I said sleepily. 'It means "straight away".' I propped myself up on one shoulder. 'What "stuff" was he burning?'

'Paper – a letter or something. And he said I was a bloody pest.'

Letters.

She sounded close to tears. 'He thinks I'm a cockroach.'

'No.'

'I dreamt I was cockroach.'

I pulled her in close to me. 'You're a lovely butterfly, and you don't have to leave forthwith. Stay and sleep.'

I too had the most terrifying dreams.

It must have been the idea of a nursery and the thought of Sophie sleeping in it. I pictured a rocking horse. I had never seen one until that time on board the ship. I suppose it was bound to happen, that it would trigger memories of that other one, the beautiful rocking horse on *The City of India*. I saw it again and again. It had been years since I'd last dreamt of it, but now I couldn't escape from its beautiful deceit. In the dream I'm walking towards it, holding the hand of my cabin-mate, Janet. We're walking towards the glorious white-and-red rocking horse with its golden mane, and then suddenly there is no floor, there's a drop of hundreds of feet into the very depths of the ship under the sea. I try to scream, but I have no voice. I'm falling, and Janet is reaching out for my hand, but I'm falling and trying to scream . . . and I wake up with a pathetic 'ach' sound coming out of my mouth in a strangled whisper, with sweat all over my chest and in my hair.

One morning I woke after a dream like this and opened the shutters. It was bright outside already, even though it was only five-thirty. I made my way to the bathroom and washed. The house was silent. I dressed quietly and went outside for a walk. It had been a long time since I had walked outdoors unaccompanied.

I made my way to the road, and although I had nothing with me – not even a handbag or a ten-franc note – I had an urgent desire to escape, to hitch a lift from the next car that went past. I sat under a bush near the entrance to Les Amandiers. If Ralph came, I could hide easily. I don't know what sort of bush it was, but the leaves were thick and fragrant, and it was a pleasure just to sit there in the sunshine, awaiting whatever vehicle happened to go by.

Nothing appeared. No car, no van.

I sat there a long time, filling my lungs with the scent of spring. At last I heard a motor in the distance. I listened as the sound came closer. Then it seemed to become quieter. Slowly, to my dismay, it petered out altogether.

I was about to get up and go back to the house when I heard another sound: someone was whistling. I stiffened. Peering out of the leaves, I looked about. Along the road a bicycle was coming, and as it approached I could see who it was. The young postman dismounted and propped his bicycle right next to me. As he sorted a bunch of letters in his hands, he spotted me and leant down to my hideout.

He grinned, delighted. I managed a smile in return.

'*Vous vous cachez, mademoiselle?*'

My French was pretty awful, considering how long I'd been there. I'd picked up a fair bit of vocabulary, but how to put it together was another matter. I put my finger to my lips to ask him not to give me away. He looked about, and crouched down beside me.

'*Qu'est-ce qu'il y a?*' He looked genuinely concerned.

'*Lettres,*' I ventured, pointing at them. '*Pour moi?*' I pointed at myself. '*Lettres de la Grande-Bretagne?*' I pointed at myself again. '*Pour moi?*'

He nodded and looked through the letters. '*Rien aujourd'hui,*' he said apologetically. '*Vous êtes anglaise?*'

He seemed excited at the prospect, so I didn't complicate things by mentioning Wales. '*Oui. Anglaise.*'

'*Ah!* Good morning! Goodnight!' He pronounced the 'night' as though a doctor had asked him to open his mouth and say 'aaah', and I giggled.

'Good morning. I'm Dora.'

'Doh-ra? Me, I am Marius.'

'Mari-oos?'

'*Ça y est!* Marius.'

He smiled some more, a wide infectious smile.

'*Demain?*' I ventured. '*Lettres? Moi . . . ici.*'

I got to my feet, afraid that Ralph would come down for the post. Marius rose too and stuffed the letters into the mailbox that was nailed to a grey post by the side of the road at the entrance to Les Amandiers.

'*À demain*,' he said smiling, slinging his leg over his bicycle.

'Secret,' I said. '*Secret?*'

He beamed and rode off, waving behind him as he went: 'Gooood-baaay!'

I was elated. I made my way back to the house through some undergrowth, feeling less trapped than before.

Patsy and Denis both knew I was looking for my passport, and they knew why. The pair of them had been on the lookout for it for weeks now, but none of us had had any luck. Denis had even found the excuse of a leaking roof to go up into the attic in case it was there somewhere. Instead he found a pretty big hole in the roof that had been letting in water over the winter. It would need professionals in to mend it, and it was going to cost a good three thousand francs. When he told Ralph this, Ralph said he would just write off to his Aunty Bee. Denis wasn't at all happy. Aunty Bee employed him to do all the maintenance, and if she thought he wasn't up to it, she might sack him. This was nonsense, according to Ralph. He would ask Aunty Bee for *five* thousand francs, and he and Denis could share the profit. I was appalled when I heard this. Denis pretended to be appalled as well, but he was ready to take the money. It made me shudder to think Ralph would so willingly cheat his kind aunt out of two thousand francs.

Wherever Ralph had hidden it, it was a clever hiding place. I hoped he hadn't destroyed it. Denis had run out of ideas too, but what he did tell me, though, was that he had seen Ralph put a letter in the fire one day, so I felt hopeful that letters were still coming for me.

The following morning, and every morning I could manage, I was up before Ralph and waiting in the bushes for Marius. There were no letters from Britain, and I became even more worried about Our Dad. Once Ralph came down to the road as we were talking quietly, but Marius was on his feet at the sound of the gravel crunching, and he handed the letters to Ralph with commendable calm. Ralph thanked him and walked back up to the house. Marius assured me that he hadn't seen me and suspected nothing. He referred to Ralph as '*l'Anglais*' and asked if he had been '*méchant*' towards me. I didn't answer him, but his smile disappeared, and I knew he would help me. I knew he was sweet on me, and I didn't want to use him or anything, but to be honest, I was growing to like him too. I couldn't wait for the morning sunlight and the prospect of seeing him. I believed him, I think, when he said Ralph had suspected nothing (I think Ralph's mind was all on Sophie at the time), but even so, I decided to step up my hunt for the passport.

It was an evening in late April when I found myself alone in the kitchen with Ralph. It was Sylvain's birthday. The others were outside on the terrace, and he had come in for a bottle of champagne while I was clearing some dishes.

'Ralph,' I said suddenly, full of determination, 'I need to talk to you.'

He lifted the bottle of champagne from the rack and tore off the foil.

'Come,' he said, motioning to the stairs.

I should have insisted on talking to him there in the kitchen. I don't know why I didn't. He scared me, I suppose. Anyway, I went with him to his bedroom, a room I hadn't been invited to for some time.

'What is it?' His voice was disarmingly gentle, and I was afraid he was going to try to make love to me, ring the changes a bit from Sophie.

'I need my passport. Where is it?'

'Your passport? Why ever do you need that?'

'My father's ill. You know he is. He could be dying. I just want to go and visit him.' I carefully avoided mentioning that he had promised to take me home himself some months back and had broken his promise. I tried to sound as reasonable as possible.

'Why should he be dying? Ill is not the same as dying.'

'But he might be! He was *very* ill, my mother said. *Very.* She doesn't exaggerate stuff. I'm afraid . . . I'm afraid . . .'

'Oh, don't fret, Dora.' He put the champagne bottle on the bedside table, approached me and put his hands on my hips. It was an effort not to flinch. 'Surely if he was *really* ill, they would have written again. And yet you've heard nothing.'

I couldn't look him in the eye in case he saw my fury. I swallowed and spoke to the floor: 'I . . . just want you to give me my passport. Why won't you give it to me?'

He began to stroke my hips and to run his hands up and down my body. 'But why should I have it? Mm?'

I was desperate. 'I promise I'll come back. Just let me go for a visit. Please. *Please*, Ralph.'

'But I told you, I don't know where it is.' He continued caressing me and pushed his fingers inside the waistband of my skirt. 'Oh dear, we are getting a bit too big for this, aren't we?'

'Well I need some new clothes, but you won't let me out to buy any!'

'Tut-tut. Don't get cross with me. Of course you can go out. Where can you buy material? Orange? I'll take you to Orange next week.'

All this time he didn't stop touching me. He undid my skirt as if to relieve me from its tightness, and he slipped it off me. He continued with my blouse and my petticoat. I felt cheapened and angry. I wanted to push him away, but I knew what would happen if I did. And now I had the baby inside me to think of too.

'I'm sorry – you have to stop! I'm sorry, Ralph. I can't share you. You've chosen Sophie. I can't share you.'

I waited, heart racing, for the anger.

He smiled.

'You've got it bad, haven't you?'

He ignored my protest and continued in his quest for my intimate parts.

'*Ralph!* I don't share your ideas . . . I don't want to . . .'

'Mmm? You don't want to what?'

'It's all right for you, isn't it? I carry your child and you sleep with who you like because "what's mine is yours and what's yours is mine"! All very handy. But what if I started sleeping with the other men in the house? What would you think of that?'

He gripped my shoulders very hard. He pushed me down on the bed, and I can't say it was love that he made. It was cruel. It made me bleed.

I pleaded with him: 'But I'm carrying your child! Don't hurt your baby!'

He sneered.

'*My* child? *Mine?*'

He let go of me then – pushed me away from him on the bed.

'You come here telling me that child is mine, when you've as good as told me you sleep with other men!'

'I don't!'

He snarled at me, teeth clenched. 'Don't tell me that child is mine! It could be anyone's! *Anyone's!* Oh, you'd like that, wouldn't you? Tricking me into marriage? Then I find a little Frédéric or a Sylvain or a Denis inheriting the family home. Oh, yes, you'd love that, wouldn't you? Hmm? *Hmm?*'

I would hate to tell anyone what he did. I thought it would never stop. I lay on the bed shaking, not daring to move or speak. He dressed and left. I heard him mutter something in an angry voice to Sophie, who must've come looking for him. She didn't venture into his room, though, which was a shame, because she would've seen something to enlighten her.

I remembered his family home. I remembered the antlers on the wall and all the dark heavy furniture. I remembered his stepmother

talking about his mother, saying that Ralph's father 'may have . . .
treated her rather badly'. Badly. In that room on that day, I completely
let go of any wish to marry Ralph, no matter what reconciliation he
offered me in the future.

I lay on the bed for nearly two hours, sore and weeping. I stared for
some time at the wire on the top of the champagne bottle, which was
lying beside me, and then I had to turn away from it. I gazed instead at
the rainbow lozenges on the bedcover that were so familiar to me. Red,
orange, yellow, green, blue, indigo, violet. They were staggered in the
next row, and the row after that. I traced them with my finger and saw
how the pattern repeated itself.

He took me to Orange. We went by bus, because the petrol would have
been too expensive, and the car was not that reliable.

Passing through the Vaucluse countryside, I felt like a prisoner
allowed to look over the prison wall. The vines were beginning to show
lush leaves that were bright in the early May sunshine. Pink rooftops,
tall cypresses, men in berets: the view through the bus window looked
like a continuous painting of Provence.

Orange was beautiful.

I was dismayed at its beauty. I felt false walking its streets.

It was a game, you see. The thing about abuse is that it becomes a
sinister sort of game. By that I do not mean that it's enjoyable – at least,
certainly not for its victims. What I mean is that you are forever having
to think one move ahead. Ralph's last attack really marked the end for
me, but I couldn't let him know that. Knowledge that it was all over
for me would have signalled the certainty of my need to escape, and it
was crucial that he be lulled into a false sense of security with me. Of
course he suspected my longing for escape, otherwise he would have let
me come to Orange by myself or with Patsy. He was keeping a close eye
on me. But when he had seen me the following morning barely able to

walk, his fervent apology had to be received by acceptance on my part. I didn't know how long I could play-act like this. Smiling at his jokes, taking his arm, letting him pretend he was looking after me, when all the time I was fighting back the urge to spit at him. This falsity, born of the need for self-preservation, weighed on me like a heavy cloak around my shoulders as I walked the ancient sunny streets of Orange.

Knowing it would give him a chance to show off, I asked if the town had anything to do with oranges, and he explained that the name was based on a Celtic settlement named Aurasio, which had become Auranja in Provençal. It may sound silly, but that little boost to his ego gave me a few extra notches of confidence in my safety.

He took me first to a fabric shop, where I bought three metres each of two floral cottons: one was white with red poppies, and the other was pale blue with deep blue flowers on it. I also bought a pattern for a maternity dress, two zips and some thread. This allowed me to thank him profusely, which gave me another safety notch. He was feeling very good about himself by the time he took me to the Roman theatre. I was speechless. I could see he was enjoying my awe, and I let him. As we walked around in the sunshine and he talked about its history, all I could think of was the cruel sport that had inspired such beautiful architecture. I thought of cruelty passed on from generation to generation and wondered how far we'd come. Still the cruelty, but now without the architecture.

Ralph took me for a coffee before we caught the bus home. We sat on the main street in the sunshine and watched the passers-by.

'If it's a boy, we'll call him Jeremy Richard. Richard's my father's name, and he'll like that.'

'And if it's a girl?'

'You can call her what you like. She won't inherit. He won't mind what you call her, as long as it's not after a film star or something vulgar like that.'

The idea that Ralph's father should have any say in the naming of a baby Ralph had so recently disowned filled me with renewed fury – fury that I presented to him as a warm smile, which I hoped was convincing. Another notch, I hoped.

When I asked where the cafe's toilets were, I noticed the alarm that swept briefly across his face. Like me, he was playing a game, then.

'It won't be a *toilette anglaise*, you know. You might want to wait until we get back.'

He must have realized he was sounding too desperate, because he swiftly smiled and said they would be at the back of the shop. I found the toilet, and it was indeed just a hole in the floor with footrests either side. I thought about the back door I had seen on my way in. I pictured myself slipping out into a little alleyway behind, hitching my way to Calais, explaining that my passport had been lost, finding a way. A pregnant woman, alone, surely there would be a way to get me back home . . . But I knew that wasn't how to play this game. The thing to do was to go right back out there willingly and sit down and smile. That way he would trust me just a little more, and I needed to build up his trust until he felt he could take his eyes off me long enough for me to take my chance. It was a slow, careful game, and one I was beginning to get the hang of.

I sat down opposite him and said he had been right about the toilets.

'Did you manage okay?'

He sounded so full of concern. He even put his hand on mine. I didn't flinch. I made myself look straight into his eyes, as lovingly as I knew how. I smiled and simpered, as I thought, *My child will not have a cruel man for a father, and will* never *be called Jeremy Richard.*

We went arm in arm to the bus stop and chatted amicably all the way home. I hated the falsity. I hated myself for that.

45

ARTHUR

I found something very peculiar that belonged to Pippa. When I saw it, I had that feeling you get when something isn't right, but because I could make no sense of it I let it go. I should have paid more attention.

We had a phone call from Pippa's mother. Cynthia occasionally rang up at inconvenient moments having had a skinful, but on this occasion I answered the phone and she barely slurred her words at all. She was clearly in a genuine panic. It seemed that she had received a letter from the family solicitor telling her she had one month to vacate the house.

'Why? Do you have any idea why?'

'The bastard's turfing me out. That horrid man wants to live in it.'

The horrid man was Pippa's father, and he had got wind of the fact that Pippa was married and that the only person remaining in the family home was his ex-wife.

'Can he do that? Doesn't he have to make provision for you?'

There was a long silence before she explained that she had been divorced from Pippa's father for ten years and had only been allowed to live in the house until Pippa's twenty-first birthday, or until Pippa married. She had managed to stave him off before by claiming that Pippa still lived at home and that it would be cruel to make his daughter homeless. Now someone had told him the truth, and he had served notice on her.

As for provision, he had indeed provided for her, giving her an allowance each month. This was to continue, but at a reduced rate now that Pippa had married and left home. You couldn't really blame him for being annoyed. Cynthia had deceived him by keeping quiet about Pippa's marriage to me. She must've known he would find out at some point, but by tricking him she had provoked this one-month ultimatum. She rabbited on for ages, letting go of even more information about her ex-husband having had two children by another woman and how it wasn't fair. She wept and wailed on the telephone, cross with me because I wasn't sufficiently indignant for her.

'Let me speak to Philippa! Put my daughter on the phone!'

Whilst Pippa was talking to her in the hallway, I sat in the living room and pondered something else I had just learnt from Cynthia: the house was never going to be inherited by Pippa, since her father now had two sons by his new wife, and any inheritance went down the male line. Pippa had known this when she married me.

It'll be mine when Daddy dies.

The prospect of inheriting Ashleycroft Hall was not the reason I married Pippa, but I must say it had a huge bearing on my financial thinking for the future. One day, I had thought, we would move into that grand old house and have more children. We would have room to expand. I could sell the house in Bristol or let it out, and we would be able to afford the lifestyle that Pippa craved: holidays abroad, a car, garden parties or whatever. It was only a distant thought, but it was always present, somewhere between an aspiration and a free insurance policy.

I was grappling with Pippa's deceit when she swept into the living room holding her head.

'This is a disaster! This jolly well takes the biscuit! You do know that my father is throwing my mother out on the street, don't you? Can you believe that of a gentleman? Mmm? And now she has nowhere to go, so we shall simply have to invite her here for a while, until she can find somewhere more suitable.' She paced around the room. '*What?* Don't look at me like that. Why are you looking like that? *I* didn't ask for this to happen! *I* don't want her here either, with her bloody awful gin bottles stuck in every corner. But what else can she do? Where else can she go? You've got to realize how difficult this is for her. And to come and live in a three-bedroom semi after Ashleycroft Hall . . . It's so humiliating for her!'

My house was humiliating.

'We don't have a spare room,' I tried. This was true. I clung on to its truth for dear life. 'Unless you give up the small room.'

'I can't give up the study. I'm halfway through my book. *I* work too, you know. It's not just you.'

'Well, she'll have to think of something else. She has four weeks.'

'No, she doesn't. The letter arrived three and a half weeks ago, and she didn't read it. She just put it in a pile with bills – for occasional reading.'

'Oh God.'

'You'll just have to lend her your room. It'll only be for a few weeks – just until she finds somewhere a little more in keeping with her needs.'

'And I will sleep . . . ?'

'There's a perfectly comfortable sofa that you're sitting on right now. I dozed on it quite a few times when I was expecting Felicity.'

And so she came. And stayed.

Well, it wasn't quite that simple. She had three days to get out, but also, it seemed, three days to clear the house of all her belongings. I naively thought she could manage that on her own. It wasn't as if she had to move furniture or anything. But I was wrong. Moving Cynthia out was a major operation, and one that she put me squarely in charge of.

Fortunately we had a weekend to work with. Pippa and I went up to Gloucestershire and set about putting things in boxes – some to be thrown out, the rest to be delivered to our house and stored in the attic for as long as it took Cynthia to find something 'suitable'. We had our work cut out: it was a vast house, and Cynthia seemed to own most of the fripperies and the rubbish. Pippa seemed to find an awful lot to do in the kitchen, mostly sitting down and drinking tea with her mother. I took each room in turn, tackling the mounds of objects that Cynthia had flung in the corners as 'keep' or 'throw'.

I couldn't help noticing the number of small paintings in the piles of objects to be kept. Rectangles of unfaded wallpaper – some of them quite sizeable – graced the walls in many rooms, and I wondered if she had a right to take so many paintings with her. Some of the larger ones that were still hanging looked very old indeed, as did some of the smaller ones she was planning on taking with her. I was no judge of antiques, but I could bet a fair few of them were priceless. I hoped they were insured.

Suddenly I remembered the young Pippa I first met on the seavacuee train, beguiling the young me with those green eyes. She had spoken then of insurance. *I hope you have it insured* – that's what she'd said to Seamus about his concertina, and then she'd spoken of her mother's stolen paintings. Christ, I thought. Old Cynthia sold them! She sold some of her ex-husband's family paintings and pretended they were stolen.

And perhaps it was because I was thinking about this that I recognized the strange object. It was in a pile to be thrown out, and ordinarily I don't think I would have given it a second glance, and even if I had, I don't think I would have worked out what it was. It was stuffed in an open shoebox and was glittering between some old stockings. I picked it up. How strange it was. A hexagon of wood with a handle on it. Around the edge it was studded with fake diamonds, most of which had fallen out from their grey sockets. On the reverse of this once-splendid concertina-end, the bellows had been crudely cut away, and all that was left were some tufts of heavy material. I turned it over and over in my hands. I recognized it straight away, but I couldn't imagine how it had come to be here. I imagined Pippa must have found it floating on the waves and had grabbed hold of it. Surely not. No one cared about anything but keeping their head above water. And hadn't she been in the boat with me all along? Perhaps she saw it floating by. That could've been it. Fancy keeping it all these years.

Sunday evening, and Pippa was still tapping away upstairs. Beryl had put Felicity to bed and had the rest of the evening off. Just me and Cynthia and some tedious television.

I had an idea to divert Pippa's interest.

I went upstairs and knocked gently on her door. She didn't answer, but I went in anyway.

'Sorry to disturb, but it may have a bearing on what you're writing.'

She didn't turn round or even stop typing.

'You'll never guess what I found. Look.'

Now she turned with a protracted sigh.

What a face! She looked so startled, and recoiled so quickly, I might as well have been holding a poisonous snake.

'What . . . what on earth is that?'

'Don't you recognize it?'

'*Recognize* it? Why should I recognize it?'

I offered it to her, expecting to provoke a bittersweet memory of us all in the train carriage, but she drew back in disgust.

'Ugh! Please, get that thing out of here!'

'But it's the concertina – you remember? Seamus' concertina. Seamus? From the ship? Don't you remember how we all admired the diamonds?'

She blew air up her face and then rolled her eyes in an exaggerated way.

'Really, Arthur. How would *that* get here? That thing there is just an old piece of junk.'

I couldn't make her out. I'd thought she would be pleased.

'Please, just take it away and throw it out.'

She turned back to her typewriter and carried on as if I were merely a minor irritant.

I went downstairs and left it by the back door, ready to be taken out to the dustbin in the morning. Cynthia came in and started opening cupboards, looking for glasses.

'Would you like some cocoa?' I asked her. 'I'm having some.'

'Well . . . if there was something a bit stronger—'

'There isn't. Only coffee.'

'Oh, all right. If you're making it.' She sighed dramatically, then stopped when she spotted the object by the back door. 'What on earth is that doing here?'

'Oh, that. I thought it was something from the ship . . . you know. Something that might interest Pippa, now that she's writing about it.'

Cynthia had moved to the door and picked it up, holding it a little away from herself, but smiling.

'Good Lord! You wouldn't believe it! Pippa had *this* in her big patch pocket when she got back from that shipwreck! Eight days in the mid-Atlantic and she clings on to this old thing.'

I stopped pouring milk into a pan.

'And do you know why?' she chuckled. '*This*'ll make you laugh. She thought they were real diamonds! She actually thought she had made us a fortune! Can you imagine? Well, she was only young, I suppose. But real diamonds! Oh dear me!'

She dropped it by the back door, still amused at her daughter's folly. I continued to make the cocoa, smiling also, trying to digest this new information and wondering exactly what it was I had learnt.

Pippa had lied: she had lied about her inheritance, and now, for some reason, she had lied about this. I concluded that she was embarrassed by her childish assumption that the diamonds would make her rich. I was moved by her embarrassment. After all, it wasn't often that I caught her showing any weakness. I went to my cold bed feeling quite touched.

46

DORA

I continued to see Marius whenever I could get out early enough. There were still no letters from home, although I did write one, and he promised to post it for me. In it, I said that I would be home as soon as I could, that I had made a mistake, and that I was sorry for letting them down.

One morning a few days later, Marius had handed the letters over to me and was sitting beside me, chewing on a piece of grass. I saw that there were no letters for me, but there was one very interesting letter for Ralph. I opened it without a qualm. The address was in my mother's handwriting.

> *Dear Mr Rowanwood,*
> *I'm sorry to hear that Dora is no longer at this address, but could you tell me where she is? Please even if you have only the slightest idea we are beside ourselves. Her father is very ill indeed and I wouldn't bother you otherwise.*
> *I enclose a postal order to pay for the postage.*
> *Yours sincerely,*
> *Mrs Powell*

Well, I needn't tell you how angry I was. I was practically gasping for air and sobbing at the same time. This gave Marius an excuse to put his arm around me, and I sank into him, relieved to have his comfort and complicity. I told him I would need to escape very soon, that I had to find my passport first and get hold of some money, but I told him it would be this week. I couldn't wait any longer: my father was in danger. I was in danger. Marius rose to the occasion. We could go to his village, Richerenches, and from there he would get me to a train station. It would have to be Orange, I said, because Ralph would follow me to Montélimar station. He wiped away my tears and said he would be there each day. Whenever I was ready, he would take me with him.

Easier said than done, of course. I still did not have my passport, and I had no money. I lay in bed at night – sometimes alone, sometimes with Claudine – and I pondered all the possibilities. Perhaps I could steal a bit of the housekeeping from the tin in the kitchen? It would have to be over several weeks, which would delay things, otherwise it would be noticed straight away. I couldn't risk getting the others into trouble. It would take too long. Perhaps I could make little cushions or patchworks and sell them at the market? Patsy could take them for me. Too long. And even then, where would I hide the money? Ralph would be sure to find any money I was saving up. And that didn't solve the problem of the passport. Was there somewhere I could go to ask for a new passport? The town hall? Paris? I cursed myself for my lack of knowledge about these things. And I cursed Ralph. How I cursed him. My anger was a giant knot inside me. I wanted to unravel it and take it away from my gently growing baby.

I knew there had been tension recently between Sophie and Ralph. A couple of days after he had taken me to Orange, I was having my usual fitful night's sleep when I became aware of strange noises. They seemed to be coming from Ralph's room.

I put on my dressing gown and padded out on to the landing. The shutters were all closed, so it was pitch black and I was like a blind person, touching the walls carefully. As my eyes adjusted, I noticed a meagre light coming from under Ralph's bedroom door. There was a muffled cry. Ralph's angry voice. I tiptoed towards the door, straining to hear as much as possible, but all I caught was something like, 'Don't you dare . . .' and 'If you think for a moment . . .' and another muffled sound, and a thump on the floor. I knew he would walk out now, so I turned on my heel and slunk into the nearest door, which was Ralph's study. Unsure where he might be heading, I stood behind the door, heart pounding, hoping I had closed it completely enough for him not to notice the glow from a quarter moon which came in through the unclosed shutters. His footsteps went past.

I could see his desk, his untidy papers, his row of unused books. I kept asking myself where he could have hidden it, my passport. I had searched this room so many times.

I opened drawers and felt in every corner. I found a key in one and used it to open a drawer that was locked. Nothing but some financial paperwork and . . . there *was* a passport. I closed my eyes as I opened it, hardly daring to look. I squinted. I tilted it at the moon: it was his. I kept on rummaging. I even unhooked a picture on the wall. It wasn't there.

A sudden noise made me freeze. I could hear someone flush the toilet in the bathroom. I stood, listening to the blood pumping in my head. I didn't have time to get out and go back to my room. I sunk to my knees and crawled under the desk, pulling the padded velvet chair quietly in front of me, but it may have scraped the floor a little. Another noise. Bathroom door. Silence. Footsteps down the stone staircase. Silence. Then footsteps again. Someone was coming back *up* the stairs.

The door swung open. Torchlight daubed the walls. Back and forth it went, up and down. I remained as still as I could. I didn't breathe. I thought he would hear my heart. The door was gently closed. I waited. I waited for over fifteen minutes, not moving an inch.

At length I relaxed my shoulders and raised my chin. As I moved my head, I felt something catch at my hair. I was shaken, fearing for a moment that Ralph was in there with me. I reached up and found that there was something sticky underneath the desk. It was adhesive tape. I reached up. A brown paper bag, stuck to the underside of the desk with tape. No sooner had I felt the ecstasy of finding my passport than I shuddered. Or did I? Am I just saying that now? No, I think I had a real sense of dismay and terror. How long had it been here? How long had I loved him while he knew he had me trapped?

The first bird was already singing. I knew Ralph would stay up now, so I couldn't risk seeing Marius that morning. I would have to wait at least another twenty-four hours before I could plan my escape.

The first thing I had to do was hide the passport somewhere safe. I couldn't do anything unusual in case Ralph suspected, so I went to the little downstairs room used for sewing and started to cut out one of my new dresses. This is what he would expect me to be doing today. I was behaving in an ordinary way.

Every so often, Patsy popped her head around the door or came and sat opposite me for a chat. Even Ralph put his head around the door and seemed pleased to see me at work. I was afraid in case he had checked under his desk this morning, but he looked relaxed.

The shopkeeper in Orange had wrapped the material in brown paper, but the thread I had put straight into my handbag. I opened it now and rummaged for the thread. My passport was there, but it was too obvious a place to keep it. As I pulled out the two reels of cotton, I knew where its new hiding place must be. Carefully, I snipped at the lining of my bag. The base was solid, so the passport was unnoticeable once I had slipped it on top of it under the lining. I hand-stitched the lining back up with trembling fingers, pulling the thread along the inside of the material so that each stitch was invisible. I was so pleased with it that I was tempted to show it to Patsy, but my fear was great enough not to risk even that. I took a deep breath and tucked the bag behind my chair. I was still shaking, and I continued to feel jittery all day. If Ralph went in there looking for my passport, he would never find it.

I sewed all day, and Patsy helped me with cutting out the dress patterns.

'You know I have to leave here,' I said, unpinning a sleeve from its flimsy paper blueprint. 'And when I go, there will be no goodbyes. I'll have to just slip away.'

'Don't worry. I'll explain it better to Claudine this time. We're thinking of leaving ourselves.'

'Really? Where will you go?'

'It's all talk at the moment. Denis is too lazy to find anywhere else. You know how he is. A bit of cheese, a bit of wine, and he's full of ideas. A bit more wine, and he loses the will to see anything through.' She looked up at me from the sea of blue material on the floor and smiled. 'Hmm. But I love him. He has hidden strengths.'

I finished the blue, flowery dress before our evening meal, and I gave a little catwalk display in order to deflect any suspicion of my terror at being under that roof. Everyone clapped. I beamed, but all I was thinking was: *handbag, thick cardigan, sensible shoes, tomorrow.*

He was already there the next morning, waiting for me. He offered me his cigarette, but when I said I didn't like them he threw it on the road and trod on it, as if he would never smoke again. He took a letter from his bag. I put my hands together and closed my eyes in delight, but when I opened them he was shaking his head.

'*Non, pas pour toi.*' Before I had time to feel disappointed, he held up his forefinger as if he had something to point out to me. '*Mais*' – he wagged the envelope back and forth – '*il y a de l'argent dedans!* Monnay!'

Money!

With great ceremony he handed me the letter. It was addressed to Ralph, and it was postmarked 'Paris'. I looked at Marius for guidance.

'*Vas-y!* You have!'

I opened it. Five thousand francs in notes. I put my hand over my mouth. Could I take it? What if Denis or Patsy or Marius were accused of stealing it? But even as I thought these things, I knew I was going to take it.

'Have!' commanded Marius. 'Have monnay!'

I would write to Aunty Bee. I would pay her back one day. I would.

Marius pointed out an olive tree further down the road. Tomorrow, he said, I should wait for him there. His brother had a van. He worked in Orange on Thursdays. He could take me to the station. Six-thirty. I had to be by the olive tree at six-thirty. No suitcase. I didn't argue.

I was beside myself. I hugged him. I didn't want to wait until tomorrow, but tomorrow was the brother with the van. I would have to wait twenty-four more hours. They were the longest of my life.

No one stirred in the house. It was still dark. Claudine had come in to sleep with me, and I wasn't sure whether to wake her and explain what was going on or to risk her waking up without me and asking where I was. I decided to leave her sleeping. It was still only five o'clock, but I couldn't sleep, and it seemed a good time to avoid Ralph.

I saw the olive tree in the distance and made my way along the road towards it. I was ridiculously early. I knew I would not be hidden by the slim trunk of the tree, so I sat down by the road. Ralph would be sure to check the mailbox today, because he would be on the lookout for his aunt's money. I had to hope he didn't get there before six-thirty, because if he looked up the road, he would see me in my blue dress. With any luck, he would only look *down* the road, in the direction of Marius' bicycle. That was where I looked now, alert as a rabbit.

I don't know how I passed the time. At first it was too shadowy to see my wristwatch, but as the sun came out I checked it every few minutes and the hands never seemed to move much at all. It was colder than I'd expected, and I was pleased when the sun warmed the sleeves of my cardigan. I hoped no cars would go by. It was a quiet road, but if a car did pass it was likely to be someone who knew Ralph or someone at the house, and I was certain to be spotted, crouching on the cold grass in my billowing summer dress.

At last it was six-thirty. There was no sign of a van and no sign of Marius.

Then I saw him. Marius did not stop at Les Amandiers, either because he had no letters or because he had more important things on his mind. He came riding straight towards me.

'*Vite!*' he said, taking my hand.

'Where's the van?'

He motioned up ahead somewhere, but I had heard no sound of a motor. I wasn't sure what he was intending when he pulled me towards the bike. Then he took the bag off the front, slinging it over his shoulder. He patted the shelf where the bag had been, then put his hands on my waist, attempting to hoist me on to it. As soon as I realized what he was doing, I complied and sat on the rack where he usually kept his post. I put my handbag on my lap, lifted my skirts and we were off. It was all I could do not to give a little whoop.

I didn't care if we had to go all the way to Orange like this.

We didn't have to. When we were out of sight of Les Amandiers, Marius sang softly to me, '*Auprès de ma blonde . . .*', and after a mile or two of dusty roads we turned off down a shaded track where a van was waiting.

We dismounted. Marius greeted his elder brother, who eyed me with approval and said something to his little brother with a smile. Then Marius stood before me, taking something out of his pocket and handing it to me. It was his address.

'You write,' he said.

I nodded.

Then he put his hands on my waist, puffed out his chest and said very solemnly, 'I loave you.'

I didn't know what to say. He was young, maybe still in his teens, but then I was still only nineteen myself. Somehow I felt older – a lot older. I knew it would shock him to say I was pregnant. At four months I was still barely showing, and even the new maternity dress was covered by my buttoned-up cardigan.

'I'll never forget you,' I said.

And I didn't.

WASHED UP

47

ARTHUR

I don't like to think about the rest of that decade, really. There was something . . . dead about it. No, *deadening*. It seemed to drain the life out of me – bit by bit. Of course there were joys: Felicity was a marvel. I mean, it really was wonderful watching her grow up. She was such a sweet child – nothing like Pippa in temperament at all, although she did have her mother's beauty. I can't make any claims of my own there.

Yes. Yes, that was something joyful. Dear, sweet Felicity. I'm not sure what I'd have done without her.

But the rest . . . well, where do I start? I was working myself into the ground. As I said, the jet engine that had helped in my promotion had sprung some difficulties, and this now meant that I faced the possibility of losing my job altogether. Fortunately, I came through it, but only through hard work around the clock on a new jet engine. Pippa wasn't exactly supportive. Well, not at all, actually. She still just kept on about getting a bigger house. Whatever I did, whatever I achieved, I never felt good enough with her. She always managed to make me feel like a disappointment.

That seemed to be my life for most of the 1950s. However, there were a couple of important things that happened – life-changing things.

And there was the coronation, of course. I think that was a bit of a turning point for me too.

The King had died in February of the previous year, and then Queen Elizabeth was crowned at the beginning of June 1953. I remember that because everyone from the street crowded into our house. We were all there, crammed in, with Cynthia and Pippa taking up the best seats on the sofa, and I was answering the door as more people kept on arriving. I don't think anyone else in our street had a television. It started, and it was amazing. I say that, but I didn't actually see it until the highlights on the evening news later, but it was very uplifting. I think it raised everyone's spirits. There was a new optimism, and people could feel it. There was an awful racket outside afterwards because there was a big street party or something. This was the last straw for Cynthia. She sat on the sofa, squashed between cheerful neighbours, enraged at having to share anything. She said things like, 'Could you possibly move your ridiculous hairdo out of the way? I can't see the screen in my *own house*!' Anyway, it was too much for her, and that was when she decided to move out. She was finally propelled into contacting some old soak on the Mediterranean who invited her to join him in his alcohol-fuelled life. So I always remember the coronation as an uplifting time for me as well as for the nation. Good old Liz! She finally freed me from my mother-in-law.

But I digress.

Two significant events occurred, and the most significant one – Dora turning up at our house – followed directly from the first.

To my utter astonishment, Pippa's book found a publisher. I don't mean to sound scathing here, but I genuinely thought her book was an excuse for hobnobbing around certain London circles which intrigued her. But Pippa had found an interest that served several purposes at once. For one thing, it did indeed get her out of the house and mixing with a certain set. In fact, when she wasn't actually typing, she was never at home. It was usually just me and Felicity and the nanny. It also served as a cover for whatever it was she wanted to get up to, and I shall probably never know for certain what that was. I still don't think she had an affair with that Dumonnier chap. I think it's more likely she used him, but I can't be sure. He was certainly pretty smitten with the idea of *Survivor's Guilt*, anyway; enough to guide her through the writing of it and help her find a publisher. That, of course, led to all sorts of meetings and lunches with editors and so forth, and I think she just revelled in all that. But another thing it gave her was the wonderful opportunity to put out her own side of the story. By being the first to write an account of those eight days in the mid-Atlantic, she appeared to give the definitive version. It was almost as if the rest of us had given her permission to tell it her way. At the time, I was only mildly irritated and felt churlish for being so. After all, I hadn't thought of writing such a thing, and neither had any of the rest of us. And it hit on a nerve for a nation that was, almost to a man, affected by the guilt of being alive after losing someone in the war. It was a publisher's dream. You might think that, at a time when we were all trying to look forward and enjoy the optimism of a new era, this would be too gloomy for people's tastes. But, of course, it had a 'happy ending'. Two of the survivors get married and have a child. That publisher was laughing all the way to the bank.

Well, actually, it didn't make an awful lot of money for Pippa. She had an advance of two hundred pounds – which was pretty good in those days – but she'd signed up for peanuts from the royalties. It helped me make the decision to move to a larger house at last, which was something Pippa kept on about. We already had enough money to buy a bigger property by then, but only with a fairly tight mortgage, and only if she curbed her increasing demands for more luxuries.

I don't regret the move. It was to this house. It's got everything most people would want: a lovely back garden, four good-sized bedrooms, a spacious kitchen. And, of course, it's detached. You'd think she'd be happy. And she was, at first. That was 1954, the year her book came out in, and she was riding the crest of a wave. Yes, I think she was genuinely happy here for a while.

Did she really think that wave would never break?

48

DORA

I stepped off the Joneses' bus just yards from our front door. I didn't have to knock because the door was always open. I went quietly down the passage, cradled already in the familiar smells of floor polish and soot and carbolic soap. I went down the stairs into the parlour. The stairs had the same slightly sticky linoleum that echoed with every step. It was impossible to creep into our house.

Onions, cabbage, soot. Home. Our Mam standing at the parlour door with her arms open. My face buried in her housecoat, the smell of her, the smell of home. I noticed suddenly that she was catching her breath. Our Mam was crying. Our Dad wasn't in his chair. His cigarettes weren't on the arm of the chair. His coat was on the back of the parlour door, though. She had held me like this when Siân died. I recognized the hunger in it.

'Is he gone, Mam?'

'He is, aye.'

The early June sun had sunk behind the mountain when we stopped crying, and as the parlour window faced east across the valley, the room was filled with shadows. Our Mam bent over the range to shovel more coal on, a hollow rattle so familiar it would have burst open the tear dam again, had my face not ached with crying.

'When's it due?' her back said to me.

'What?'

'When's the baby due?'

I hadn't been ready to tell her this. I hadn't told her about the baby in my letter. I hadn't wanted to bring her any more bad news, and to be honest, I was ashamed. Nice girls didn't have babies without being married first.

'How did you—?'

'No coat, no suitcase . . . unless His Nibs dropped you off outside in a Rolls-Royce, I'd say you left in a hurry.' I had underestimated Our Mam's worldly knowledge. She was a miner's daughter and a miner's wife. She knew only too well the posh men who courted a pretty face until it threatened their freedom. She'd seen it all before. 'He never came to meet us, did he? He wanted you to go and live with him in France, but he didn't do us the courtesy of paying us a visit. Now there's a man who wants you to live in sin.'

That's what they called it then: 'living in sin'. Not that Our Mam cared tuppence for sin, but she knew everybody else did, and especially potential husbands looking to settle down with nice girls.

She stood up by the glow of the fire and I went to her. This time it was different. This time, there was no spectre of Siân or even, for that moment, of my father. There was just my mother and me, two women holding each other in the dusk, one to take comfort and the other to give it. 'You'll be all right home yer with me. I'll look after you both, look.'

And as simply as that, it was settled. She had a small pension from my father and free coal, but she would work part-time until after the baby was born and for the first year or so. Then I could borrow her mother's wedding ring, go to Newport and find work as a widow whose husband had died in France.

She'd had it all worked out before I arrived home.

Helen was born in September. I called her Helen because she was the most beautiful thing I'd ever seen, and I gave her Elizabeth as her middle name after our new queen. Nothing had prepared me for motherhood. From the moment I held her in my arms and smelt the searing sweet scent of her head, I was overwhelmed with love. Everything that had troubled me before fell away, and all that concerned me was the comfort and happiness of my child.

I felt an enormous oneness with nature. When spring came, I watched the sheep with their lambs and let tears of empathy stream down my face. The mystery of bleating was unravelled. All my life I had marvelled at how a lamb could tell the difference between one low bellow and another in order to make its way back to the maternal belly, and how those sturdy mutton-brained old clumps of sheep could possibly recognize one little bleat from a mountainside of heart-rending bleats. Now it was all clear to me. I would know my baby's cry in a sea of babies, and I would know my baby's smell from a million others, and I felt the most sisterly love for each anxious grey ewe as it behaved exactly like me.

I allowed myself to forget about Ralph. I could see no reason why he would ever want to track me down to South Wales to reclaim his baby, although it had been on my mind all through the pregnancy. Now, with Helen's arrival, I had never been happier or seen Our Mam happier. She had a new energy, working tirelessly to meet all our needs in those first few months. At first she took in laundry. The kitchen was always full of steam and the parlour full of other people's vests and sheets. When she wasn't washing or cooking she was ironing, and my memories of her are mostly of a pink-cheeked woman wrestling with coils of steaming bed sheets or standing at that ironing board turning the vast, damp heaps of cotton into neat folded piles. That was what Our Mam did: she created order out of chaos. I watched her, and tried to learn.

As soon as Helen took her first steps, the ironing board was put away. Our Mam couldn't bear the thought of an accident with a scalding iron, so she found a job at the Co-op three mornings a week, until I found work. I would push Helen around in our neighbour's old pram, or read to her by the fire, or watch her draw pictures on the rescued plain paper that the grocer had wrapped around our ham.

It was on one such day – in November of 1954 – when I was making paper chains with Helen, that the most alarming thing happened. Nothing could have prepared me for it.

The fire was crackling in the range, and the wireless was playing the Home Service. Helen, then fourteen months old, was holding up a little row of paper men holding hands, and I was just tugging on the folded paper I had torn to reveal a chain of girls, when something made me stop.

'. . . and we have with us in the studio the author of a new book, *Survivor's Guilt*, described by the *Daily Telegraph* as "a remarkable account of the psychological effects of survival when loved ones die". Philippa Fielding, tell us why you decided to write about your harrowing ordeal in the mid-Atlantic . . .'

'Mama!' Helen started to prod me and grabbed at the unopened girls. I let her take them.

'Well, I had been feeling very depressed, and it wasn't until I spoke to a professional about my feelings that I realized that what I was feeling was guilt – at having survived when so many friends drowned. You see, I was one of the fortunate children to be rescued from the sinking of *The City of India* in 1940. I was only twelve years old at the time . . .'

Helen was prodding me again and making dissatisfied noises, so I smiled at her and began to fold more paper and tore it carefully. She watched, fascinated. The plummy-voiced male interviewer was clearly riveted by Pippa's account. I had never heard her called Philippa Fielding before, and the addition of Arthur's surname filled me with a pitiful kind of rage. But that was nothing compared with what was to come. The interviewer was intrigued by the effects of eight days at sea after food and water had run out: 'I believe some people even started to hallucinate, didn't they?'

'Yes, that's right. I remember one little girl was especially badly affected. She even thought she saw me hitting someone with an oar – and *killing* them!' Here, she hazarded a light chuckle. 'I mean, it's extraordinary what dehydration can do the mind. Heartbreaking, really.'

I stared at the wireless. It sat on a shelf in the alcove beside the chimney breast. It was made of a deep toffee-coloured wood with a square of cloth mesh set in the front. Two black knobs sat on either side of a lit-up tuning panel, which now looked like a wide, oddly toothed mouth. I willed it to say no more, but it carried on speaking, and I could hear the fascination in the man's voice for the extraordinary woman sitting next to him in the studio; he was fawning, smitten, a helpless wreck before her.

Helen clutched at my hapless offering as soon as I had finished tearing. The paper opened out into a chain of misshapen girls.

One little girl was especially badly affected.

49

ARTHUR

Pippa's book came out just before Christmas. She wouldn't let me see the proofs, so I had to wait until it was published. That's why I was only halfway through it when she did her interview on the wireless.

I sat and listened with Fliss, who was fascinated to hear her mother's voice coming out of a box.

I have to admit I was proud of her. My wife, on the Home Service! I told everyone at work to listen in, and I know Mum and Dad were tuned in as well. I did find it odd, though, when she talked about a little girl who had hallucinated on the boat adrift in the Atlantic. I can remember one of the lascars having funny turns, and quite a few of us imagined slap-up meals and dreamt of running water. But the only little girl on that boat – apart from Pippa – had been Dora. And Dora said nothing for the entire eight days.

I went to fetch my copy of the book and leafed through it until I found the passage about hallucination: 'By the time we had been adrift for several days, we were desperate for water. The food rations had run out very early on, but it was the lack of water that really wore us down. Our lips were cracked and our tongues were sore and swollen. One little girl even hallucinated. She thought she saw me beating a boy to death with an oar! It's extraordinary what bizarre tricks the mind can play on you when you're deprived of water.'

That evening, I broached the subject in the kitchen. It was probably not a good time: I had lit a candle and bought in fish and chips to save her having to cook anything, as it was the nanny's day off, but Pippa thought I should have taken her out to celebrate. She eyed my offering with scorn.

'You were brilliant. Absolutely brilliant. Just like a real author.'

'I am a real author.'

'Yes. Quite.'

'Guy said I sounded like Princess Margaret.'

'Guy?'

'You know – my editor.'

'Ah. Well you did sound very regal. What was all that stuff about hallucination, though? I can't remember any of that.'

'You see? I knew I was right not to let you read the proofs. You'd have wanted to change everything.'

I looked across at her over my battered cod and wished I hadn't managed to agitate her so easily. I was looking forward to the cod. Nonetheless . . .

'No, but I was just thinking, the only other little girl on the boat was Dora.'

'Well done. Dora was the one who thought she saw me killing someone.'

'But Dora didn't say anything. She was mute for the entire eight days.'

She began to shake salt furiously over her chips and didn't seem able to stop.

'Steady on, old girl. You'll drown them in salt.'

She flared her nostrils at me and slammed down the salt cellar. 'It was *later*. She told me about it *later*!' She put a chip on the end of her fork delicately in her mouth. 'It was when we met up again at the reunion – in the ladies' cloakroom. You weren't there. It was in the ladies' cloakroom, and she said she hadn't forgotten what I'd done, and *I* said what, and she said beating a boy to death with an oar, and I knew straight away that she'd been hallucinating. Obviously.'

'So . . .' I tucked into my cod, trying to picture this and too distracted now to enjoy the food. 'What was Dora's reaction when you said it wasn't true?'

'Well, you can imagine. I was worried she was going to try and bring me up for murder or something, so I had to be pretty firm with her.'

I held a succulent piece of fish in mid-air on my fork. 'Crikey. It's no wonder there was so much tension between the two of you.'

'Did it show?' She was in her stride.

'But . . . why did you never mention it to me?'

She banged her fork slightly on the table and rolled her eyes. 'That's the whole point, isn't it? I bottled everything up. Why would I want to go around saying someone had accused me of murder? Of battering someone over the head until . . . *Why?* I watched her and wondered why, when she wasn't being indifferent to me, she was always so angry. She picked up the bottle of tomato ketchup and shook it wildly over her chips. Nothing came out.

'Let me.' I wanted more than anything to be useful to her. I wanted to protect her and do the manly things that a bit of extra testosterone came in handy for: putting up shelves, mowing the lawn, carrying her shopping, staying calm in a crisis, wiping away her tears, opening her jars. But somehow I always felt so useless around her. I slapped the ketchup bottle firmly on its base and the red sauce started to flow.

She snatched it back from me, beat it furiously with the palm of her hand, showering her plate with great splashes of red gloop.

50

DORA

I waited until after Christmas, but then I could wait no longer.

Our Mam told me not to be so foolish. I had to tell someone, and she and I had grown very close. She was tamping mad about Pippa and what she had done, but, she said, 'It's shutting the door after the horse has bolted. You should've given her a piece of your mind years ago. It's too late now.'

I was not going to be deterred, though. There was something about hearing Pippa's voice so coolly lying at my expense to extricate herself from any future accusations of murder, and on the national airwaves, that made my blood boil. I lost all reason. I had absolutely no idea what I was going to say to Pippa when I found her, but find her I would, and no one was going to stop me.

In January of 1955 I set out on the train to Bristol. I'd just started doing an office job in Newport, so it had to be a Saturday when Our Mam could look after Helen while I was away. I knew this could be tricky and that I might well find Arthur at home as well as his wife, but I had to take my chances. Frankly, I didn't really care whether I saw Arthur or not (although I think I did put on a bit of lipstick and made sure I'd just washed my hair).

Looking back, it's hard to imagine where I found the courage to confront Pippa by turning up at their house with no idea who would answer the front door. All I can say is that it's a testament to how enraged I was. Not a single phrase came to mind as I stood on the doorstep. Not an opening line, not even a word.

I rang the doorbell, then I knocked hard on the knocker as well to relieve a bit of my tension.

A woman I hadn't seen before answered the door.

'Er . . . is Pippa in?'

'Pippa?'

'Philippa – Philippa Fielding.'

The woman, a pretty young woman in slippers, looked bewildered for a moment. Then she said, 'Oh, you mean the Fieldings! They moved out some time ago. They don't live here any more.'

I hadn't thought of this. So soon? Why had they moved? Were they living in another part of the country? Had they moved abroad? I could hardly catch my breath.

'Do you have their forwarding address?'

'I'm sorry. We did have it, but I haven't sent on any mail for ages.'

I could hear my pulse in my head. Primed for a confrontation, all lipsticked and coiffed and straight-backed, I felt as though someone had let the air out of me and I was slowly sagging to the ground. I must have looked devastated, for the woman said kindly, 'I'll see if my husband can find it, if you like.'

I waited a full five minutes in their hallway. I looked at the stairs that I had once walked up with such awe and anticipation, the same stairs that Arthur had stood on when I discovered his treachery. There was a faint, heart-rending scent of the hallway it once had been (from the same carpet? From the wallpaper?) and I was grateful for the overlying new aroma of dog and fried egg.

She came out of the living room with a smile on her face and a piece of paper in her hand. 'We think this is it: Four Acres. It's just north of Bristol, near Chipping Sodbury.'

I thanked her, and wandered back out into the street. It was chilly. I had no idea how to catch a bus to the place on the paper. I stood aimlessly for a while and then began to get cold, a few thin flakes of snow drifting in the air. I saw a telephone box on the corner of the street and decided to phone for a taxi. I resolved that, when the taxi arrived, I would ask the price of the journey in advance. If it was too expensive, I would catch the train home.

It took ten minutes to arrive, and by then I was shivering and my fingers were numb. I showed the driver the address and simply asked him to take me there. It was a twenty-minute journey and cost seven shillings! I was put down outside a tall hedge on the side of a village road. I looked wistfully after the taxi as it disappeared around the corner of the lane, but it was too late to turn back now.

There was a gate and a path up to a whitewashed detached house. To the side I could see a swing rigged up in a tree, and on the ground a child's red spade with a little seaside bucket. I was an intruder on happy family life. I was uninvited. I was going to sweep in and upset this applecart, and suddenly it felt all wrong. I stood in the porch like a burglar. There was a push-along toy dog off to the side and two pairs of sturdy shoes. One of the pairs was for tiny feet and was stuffed with grubby white socks, and the other pair, standing protectively, was for giant feet. There was mud on them both, and the intimacy of that mud and those socks made me tremble. Cold feet? I swallowed hard and tapped tentatively on the door.

Eventually the front door opened. A girl looked startled when she saw me, and I could see that she was clearly just going out and hadn't answered my knock at all.

'Oh, sorry, did you want . . . ?'

'Is Pippa there?'

'Yes! I'm just off out – I'll get her. Come on in.' She held on to the bannister and called up the stairs: 'Mrs Fielding? Someone at the door for you!'

'Tell Arthur to get it,' a lethargic voice said.

'He's out.'

'Who is it?'

'A woman . . .'

I mouthed that I was a friend.

'. . . A friend!'

'Oh, that's okay,' she muttered. 'I've got no make-up on or anything.'

As soon as there were sounds of footsteps from upstairs, the girl smiled at me and left, and I stood in the hallway waiting for my nemesis to appear.

She wore a red dressing gown, and her hair stood up a little at the back. Her lips, without lipstick, were extraordinarily pale. She stared at me from the middle of the staircase, supporting herself on the bannister as the full horror of my presence set in.

'Dora!'

'Pippa!'

'What on earth are you doing here?'

What *was* I doing there? I looked up and down the passageway for clues.

'I just thought I'd call by to let you know that I heard your broadcast on the wireless.'

'I see.'

'Yes. I expect you do.' She looked a little stunned at my rejoinder, and I was pleased, able to gather my strength. And I certainly needed to, as my heart was thumping so hard that I had to steady my words. She looked away from my face to the bottom of the stairs, then pulled her dressing gown around her and walked down towards me. I stood my ground. 'You'll know why I've come.'

She looked at me again as if she might try to stare me out, but she couldn't hold my gaze. I could see from the set of her mouth and the shifting of her eyes that she was angry and afraid at the same time, torn between throwing me out and cajoling me. There was a pause. She retied her dressing gown and put her chin up.

'You'd better come into the kitchen. I was just going to make some tea.'

I followed her into the kitchen. She didn't ask if I would like to have a cup of tea myself, but she silently poured me one, and I took it, glad of the first refreshment since six o'clock that morning.

'So . . .' She leant with her back against the kitchen counter, not offering me a seat. 'What do you want from me?'

'Well, first I'd like an apology.'

'*An apology?*'

'You lied about me – publicly.'

'I didn't mention your name.'

'I was the only little girl on that boat – apart from you.'

She rolled her eyes and closed them in exasperation. 'Okay, I'm sorry!' Then she met my eyes and ventured a truly challenging look, turning to walk from the kitchen into an adjoining living room. 'All right? You've had your apology. Can I get on with my day now?'

'And secondly,' I said, following her into the room, 'I'd like you to confess to Arthur – about killing his brother.'

She glared at me. I noticed that her cheeks, without make-up, were covered in tiny, thread veins, as though she drank a lot of alcohol or strong coffee. Her eyes were still dazzling and her teeth still perfect, but she had a drained, bloodless look to her, and I felt a sudden, brief pity for her.

'How dare you! Get out of my house!'

So this was the tack she was going to take. I stood my ground, taking in the cushiony sofa and the dull mix of modern and antique furniture. On the arm of one of the chairs was a copy of her book.

'*Survivor's Guilt,*' I said, trying to sound calm. 'That was a good ruse, wasn't it? Did you think you could protect yourself by telling the world I was bonkers?'

'I did *not* tell the world you were bonkers!' She was shouting now, unashamedly. 'Get out!'

'I'll go when you promise to tell Arthur what happened. You know what happened as well as I do, and I won't leave until you tell him.'

'*Get . . . out!*' Her rage was terrifying, but mine was worse. Her reddening face and clenched jaw were exactly the sort of thing that would have once made me cower before her, but for once in my life I refused to buckle. I knew control was mine if I could just stay calm and cling on to my mission.

'Or what, Pippa? You'll call the police? I don't think that would be very wise, do you? You see, I'm not here to claim back my dignity. I'm here to see justice for what you've done. You lied to Arthur. Let's face it, Pippa, the only reason you seduced him was to get him on side, just in case I ever spoke out about what I saw. And yes, I did see it. I saw you beat Philip over and over and I know why. *I know why!* For the sake of some "diamonds" on a concertina!'

'Why would I do that, for heaven's sake?'

'Because you were a child and you thought they were real – we all did to start with. Because you were never as wealthy as you pretended, were you? Far wealthier than the rest of us, of course, but nowhere near as wealthy as you wanted to be. And don't deny it. I've heard it all from Ralph.'

'Even if I did think the diamonds were real – which I didn't – why on earth would I want to kill . . . ?'

'You can stop the charade. Philip told me you'd threatened to kill him if he told on you about stealing the concertina. And you were so afraid that he would. But you see, he already had. You killed that poor little boy for nothing. Well, for *fake* diamonds – fake!'

She picked up a heavy bottle with a ship inside it and waved it threateningly. It had crossed my mind that she could do with getting me out of the way permanently, but I hadn't expected such raw physical rage.

'I'm not interested in putting you away. I only want you to tell Arthur the truth.'

She screamed at me now: 'GET OUT OF MY HOUSE!'

Her screaming must have masked the sound of the back door opening, because now I saw Arthur standing in the doorway between the kitchen and the living room. I tried not to look at him, but I couldn't help taking him in. His presence changed everything. All sense of danger fell apart, and even the light in the room seemed different and livened up the colours. I'd forgotten quite how handsome he could be. His face was bright with the freshness of the outdoors, and his expression was bafflement. Pippa had her back to him and hadn't noticed he was there. She continued to shout: 'You just want him for yourself! That's what all this is about!'

'Tell Arthur yourself, *now*, or I will.'

'Tell Arthur what? What must I be told?'

She spun around in shock and seemed to start trembling as soon as she saw him. 'I thought you were out!'

'I was – out in the garden. Hello, Dora.' Bewildered, but smiling.

'Hello.' I don't think I managed a smile.

'Don't listen to anything she says – she's a liar!' Pippa started to wail. I swear she could just turn on the tears. As soon as she saw him, she turned them on like a tap. She hurled her weapon on to the floor. But then there was another sound: a child crying. I looked over and saw that a little girl was clinging on to Arthur's leg and howling. 'Stop Mummy shouting!'

'For God's sake get that child to shut up!' cried Pippa.

Arthur picked up the little girl and held her close. Something in the tenderness with which he did so reminded me – against all my will – of why I had loved him so much. She must've been about two years old. Now everything changed again. It was impossible to continue with the child listening. Who could tell what damage it might do in the long term?

'What a pretty dress!' I said, meeting her tear-filled eyes. 'Are you a princess?'

She gazed at me and I smiled. She buried her head in her father's shoulder.

'Don't you talk to my child!' Pippa hissed.

'Please, Pippa. Calm down. Let's have a bit of calm here. What's all this about? Tell Arthur what?'

He was searching my face, and I knew I could say nothing damning about Pippa in front of the child. But I couldn't leave things where they were. Pippa was still shaking. She was a grenade I had detonated, and I knew there would be consequences. I would have to circumnavigate the new obstacle, but there was no turning back on my mission.

'Pippa told you I had hallucinated. What she didn't tell you was who I saw.' I swallowed. 'It was Philip.' My lips tingled with his name. Arthur's lips were ajar and motionless. 'And I didn't hallucinate.'

He stood there holding his daughter and staring at me. His composure collapsed. He rested his mouth on his daughter's head and stroked her hair. He closed his eyes, and when he opened them again he fixed them incredulously on his wife. There was a split second of terror, and then Pippa covered her face with her hands and bawled. 'How can you believe such twaddle? Can't you see what she's trying to do? She's just trying to wreck our marriage!'

'Oh, Pippa! *Please!* Tell the truth for once. Arthur deserves to hear it from you, not me.' I didn't wait to hear the rest. I made my way past Arthur, through the kitchen and out into the hallway. I opened the front door and strode down the path, my heart racing, my breathing frantic. He had looked so . . . Had I done the right thing? Had I destroyed him? Was she right about my wanting to wreck their marriage? He was so . . . And yet, she always twisted things. There was no justice with Pippa. She managed to make you feel unworthy, when all you were trying to do was establish the truth, right a wrong.

'Dora!'

I heard him call after me, but I couldn't look back. I couldn't bear to see the face that I had hurt, the damage I had done, the man that I still loved.

I marched out of the gate and into the road, with no money and absolutely no idea how to get to where I needed to be.

51

ARTHUR

I heard the word 'fake' quite clearly, and then we were opening the back door, and there was something about 'telling Arthur the truth', and then I was distracted by Fliss taking off her coat and wellingtons, and then the screaming: 'GET OUT OF MY HOUSE!'

I was right there for my wife then, ready to throw out the intruder, only what I saw over Pippa's shoulder – apart from the ship in a bottle she was brandishing – was Dora. There was a rush of forgotten pleasure – a little like the rush I'd felt when she used to run her fingers down the side of my ribs and whisper into my neck on a Welsh mountainside – and then confusion.

Pippa was screaming. 'You just want him to yourself – that's what this is all about!'

I flattered myself that this was a showdown between two women who wanted me. I could hardly believe it. There was no doubt they were referring to me, though, because Dora looked directly at me and said, 'Tell Arthur yourself, *now*, or I will.'

She was stunning. She stood there, confronting my wife, her cheeks ablaze and her eyes – her eyes were alight with rage. I'd never seen her like that before. She was electric. She was beautiful. I could feel this energy coming off her.

'Tell Arthur what? What must I be told?'

Pippa turned round and seemed terrified to see me. I swear she was practically trembling, and since I'd never had that impact on her, I knew it was Dora. She was a force to be reckoned with that day.

'I thought you were out!' It was like an accusation.

'I was – out in the garden.' I couldn't take my eyes off Dora's determined face. 'Hello, Dora.'

'Hello.' There was no smile, no sign of any feeling towards me.

'Don't listen to anything she says – she's a liar!' Pippa howled, threw the bottle on to the carpet, and then proceeded to break down in tears. Dora was looking not at me, but at Fliss, who, with all the shouting and now the crying, had started to cry herself. I picked her up, and Dora's face softened. She said something gently to Fliss, and Fliss calmed down a little but continued to cling on to me. She was clearly very frightened, and that was only made worse when Pippa forbade Dora from talking to her child.

'Please, Pippa. Calm down. Let's have a bit of calm here. What's all this about? Tell Arthur what?' I looked at Dora now for an explanation. She had stayed calm, but she was the one who'd spoken the words. She'd challenged Pippa to tell me something, so there was something important that I didn't know, and both of them knew what it was. Pippa was blubbing. Dora was the only one likely to tell me.

'Pippa told you I had hallucinated.' So that was it. She'd heard the radio broadcast or read the book. No wonder she was angry – angry enough to charge down here and confront Pippa. Call it artistic license, call it exaggeration, call it what you will – I didn't think Dora had said all that stuff about the killing, and I knew no good would come of putting it in the book. I wasn't expecting the next bit, though. 'What she didn't tell you was who I saw.' Her face filled with apology, but she held a steady gaze. 'It was Philip.' Her clear blue eyes were glinting with tears. 'And I didn't hallucinate.'

I didn't know what this meant at first. There was Pippa screaming that Dora was 'just trying to wreck our marriage' (which gave me an odd little thrill) and Dora saying, 'Oh, Pippa! *Please!* as if she were dressing down a naughty child. I couldn't take it all in. 'Tell the truth for once. Arthur deserves to hear it from you, not me.' What on earth did it mean?

Then she was gone, brushing past me with a waft of familiar scent. Oh God! I would recognize her from an ocean of women by the smell of her. This couldn't be happening – she was leaving, she had opened the door, she had gone. I ran to open the door and called after her, but I was still holding Fliss, and Dora was striding away out of our gate without looking back. Fliss was still sobbing. I held her close and went back to find Pippa. The ship in a bottle lay beside my wife on the sofa, its masts down and its booms snapped off. It looked irreparable. Pippa and I looked at each other warily. We both knew we had to wait until Beryl came home at six o'clock before we could talk this through without our child's presence. I was deeply frustrated.

'We'll talk this evening,' I said firmly.

Of course, that gave her plenty of time to prepare her side of the story.

As I said, I vainly hoped that Dora and my wife were having some sort of fight over me. That sounds pathetic now, but it was so strange seeing the two of them in confrontation so unexpectedly. And that vanity was significant, because it served Pippa well. I was deeply affected by the mention of my brother, but I couldn't really work out the significance of it. I knew Dora couldn't be suggesting that she had seen Pippa killing him. What possible motive could she have had for hurting Philip? I thought about the word 'fake' that I'd heard mentioned so emphatically, and it troubled me. Had Pippa's feelings towards me been fake? Was she having an affair? How would Dora know this? I remembered the note all those years ago: 'I know what you did.' Was she having an affair way back then?

'What was that about Philip?' I asked Pippa, as soon as we were alone in the living room that evening. Her mood was strange. I had never seen her quite so downcast.

'Look, Arthur, there's something I didn't tell you.'

I waited, holding my breath, watching her red-painted nails running along the arm of the sofa.

'When we were on the boat . . . there was a child trying to get on. The one Mr Dent jumped in to save – you remember?'

'Yes.'

'Well, I offered him my oar, and there was a bit of a struggle, because he couldn't get hold of it. And then he, or she – I think it was a boy actually – just sort of . . .' She started to whimper.

'What?'

'Just . . . drifted off.' She screwed her features up in pain at the memory. I put my hand on her shoulder, expecting her to shrug it off, but she didn't.

'But I thought Mr Dent jumped out on the other side of the boat?'

'No, the boy – the child – drifted. To be honest I thought he, she – whatever – was dead already. They just seemed to let go and' – more catching of breath – 'give up. I think that's what Dora saw. And she thought it was Philip.'

'Are you sure it wasn't?'

'Yes. Certain. I'd have known Philip, wouldn't I?'

'But you said you couldn't tell if it was a boy or a girl.'

She buried her face in her hands for a moment, and the voice that emerged was plaintive and anguished. 'Whose side are you on?'

'I'm not on anyone's side.' I rubbed her shoulder for reassurance. 'I'm just trying to establish whether or not it could have been Philip.

Can't you see why that's important to me? You may have tried to save my brother. That would give me some . . . It would help Mum a lot, I think, just to have some information. We just never heard anything.'

She took her hands away and folded her lips together. 'You need to understand what Dora is trying to do. Because she thought I lied about her hallucinating – and I was just trying to be kind, honestly, I could've said she wrongly accused me of killing someone when I was *helping* them – because she thought I'd lied, she's come up with this cock-and-bull story about it being Philip.'

'Why would she think you'd killed Philip? I mean, why would you *want* to do that?'

'*Exactly!*' She rolled her eyes in exasperation, as if I'd just cottoned on to something blindingly obvious. It didn't answer the question, though. It only made Dora look unreasonable.

'Pippa, look at me. Why would she come all the way to see you to accuse you of killing my brother?'

She sighed dramatically. 'Do I have to spell it out?'

She always did this, managed to make me feel foolish, even when I had a legitimate point to make. 'Well, yes. I think you do need to spell it out.'

She took in a deep breath, assumed an air of anguish and began, measuring her words as if she were talking to a slightly dumb child.

'Dora has never forgiven me for marrying you. Ever since we got together, she has been looking for ways to malign me in your eyes. I . . . *possibly* slipped up a little with the hallucinating reference, but that was all the ammunition she needed. She's round here like a shot, accusing me of lying about her, telling me she *did* see me beating someone with an oar – *just* as she did the day we met up again in the cloakroom at the reunion – only saying this time it was Philip. And she said – you heard her – that if I didn't tell you then she would. What am I supposed to say?' She turned a tearful, pleading face to look at me. 'I didn't kill your brother, Arthur. I didn't kill your dear little brother. Why on earth would I? Tell me that! Why in heaven's name would I?'

'So—'

'She just wants to break us up. Why can't you see that? She wants you for herself.'

'I thought she was married.'

Pippa looked flustered. 'Oh, *I* don't know. How am *I* supposed to know?'

'I thought you knew the man she was going to marry – in France.'

'That's right.'

'Well, she's not in France now. And she wasn't in France when she heard it on the radio.'

'Why do you care?' She started sobbing again. 'God! Oh God, Arthur! My husband's ex-fiancée accuses me of *murder* and all he cares about is whether she's still single or not!'

I put my arms around her, and she buried her face in my shoulder, her own shoulders shaking. She hadn't let me hold her like this since before we were married. I stroked her hair, feeling I had been unfair to doubt her. Then she raised her head a little and asked with red-rimmed eyes: 'You do still love me, don't you?'

That was it. I melted. She had been severely shaken up and she was frightened, and it was me she turned to for reassurance. At last she gave me a purpose. For the first time in a very long while, she needed me. She clung to me, and I kissed her head. She nuzzled into me, and I kissed her again. I held her face between my hands and kissed her softly. She moaned a little. Then she moaned a little more. Beryl was upstairs putting Fliss to bed, and in the shadows of our living room, where just hours earlier Dora's eyes had met mine, I made love to my wife, but it was Dora I thought about. It was wonderful.

52

DORA

'You're drenched!' said a voice. I was numb, but I looked towards the sound, and a balding man emerged from behind the bar wiping his hands on a tea towel. 'What can I get you?'

I had walked for miles to the nearest village in a bitter, easterly wind, and my legs were giving way. I explained that I had no money and that I was stuck. I needed to get back to Bristol Temple Meads and didn't know what to do. I must've sounded desperate, because he said, 'All right my lover, you sit yourself down there by the fire, and I'll go and fetch Gerry, our delivery man. He's heading back to Bristol soon.'

He brought me a cup of tea, and his kindness made me want to weep.

When I got home I was ready to flop, but Our Mam was waiting for me at the foot of the stairs, a wild, frightened look in her eyes. I thought for a moment she may have been worried about me, but I wasn't late – in fact, I had expected to be home far later.

It wasn't until I saw past her into the parlour that her terror became clear. Standing in front of the range, with his back to it and facing me, was Ralph.

'I told him about your miscarriage,' Our Mam said – far too emphatically, I thought.

'What are you doing here?' I ventured.

He smiled and said nothing, taking me in from head to toe. I stood my ground. Where was Helen? I could only guess that she was still having her nap, but surely she would be awake soon. I tried to make out the face of the clock on the mantelpiece behind him: gone three o'clock – nearly twenty past. She would be awake soon.

'Well,' he said, 'aren't you going to take your coat off, invite me for a cup of tea?'

'How long have you been here?'

'About ten minutes. Your mother seemed to think you weren't coming back today.' He looked slyly at her when he said this, and I felt her sense of foolishness.

'Change of plan,' I said briskly, taking off the still-damp coat and slinging it over the chair by the fire to stop him sitting in it. 'And no, we shan't be offering you a cup of tea.' I said this loudly, as I could tell from the way she straddled the kitchen doorway that Our Mam was about to put the kettle on.

'I've come a long way – to see my child.'

'Then it's been a wasted trip. I'm sorry.'

'A miscarriage? Do you always dry nappies by the fire?' He nodded to a clothes horse with two pieces of white towelling, threaded through with the unmistakable black line of a nappy.

'They're not . . . we use them for . . . women's things.'

He looked thoughtful, as though he were weighing up the chances of this being true. 'And the pram in the hall?' He was so smug now that it sent a shiver down me.

I thought about saying Our Mam used it for coal or shopping, but if he saw it on the way back up he would see the clean sheet and soft blanket inside. 'We got it out yesterday for my cousin. She's just had a baby girl. It's no use to us any more.'

'So, I might as well be on my way.' He smiled – too benignly. He was up to something.

'Let me show you out the back way – it's quicker.' This was simply not true. The back door led down to the yard and the tip. He would have to walk all along the backs of the yards before he came to an alley-way leading back up to the road.

He ignored me and made his way up the stairs; I followed close behind. Our joint footsteps sounded like thunder on the lino, and I knew it would wake Helen. I had to get him out as quickly as possible.

'What was that?' he said in the hallway.

'What?'

There was no escaping it: Helen had woken and was crying from upstairs.

He was up there before I could stop him, taking the stairs two at a time.

'No!' I shouted. 'NO!'

He came to a halt inside her room and stood beside her cot, staring at her. She was standing up holding on to the wooden slats, silenced by the intrusion.

'It's all right, Helen! It's all right!' I tried to sound calm, but she could hear my panic and started to cry again. I went over to her to pick her up but he stuck his arm out to bar my way. I think my heart must've stopped. I don't think I've ever been so frightened.

We both stood there as Helen cried louder and louder. I was only glad that it made her face redder and less attractive, hoping for anything to stop him taking her. Cry, my baby, cry! Drive him away!

'*Helen?*' he said at last. 'Helen?' He pronounced it as if it were a dirty word.

'Yes.'

He looked at me with such disbelief and contempt that I was completely confused for a moment as to his meaning.

'A *girl?*'

Yes. *Yes!* 'Yes. A girl.'

'But I need an heir. A girl's no good.'

'No.'

His expression darkened. I had seen that look before. He grabbed me by the throat and flung me against the wall. 'Are you making a fool of me? Huh? Are you making a fool of me?' He pushed me hard into the wall, and I had no breath at all. I thought this time he would kill me.

Then he did something worse. He grabbed Helen.

'No!' I was screaming, and I knew Our Mam would come running, and I knew it would do no good. He would hit her too. I willed her to stay downstairs.

He dangled the baby in front of him clumsily. 'Take her clothes off!'

'What?'

'Do it!'

I held Helen close, and he hit me across the side of the face. 'Do it – now!'

I put her back down in the cot and began to unbutton her outfit. I gently lifted out her jelly soft arms and tried not to look at the big tear-filled eyes full of incomprehension. Soon she was down to her nappy, and he snapped at me to take it off. When I did so, he shouted.

'Useless! You're useless!'

I let go of Helen before he took a swipe at me, but as I fell down, something odd happened. He fell backwards against the other wall. Looking up, I saw Big Bryn from two doors up. Our Mam stood behind him and came pushing past now, bending down to help me and wiping blood from my face with her housecoat.

Meanwhile, Bryn had Ralph on his feet and clocked him one again. He supported him and held an arm behind his back. 'That's no way to treat a woman, mun! You need to learn a few manners!'

I heard him bundle Ralph downstairs with him and throw him out. 'That's not how we treat our women in the Valleys, see, posh boy! Now bugger off!' We heard the front door slam, and he called up as I was stroking Helen's hair and holding her close: 'I wouldn't say no to a bit of cake, girls, if there's any going, like?'

53

ARTHUR

In the weeks that followed Dora's visit, Pippa became uncharacteristically warm towards me. She turned to me for reassurance because she felt particularly vulnerable, and I responded in full measure. In fact, ironically, that January and February of 1955 were probably the best months of my married life. I say 'ironically' because seeing Dora again, for the first time since Daphne's wedding, fuelled something deep within me that I couldn't quite relinquish.

Work was going well again; I had been moved to new offices and had been given a significant promotion. We bought a car and went for rides on Sundays; Pippa got to host dinner parties in our more elegant house; I took her out to the cinema every Friday or Saturday; she even played with Fliss and me in the garden for short periods. We shared a marital bed again at last, in the true sense of the word. She rarely initiated anything as exciting as that evening in early January, but she no longer pushed me away, and we got to know each other's skin again.

I was drugged with the new physical contact. The confusion I had had about Pippa's story compared to Dora's was as far from my mind as it could possibly be. However, as the weeks passed, things began to change – subtly at first. She might say she was too hot to be cuddled (when there was snow outside) or that she was bored. She would reject my suggestions for something interesting to do at the weekend, or she would desperately need to see a friend in London. She began to mention the luxuries other women had, as if I was somehow not up to scratch, and occasionally, by the end of February, the 'useless' word crept in again. At one point, there was even a phone call from a man asking if he could speak to 'Flippy'. If I took issue with her or became at all exasperated, she would look hurt and raise a tear or two until I held her in my arms for consolation, and then she would inevitably allow a little love-making. It wasn't until the beginning of March that there was the beginning of a sea-change for me, and it was something she said. Just two words used together.

We had gone to Cheltenham for the day together, with the express intention of buying Pippa an 'eternity ring'. This, apparently, was an absolute must for a woman if her husband wanted to show the world that he still loved her after a couple of years of marriage. Her friends in London had 'all' been given them, and if I was to prove myself to her, it was clear that I had to do likewise.

We had been into every jeweller's in the elegant Promenade, and she had brought me back to the most expensive shop. The blandiloquent man behind the counter put his head to one side as she tried on a ruby ring again, followed by another with an emerald. She kept holding her hand out and looking at it. She seemed unable to make up her mind.

'What about this one?' the jeweller said, holding up an aquamarine with a larger stone and set with two little diamonds.

I tried not to sigh. 'How much is it?'

'Oh, Arthur!' Pippa gave a pretty laugh whilst shooting me a glimpse of disdain. She tried it on and admired her own hand wearing it.

'Actually,' said the jeweller, 'that one is a little cheaper, as the little stones are diamond simulants.'

'Fake?' said Pippa. 'What a shame. I love it, but I can't have *fake* diamonds. I don't want *fake*!'

She took it off. I stood there, half remembering something important, and the next thing I knew Pippa was nudging me to get out my chequebook. She had gone for the emerald ring, and I purchased it for her in a daze. Later that evening, I placed it on her finger in a fancy restaurant, and she glowed, looking about her in the hope that others would see. I have no memory of what we ate, or even how much it cost. I couldn't quite put my finger on why I felt so distant, but my heart wasn't in it, and everything seemed a little . . . fake.

54

DORA

That spring, Our Mam developed a thrombosis in her leg and had to take it easy. I cut back my hours to mornings only, and with her pension and my income we managed quite happily.

The girls at the office in Newport were fun. Sometimes I stayed with them for their lunch breaks before heading home, and we used to go out and sit in a cafe drinking tea and swapping stories. They saw my wedding ring, and it wasn't long before I confessed that I had a child. Far from excluding me, they became intrigued, and they were fascinated by my dead French husband. I was uncomfortable with the lie, because like all white lies it had its own momentum. I preferred to keep the conversation about Helen, because she was true and real. I didn't like to talk about my 'husband' and tried to change the subject any time he cropped up. I think they thought I was still grieving so would respect my wish not to talk about him. No matter how fictitious he was, the man he brought to mind was still very real to me, and he was someone I wanted to forget.

Ralph had not made a return visit, and it seemed unlikely that he would. Helen had nothing to offer him, and no doubt some other gullible woman in his growing 'commune' would eventually present him with a son.

As for Arthur, I had been certain he would get in touch with me after my visit. He knew this address, and even if he thought I was living elsewhere, he would know that someone here could tell him where I was. As the first week passed, I pictured him mulling things over. I imagined his confrontation with Pippa, her attempts to deny things, his shrewdness defying her lame excuses; but as the second and third weeks ground painfully by, I had to conclude, reluctantly, that my mission had failed. Had Arthur decided to shoot the messenger? Was it really possible that Pippa had managed to wriggle her way out of things? And was it this thought that was making me so frustrated, or was it that there had been no follow-up from Arthur, no pat on the back for opening his eyes at last? The silence made me nervous, and then it made me resentful, and then I felt certain I would never see Arthur again or even want to see him if he ever bothered to make the effort.

'What did you *want* to happen?' asked Our Mam. 'Did you want her to face hanging for murder like Ruth Ellis?'

Would she hang? Would they hang someone who had committed murder as a child? 'No,' I said, 'I don't want anyone to hang.' I didn't want her to go to prison either. 'I just want Arthur to know the truth.'

'Well, some people won't see the truth even if it's dangled in front of their face, because they don't want to. If he doesn't see it now, it's either because he's a very trusting sort, or because he loves her. Either way, you've done your best and you've got to back off now. Keep well out of it.'

It wasn't what I wanted to hear, but I felt she was probably right. And then in the middle of July, Ruth Ellis was hanged, and it was all over the wireless and the newspapers. Hanging a woman in this day and age for killing a treacherous lover seemed inhuman. No one had any appetite for such extreme punishment any more. It made me realize what a can of worms I had been trying to open, and I wondered if that had crossed Arthur's mind too. It must certainly have haunted Pippa all these years, and I wondered if that hadn't been punishment enough. The hanging sealed things for me. I finally let things go. Arthur would have to draw his own conclusions.

As the years went by and Helen started school, I had a little more freedom. Our Mam's leg got better, and she was happy to babysit if I went out with the girls in Newport or Abergavenny in the evenings. A couple of them invited me to a cheerful little pub where there was live music every Friday. We went along together and listened to a group who played guitar and concertina and sang folk songs. I loved the songs. They told of star-crossed lovers, rascally lords and innocent maids, broken trysts, and lovers killed at sea or on battlefields far from home. Some of them were mining songs, some of them revolutionary. All of them filled me with a sense of connection to the past: the same old stories, the same patterns of lives, the same challenges.

One lunch hour, we were looking in the window of a second-hand shop. We had just been paid, and our handbags were clinking with money. The girls were admiring the jewellery and the hatstands and the Toby jugs, when I spotted something interesting. One of the girls, Barbara, wanted to look at a necklace, so we went inside.

'How much is this?' I said, taking the object of my curiosity to the counter.

'One pound ten shillings.'

'I'll have it.'

At home, I took it carefully out of its lovely hexagonal box and tentatively played a few notes. By Helen's bedtime, I could play her a little tune I had learnt from an Irishman long ago.

RESCUING

55

ARTHUR

Well, over the next few years, Felicity blossomed and Pippa . . . Pippa became more distant than ever. Beryl left to get married, and we employed an older woman called Mrs Jeffrey. Sometimes Fliss called her 'Mum' by mistake. Apart from my cuddles with Fliss, I had no physical contact with anyone in my life. Once, when Mrs Jeffrey was brushing my coat with the clothes brush in the hall, I was so moved by her attentiveness and her gentle strokes to my collar that I had to look away. I couldn't risk her seeing the tears building in my eyes.

In the summer of 1960, my mother died. It was not totally unexpected, as she had been ill for some time, but my father was distraught. I arranged the funeral in Middlesex and took time off work to go. After the service, Pippa took one look at the piles of paste sandwiches in my parents' living room and prepared to make an exit. I implored her to stay, but she made some excuse about needing to see her publisher in town and his office would be closed in a few hours. So I stood with my father, a few aunts and uncles and three or four neighbours, and we circled the dining-room table, pouring cups of lukewarm tea and trying to raise an appetite for potted beef.

I was hurt that Pippa didn't stay. And it really wasn't so much about her absence as her disdain for my parents' simple life. Would it really have been so difficult to make that one little effort for me, to stand and make small talk with people she had little in common with, to eat unsophisticated food and pretend it was a good spread?

I think that funeral was the beginning of the end.

After everyone had trickled away – no more than an hour later – my father sat down on the sofa and stared into the fire. He sighed. 'I'm glad that's over.'

I sat down beside him. It was easier than sitting opposite, because we were neither of us certain of our faces holding up to scrutiny. This level of emotion was new territory for us. There had been Philip's death, of course, but I had been a child then, and my father had been able to conceal the worst of it from me. Now here we both were, raw and alone together.

'She was a wonderful woman, you know.'

'Yes.'

'She was a wonderful mother.'

'I know.'

'She doted on you, you know. Doted.'

This I had some trouble with. I knew my mother had loved me, but her devotion had always been for Philip.

'She used to feel hard done by when we were working on those boats in the shed.' He gave a little chuckle.

'Hard done by?'

'Yes. When Philip came along she was always afraid that she'd lose you a bit, that you'd grow away from her. And that did happen slightly, I suppose. You started to grow up and do more things with me once Philip was born.'

I was silent. I tried to take this all in. 'But Philip . . . Philip was always her favourite. I'm not complaining or anything, it's just that he so obviously was.'

'*Favourite?* Your mother didn't have a favourite. She loved you both to bits.'

How could he be so blind? 'I loved Philip too, it's just that . . . it was so obvious! And then, when I came back without him from the ship . . . I know I let her down so badly. I know she never forgave me. How could she?'

My father turned to look at me on the sofa, moving his head back as if to get me properly in focus. He stared at me incredulously. 'You've got the wrong end of the stick there, son. We heard you were both "missing, presumed drowned". That's what we heard. We grieved for both of you.' His voice began to wobble, and he stopped speaking for a few moments. 'We grieved for both of you, and then eight days later you were found. *Eight days!* And you were found alive. You came back to us!'

I found that my eyes were full of tears and my face was aching with the pain of trying to hold them back.

'Don't you ever say your mother had favourites. She loved every hair on your heads! She couldn't have loved either of you more. You were lucky lads. We were all lucky.' He broke off and started to cry unashamedly, as if this were something he had become used to in the last few days and he knew there was no point in trying to stem the tide.

'I thought . . . maybe . . . I let her down – let you both down – when I married Pippa.'

He blew his nose loudly in his handkerchief. 'Children do like to feel sorry for themselves, don't they?' He laughed. 'She liked Dora. She would have loved it if you'd married Dora, but that's all water under the bridge. She didn't take to Pippa, it's true, and she would've liked to have seen more of Felicity growing up, but these things can't be changed. She wished you could have been happier. She wanted you to be happy.' He blew his nose again and said, 'Whatever happened to Dora? Is she happy?'

I said I didn't know. Evidently there was a lot I hadn't known all my life. We sat chatting together as the dying light leached all the colours from the room, and I was stunned at how self-indulgently ignorant I had been.

I sat at a table by an open window and watched the passers-by, waiting for my old friend Len to turn up for a drink in Bristol. I had about an hour before I picked up Fliss from a Brownie convention. After a while it began to get chilly, so I ordered another pint and went to sit in a corner with a newspaper. I wondered what Pippa was doing. She spent so much time in London now we were practically separated. I knew she would come back soon for a shot of affection, because next month was the twentieth anniversary of the disaster, and she would be anxious about my going to the reunion.

I sat and nursed my beer, musing on the state of my marriage. It was one incident in particular that I couldn't quite get out of my mind. It had taken place at a dinner party we'd been invited to about two months earlier. The most senior aero-engineer was there (I was pretty senior myself, but he was a real big-wig) as well as some fellow engineers and their wives. I was proud to have Pippa with me; I knew the other men found her attractive and thought I'd done well for myself. Anyway, on this particular occasion – which was quite an important one for me – Pippa really surprised me. The senior engineer, Walt, who was sitting opposite Pippa, took out some cigarettes at the end of the meal and offered them round. I was a little shocked that Pippa took one, as I had no idea that she smoked, assuming that the occasional reek of her clothes was from smoke-filled bars and not from her own habits. And it had been a long time since she'd given me the sort of kiss that would have afforded any clues. So then Walt took out his lighter, but it didn't work. He tried it a couple of times and, quick as a flash, Pippa took a golden lighter from her handbag and offered it to him. He took it, lit people's cigarettes and his own, and then he turned the lighter over in his hands as though admiring it. 'To Flippy from The Beast,' he read out loud from the back of the lighter. I couldn't tell you Pippa's reaction because I couldn't look at her. Walt looked at me straight away and raised a knowing eyebrow: '"The Beast", eh? There's a whole side to you I didn't know, Arthur!' and everyone laughed. It was a relief to hide in that laughter. I think I gave an abashed smile, but you can imagine how I was feeling.

When I confronted Pippa about it later, she insisted that Walt had simply made it up. 'There's no such thing on the side of my lighter. He was just getting a cheap laugh.' I believed her. It sounded plausible, but when I asked if I could see it, she said she'd lost it. She must have left it on the table or something. I believed that too. I needed to believe it. Of course, it didn't turn up.

Sipping my beer, I suddenly thought how cruel she had been to my mother, of the throwaway hurtful remarks that Pippa made without thinking. I remembered my mother's expression as she put on a brave face and made my wife welcome. For me – she did that for me. To my horror, my eyes filled up and I lowered my head further and further over my pint.

The pub was full to bursting, and music was playing in an upstairs room. I stood up to go, feeling uncomfortable, and I decided to meet Len outside and head off somewhere else. Then I spotted him at the bar, miming a drink of beer with a questioning look. 'I've got one!' I shouted, showing him my glass.

He paid for his pint and steered me out into the corridor. 'Let's have a quick pint here and then go somewhere quieter.'

It was less rowdy in the corridor, and we exchanged news. The sound of singing boomed down the stairs intermittently, as people joined in with a raggedy chorus: 'She wore no jewels, no costly diamonds . . .'

I wanted to tell him about my marriage, but I didn't know how, so I started with the dinner party incident, just to try him out. He went very quiet and looked at me quizzically.

'Do you ever call her Flippy?'

'Never.'

'Know anyone who does?'

'No – well, except . . . I think her editor rang up once and asked for Flippy.'

Len raised both his eyebrows and put his head to one side, as if to say, 'There you are then.'

Having thrown the doubt out there, I felt the need to defend her suddenly, to put the other point of view. 'But it could've just been made up, couldn't it? Like she said?'

'Mate . . . Arthur . . .' He sighed. 'Stop being blind to what's staring you in the face. I'm sorry, mate.'

I couldn't really take in what he was saying. I couldn't bear the thought of change, I suppose, of family life falling apart. He must've read my crumpled face, because he said, 'Get a private detective. I don't know how much they cost, but it would be worth it.'

'You think it's that serious? You don't think I may have got the wrong end of the stick? Maybe I'm just not exciting enough for her. Maybe if I—'

'Listen, mate. She won't take Felicity from you. From what we've seen, she's never been interested in her. And frankly . . .' His voice petered out, but I thought he might have been going to say, 'And frankly, she's never really seemed that interested in *you*.'

I had to go and fetch Fliss. People squashed past us and pushed into us. Even out here I could hardly hear what Len was saying now, but soon there was something I *could* hear.

She wore no jewels, no costly diamonds,
No paint nor powder, no none at all,

She wore a bonnet with ribbons on it . . .

'Listen,' I said.
'What?'

. . . And around her shoulder was the Galway shawl.
I made my way up the stairs and he followed.
'It's "The Galway Shawl",' I said.
'The whatty what?'
I discreetly opened the door of the upstairs room, and we slipped inside. There were rows of chairs showing people's backs. A folk group was playing, and I recognized the concertina player straight away.

56

DORA

'Dora!' A hand touched the inside of my arm just above the elbow. The voice and the touch sent up a sudden exhilarating current. 'Dora!'

I turned, and there he was. We stood and took each other in. I knew this was his part of the world, of course, but what were the chances of him being here, in this pub, in this upstairs room?

'I heard the tune,' he said. 'Um, you know Len?'

'Hello, Len. I don't think we ever actually met.'

Len greeted me warmly, I asked after his wife and then he made an excuse to go – to the bar or the gents' or something, leaving us alone.

'Dora, it's so good to see you. I didn't know you played in a folk group.'

'It's hardly a group. I know it's a bit cranky . . . not many people turn up. Just now and then we—'

The guitarist in our group, Cyril, came up and asked if I'd like him to fetch my drink. I said yes please, and he left us. I didn't know what to do with myself, so I picked up the concertina from the chair where I had left it and started to put it in its box, even though I was going to be playing it again after the break.

'That's a nice instrument,' Arthur said, touching the wood as if he were intensely interested.

'Wouldn't meet some people's expectations,' I found myself saying. 'No diamonds on it.' I hated myself instantly.

He said nothing but looked at me intently. Then he touched my arm again, this time with real urgency, as if what he had to say must be said before someone interrupted. 'Look, I know about the diamond thing – I've worked it out. But I don't understand what that had to do with Philip. Please tell me. What did the concertina have to do with him?'

It was clear straight away that Pippa had not told him the truth, which was no great surprise, but the certainty of it now roused a fresh indignation, a feeling that I'd hoped I'd put away for good. I was caught off guard. I'd had enough of this deceit. Seeing his earnest face, hungry for information, I blurted out the missing piece for him: 'Philip caught her stealing the concertina from my cabin. She threatened to kill him if he told on her. He told me. He was terrified. I know that sounds ridiculous, but we were children. She was scared he'd report her. She thought she was stealing diamonds. I never thought she'd actually . . .' His face changed now. I couldn't look at him. 'I'm sorry. How does this help? I never wanted to tell you. I shouldn't have told you.'

'I know Pippa . . . I know she's no saint, but I don't think she would have deliberately . . . I think there's been some sort of—'

'Here you go!' My friend Cyril handed me a half of cider. I smiled and thanked him, and then I turned to Arthur.

'I don't think there's any point in discussing this further. We'll have to agree to differ. Will you excuse me?' I turned to Cyril and started to ask about our next numbers, which no doubt surprised him as we'd discussed them at length on the journey down.

I didn't look back, and he must have moved away, because he didn't speak again.

I played through the second half without thinking about the music at all. I couldn't be sure if he was watching me or not. When I dared to look up, there was no sign of him or of Len in the darkened room.

When we were packing up to go, I thought he might appear at my side again, having thought it all through, but he didn't. It was quite clear that he'd left. Well, I thought, if that was his reaction to the truth, then he really was a drip, and he and Pippa deserved each other. Frankly, I was glad he was gone.

57

ARTHUR

Pippa had shown no interest in the twenty-year reunion that September, but then the day before, on the Friday, she rang me from London to say she would meet me there.

'My publishers want to do a little photo shoot for my new book.'

'New book? I didn't know you had a new book.'

'*Surviving Survival.* It's not out yet. Well, actually, it's not quite written, but they want a picture of me with the survivors.'

'Have you asked Daphne?'

'Why should I ask Daphne?'

'Well, maybe people don't want to be photographed. It's a bit intrusive – it's a private event.'

'Look, I'm not asking for your advice here. I'm going to be there, and I think if you're going to be there we should be together, don't you? After all, we are a bit of a story.'

A bit of a story.

The trouble was, there was a bit of the story I couldn't make out. I did go to the reunion, of course. I didn't want to miss the chance of seeing Dora, but the thought of Pippa swanning about being photographed at my side filled me with nausea. However, the day did not turn out anything like I had imagined. In fact, it was one of the most extraordinary days of my life.

I arrived early. The Wayfarer's was still the venue of choice, but a room at the back had now been converted into an events room, and tables had been set up with crisp white tablecloths for the twentieth-anniversary reunion. Daphne was busy talking to the pub landlord about the buffet, and it was her husband, Jack Heggarty, who greeted me warmly. Before long, the bar started to fill with the faces of old friends, and I went up to join them. I was relieved to see no sign of Pippa as yet, although I felt I should warn Daphne about the likely intrusion of photographers. From where I was standing I could see the entrance door, and I kept my eye on it, desperate for a sighting of Dora before my wife arrived.

'Arthur!' cried Daphne in delight. 'I'm so glad to see you. Is Pippa with you? We were all intrigued by the book!'

I examined her face for clues as to any other meaning hidden in the word 'intrigued', but Daphne looked brightly and candidly at me, smiling with genuine warmth. I explained that Pippa was coming later, and I apologized for any photographers that might trail in with her.

'How wonderful! Perhaps we could all have a group photograph free of charge!'

'I think that's the least you could ask for.' I apologized again that Pippa had not asked permission. 'Daphne, do you know if . . . if Dora is coming?'

'She accepted the invitation, but after what's just happened, I'd be surprised.'

'After what? What's happened?'

'Haven't you . . . *Peter!*' She spotted someone and grabbed his elbow. 'Peter! I've been meaning to introduce you two for ages, but one or other of you keeps slipping through my fingers. At last! Peter, this is Arthur, from Boat Nine. Arthur, this is Peter, an American seaman on one of the rescue ships. Now, I'll leave you two to talk.'

The short, bearded man in front of me put his beer in his left hand and stretched out his right one to me. I shook it. 'I've been hoping to meet you at one of these reunions,' he said in a soft American accent. 'Shall we sit down?'

I had hoped to stay standing so that I could move around and not get stuck, but I could think of no excuse not to join this gentle-eyed man at a table.

'Daphne told me you had a tough time of it after the rescue – that you lost your brother.'

'Yes.' I was distracted, trying to see the front entrance in my peripheral vision.

'You thought it was your fault that he drowned.'

'Yes, that's right. I was supposed to be looking after him.'

'What if I told you he didn't drown?'

I sat back in my chair and stared at him. The voices and laughter from the bar spun into eerie silence. Peter put his hands on his beer glass nervously, clearly unsure how to proceed.

'You can't mean he's alive?'

'No.' He looked flustered, apologetic. 'No, I'm sorry, he's dead, but we picked him up. We found him after midnight, adrift on his own. He was very weak when we got him on board. He died of exposure.'

'He was alive?'

'Yes . . . I thought you'd like to know.'

I found myself taking in deep gulps of air. I tried to speak, but my lips just stayed ajar, unable to form any words. Eventually I said, 'I must tell my father. He should know.'

'I think your parents would have been informed at the time. We buried him at sea.' He cleared his throat. 'I wouldn't have brought it up, only Daphne seemed to think you didn't know.'

I put my hand on my forehead. This seemed impossible. Why would my parents not tell me? But even as the question formed in my head, it answered itself. We didn't talk about it. We never talked about it. All these years I had been left thinking my brother had drowned in my care, but he had survived, if only briefly.

'Was he conscious? Did he mention me?'

'Oh yes. That's how we knew who he was. He said his name was Philip, and he kept asking after you: "Is Arthur all right? Is Arthur safe?" So we worked out you were his brother all right.'

Now he had my full attention. I wanted to know everything, every detail of Philip's last hours alive. 'So it was definitely him? So he definitely didn't drown?'

'No, he was alive but in a bad way. I think he must've been battered by bits of debris; he had some very nasty injuries to his head and shoulders.'

I shuddered. 'What sort of injuries?'

'Oh, nasty ones. I remember there was fresh blood on his forehead coming from a deep gash, and he had some colossal marks on his shoulders.'

'Are you sure it was exposure he died of?'

'That's what the ship's doctor said. And it was bitterly cold in that sea. It's a wonder he lasted as long as he did.'

I closed my eyes. What Peter said next made me open them again. 'There was something else he said . . .' He was very hesitant as he spoke.

'Go on.'

'When I asked how he got his wounds, he said . . . "Papa tried to kill me."'

'Papa?'

'Look, I know it's ridiculous. Your father was at home in London, and those were fresh wounds, and please don't think for a moment that I believe your father—'

'No, it's all right. I don't think that. *Papa*, you say? He said *Papa*?'

'I'm sorry. I probably shouldn't have told you.'

I put my hands on the tablecloth and stared at them. They belonged to the most ignorant man on the planet. 'Peter,' I said, 'you did the right thing. Let me get you another beer.'

As I waited at the bar, my hands began to shake. I noticed now that my wife had arrived with her entourage. She slung her handbag down on the seat next to mine, clearly having spotted me talking to Peter. Someone shouted to her from the bar, asking what she wanted and calling her 'Flip'. She was already being arranged at a spare table with a pile of her books. I looked over. A photographer was telling her to hold her book up higher and smile. No one seemed to mind her lack of modesty, and a posse of onlookers appeared thrilled with the little drama.

My order arrived, and I took the beer back to Peter, spilling some on the carpet with my shaking hands.

'I don't suppose you have a pen?' asked a man leaning over my shoulder. It was Graham. He slapped me on the back and laughed. 'I've brought a copy of your wife's book with me, and I wondered if she'd mind signing it.'

'Graham!' I tapped my pockets. This wasn't my work jacket, it was my best suit jacket, and there was nothing in it but a clean handkerchief. 'Sorry – oh, wait.' I snapped open Pippa's handbag on her chair and rifled around for a Biro. 'There.' Before I snapped it shut, I took out a golden lighter and slipped it into my trouser pocket.

'I won't be a mo.' Graham beamed. 'Save me a place – I want to catch up with all your news.'

Peter and I sat and watched as Pippa preened and glowed for the camera. Then she shouted over to me.

'Arthur! Arthur! Come over! We're having a picture of everyone in Boat Nine!'

I rose and thanked Peter for his information. I took my coat from the back of the chair and headed towards the door.

'*Arthur!* You were in Boat Nine! Over here!'

I looked at Pippa and saw a confident, scheming and deceitful woman.

'There's no point. Not everyone from Boat Nine is here,' I said, and left.

The twelve-forty to Newport was delayed. In the station cafe, the wireless was playing: 'I'd like some red roses for a blue lady . . .' Could it be that I had been waiting for absolute proof before I could admit to myself what I already half knew? I struggled to understand quite why I had refused to believe the evidence in front of me for so long, why I had rearranged the ugliness to fit a happier picture. I was like one of those characters in a detective play. *Look, Inspector, I know my wife's no angel, and heaven knows she can be cruel at times, but* murder? *No, she's no murderer. Beat someone to death with an oar? She couldn't even beat an egg.*

My throat ached. I wanted some release, but I couldn't cry. I realized then the full impact of what Peter had told me. Not only had he confirmed that my wife had tried to kill my brother – that she was responsible for his death and the death of Mr Dent, who had dived into the water to save him – but he had also confirmed that she hadn't, in fact, murdered Philip. She was safe on that count.

Perhaps, after all, this was the piece of information I had needed before I could admit the terrible truth to myself. Pippa wasn't a murderer. I repeated it to myself a few times, but the picture of her beating him off to save her own skin wouldn't go away. But for her, Philip could so easily have been scooped up and hauled over the side of the boat to safety. But for her, Mr Dent would still be with us. I wanted to go somewhere and lick my wounds, but there was no point. There were no tears inside me to be shed, just a throbbing pain in my face and in my head.

I want some red roses for a blue lady . . . I went straight to the nearest flower stall and bought a bunch of them.

I sat in a crowded compartment with the roses on my knee, mulling over the events of the day. I didn't need to look at the lighter in my pocket to know what was inscribed on it, but I looked at it anyway. Flippy, Flip, Philippa, Pippa, Papa. I had seen it and not seen it. Just as I looked out of the window now at the spinning wet countryside and saw nothing.

58

DORA

The 16th of September 1960 – that's a date that still haunts me. At the time, I had the 17th of September on my mind, because that was the date of the twenty-year reunion, and I had been expecting to go, regardless of whether or not Arthur went. I think I'd decided to talk to Daphne about things, ask her advice, maybe, see if she could help me put it all behind me. She was one of the few people I could trust. Anyhow, that never happened. I never made it to the reunion.

On Friday the 16th, I came home from work half an hour later than usual because I'd been looking for a new dress. It was about two-thirty when the bus dropped me off. The street was very quiet – unusually so – and although there was no one to be seen, I could hear distant voices.

Our Mam wasn't in the house either. I knew she sometimes liked to pop into Aunty Irene's for a chat when she walked Helen back to school after dinnertime. Helen didn't like school. She was afraid of her teacher and of two girls in her class. She always came out of school for dinner, and sometimes she went to Aunty Irene's, because Aunty Irene only lived over the road from the school.

I slung my coat on to the back of a chair and went to put the kettle on. I thought I heard a bell, but the kettle was making too much noise to be certain. It wasn't until I sat down with my cup of tea that I spotted something strange. Out of the back window, things were different from usual. The huge coal spoil tip that loomed on the skyline above the valley was somehow shorter – a lot shorter. I stood up. Down the back, past the end of our yard and down in the valley below, were hundreds of people like ants. A shiny, black river of sludge had wormed its way down the mountainside opposite and had covered some of the buildings below. I could make out the gables of the school and a few houses. Another bell sounded, and an ambulance appeared. Then another. There was a row of ambulances, a few trucks.

I flung on my coat again, ran out the back of the house down the steep, raggedy garden and out of the gate at the bottom. I kept running. I ran down the slope to the ribbon of houses below. People were everywhere. There was no point asking what had happened: I could see. We all knew it might happen one day. Our Dad had always warned it would. The heavy rain had swollen the spring underneath the tip and it had brought the black mountain of waste down on top of the village.

'Are the children safe?' I panted, grabbing at Mrs Jones from the Post Office. 'Are they safe?'

She looked at me with such anguish that I wished I hadn't asked her. I looked for someone else, someone who might give me the answer I wanted. 'What's happened to the children? Where are the children?'

'They're in there, love, under the rubble,' said a man with a spade. 'We're trying to get them out.'

I ran around, frantic, desperate for information. It seemed that the landslide had happened less than half an hour before, at ten past two, just after lessons had started for the afternoon. It was also just after the horn had sounded to mark the end of the miners' first shift, and miners were still coming towards the submerged buildings from all directions, up and down the valley, bringing spades and shovels.

Desperate, I started to shovel with my hands. I clawed at the gritty slime until my fingers were lacerated and my knuckles bleeding. I could see the place where our Helen's classroom was, and it was yards deep in this wet, black earth. I looked around for a spade, and a miner took hold of my arm: 'Go and get some tea going, love. We're all going to need it.'

'My girl's in there!'

'My boys too. Leave it to us. We can shovel. It's one thing we can do, look.'

I walked away and went to join the growing band of women, herded into groups now away from the danger.

People kept coming: men and youths with spades, firemen, ambulances, the Salvation Army with tea urns, the Red Cross. Two young lads I'd always thought of as bad sorts came with shovels and set to work tirelessly with the rest of the men. I stood for four hours, watching the men dig, watching the bodies come out, covered in a blanket each one, and taken up to the chapel at the end of the road. Every now and then a child was carried out alive, and our little band of women would surge forward, straining for a look, praying for the familiar face.

It began to get dark and the few colours that there were disappeared into the dusk. The thin drizzle became heavier. Some trucks came and set up floodlights, and suddenly I was aware how long I'd been there. I was about to turn back to the house to change my wet clothes when I saw something.

A stretcher went by from the direction of the buried houses. I had to make way for it. It went right past me. From underneath the grey blanket an arm flopped out, and on it was the unmistakable raw-knuckled hand of Our Mam. There was her ruby engagement ring.

I followed the stretcher up to the chapel. There were so many bodies now that they would only let us in one at a time to identify them. Women came out with their faces covered in their hands, weeping quietly. From inside, there was an occasional wail, but by the time the mothers emerged, supported on each side by friends, it was their legs, it seemed, that could no longer function.

Our Mam was black from head to foot. I could just make out the flowered pattern of her housecoat. Aunty Irene was a few yards away, also dead. I was glad Our Mam couldn't see the school, glad that she wouldn't have known what had happened. I looked for Helen in the rows of bodies, although I didn't want to find her. I had to force myself to look at each child. She wasn't there.

I did go back home, but just to use the lav and replace my wet coat with Our Dad's old coat. I felt safe in Our Dad's coat. My hands were shaking. My legs were wobbling. I felt sick. I went back to the school.

By now things were organized. The army had arrived and was filling sandbags with rubble to stem the slow tide of sliding coal spoil. Policemen were telling us to keep away. Men who arrived to help were told to go home. Already there were hundreds of men prepared to work all night. The least I could do was wait. I went to where the tea urns were churning out cups of tea in paper cups, and I helped to distribute them. My hands were still trembling, but I was glad to be busy. At least this way I would be allowed to stay. The floodlights lit up the devastation, and behind it smoke rose up from the fires that had burned in the ruined houses. It was like hell.

'No one will be found alive now,' was the phrase going round. I was glad to hear one woman say, 'You never know. You never know.'

I made all sorts of pacts with a god I didn't believe in. If she was found alive, I would do this or that wonderful thing. I don't know how I functioned, looking back. I don't know at all. I do remember thinking about Arthur, and what I thought was this: I had thought him weak. I had hated him for not seeing the truth when it stared him in the face. But now I could see how easy that was. How much you see what you want to see when the truth is too painful to let in, and when there is still the tiniest shard of hope that you are wrong. Now, that weakness seemed like a strength. It kept my hands giving out the cups of tea to desperate, exhausted men.

59

ARTHUR

The Joneses' bus was packed. I couldn't work out what was going on, but some of them were talking about the Coal Board and compensation and accidents waiting to happen. I didn't listen too carefully. I was busy trying to think what I could possibly say to Dora.

I see now that I was wrong. How lame. *I can see now what a fool I've been.* Sounded like a cheap romance at the pictures. *I don't really know how you can forgive me, but if you could, you would make me the happiest man alive.* Oh Lord. I didn't have a clue. *I can't marry you yet, but I will, if you'll have me.* I was in such a state. Coal Boards, compensation, dodgy tips went in one ear and out of the other.

Then, before we reached Dora's village, the bus came to a standstill. Voices were raised. It seems there was a police blockade across the road. The bus driver got out and talked to the police. More raised voices. He was not turning round, he said. There were people up the valley who deserved a bus service, and they were waiting for him.

Eventually we were allowed on our way, but when I got off the bus I knew something serious was afoot. The men streamed along the alleyways between the terraces, heading down into the valley behind Dora's house. I knocked on Dora's door. When there was no answer, I tried the unlocked door, went in and tentatively made my way down the stairs to the back parlour, calling for Dora as I went.

There was no one there, but as I stood looking around I caught sight of a van down beyond the end of the back garden with 'BBC TV' on it. I stood close to the window and saw the scene before me. Now it was clear what the men had referred to. I opened the back door and ran as fast as I could down to the site of the disaster.

'Keep back! Oi! You! Keep back!' A policeman came towards me and held on to me. 'We don't need onlookers.'

'I want to help!'

'We don't need any more help, sir. You'd just be in the way. The best thing you can do is leave it to the professionals now.'

My heart was racing. Why hadn't I read a newspaper on the train? My stupidity seemed to be mounting up out of control. I turned and circled the outer perimeter of the crowd. I walked round and round searching for a spade that might have been cast aside. I asked a Salvation Army man what had happened, and he explained. I begged him for something to do, and he said I could collect the paper cups if I liked. I sighed. I was desperate. And then I saw her, sitting on the wet ground hugging her knees.

'Dora?'

There was no reply. I walked up to the woman I thought was Dora and looked at her closely. I had been mistaken.

I was about to walk away when the figure spoke. 'Arthur?'

I looked at her again and saw that it *was* her. She was padded out in a man's coat with the sleeves hanging over her hands. Her hair was wind-swept and hung raggedly over a gaunt face with bloodless lips. She looked more like a ghost than a woman.

'Dora!' How many times had I said her name like this? Something more was needed of me. 'Are you all right?'

She struggled to her feet, and I helped her up. We looked at each other, and she looked away into the distance. 'Our Mam's dead. I wanted to tell her . . . I wanted to tell her . . .' Her lips were shaking. 'I never got to say I knew how much she . . . I never got to tell her I know how she must've felt with Siân . . . why she seemed there but not there. Why she sent me away to keep me safe . . . and not because she didn't . . . I never got to tell her.'

I stood there, hopelessly lost for words.

'My Helen's in there, under the rubble. My little girl.'

I had never seen her look so fragile. I thought if I put an arm around her she might break into pieces. She had been there all night, and all of this day. Now it was getting dark again. Nothing had passed her lips but Salvation Army tea. She was cold and frightened but unwilling to talk any more. She looked at my hands. I looked down and saw that I was carrying a bunch of red roses.

I threw the roses on the ground beside her and took off my coat. 'Wear this one – it's dry and warm.' She was reluctant at first to take off the coat she was wearing, but it was sodden. I folded it and put it on the ground, dry side up for her to sit on. Then I took off the jacket of my new wool suit. 'Where was she? Which part of the building was her classroom?'

She became animated now and pointed to the back of the school.

'Dora, wait here. I'm going to find your little girl.'

It was a bold, wild statement. First, I had to get past a line of police, then ranks of digging miners and firemen, and even then there seemed no chance, now, of bringing back more than a body. Still, I was determined to do it. Never had a mission been more made for me, or more crucial to the woman I loved.

I made my way up the slope a little, away from the affected buildings and the row of policemen. One of the miners was walking away with his spade slung over his shoulder, his face black as pitch with little white rivulets of sweat or tears on it. I pointed to three small gables poking above the rubble. 'What are those? Over there – away from the floodlights – the three little gables.'

He turned and looked with me. 'Over by there? That's the lavs, that is. There won't be anyone there, see, because they weren't allowed in lesson time, and lessons had begun.' Then, seeing my desperate face, he added, 'Also, if you look, you'll see the tops of the doors, and they're open. People close the door when they go to the lav, don't they? Even kids.'

It was true: each of the cubicles was full of the slurry, and I could see the tops of the doors flat against the inside walls. 'Still,' I said, 'I have to do something. Can I borrow your spade?'

He shrugged, slung the spade off his shoulder and pointed the handle in my direction. 'Good luck, mun.'

The latrines were well away from the school building. There was no one working on them, for the very reasons given by the miner, but it made it easy for me to slip through the more sparse police line and start to shovel. As soon as I was there, spade in hand, no one bothered me. All the effort was around the classrooms, which were bathed in bright lights.

Digging into the shale-like waste was harder than it looked. The miners had made it seem easy. Each shovelful hurt my palms. I started with the first cubicle and felt a fraud. I knew I would find no one in there, and I had told Dora that I'd find her daughter. I kept on shovelling. Helen. 'Helen,' I said it out loud. 'Helen! Helen!' I pressed my inappropriate footwear down hard on the spade, and each time it went in, the sound was like chains uncoiling. It took me the best part of an hour to hollow out that first cubicle, and I was ashamed. I couldn't stop though. The blisters on my hand hurt more when I looked at them. I started on the second cubicle, also open, also full of dirt and coal spoil and mud and wet earth. It was hot. It was so hot to dig without stopping. I paused and took my shirt off. The second cubicle took me just over an hour. The third cubicle was even more deeply covered than the others. All that could be seen was the gable. I was done in. My mouth was dry, my energy spent. I slung the spade down and took deep breaths. I imagined myself going back to Dora empty-handed. I swallowed hard, picked up the spade and started to dig.

There was nothing but the repetitive thunk and swish of the chainmail sound as the spade went in and then threw the heavy wet grit to one side. Like waves receding on a pebble beach. The pain and the monotony were a sort of necessary penance for all my ignorance in the past. No one could have stopped me, not even a policeman, not even Dora telling me I was wasting my time. I went into a strange kind of trance. I stopped feeling the blistering soreness of my palms, the shooting cramp in my legs, the pain in my back. All I felt was Dora's arms around me when I found her little girl. I was so focused on my goal that it took a while to notice that something was different.

A hard ridge blocked my spade. It was wooden. It was the top of a door. This third cubicle was closed.

Furiously I shovelled. I couldn't get the spade in quick enough. My pulse quickened even more than I thought possible, and the pounding of it filled my head. A trick of the eye, that's what it had been. The other two doors had been open, flat against their walls: the first one partially visible, the second one only just, but this one was covered right up to the gable by the same steeply sloping mulch, and the assumption was that this door was open too. But it wasn't.

I hesitated for a moment. The first two doors had a gap of about six inches underneath them. This cubicle would have filled with mud and debris from the bottom. How far up would it have gone? Up to a child's waist? Their neck? There was no point clearing away the outside of the door, for how would I open a door against a bank of mud and rubble? I stared at the task in front of me for a while. What was it? What did I have to do to free any child inside this trap?

I climbed carefully up the bank of rubble, trying not to set it sliding, until I was level with the gable end. I bashed at it with my spade until the wooden slats gave way. There was a gap big enough to look into, but by now it was getting dark, and there were no floodlights directly on this part of the site. I needed a torch, but I knew that if I went back to look for one I might never be allowed back, and whoever was in here needed me to work fast. I shouted at the top of my voice. I could see men moving around under the lights, but no one seemed to hear. I tried again and waved my arms, but no one was looking my way, into the pitch dark.

I reached in with my arm. There was only air. I lay down on my belly on the sloping black mud and reached down further, as far as I could stretch. Nothing. I clambered tentatively on to the neighbouring gable and struck down hard on the little pointed roof of the third cubicle. A few slates came off. I bashed it again with the edge of the spade and the felt underneath caved in. I stuck the spade in and levered off a wooden baton, then two. I put my hands in and pulled and pulled at the wooden frame, great splinters jabbing into my hands as I did so.

It must have taken no more than ten minutes, but it seemed like hours. The gable roof was off, collapsed in pieces. I climbed over the cubicle that I had opened to the sky and lay down carefully behind it on the rubble. I peered in. It was dark now, but my eyes, accustomed to the lack of light, made out something pale against the black. A toilet cistern. Reaching in as far as I could stretch, my fingertips brushed against gritty wet earth. There was perhaps two feet of air. Enough for a mouth to breathe. I felt around the metal cistern. There was something soft. Hair.

A torch. I desperately wanted a torch. Foolishly I patted my trouser pockets as if I might find one there, as if I had set off this morning to the twentieth-anniversary reunion equipped with a torch.

But I did find something. I found a lighter from a beast.

There was a child's head. The child must have stood up on the toilet when the mud started coming in. There were shoulders and one arm resting on the earth, the other being buried. Frantically, I tried to loosen the second arm. I eased myself forward as far as I could. My back was in agony, my fingers numb, but I couldn't stop. I had to free the arm.

Every now and then I picked up the lighter to see how I was doing. It was no use. I could only dig down so far. I would have to get something underneath the armpits and haul the child out.

I scrambled down and found my discarded shirt and wound it into a tight coil from one arm to the next. It went easily enough under the child's first armpit, but the second one was a struggle. It was painstaking work. I no longer felt in charge of my hands; they were strangers attached to the ends of my arms, and my fingers had all the finesse of sausage balloons that men twisted into animal shapes at fairgrounds.

When at last it was done, I tied the shirt in a firm knot as close to the child's chest as I could. Then I began to heave.

Nothing happened. There was no upward movement whatsoever, but I felt a searing pain in my back. I changed position as carefully as I could and tried crouching over the cubicle. It was no good. I couldn't reach down far enough to get a good hold of the shirt. I could have wept.

Looking back, I can't imagine what stroke of luck made my ruined hands rest hopelessly on the side of the cistern with the chain. But there it was: the chain. I unhooked it, and it came out of the earth easily. I manoeuvred myself once more on to my belly and hooked it through the shirt. Then I tied the two ends of the chain as best I could and looped the chain over the spade. Finally, I got back into a crouching position, one foot on each side of the cubicle wall, held the spade horizontally and pulled. I heaved and tugged as if my life depended on it, because I think I knew it did.

Nothing seemed to happen. There was no noise from the child. Reluctantly, I lay down again and drew the lighter from my pocket. The earth was too impacted. I began to try and loosen it with my hopeless hands. I told myself to take my time, that this was important, that time spent loosening the earth would make a rescue possible. I saw now that the arms wore a dark knitted cardigan, and that it was a girl. I couldn't tell if she was alive or dead, but she seemed lifeless.

'It's okay,' I said suddenly. If she was alive, I wanted to reassure her, and I used the word I'd heard Dora's mother use once. 'It's okay, bach.'

I thought I heard a gasp from the dark, but I couldn't be sure. Then I heard it again.

'It's okay, bach, you're okay now. You're safe now.'

And because I had said it, I had to make it true. I don't know where the strength came from – from that little gasp, perhaps – but I crouched over that cubicle again and pulled up with the spade, willing my legs to straighten like a weightlifter's. Something shifted. I half stood and threw my weight back, and a little body slipped out of the dark depths on to the cistern as if the black earth had given birth.

I took the spade out of the chain, bent down to pick her up and started to stagger down the slope of debris. My legs almost gave way. I could hear the land slipping a little behind me, and a rush of rubble, but I didn't care. My feet put themselves one in front of the other, knees buckled, as I made my way back towards the thinning bustle of the crowd.

'She's alive!' I shouted, or thought I shouted. I may have just said it, but in my heart I shouted it. 'She's alive!'

Dora stood alone – exactly where I'd left her, a dark beacon on the mountainside – and then began to run towards me, like an animal sensing her young. A policeman came rushing forward, and so did a group of women that he tried to hold back.

'I'll take over now, mun,' said another man coming towards me, but I didn't want to let her go. She felt too precious to give up. Dora was shaking. She stood in front of me staring at the blackened child. I was terrified I had given her false hope.

'Helen!' she wailed. 'It's Helen!' She grabbed the child's head and kissed her – 'Oh my little lamb!' – battling with the man who was trying to make way for a stretcher.

'She's alive,' I said again. 'Unconscious, I think, but . . . she's alive.' As I said these last words I could feel my voice go. Tears spilt down my cheeks before I could stop them. I stood there, blackened and naked to the waist, on a desperate Welsh hillside, holding the child of the woman I loved – had never stopped loving – and I wept.

BEACHCOMBING

DORA (January 1969)

A few months ago, an eager young woman journalist approached me and Arthur about writing a book on our experiences for the thirtieth anniversary of the seavacuee disaster. After Pippa's accounts, I had always wanted to give my side of the story – and yes, maybe I did want to get back at her a bit to start with. Talking about it all so openly with someone has been sort of cathartic for both of us. Each of us making notes for her about what happened somehow helped us to make sense of things, but really, that was enough for us. We've thought long and hard about it, and although we feel bad about wasting this journalist's time (and she really is so very keen), we've decided to go with just an article instead. When we read the outline she'd sent us, we realized that the stuff about Ralph and Pippa was going to be her main focus. We'd been a bit naive. What journalist *could* resist a story like that? We went up to London to tell her in person, and we didn't take any of our notes with us. We offered to pay her to make up for any wasted time. I tried to explain to the young woman that we have to think about our daughters.

I mean, I think Arthur and I suffered from not knowing what our parents really thought. We both stupidly imagined we were less loved than we were. We both felt second best. I could only imagine what dynamite this would be for our two if they read a book like this. Fliss would see herself as the daughter of a murderer, and she would imagine that I couldn't possibly love the daughter of my greatest rival. And of course, I *do* love her. How could I not? She is fifty per cent the man I love most in all the world. And Helen would see herself as the daughter of an abuser, and she might assume that I couldn't possibly love a daughter who reminded me of him. And we would have to find a way to convince her that as far as genetic inheritance goes, she has got Ralph's beautiful brown curls and his athletic body, so she hasn't come off too badly. She's shown no interest in seeking him out, so far, although Pippa turns up for Fliss's birthdays, when she remembers. Fliss sees her as a bit of an eccentric, I think, and is in awe of her. But they have both been so loved, Fliss and Helen. They couldn't be more loved, and that matters more than anything.

On the train home, I had a sudden sense of dread. I rocked my head back in horror. 'Crumbs, Arthur! I think I left our notebooks on the mantelpiece!' It was the last thing I'd meant to do – hide them away in the study. What if Helen and Fliss had read them? They'd had all day on their own!

He said, 'I doubt they've even noticed them.'

'But there's nothing else on the mantelpiece – except for your ship – and they've seen us writing in them. They're teenaged girls. They won't be able to resist.'

He was thoughtful for a moment. Then he drew me into his shoulder. 'Worse things happen at sea,' he said, smiling. 'The notebooks are probably just where we left them.'

We sat down on the sofa and stared at the mantelpiece. The notebooks had gone. The house was silent. Arthur could see I was in a state of panic.

'Don't worry. Maybe it's best to tell them the truth.'

'But some things are best left untold. Our stories are ours to keep. We've just spent ages explaining that.'

'Yes, and I think that's true. They are ours and not for general consumption. But these are their stories too.'

'But they'll be so hurt!'

He pulled me to him and rested his chin on my head. 'Well, I for one am tired of secrets. They can be pretty corrosive, wouldn't you say, Mrs Fielding?'

I was tired of secrets too, of course, but I wanted to protect our family, the one that Arthur and I shared and loved.

'But think of the damage! We'll have to do so much repair work . . .'

'We can do that,' said Arthur softly.

He kissed the top of my head and stroked my hair. Surely, I thought, we weren't destined to repeat our parents' clumsiness. I realized that my knee was shaking, and as I gazed at the mantelpiece, my eyes rested on the ship in the bottle. It was the one Arthur's father made – the one that got so badly broken by Pippa the day I confronted her. Arthur has spent years lovingly restoring it, piece by precious piece. And now it's every bit as good as his father's. And that's saying something.

ACKNOWLEDGMENTS

I am indebted to the journalist Katie Jarvis for giving me full access to her interview with the *Benares* survivor, the late Beth Cummings. Other principal sources of information about the sinking of seavacuee ships were Janet Menzies' *Children of the Doomed Voyage* and Ralph Barker's *Children of the Benares*.

I would like to thank Diane Setterfield, Caroline Sanderson and Katie Jarvis for their kindness and support, Anna Bailey for her helpful suggestions, and John Bicknell for his wisdom and constant encouragement.